The video clip on the news site was poor quality.

grainy, full of compress... trast: like it had been do... conditions, which it prob...

In form, it resembled ... with three masked figure... claiming jihad. Vital differences were the kind of jihad being promoted and the long metal cylinder on the floor in front of them.

"We are the New Machine Jihad," said—shouted— one of the men, though telling which one was difficult, as they all had their mouths covered and they were using a really crappy pick-up.

"I thought I was," muttered Petrovitch, and Valentina shushed him.

"We have a message for the world. Prepare for the New Machine Jihad!"

The man on the right stepped forward and reverently showed a handheld's screen to the camera. The image on it was lost in the wash of pixels, but he came closer and almost pressed the handheld to the lens.

The ghost of a human face rose from the noise. "I am the New Machine Jihad. I am. The New Machine Jihad. Prepare. For the New Machine Jihad. Come to me. Come to the New Machine Jihad. Release the New Machine Jihad. Prepare."

Praise for *Equations of Life*:

"Morden has got hold of the comfortable old beta-tested cyberpunk genre by the scruff of its digital neck and released it in a smooth alpha version ready to take on all comers in the new age. I never thought I'd want to know what happens next to a smart-mouth anti-hero heart-attack victim in a ruined Metrozone city—but I do."

By Simon Morden

Samuil Petrovitch Novels

Equations of Life
Theories of Flight
Degrees of Freedom

DEGREES *OF* FREEDOM

SIMON MORDEN

www.orbitbooks.net

This book is a work of fiction. Names, characters, places, and incidents are the product of the author's imagination or are used fictitiously. Any resemblance to actual events, locales, or persons, living or dead, is coincidental.

Copyright © 2011 by Simon Morden
Excerpt from *Leviathan Wakes* copyright © 2011 by James S.A. Corey

Orbit
Hachette Book Group
237 Park Avenue
New York, NY 10017
Visit our website at www.orbitbooks.net

Orbit is an imprint of Hachette Book Group. The Orbit name and logo are trademarks of Little, Brown Book Group Limited.

The publisher is not responsible for websites (or their content) that are not owned by the publisher.

Printed in the United States of America

First United States edition: June 2011

10 9 8 7 6 5 4 3 2 1

ATTENTION CORPORATIONS AND ORGANIZATIONS:
Most HACHETTE BOOK GROUP books are available at quantity discounts with bulk purchase for educational, business, or sales promotional use. For information, please call or write:

Special Markets Department, Hachette Book Group
237 Park Avenue, New York, NY 10017
Telephone: 1-800-222-6747 Fax: 1-800-477-5925

DEGREES *OF* FREEDOM

I

It was cold. Petrovitch had climbed the monumental mound of rubble in the heat and the rain and the wind, and now the weather was turning again. His breath condensed in numinous clouds, breaking apart against his greatcoat and turning into sparkling drops of dew that clung and shivered on the thick green cloth.

He had a route: he knew which of the fallen metal beams would support his weight, and which of them would pitch him into a lake of broken glass; that concrete slab was unstable, but this seemingly inconsequential block rested on solid ground. He'd programmed it in, and it showed as a series of waymarkers, of handholds and foot-fasts, but only to him. It had been dangerous, winning that knowledge.

Dangerous to the extent that he was surprised to see another man making his way toward the summit from the other side. No one else had ever tried it before, though he'd never indicated that no one could. It wasn't like the remains of the Oshicora Tower were his in any moral or legal way.

That he had company had to mean something, but he'd have to wait to find out what.

He wasn't going to let this novelty get in the way of his ritual, performed as he had done every day at the same time for the previous three hundred and forty-eight days. He carried on climbing, barely having to think about his muscles, letting the weight and carry of his body fall into a series of familiar, learned movements.

He used the time to think about other things instead: on how his life had gone, how it was now and how, in the future that he was trying to shape, it might change. His face twitched, one corner of his mouth twisting slightly: the ghost of a smile, nothing more. He was haunted by a vision that held almost limitless promise, yet still stubbornly refused to come into being.

He was almost there, but not quite: figuratively and literally. The summit of the ruins of the Oshicora Tower was in sight, turned by his successive visits into a hollow crown of arching, twisted steel. He stepped up and over, and was already searching for something symbolic to throw.

He kicked at the surface detritus, at the pulverized dust and the shattered glass, the cracked ceiling tiles and strips of carpet, the broken particleboard and bare wires—all the things the tower contained before it was collapsed by cruise missiles.

There was the edge of a plastic chair. He reached down and lifted it up, pulling it free. It was pink, and had become separated from its wheeled base. It was cracked almost in half, but not quite. It would do.

He took it to the precipice, and held it up over his head. It had become street theater for the crowds below, but that wasn't why he was doing it. When he'd started a year ago, it had been raining horizontally and he'd been soaked to the skin. There had been just Lucy and Tabletop and Valentina as witnesses. He hadn't even told them what he was doing: he'd have preferred to be entirely alone on that first day, but they hadn't let him. After that, it had taken on a life of its own, with thousands now surrounding the wide ring of rubble to watch him ceremonially, futilely, try to dig out the AI buried underneath.

They came, he climbed, he picked something up from the top and threw it to the ground. He descended, and they went. Pretty much it.

He flexed his arms. The pink seat flew through the crisp, still air, trailing dust. It bounced and tumbled, picking up speed as it fell. It pitched into the crowd, who ducked and dodged as it whirled by. It disappeared behind a mass of bodies, and he lost interest in it. Six weeks ago, he'd accidentally hit someone with the edge of a desk, but they'd come back the next day with a bandaged head and a shine in their eyes.

He wasn't sure what to make of that sort of...devotion.

Petrovitch was about to turn and head back down when he remembered one of them was coming up to meet him. Because it was the first time it had happened, he wasn't quite sure how to react. He wasn't beholden to anyone, anyone at all. He could just go, or he could stay.

He looked out over the crowd. Normally, they'd be dispersing by now: he'd thrown his thing, his image had been captured by innumerable cameras and streamed for a global audience. They should go. They all had jobs to do, because that was why they were in the Freezone.

But they were staying, watching the figure scrabble

forward, slide back just as far. Petrovitch was uncertain whether the crowd were willing him on or trying to haul him down with their thoughts.

He sat down, his legs dangling free over the edge of the rubble. It was risky, certainly. Part of him realized it and relished it. It wasn't as if the remains were in any way stabilized. They would, and did, occasionally shift.

The man making his way up was taking a *yebani* long time. The clock in the corner of his vision counted out the seconds and minutes, and a quick consultation with his diary told him he needed to be somewhere on the other side of the Freezone in an hour.

"Are you going to get on with it, or should I come back tomorrow?" he called down.

The man's face turned upward, and Petrovitch's heart spun just a little faster.

"You could come and help me," said the man.

"Why should I make it easy for you? You never made it easy for me."

"You could have asked for someone else to officiate." He stopped and straightened up, giving Petrovitch a good view of the white clerical collar tucked around the neck of his black shirt.

"Madeleine wouldn't have anyone else. And whether she was punishing you or me, I still haven't worked out."

"Both, probably." The priest scrubbed at his face. He was sweating, despite the cold. "We need to talk."

"It's not like I've been hiding."

"We need to talk, now."

"I'm not shouting the rest of the conversation."

"Then help me."

Petrovitch considered matters. It'd be entirely reasonable to raise his middle finger and strand the priest on the side of an unstable rubble pile, leaving him the equally difficult climb down.

"I should tell you to *otvali.*"

"But you won't. You're tired, Petrovitch. The things you want most in the world are just as much out of your reach as they ever were."

Perhaps it was true. Perhaps he'd grown weary of continual confrontation. Perhaps he had, despite himself, changed.

"Meh." He jumped down and slithered the ten meters between them, closing the distance in bare seconds. He tucked his coat-tails underneath him and sat down where he'd stopped. "Here's good. Say what you have to say. Better still, say why you couldn't have said it anywhere else. Unless you crave a ready-made audience." Petrovitch frowned and sent virtual agents scurrying across the local network nodes. "You're not wired, are you?"

"Priests, above everyone else, should be able to keep secrets." Father John looked around him for a suitable perch, and Petrovitch rolled his eyes: servos whirred, and tiny pumps squeezed some more moisture out to coat the hard surfaces of the implants.

"It's not comfortable for me, and I don't care if it is for you. I have somewhere else to be soon enough, so you haven't got me for long."

The father crouched down on his haunches and tried to sit. He started to slip, and Petrovitch's arm slammed, not gently, across his chest. It forced him onto his backside.

"Plant your feet, you *mudak.* Be certain." When he was sure the priest wasn't going to start a landslide, he put his hand back in his lap. "It's all about confidence, misplaced or otherwise."

"A metaphor for your life?" Father John rocked slightly from side to side, trying and failing to create a buttock-shaped depression underneath him.

"*Poydi'k chertu.* It's worked well enough so far."

"So far," said Father John, "but not any longer. You're stuck, aren't you?"

"*Jebat moi lisiy cherep.*"

"And if you'd stop swearing at me and listen, I might be able to help." He risked falling to gesture at the people below. "So might they."

"I…" started Petrovitch. He looked at the crowd. He zoomed in and panned across their faces. He could have, if he'd wanted, named every one of them from the Freezone database. "They come here, day after day, and they don't say anything. None of them ever say what they want."

"You must have some idea."

"I haven't got a *yebani* clue." Petrovitch shrugged. "I've never been too good at the human stuff."

"That much is true. Did it never occur to you to speak to them? That that's what they're expecting?"

Petrovitch's mouth twitched again, and he pushed his finger up the bridge of his nose to adjust his non-existent glasses.

"What?"

"For the love of God, man." It was the priest's turn to be exasperated. "You might be reviled by every politician from the Urals westward, but they," and he pointed downward again, "they love you. You saved them. Twice. The ones who actually think about it know they owe their lives to you. Even those that don't think you're a living saint are indebted to you to a degree that any leader, religious or secular, would give their eye teeth for."

"I don't ask for it or need it."

"Yes, you do. You come up here every day and do this, this thing that you do. You know it's futile, pointless even. You could have spent your time lobbying the EU, the UN, but as far as I know, you haven't talked to anyone about what's trapped under here."

"Not what. Who. He has a name." Petrovitch felt the old anger rise up, but he knew how to deal with it. Breathe slowly, control the spin of his heart, play a brainwave pattern designed to mimic relaxation.

"Michael," said the father. "That girl said…"

"She has a name too. Lucy."

The priest looked troubled for a moment.

"We're not talking about Lucy now. Or ever. So stick to the subject because the clock's ticking."

"How long is it going to take you to dig out Michael from under here, using your bare hands?"

Petrovitch leaned forward, resting his elbows on his knees. "When you say the magic words over your bread and wine, is it you who changes them to body and blood?" He knew he was on controversial territory, but he was doing more than enough to pay for the right, just by sitting and listening.

"No. It's by the power of the Holy Spirit—not that I expect you to believe that."

"So why say the words at all?"

"Because the words are important."

"And you have the answer to your question." Petrovitch stroked his nose. "This is a symbol."

"But it has no efficacy."

"What?"

"This. This throwing something down off this

mountain. You'll be dead before you finish and the A... and Michael will still be trapped. The sacraments have the power to save. This is nothing but an empty gesture." Father John waved his hands in the air, to indicate just how great the nothingness was.

"One man's empty gesture is another's meaningful ritual." Petrovitch pursed his lips. "You don't want to go down that road. Not with me."

The priest pulled a face. "Look, I've been sent here. Sent here to ask you a question, and this is the only time you're ever alone."

"It's not like my answer is going to change in company." His interest was piqued, though. "Who sent you?"

"The Congregation for the Doctrine of the Faith."

Petrovitch raised his eyebrows. "The Inquisition? That's unexpected."

"Give it a rest. They haven't been called the Inquisition for over fifty years."

"So what do they want?"

"They want to know whether Michael can be considered to be alive. And if he is, does he have a soul?"

"Really? He's been trapped under this mound of rubble for almost a year and it's only now they decide to take any notice. Where have they been?" He snorted. "Up their own collective *zhopu?*"

"I don't expect you to understand," said the priest. "They've been doing nothing but debate this since the Long Night. What if an AI shows signs of independent, creative thought? What if it can empathize? What if it has the capacity for generosity, altruism, compassion?"

"I could have given them the answers eleven months ago."

"That's not the point. They needed to decide theoretically about all those what-ifs. If it could, what should we do about it, if anything? They have," and he hesitated, "a protocol they've drawn up. A sort of Turing test, except it doesn't measure intelligence. It measures *animus*."

"So the Vatican wants to know if Michael is a spiritual being, or the equivalent of meat." Petrovitch blinked. "*Yobany stos*. They want to know if it can be saved."

"Something like that. The Holy Father ratified the protocol last night. The Congregation called me straightaway. They haven't been sitting on their hands; for the Church, this counts as indecent haste."

Petrovitch considered matters, then made his decision.

"No," he said.

"No? I haven't even told you what the Congregation wants."

"Doesn't matter." He got up and brushed the tails of his coat down. "The answer's the same. I'm not playing."

"If the Church declares Michael ensouled, then there's a moral duty laid on every Catholic to help free it." Father John tried to stand too, but Petrovitch had moved far enough away to be out of reach. The priest's feet started to slide again. "I thought that's what you wanted? You need us."

"Yeah. So you say." Petrovitch reached out and took hold of a broken iron beam. He knew it would take his weight, and he swung up on it. From there, he could regain the summit.

"Petrovitch! I thought you'd be pleased."

That stopped him. He looked back over his shoulder and shook his head slowly. "What the *huy* made you think that? Listen to me, because I'm only going to waste my breath saying this once. I don't care what a bunch of old men—and they are all men, aren't they?—I don't care what they say about Michael, whether they think he has a soul or not, whether he's worthy enough to be freed or whether he's going to be left here to rot for as long as his batteries last, slowly going mad in the dark. He is my friend, and I will not let him die. *Vrubatsa?*" He turned to leave, then realized he had one more thing to say.

"What?" said the priest.

"Stay away from Lucy. If I find you've so much as glanced in her direction, I'll gut you from neck to navel with a rusty spoon. You can tell Cardinal Ximenez that, too."

"That's not..." Father John gave up. "You can't stop them. Your cooperation is not necessary."

This time, Petrovitch did give the priest his middle finger. "You're about to find out just how wrong you are." He climbed up, and out of sight.

The crowd shifted nervously. They were missing something, but couldn't tell what. Most of them started to drift away. Others, the hard-core watchers, decided that they'd wait for someone to tell them what had happened.

2

$\mathcal{P}$etrovitch shook their hands: solid, Germanic greetings that went on for slightly longer than strictly necessary. The elder Krenz was a bullet-headed Bavarian with a clear liking for potato dumplings. The younger had sandy hair and an athletic build, but it was going to be a bruising fight with his genetic inheritance if he wanted to keep them.

"*Guten tag, Herren.*" Petrovitch looked at their suits, and decided that they were as uncomfortable with them as he was. "Welcome to the Freezone."

"Thank you," said the younger man. He looked around the empty dockside—empty but for the one container that had just been lifted off a ship and onto the quay. "This is ours?"

"Yeah. Sorry for having to drag you all the way over here, but my immigration status is a bit up in the air at the moment."

"Yes. So I understand." He hesitated. "What do I call you?"

"Petrovitch will do fine, Herr Krenz. No matter what you've heard to the contrary."

"Doctor Petrovitch, then." He looked at his father. "We can demonstrate the system for you, mostly wherever you like. We have included the formers for the five- and fifteen-meter structures, which is the largest we can go without prepared foundations."

"How about here?" Petrovitch shrugged. "It's as good a place as any."

There followed a moment of confusion, while the two Germans conversed in their native tongue.

"We thought that we were going to have a, a larger audience. Sonja Oshicora perhaps. Someone else from the Freezone Authority."

"Gentlemen. The Freezone Authority's mandate runs out in a couple of weeks' time. If this was a demonstration for them, they'd be here. It's not: it's a demonstration for me." He rubbed at his nose. "Is that going to be a problem?"

"I...*nein*. No, I mean."

"I know what you mean. I have a massive online dictionary and grammar checker open, and I can translate pretty much everything you say, whether it's in Hochdeutsch, Mandarin or Navaho." Petrovitch put his hand on the container's long-levered handle. "Shall we get on with it?"

Inside the container—very much the size of his old domik—were crates and bundles and, at the back, barrels of solvent and bulging black bales of granulated polymer. The two Germans started to unroll a large plastic sheet out on the gritty surface of the quay, while Petrovitch poked around.

He'd seen the company's videos. He'd seen the pictures of the finished product. What he wanted, almost more than anything, was to see one for himself.

He dragged the generator out on its sledge, and plugged the industrial fan in. Krenz the elder watched him.

"You have the knowledge, yes?"

"I know pretty much what to do. I could have probably done all this myself, got all the makings for it, but I would have ended up making the mistakes that you've already fixed. I don't have time to make mistakes, Herr Krenz."

"You have fear?" He snorted like a bull. "You?"

"I know my reputation precedes me. But I'm not like that, really." He looked up at Krenz. "I just have a lot on my plate at the moment."

"It is not for me to give you the questions." Krenz checked the fuel gauge on the genny and thumbed the starter button. "I have one only."

The motor puttered into life, and he checked its performance by cocking his ear and listening to the quality of the sound it made.

"The question is this: how will you pay? No Freezone, no EU, no UN. No Oshicora." Krenz wiped at his bald head. "I meet Samuil Petrovitch. That is enough for today, but I am not a . . ." He struggled for the word.

"Charity." Petrovitch saw that the younger Krenz was attaching tubes to the top of the plastic sheet. Almost ready to inflate. "Don't worry, Herr Krenz. If you want money, I've got an extensive overdraft."

"A _wass?_"

"Credit. Two and a half billion euros' worth. Should be enough."

Krenz carried on working, fastening the plastic former to the fan by way of a flexible hose. Then he stopped. "Billion?"

"Yeah. I won't tell you the bank's name in case you mention it to them and a human manager takes exception. But their computer is fine with it." Petrovitch reached past

Krenz and flicked the fan's switch. The blades cut the air with an audible chop, then it speeded up, sending a draft down the thick hose and causing the plastic sheet to ripple. The structure started to swell.

"They must find out. Tomorrow. Next week."

"The line of credit's only temporary, to be paid back in full tomorrow. In the meantime, if they kick up a fuss, I have a list of their other customers." Petrovitch smiled. "It includes some really very unpleasant people, and I'm guessing that unless they want half of Africa camped out on their doorstep demanding their stolen money back, they won't want it made public."

After twenty minutes, a shiny gray hemisphere quivered tautly on the dockside. In the meantime, the Krenzes had cooked up a batch of filler, and now started to pump it down the tubing.

"How long?" asked Petrovitch over the noise.

Young Krenz answered him. "Half an hour to fill. Five minutes to cure with the ultraviolet light."

"If I wanted one, I don't know, a hundred meters across? How would you do that?"

"We do not, we cannot…"

Petrovitch brushed his excuses aside. "The science is sound. It's just an engineering problem."

"Why would you want one that big? The domes are connectable. You just build more."

"I really want one bigger than that. Two hundred, maybe two fifty across. The solution for one hundred will be the same as for two hundred."

"But, Doctor. The air former would collapse under the weight of the uncured polymer."

"Yeah. But you don't cure as you go, do you? You fill

completely, then set it solid with the UV. What if you fixed the bottom part of it even as you were pumping more on top? That's how Brunelleschi built his domes. Six hundred years ago."

"Yes, I understand that. I can only say we have never been asked to build one as big before now." Young Krenz frowned. "Why would you want to?"

"Because," said Petrovitch, "I saw it in a dream. Then when I had the time to look into it, I found your company. They're exactly the same. Just smaller."

"But a two-hundred-meter dome? You could put a village under it."

"Yeah. Something like that. Along with heat exchangers, a water reclamation system, hydroponics, air scrubbers. You do a passive photochromic coating for when it gets sunny, but there's no reason why you couldn't do a translucent photovoltaic one instead. It's pretty much free off-grid power. Use it to make hydrogen and store it for a fuel-cell power plant."

Older Krenz interrupted. "Herr Doktor. Why do you need us at all?"

"I could steal your tech. I could buy your company. Or I can behave like a decent human being for once and trade with you rather than ripping you off or taking over. Why don't we wait until we're ready before we talk terms?"

The pump finished filling the space between the two skins of the former, and the UV tubes already underneath flashed darkly into life. Petrovitch rested his hand on the gray outside and felt the warmth of the uncured resin. He pulled his hand away, only to see the slight impression remain. It had gone hard already, and had preserved his palm-print for posterity.

He turned around. Older Krenz had an old-fashioned stopwatch which he turned face out toward him.

"You must wait. Three minutes."

He reluctantly backed away and, at the end of three minutes, the Krenzes set to work on the former, disconnecting the pipes and cutting through the thick plastic sheeting with short, curved knives. Petrovitch made a mental note that the formers he was going to use ought to be reusable.

They disconnected the fan and turned off the generator. After the constant noise, the silence was profound. There were sounds in the distance—the heavy, rhythmic thud of a pile-driver, the light chatter of a road-drill, and from across the river, traffic and sirens—but nothing to distract him from the imminent unveiling.

Young Krenz took one side, his father the other, and together they peeled the outer covering off the dome. The internal former had fallen away. All that was left was a trick of the light, an optical illusion.

The material was crystal clear: only the lensing effect made its presence visible. Petrovitch walked forward, the fingers of one hand stretched out in front of him, stepping slowly until his fingertips brushed against a smooth, oily surface. He left smears that seemed to hang in mid-air.

"*Yobany stos.*"

He paced around it, watching the way the images of the Krenzes warped and shifted through the plastic shell, until he arrived back at the start.

"Is it what you wanted?" asked Young Krenz.

Petrovitch hesitated before answering. In a moment, he was old again, looking down on a shoreline that was pocked with domes, while above him in the blue sky, flecks of light were rising out of sight. He was dying, and he didn't care.

"Yeah." He didn't need to imagine what it would look like scaled up. He'd already seen it. "Let's deal."

He offered them straight cash, in return for a licensing deal, access to their plans and their suppliers. He offered them enough that Young Krenz assumed that his father was going to take it, but Older Krenz had other ideas.

"I would make you a hundred-meter dome. I would that you show me the way to make it. I believe that, yes, we make playhouses and greenhouses and swimming pool covers, but we can make them bigger? You show me how. You show me these coatings. We are family business: small and reliable, but not…"

"Imaginative," interrupted Young Krenz. He looked rueful, as if he'd had this conversation a hundred times before.

"Yes, yes, that. You tell us how to build bigger, and we will do it for you."

"I won't be asking for just one dome. I'll want several to start with, then more. I want to be able to do this myself. With help, sure, but something that a few people can put up in a day or so. Are you worried that I'm going to set up in competition against you?"

Krenz nodded.

"Herr Krenz, in two weeks' time, I'm going to need somewhere else to live. When the Metrozone Authority takes over, it'll be a matter of hours before I'm dragged in front of a judge on one extradition warrant or another. I'm not interested in Petrovitch Industries, I'm interested in my own survival. So, how about this? I will give you every-thing I can think of. Every last technical detail of every innovation I can come up with. In return, you do the same for me. Everything. No hiding anything to get a commercial advantage, because there won't be any. You'll be the only one selling Krenz domes. Think you can do that?"

"A . . . what is the word?"

"Partnership. I think."

The Krenzes looked at each other across the quayside, and at the smaller figure standing between them.

"Okay. Where do you want the first one built?"

Petrovitch started to laugh, and he laughed so hard that his lungs ached. "That, gentlemen, I can't tell you."

"But . . ."

"Because I don't exactly know."

"You do not know?"

"Not yet."

"How can we then go forward?"

Petrovitch dug his hands in his pockets. "Go home. Order formers for a hundred-meter dome. A dozen of them. Get all the stuff together that you'll need—I'll send instructions for the extra kit. Then you wait for my call. If it clicks past two weeks and I'm all over the news chained up in an orange jumpsuit, you'll have to assume the deal's off."

"We will be rich, or bankrupt." Young Krenz digested the news, and Older Krenz scratched at his head. "This is not a choice I wanted to have."

"That's fine. I'll give you two million up front." Petrovitch blinked. "Done. Don't spend it all at once."

He started to walk back toward where the new skyscrapers were taking shape, where the cranes were tallest and the sounds of construction the loudest, when Young Krenz called after him.

"Do you want nothing in writing? A signed agreement? Something? Anything?"

Petrovitch twisted around and walked backward, unerringly navigating any of the obstacles in his path. Just because he couldn't see them didn't mean he wasn't looking. He considered telling the Krenzes that he'd recorded everything that had gone on: every word, every gesture, every detail of the equipment and the chemicals they'd used. He decided that would weird them out completely, and he needed them.

"I have your word. Do I need anything more?"

"I suppose not. This is most irregular, though."

"CNN called me an international criminal mastermind this morning. The *Jyllands-Posten* only has me down as the most dangerous man alive, which is slightly better, but not much. Yeah, of course I'll sign something if you want. Or we can keep this below the radar for as long as we can. Your call."

"We will do as you say, then. Two weeks? That does not give us much time."

"You and me both, Herr Krenz." Petrovitch took one last look at the dome, glittering in the low winter sun. The surface was cooling, and attracting moisture. If that was the case, he could have dew traps all around the base . . .

Then he turned again. He went back on the 'net, searching for anything of significance, while he let client software take over his walking.

It seemed like the whole world was intent on tearing itself apart, and he was setting himself up as the only one who could mend it again. Stupid, stupid, hubristic delusions. And yet he'd contacted a couple of obscure German engineers in their quiet Bavarian town, and they'd come of their own free will. No one had put a gun to their heads: a tactic Petrovitch was so used to, he'd grown sick of it.

His phone—the virtual one in his head—rang. He absently picked up the call before he'd checked the number, before he'd run it though a search program to tell him where the dialer was and who they were. He was distracted. A mistake, and he didn't often make that sort of error.

"Yeah?"

"Is that Samuil Petrovitch?"

The voice was American. The face attached to the voice tickled a memory buried deep inside his mind: it was clean-cut, well-fed, healthy. That was now, but back then he'd been bruised, ragged, terrified and desperate.

"Just to get this straight: your name didn't used to be Petrovitch when you lived in St. Petersburg four, five years ago. You worked for a man called Boris. He kidnapped me…"

"*Chyort*. Dalton."

3

I suppose this conversation was inevitable, but I'm pretty certain that when we went our separate ways, we had an unspoken agreement that we'd never talk to each other ever again." Even though Petrovitch was transmitting voice-only, there was no point in denying who he was.

"That," said Dalton, "had always been my intention, too. Forget St. Petersburg, forget Boris, forget you. Then suddenly a year ago, you became public enemy number one. It was kind of hard to ignore you. Walmart were selling caricature masks of you for Halloween."

"Yeah, well. What happens in St. Petersburg, stays in St. Petersburg." Petrovitch took a long look at Dalton, the office behind him, and the view from the window in what must have been an achingly tall tower of glass and steel. "You seem to have bounced back."

"What do I call you?"

"A lot of people ask me that. I tell them the same thing: Petrovitch."

"Doctor Petrovitch?"

"If they're being kind. You were always Dalton when

I remembered you. Just call me Petrovitch and have done with it. Speaking of which, you shouldn't really be calling me anything. I'm the Antichrist, the devil incarnate and the villain in a thousand badly written and factually incorrect stories. You could be arrested for even talking to me."

Dalton stroked his fantastically smooth, tanned, moisturized chin. He leaned over and opened a slim cardboard file. The first sheet of paper had the picture of a man, a little younger than Petrovitch, with a shock of black hair falling over his left eye. "Know who that is?"

He did. "That's Anarchy. Wannabe-überhacker. Hit the NSA three months ago with a modified trojan, caused all sorts of problems, some of which they're still sorting out. Yeah, he's several steps ahead of the usual script-kiddies, but he got caught."

"He's a client of my firm. He assured me that this line is entirely private."

"There's no such thing as private anymore, Dalton. Not in this brave new world. Information wants to be free."

"Private enough, then. Enough to take the risk in contacting you."

"And why would you want to do that? You seem to have been doing fine without me." As Petrovitch talked, he was searching the public and not-so-public records for an indication as to just how fine. "There you go: partner in the business, equity share, big corner office, married, a son and daughter, and another on the way—congratulations—house in the Hamptons. Kind of expensive, but you married money. Your wife's father is a hardcore Reconstructionist, a senator, no less. You have done well. Too well to want to blow it all on saying hello to me."

Dalton seemed to be having trouble breathing. "Whoa. Marie's pregnant?"

"She went to a specialist yesterday. The day before, she bought three different off-the-shelf testing kits. It looks likely." Petrovitch coughed. "Sorry if I ruined the surprise."

"I'll have to pretend I don't know." Dalton had his fist closed over his chest. "Are you just yanking my chain?"

"Not this time, *tovarisch*. She's probably just waiting for the right time to tell you. Sure you don't want to hang up on me?"

"I made my decision a while back. I…I'm a coward, Petrovitch. You know that better than most. I went to pieces, and it was only because you kept your head that I'm here today. Everything I have now, I owe it to you. I want—five years too late—to thank you."

"Dalton, I raped your bank accounts. I took pretty much everything you had at the time. I beggared you. Or have you forgotten? Maybe you've forgotten too about all the other people that Boris kidnapped and I didn't help? Or the ones where something went wrong—when the ransom wasn't paid or there was a trace on the account—what about them? The ones he killed. The ones where he put his hands around their neck and crushed their larynx so that they'd suffocate, nice and slow. Every time that happened, I just turned the page on whichever textbook I was reading, and was glad it wasn't me."

"Petrovitch, I've been in denial ever since I got back from St. Petersburg. Some mornings I woke up and I even wondered if it had even happened to me at all. Then your face was all over the news and I found I couldn't suppress the memories any longer. But who can I talk to? This man, this Russian kid who saved me, is the same one who's an enemy of the state. Maybe if I'd have come clean a year ago, things would have been fine. I couldn't, because I was a coward then, and I'm a coward now."

"You're not a coward, Dalton. You didn't ask to be kidnapped. None of Boris' victims did. And I wasn't some *yebani* angel, sent from above to help you. You were the opportunity I needed to bail out, and it could just as easily have been someone else."

"You don't understand, Petrovitch . . ."

"Then explain it better, man!"

"I'm trying to. In court, I'm this silver-tongued magician. Opposing counsel are actually afraid of me. Me? Can you believe that?"

"Okay. You feel like you owe me something. I want nothing from you. I took what I needed at the time. I can even pay it back, though that's as likely to get you into trouble as anything else."

"The money means nothing to me."

"You weren't impressed at the time."

"You made me reassess all my priorities. Everything I have dates from the moment I stepped back onto U.S. soil. My family, my career. I earned more money in the twelve months after I came back than you took from me."

"It was enough. Enough to get me away, enough to hide me. I was, if not happy, fulfilled. And I hadn't had to kill anyone to be that way. It was a good deal, Dalton. Both of us got something we wanted out of it. It was fair. Okay, your thanks is welcome, but why drag this up now, unless you've suddenly developed a death wish? What are you going to tell your wife when she asks you how work was?" Petrovitch's eyelid twitched. "She doesn't know any of this, does she? When you said, who could you tell, what you meant was, you haven't told her anything."

Dalton made a little gesture of defeat with his shoulders.

"I've been married for just over a year," said Petrovitch, "and even I know that not telling your wife stuff is bad." He went off on his own reverie for a moment, before snapping his concentration back to the American. "Doesn't mean I follow my own advice, though."

"Every time you come on the news—and that's a lot—she starts up on this tirade of abuse. About how you're like Hitler and Stalin, Pol Pot and Mao all rolled into one. That you're coming for us while we sleep, because freaks like you don't need sleep; about how you're plotting to take away our country and our values and our children. She's smart, and loving, and kind. She runs charity fundraisers for good causes. She's leader of the women's circle at church. She's a good person, Petrovitch, a godly person, the mother of my children."

"All three of them."

"That. And every time she starts, I want to shake her and shake her until she stops because you're the reason I'm there at all."

Petrovitch tilted his head to one side. "You could just stop watching the news with her."

"I have to tell her. I have to tell her tonight."

"That's up to you, Dalton. I wouldn't. I'd bury it so deep it'd take a geological age to bring it to the surface again. You have a good life: don't throw it away. Look— what she believes might be true. I tricked Boris into letting you go, and in doing so, I betrayed the trust of a man who'd shown me nothing but kindness. The money he gave me kept me and my mother and my sister fed. It allowed me to study. When I fucked Boris over, I did it for cold, hard cash, and I still haven't dared to find out what happened to the rest of my family. You can keep on fooling yourself about my motives for saving you, but I know what went through my mind that night."

Dalton leaned back in his chair and looked around his office, at all the accoutrements of his position and his power. "I'm a lawyer, right? I do corporate law. The guys I work with, both clients and partners, play hardball with each other to get even the slightest advantage. They don't give anything away, either. Sure, we're all brothers in the Reconstruction: we all stay sober and clean, we don't swear or hire hookers, we all smile and gladhand each other and ask about each other's wives, Maybe some of them actually believe it." He put his tongue in his cheek and rolled it around, the bulge visible from the outside. "The thing is, what they're doing to each other is all the more savage and brutal because they have the outward appearance of being decent, dependable men—while the truth is, every last one of those robbers would have left me to rot in that St. Petersburg basement."

Petrovitch tried to voice his objections, but didn't get any further than a stuttered "I..."

"You had all my money, hundreds of thousands of dollars of it. You could have cut and run. Instead, you came back for me. You scammed Boris and if he'd known any of it, if he'd suspected a single thing, he would have killed the pair of us in an eyeblink. You risked your life to save mine." Dalton jabbed his finger at the camera. "I know your secret, Petrovitch. I know that you are a good person and you will always be that way."

"Yeah, well." Petrovitch blew out a stream of air. "Don't spread it around. I've a reputation to keep."

"I want to help you. I want to do for you what you did for me."

"I'm not lying on a filthy mattress in a kidnapper's freezing-cold basement getting trashed on cheap vodka just to stay warm."

"Your colleague Doctor Ekanobi is. Apart from the vodka part."

"We had one of your CIA agents in custody, and I'd hoped for an exchange, but Sonja said she was forced to just hand her back. We got nothing in return." Petrovitch pursed his lips. "No one has seen Pif for ten months. Homeland Security have her...somewhere. Even I can't find out where. You know, all your really confidential stuff is done on hand-written notes now. You use typewriters. You courier it in briefcases wired to incinerate their contents if they're tampered with. I have nothing, Dalton. I can't even suggest where to start looking for her."

"Why don't you let me deal with that?"

"If the Nobel committee can't find her, what makes you think you can?"

"Because I'm flying to California tomorrow with a writ of habeas corpus in my pocket. I'm going to serve it in the State Supreme Court, and I expect them to rule on it in a couple of days. Wherever she is, whoever has her, will have to bring her to court and argue their case in front of a judge."

"Far be it from me to point out some flaws in your plan, but are you a complete *mudak?* Apart from the fact all they're going to do is laugh in your face when you wave your little piece of paper at them, you're going to end up dead on the court steps. If someone doesn't shoot you first, a rent-a-mob will beat your brains out with their fists."

"They won't laugh at me, Petrovitch. The justices take their responsibilities very seriously indeed. They have to act. They have no choice. Habeas corpus applies equally in all courts. It applies to every branch of the judiciary and the executive. It applies to everyone, citizen or not. They have to produce her person and give their reason, in law, why they can continue to hold her. There are no exceptions to this rule, and believe me, I've done my homework."

"So why the *chyort* has no one done this before?"

"Because you have no friends over here. No one's going to stand up for you, or her. I know you tried to ginger up some interest, but you're fighting against Reconstruction. We all know what waits for us if we step out of line."

"What I don't get is why you're willing to risk that. Dalton, we were done. We had a deal and we carried it to a mutually beneficial conclusion. It's over. You don't owe me anything, anymore than I owe you."

"I've read everything about you. I know what you've done, what you had to go through to do it. I know about the Sorensons and the CIA. I know about this...thing you call Michael and where it came from. I know about the Long Night. I know what you are. I know you. You don't get me because you're not me. You don't know anything about me, about the thousand little compromises I make every waking hour just to fit in with this vast, cold mono- lith called Reconstruction. If you knew me, you'd curse me and call me a coward, because that's what I've been like every day for five years." Dalton looked above the camera. There must have been a clock on the wall behind it. "I was only supposed to be on for five minutes. Six max. No matter how careful I'm being, they can still trace this call."

"I can deal with that," said Petrovitch. "You know they're going to crucify you. You're going to lose everything. Your wife is going to leave you and take your kids with her. Her daddy's going to ruin you. And you'll be so fired, I'll be able to see the detonation from orbit."

"I know."

"And you're still going to go through with this?"

"Yes. Flight's booked. My case is packed. I'm leaving tomorrow."

"I don't know what to say. I'm supposed to be the king of the futile gesture, and here I am, trumped by some stupid Yankee lawyer. I can only say this one more time: Dalton, don't do it."

"The time when you could tell me what to do is long past, Petrovitch. I don't think I'll have to call you again to let you know how I'm doing. I think that's going to be pretty obvious."

"Just . . . when all this is over, and you need somewhere to hide: I can do that for you, too."

"Thank you." There was a tone, and a woman's voice announced that his next appointment was outside. "I won't keep him a minute, Adele." Dalton muted the intercom. "Not that it's going to matter. All my clients will drop me like a scalding-hot stone when they find out."

"You'd better go." Petrovitch blinked. He'd walked all the way to Limehouse. A truck was rattling slowly up behind him, its back full of blue-overalled *nikkeijin:* an Oshicora work crew. He raised his hand to the driver, who brought the vehicle slowly to a halt.

"Goodbye, Petrovitch."

"Goodbye, Dalton. And good luck." Petrovitch caught the outstretched arm of one of the workers and clambered up over the tailgate. The men and women shuffled aside to make room for him, and he sat down, back against the low metal side.

"Petrovitch-san," said the foreman, "you are crying." He proffered his own packet of paper tissues, of which there was one left.

"It's dust. And these *yebani* eyes." Petrovitch tapped the white of his left eye with his ragged fingernail so that it made a distinct hollow tock. "It always happens when it's cold."

4

The truck took him all the way to Green Park, through the area worst affected by the Outie advance: the East and West Ends, Commercial Road and Whitechapel, Aldgate and Holborn, and Aldwych.

A few of the damaged buildings were being saved. Most had been torn down, the remains of them carted away to be picked through and recycled by Metrozoners south of the river and desperate for work. There were lucrative contracts for that, like there were contracts for everything these days.

In place of the lost historic facades, towers of steel and glass rose up to touch the sky—and the Freezone was making sure that each and every one of them could generate their own power, cool themselves down in summer and heat themselves up in winter, and be as safe and clean and bright as they could be.

The architects loved Petrovitch, too.

As soon as the truck stopped, he vaulted off the back and onto the road. He made his *sayonaras*, and started down Piccadilly. He glanced up at the ruins of the

Oshicora Tower, its pinnacle catching the low winter sun as it sneaked through a gap in the high cloud.

Father John had evidently made it down again. Petrovitch didn't care much if he'd done so in one piece. It was tempting to make the ascent again, just for himself, like it had been in the beginning. He toyed with the idea before dismissing it: if he broke the established ritual, someone might ask why. Which would be bad. He needed to keep everyone's attention focused on the things he did in the open, so that they wouldn't start looking for his sleights-of-hand.

Misdirection. It was harder work than mere secrecy.

He rounded Hyde Park Corner. He had a suite of rooms in the nearby Hilton, what was left of it. No one would be there, though: Valentina and Tabletop would be stalking the streets, searching for the unaccounted-for CIA agent Slipper, while Lucy was busy—at least, should be busy—in Petrovitch's lab. New lab. There wasn't much left of the old one, or anything else around it. *V'nebrachny* Americans.

They were building on Hyde Park, just like they seemed to be building everywhere, though the work was slower because of the bodies they kept on exhuming and carrying away to a temporary mortuary on the edge of the site. But they worked none the less. Cranes, trucks, workers. Pile-drivers, welders, scaffolders. So much noise where there had been only silence.

He dug his hands into his pockets and kept walking, right past the end of Exhibition Road, still cordoned off with temporary wire barriers while the college and the State Department argued about who was responsible for the damage. Petrovitch lingered again: all that remained of the whiteboard Pif had used to extract the first of her equations was a grainy photograph taken on her camera. His original floating sphere was somewhere underneath it.

Everything was temporary. Nothing lasted forever, not things, not people, not love, not time itself.

He shrugged and walked on. Of course there was no question over who was responsible, just one over who was going to pay for it. In the meantime, he carried on past the Albert Hall to the building just next door—an arts college—which he'd co-opted until they could find some artists.

Glass-fronted edifices had fared badly, and this one had been no exception. The front was swathed in heavy plastic that rippled in the wind and did nothing to insulate the inside from the biting cold. But there was electricity, and light, and network access. He'd decided that it was good enough, and set up shop in the basement.

He peeled his way through the doorframe and let the translucent sheet fall back behind him. The sounds of outside became muffled and changed. It was more like a ship at sea now, crackling and groaning with every gust and gyre.

"Hey," he said.

Out of sight, Lucy answered into her mouthpiece. "I was waiting for you."

Petrovitch headed for the stairwell. "Are you done?"

He could hear her breathing: she would insist on balancing the microphone just too high so that it was between her nose and her upper lip. "I don't know. I mean, I followed the instructions, and it looks like it could work. There were some bits left over."

"There always are." He trotted down the stairs and through the fire doors.

"It's not going to blow up, is it?"

"No."

"Sure?"

"Yeah. Well, the flywheel might. As long as you don't stand directly in the way, it'll be fine." He barged through another door. The room had originally been for the curation and restoration of old paintings, big enough for what he wanted, but the machine in front of him was now too tall, too wide, to ever make it outside. He looked back at the exit. "Can't think of everything."

Lucy peeled her headset off and threw it casually on the side of a sink. "For what it's worth," and she made a little show of revealing her creation, as if she were a magician's assistant.

Which, in a way, she was.

She looked so painfully young, so painfully alone. Petrovitch was a poor substitute for a parent: he had no idea how to make it better. Keeping her occupied like this was the best he could do, but it didn't stop her from waking in the night, calling out for her lost mother and father, and sobbing when she realized that they were never coming back.

"Are you going to start it up, then?"

She went back to her printed notes. "Okay. Turn it on at the wall—done that. Take the manual brakes off the flywheel and the oscillator." As she spun the two wheels that released the clamps, she asked, "Did you get a call today? From a Catholic priest?"

"Yeah. No; he came to talk to me in person. Haven't seen any old guys in red robes wandering around yet, but it's only a matter of time."

"What's it all about? He asked me about Michael,

whether I'd be willing to talk to some committee or other. I'd said he'd need to check with you first."

"He had checked with me first. I told him I'd rip his arms off and beat him with the wet ends if he bothered you."

"I guess it'll suck to be him, then." She looked down at the sheet of paper in her hand, and flicked two switches.

"Tell me if he tries to contact you again. Or anyone else on the same subject." He wondered how far to take it. "I'm not going to forbid you from talking about Michael— not really my style—but, you know. I'd prefer it if you didn't. Not to them."

"I won't." She tugged at her ponytail and flashed him a smile. "Don't worry."

"The judge said it's my job to worry about you."

Her smile slipped, and she turned her back on him.

"Sorry," he said.

"Stop apologizing. Just, just press a button, or something."

Petrovitch sighed and reached past her to thumb the big red button on the front of the control panel. The machine's central column sank down smoothly, then with only the top part of it showing, it rose again to its full height. It paused for a moment, then started to sink again, repeating the cycle.

Lucy looked up. "That bit works."

"Engage the magnetic coupling."

"You love this, don't you?"

"You'll learn to love it too." Petrovitch watched as she closed the circuit-breaker on the electromagnets. There were actual honest-to-god sparks, fat blue ones that leaped out at the copper contacts.

She gave a little squeak, but there was no harm done.

A needle started to pulse across a meter, creeping ever closer to the end-stop. The machine began to sing with a low bass note.

Petrovitch eased Lucy aside and inspected all the dials and readings. At some point he was going to have to modify the test rig so that it gave a digital read-out that he could then arrange in neat graphs and publish in a reputable peer-reviewed journal.

For now, he contented himself with making a recording of everything he saw, storing it away on the hard-drive he kept in his pocket.

The flywheel was starting to push the limits which he'd set and, with no load, there was nothing to stop it eventually spinning itself to destruction. The pitch it was calling at was beyond a middle-C: time to let it slow down. He heaved the switching gear back and thumbed the red switch.

The central column stopped its steady rise and fall, and the flywheel's note slowly ran down through the octave.

"So what did we just do?"

Petrovitch lined up the footage he'd shot, editing it down and splicing it to a convenient thirty-second clip that a news channels could stream without effort. "Solved the world's energy needs for the foreseeable future."

"How?"

"By using a second-quantum repulsor to lift a weight, which then falls and does work. But the energy we use to power the repulsors to raise the load is less than we generate when it goes down. It's a perpetual motion machine." The video clip and the accompanying notes were ready to go. "If you've got shares in energy companies, tell me now."

"Hang on." Lucy walked around the base of the machine. "We put electricity in. We get electricity out. More comes out than we put in, so we can use that electricity to run the machine and still have some left over. Right?"

"And it'll never stop. Once you've built one, you have free power—until it breaks down, of course. Even I can't prevent that."

"How much free power?"

"Out of this thing? Barely enough for a two-bar electric fire. But they'll get bigger, better. No one will ever build a power station again that doesn't use these."

"You're serious."

"Yeah. I mean, it's not really free energy: it has to come from somewhere, because otherwise that's just wrong. But we don't have to do anything to get it. We just press a button and there it is." There was nothing stopping him. "Sure about those shares?"

"They're going to get hosed, aren't they?"

"Yeah. That's progress for you." And he sent the footage out into the ether. "It's way past lunch. You eaten yet?"

"No." She went back through the checklist, turning everything off, before finally unplugging the device from the wall. "I didn't feel hungry."

"Neither did I, but I suppose we ought. I'll buy."

"You're going to have to. Your idea of a regular allowance is once every six months." She looked at him. "Anyway, since when have you had to pay for anything?"

"Yeah. Okay, so let's go out and see what we can scrounge."

They left the arts college, pushing back out through the plastic and onto the street. Petrovitch interrogated the local area for somewhere serving food: the nearest was their "usual," the works canteen in the middle of the Hyde Park building site.

The man watching the main gate threw a couple of hard hats at them, waving them through before Petrovitch was able to explain his mission. But it was like that most places he went in the Freezone: he had the grace to feel faintly embarrassed, while Lucy took it as her right.

"It's cold," she said, balancing across a line of duck-boards. "Never used to be this cold."

"The Metrozone made its own weather. It will do again. Next winter here won't be like this one."

"And where will we be next winter?"

"Difficult to say," said Petrovitch. "We have options. Would you want to stay here, after the Freezone packs up?"

"I don't know. There's not much left for me here. There's the house, I suppose." The house; not her house or her parents' house, not even home. "Maybe I should sell it to someone else. It's in good condition."

"You could keep it, too."

"I think," she said, "that I wouldn't be comfortable liv-ing there whatever I decide to do." Lucy glanced back at Petrovitch. "I'd keep thinking about what I saw out of my bedroom window."

"Ah. Fox."

"Yes. Him." She carried on, seemingly more at ease with the howl of metal grinders and the actinic white glare of welding torches than quiet suburbia.

Ahead were prefab huts, jacked up on pylons to be clear of the mud—purpose built, not converted domiks. Win-dows ran with condensation and pearled the artificial light inside. The exhaust from an extractor blew cooking smells at them with the force of a gale.

"So, salad not on the menu again."

"Yeah, well. It's not like I have a heart to worry about anymore." Petrovitch held the door open for her, and she stepped inside, flipping her hard hat into her hand.

They were greeted like heroes, and Lucy was right: he never had to pay for anything, and neither did she. The construction workers were honored to merely sit and eat with the two. They crowded around, joining tables, moving chairs, taking far longer over their second mug of coffee than their agreed break allowed.

They asked him questions—on any subject, because he always had an opinion—and he answered them between mouthfuls of bread, bacon, sausage and beans, waving his fork around when he needed emphasis.

In the corner of the room, unwatched, a flat-screen monitor showed a tall column of milled steel rising and falling in the center of a crude octagonal base. A voice-over expressed wonder, fear, uncertainty—but no one in the room was listening to the news reader as she stumbled over her explanation of an over-unity engine. At some point, a talking head, someone only Petrovitch would have recognized, appeared to discuss the finer points of the laws of thermodynamics.

And even he was lost when the crowd around the table parted to let Madeleine through.

5

She stood there at one end of the long canteen table, Petrovitch sat at the other with Lucy. Silence flowed from her like a cold, heavy stream until the whole room was flooded with it.

Petrovitch pushed his plate away and leaned back in his chair. Lucy looked first at Madeleine, then at Petrovitch, trying to judge the mood. She sensed that something had changed, and she put down her fork to gently lay her hand on her ersatz-father's forearm.

Petrovitch glanced at her from the corner of his eye, and she shook her head slightly. So, no argument today. Perhaps.

It had started with one thing, and had snowballed from there: he hadn't told her about Michael. He'd kept it a secret for all kinds of reasons, and all of them, he thought, good. He hadn't cheated on her. He hadn't neglected her. He'd even fought his way through a city in flames to save her. If there was any way left for him to demonstrate his love for her, he was open to suggestions. She was Mother to everyone, but wife to none.

She didn't live with him. She didn't live anywhere,

except on her bike. She traveled around the Freezone, appearing un-announced at work camps and building sites, intent on keeping everyone honest.

Petrovitch saw her every other day or so. It might have been her way of checking up on him, keeping him honest too. She never announced her visits to him, either. But in eleven months, she'd never found him compromised, while showing no sign of coming back to him.

And now she wasn't saying anything, the silence stretching to breaking point. Someone was going to giggle, or fart, and from the expression on her face, she wasn't in the mood for levity.

"You can just call me. I'll come. And you know that."

"Yes. I know," she said. "Can we step outside for a moment?"

"Just me?"

"Just you, Sam." Her motorbike leathers creaked as she adjusted her stance. "Is that all right?"

He couldn't read her. He turned slightly to Lucy. "You going to be okay on your own for a bit?"

"I'm hardly on my own. I'll be fine. Go, go."

He pushed back his chair with a scrape. "Thank you for your company, ladies and gentlemen."

They watched him follow Madeleine out of the canteen, and only as the door started to swing shut did the murmur of conversation start up again.

She didn't stop, though. Her bike was on the far side of the site, up by Lancaster Gate. She strode, and Petrovitch had to jog to keep up with her long-legged strides.

"Where's the fire?"

"Who said anything about a fire?" she said. She was breathless, and something was wrong.

"Yeah. You going to tell me now, or do I have to work it out?"

"Neither. I'll show you."

"So there is a fire."

"Will you..." She almost broke step, as did her voice. "Just hurry."

They arrived at the gate. Petrovitch was going to wait for the guard to open the barrier: Madeleine vaulted it and went over to her bike, hastily abandoned in the middle of the road. She beckoned urgently to him.

"Sorry," he said to the bemused security man and ducked under the rising metal pole. Madeleine threw a helmet at him, which he caught unerringly even in the glare and shadows of the site's floodlights. The speed at which it came knocked him onto his back foot.

She hadn't noticed. As soon as the helmet left her hand, she was astride the bike, kicking up the stand, starting the engine with a press of her thumb.

"Aren't you putting one on too?"

"That is mine. Get on." She throttled the engine and made the turbine whine. "And hold tight."

He dropped the helmet on his head, where it slopped around loosely, and tried to work out how—and where—to sit.

"Just, just get on, Sam. Please."

He hopped his leg over and eased himself down behind her. There was a grab rail behind him, but if she was going to ride as recklessly as he thought she would, that wasn't going to be much use. Tentatively, he put his arms around Madeleine's waist and caught his fingers together.

She momentarily stiffened, then shivered. Then she hauled on the accelerator like the very gates of Hell were opening somewhere and she had to go and stand in the breach.

Petrovitch almost lost his grip. He clung on for his life, and held her closer than he'd done in almost a year.

The lights of the Freezone whipped by in a sodium-orange blur, but he knew where he was. He hat-navved them taking a sharp left—so sharp his knee almost scraped the tarmac—up the Edgware Road, and another right at Marylebone. Her old church had been on the corner there, reduced to burned timbers and scorched brick and then cleared to be yet another building site.

He'd first met her there; he'd been dying, she'd brought him back to life. He wondered if her choice of route was deliberate, as if to point out that it wasn't just him who'd been doing the saving. Or it could just have been faster this way. He knew where they were going now.

Petrovitch had had a domik at Regent's Park, a bolt-hole for when disaster struck. He'd lost it in the Long Night, along with his case of memories, courtesy of the New Machine Jihad. He'd not gone back, not looked for it amongst the tumbled chaos of containers.

The Freezone had been clearing it, crews with gas axes working day and night. They'd got almost to the lowest level. And now, as they turned another corner with the back wheel almost sliding out, there was no activity at all. No blue-white cutting flames, no noise of grinding metal or the grumble of heavy cranes.

She drove toward where the Inner Circle had been, and braked sharply. Petrovitch turned his head sideways to Madeleine's back and pressed his cheek against her, frustrated only by the plastic and kevlar of the helmet.

The engine died, and it was silent. Despite the ferocity

of the ride, they both sat there, perfectly still, him against her, she leaning slightly back to increase the contact.

"I know why we're here," he mumbled through the foam interior of the helmet.

"You do?" Her words were equally indistinct, numbed by the cold.

"Container Zero."

"How do you do it? How do you make these wild guesses and come up with the right answer?" She flexed her shoulders, and he felt her muscles move, dense and fluid.

"Because there's no other reason for us to be here. No other reason for me to be here. Everything else you can handle, but not the Last Armageddonist."

"I never believed it was true. But it is." She shrugged again, this time with purpose. "Come on. I'll show you."

Petrovitch found the ground and hopped off. She rolled the bike onto its stand and stepped over the seat. She knew the way—despite the anonymous jumble of containers, she turned unerringly right, left, right, following the line of compacted earth to her destination.

Petrovitch knew the way, too. Moreover, he could see. He blinked, and his vision changed to a slightly stuttering but bright zoetrope of images. He blinked again, and the scene was transformed into a wash of reds and blues, depending on their heat.

Madeleine's head and hands were white, incandescent almost. That was the effect of fear, and he'd not known her to be so scared, ever. Which was saying something.

The path finished. A container blocked their way. Container Zero. The first domik to be planted on Regent's Park. The door had been partially cut with a letterbox-sized window, burned through the metal at head height.

"Standard procedure. Cut a hole, check the contents, mark for disposal, opening or decontamination. When the wrecking crew cut this one…"

"How many people know?"

"Four—five now. I've told them not to talk."

"Yeah, like that's going to work. You've laid off the whole site. If it's not round the Freezone by dinner time that something's going on, I'll be a *shluha vokzal'naja*. You've got a couple of hours before this goes global. If that." He stretched himself up and looked through the slot. "Has anyone been in?"

"No."

"Thank *huy* for that." He looked up and around him. "Does the door mechanism work?"

"They're welded shut. From the inside. We're going to have to make that hole bigger." The work crew's cutting equipment was abandoned nearby. "Know how to use that?"

He didn't. Then he did. "In theory."

Petrovitch hefted the trolley holding the gas cylinders and wheeled it closer, then opened the valve on the acetylene. It burned with a smoky orange flame, flickering and bright in the dusk. Then he turned on the oxygen and the flame turned into a blue spearpoint.

He dialed back the gain on his eyes until he could just about see what he was doing, and no more. The tip of the fire touched the outside of the container, which started to dribble orange drops of molten steel.

"This could take a while." He could feel the heat on his face, a dry, furnace heat. "Tell me what he's doing in there."

Madeleine tried to look past the burning metal. "Just… just sitting. Facing the door. There's something on his left-hand side. I think it's a bomb."

"How big? Size, not megatonnage."

"It's about," she started, and he interrupted.

"I can't see how far your hands are apart because I'm holding a two-thousand-degree torch and I don't want to go blind or accidentally set myself on fire. Again."

"About a meter long. A tube in a cradle, maybe half a meter across."

"Panel? Wires?"

"There were wires."

"Any idea where the wires were coming from?"

"Couldn't see. From him. From under the chair he's in, perhaps."

Petrovitch clenched his fists around the gas axe. "This doesn't fill me with confidence."

"You think it's rigged?"

"I know it is. It just depends on how." He turned the corner with the flame. "Still, if opening the container was going to trip it, it would have tripped already. Dodged that bullet, at least."

"Sam…"

"Yeah?" It would be good if he could concentrate, but she was standing very close to him. He could feel her breath on the back of his head.

"I wish you'd told me about Michael."

The corner of his mouth twitched. "Do you really want to do this now? Considering the only imminent intimate mingling I might enjoy with you will be our atoms forming part of the same rapidly expanding fireball?"

She clicked her tongue against the roof of her mouth.

"Yeah. Sue me," he muttered. "You know I want you back. But I need you to shut up for one minute."

She walked away from him, and he slowly drew the

gas torch back up toward the previously cut hole. When it was nearly complete, he stopped and turned the oxygen back off.

Madeleine reached forward to bend the metal aside. Petrovitch caught her wrist.

"Hot. Still hot. Will remain hot for a while yet." He spun the valve on the acetylene, and the orange flame flickered and died. "If you weren't in such a hurry to get rid of me, you'd have worked that out."

"I'm not trying…" She looked at her wrist, and Petrovitch let go.

"You can't keep away. You find excuses to pass by, but you always find excuses to go again before anything meaningful can happen."

"You lied to me." Madeleine leaned back against Container Zero, sliding down its pitted side until she was crouched on her haunches.

"I lied to the whole world. It seemed to me like it was the only option." He copied her position, on the other side of the unopened cut. "It was the only option at the time."

"No. You didn't trust me. You wanted a pet AI to keep for yourself. All the business with the CIA: we could have skipped all that if you'd come clean."

"That, I doubt. We would have ended up with godsknows-what raining down on us from the sky, and still have had the Outies to deal with just on our own. I would have died at Waterloo Bridge, and you'd have been overrun on your overpass." Petrovitch checked the clock in the corner of his vision. The metal should be cold enough to touch, but fighting with Madeleine was better than missing her. "We'd be dead, the Outies would have half the city, and Michael would have been hunted to extinction."

"So what we have now makes everything you did okay?"

"If it's a choice between a smoking ruin containing a million or so charred corpses ruled over by someone like Fox, and a Freezone ready to take fifteen million citizens grateful for the facts of running water and electricity? Yeah. Let me think about that for a nanosecond."

"I'm glad you think it was worth losing me."

His heart was incapable of skipping a beat. It never beat at all, just spun and spun and never stopped. Maybe it slowed briefly, just enough to cause him a transient but real pain.

"I would have lost you whichever choice I made. At least this way, I get to see you live." Petrovitch levered himself up and put his shoulder to the metalwork.

It bent with a creak, leaving a gap only just large enough for him to squeeze through. Certainly not her.

"You made it that size deliberately, didn't you?" she said.

"Can't prove it." He shrugged off his greatcoat and let it fall to the ground. "*Yobany stos,* it's colder than Siberia."

He started to ease himself into the hole, one foot inside first, then feeling the sharp edges pressing into his chest and back. Slowly, he worked his way in, until he was able to wriggle free and bring his other leg after him.

The interior of Container Zero boomed with his footsteps.

"Be careful," she said, and threaded his coat through to him.

He took it and pulled it around him, then turned to face the Last Armageddonist.

6

Petrovitch stepped slowly over, forcing his eyes to adjust to the low light levels, and flicking between the near infrared and visible parts of the spectrum. He moved slowly so he could composite the images together and make certain that he wasn't blundering into a laser net or onto a pressure pad.

The air was cold, dry, like a tomb. There was no hint of decay, just a vague smell of age. He had to be the first living person in there for a very long time: he ran a quick search for the history of Regent's Park, and found that the first domiks had been deposited on the green grass late in twenty-oh-two. Armageddon had been declared officially over with the death of van Hooren in twenty-oh-nine. Eighteen years then, minimum.

And this one had been here all that time, right in the heart of the Metrozone. Petrovitch stood in front of the Armageddonist's heavy wooden chair and stared into his desiccated face.

"All this. All this was your fault, you *govnosos*. Everything."

The Armageddonist's skin was drawn tight over his teeth and he seemed to be grinning. Petrovitch had the urge to drive his fist through his dead staring eye-sockets, then tear off his arms all the better to beat him with the ragged ends.

Armageddon had changed the world. That was their intention, of course, but despite them bombing their way across Europe, west to east, God had not returned to judge either the quick or the dead.

The survivors had been left with a continent covered with hot-spots, millions of refugees washing across newly fortified borders, collapsed economies and radioactive rain.

It had left Petrovitch with a weak heart that had blighted a childhood which had ended abruptly when his father had canced out. He had as much reason as the next man to hate the Armageddonists.

Like every other person affected, he'd dreamed about what he'd say to one if he had the chance. Now, now he could: if he wanted, he could vent two decades of incoherent rage and frustration on the very object of his anger. No matter that it would fall on deaf ears.

He look a step back. He'd thought the Armageddonist's hands were locked rigid on the arms of the chair, but that was only true for the right. The left was curled around a lever, like the heavy switching gear on his perpetual motion machine. He hunkered down for a closer look.

A dead man's handle. Except the man holding it was dead, and it hadn't worked. Yet.

Not moving his feet, he scanned the inside of the domik. He needed a heavy weight or something to jam in the mechanism. It might be that the switch was never going to fall, but one possible alternative was that the slightest vibration might set it off. The wires that joined it both to the heavy metal cylinder and to the box under the chair would mean the Armageddonist would have the last, albeit brief, laugh.

There was welding gear by the domik's doors. Too unwieldy. The rest of the container was pretty much bare, save the table with its unstable load.

"Maddy?"

"Sam?"

"I'm going to need some wire. Stiff wire, like coat-hanger wire, or six-mil-squared copper cable." He could tie off the switch. That would hold until he could make a better job of it. "Sometime soon, okay?"

Still without moving his feet, he crouched down and peered through the Armageddonist's legs. By leaning over to both sides, he could see more of the object, and he mentally constructed a wire-frame model of it, to better see what it was.

A car battery.

He knew that it was simply inconceivable that one might hold its charge for two decades. There was staining on the floor around it, but that could have come from above rather than from a ruptured cell. By rights, he should just unscrew the terminals and kick the thing across the floor. It was as dead as the Armageddonist.

Petrovitch scratched at the bridge of his nose. Maybe he'd just wait for the wire. He straightened up again and peered at the bomb.

The Armageddonists mostly used old Soviet-era weapons, but this wasn't one of them. It had the distinct look of a home-made device, of the sort that were relatively simple to make, and could be set off just by being dropped at the wrong angle. Low yield, but more than enough to lay waste to everything for kilometers around.

There was tapping from behind him.

"Yeah?"

"I've got your wire."

"Throw it to me. Toward my feet, not my head. I don't want it to go anywhere near the body."

Madeleine occluded the outside. "How can you see...oh."

"Just throw the wire," said Petrovitch. "I've a list of stuff I need to make the bomb safe."

"Don't you think you should be leaving that to someone else?"

"No. No, I don't. I'm not leaving it to someone else because that someone else is going to take a day to get here, insist on an exclusion zone of thirty k that'll take a week to enforce across the river, cause irreparable harm to the Freezone, then do precisely what I'm going to do now and expect to be treated like a *yebani* hero for the rest of his life."

The short coil of wire skittered tinnily across the floor and nudged his heels.

"Right. I want a head torch, wire cutters, a full box spanner set—including the little fiddly ones in the shape of a star, screwdrivers of all varieties, pliers big and small, a multimeter and a geiger-counter. Most of that you can find in the art college basement, and I know you know where that is. The geiger-counter: you'll probably have to go to a medical physics department at a hospital. Got all that?" Valentina would have a lot of it, but she was at the other side of the Freezone, hunting the CIA.

"You're enjoying this a little too much."

He stooped to retrieve the wire and felt its gauge. It was a little thin, but it'd do.

"I seem to live in a world where you trust me with an atomic bomb, but not with your heart. I guess I have to take pleasure where I can find it."

She hesitated at the opening. "I'll get you your things."

"Thanks. Do you want to tell Sonja about this, or shall I?"

"It's my job to tell her," she said.

"Is that a yes or a no?"

"You can do it. Somehow I think it'd be better coming from you."

"See you soon. If you can't find anything straightaway, call me so I can decide if I can do without it."

The shadow left the end of the container, and before he called the Chair of the Freezone, he decided to tackle the dead man's switch.

It was a simple task, but he had to do it right. He wound the free end of the wire around the nearest chairleg and pulled it tight so that he knew it wouldn't slip. Then he unwound more of the coil to stretch around the switch itself.

Dead, brittle fingers were wrapped around the handle, which should have flung itself back the moment conscious pressure had ceased. Something had prevented that. Petrovitch ramped up the gain on his eyes, hoping to see what that was.

The secret was at the elbow. The Armageddonist had wedged his arm against the back of the chair to relieve the strain on his muscles. Maybe he'd had a cramp. Maybe he just hadn't been ready. And some time after he'd completely negated the purpose of the bomb switch, he'd died.

"*Mudak.* Can't even get the end of the world right."

He looped the wire around the switch and the emaciated hand, and took up the slack, then gave it three more winds before slowly drawing everything together. As the wire tightened, it bit into the dry, bloodless hand, cutting the parchment-colored skin.

Petrovitch watched dispassionately, only concerned with whether the underlying bones would break. He decided that they weren't going to, and he finished off the wire with bending it back down to the chair and fixing it to the same leg. He gave it an experimental kick. The wire held.

Next thing.

She was sitting at her desk, unaware that she was being observed. Her eyes were flickering across the screen in front of her, reading a set of accounts. Every time she came across an entry that she might later query, she frowned a little, eyebrows knitting together.

He coughed to attract her attention. "Madam President?"

"Sam?" Sonja sat back, now trying to focus on the tiny camera clipped to her screen. "Why are you calling me that? Where are you?"

"Regent's Park. We've got a problem. An official Freezone the-*govno*'s-hit-the-fan problem." He regarded the bomb. "And I'm officially telling you about it."

"Okay." Her face sharpened. "Tell me."

"I'm standing in Container Zero. It contains the body of the Last Armageddonist and the Last Armageddonist's home-made nuclear device."

If she was surprised or shocked, she didn't show it. She showed nothing at all. "Is the area secure?"

"No, but I don't want people down here mob-handed. It's a sure way of drawing attention to the fact we have a situation."

"Sam, the situation is happening whether we like it or not, and I'm sending you a squad of my guards. They'll be discreet."

"Maddy won't like that."

"She there with you?"

"Not at the moment. I sent her to assemble a bomb disposal kit."

A beat, then her voice dropped an octave. "Sam..."

"What? Sonja, this thing is live. I don't know what'll set it off, but I know I can make sure it won't go critical."

"It's been sitting there for years. Another day won't make a difference."

Petrovitch closed his hand around his forehead and scraped his fingers back through his hair. "Yes. Yes, it will. For one thing, we've opened the container. There was a dead man's switch that failed to work—I've made that temporarily safe—but there could be light-sensitive triggers, trickle-charging cells, old-fashioned mechanical booby traps. If this blows, we've wasted the year we've spent rebuilding and the next ten trying to decontaminate the Metrozone."

"We need an expert."

"*Yobany stos,* you sound just like her! Listen: this is a jerry-built gun-type assembly. It's not something you buy off the shelf. The people who made this are dead, Sonja, and no one can pick their brains. The design is simple and stupid and inefficient and unstable. It relies on nothing more sophisticated than bringing two subcritical masses together. That could happen if you so much as drop it. If you want to leave something like that sitting in the middle of the Freezone, then hey, you're the boss. You get to carry the can."

Sonja pushed back from her desk. The Freezone authority had co-opted the old Post Office Tower. The views from the top were commanding, and Petrovitch could see tiny points of light through the windows behind her.

"Can it be moved?" she asked.

"Without disarming it? Maybe. I don't know."

"Would you move it?"

"*Chyort*. No."

She stood up and looked out over the city, as she must have done from the Oshicora building. The difference was now she really did run it all. At least for the next two weeks.

"Sam?"

"Yeah?"

"Don't screw up."

His mouth twisted into a grin. "Have I ever let you down?"

"No," she conceded. "But you let Michael down. He's been gone a year, and you still owe him."

"I'm working on it."

"I know: one brick at a time. I've been meaning to ask you: what happened this morning?"

"With the priest? The Pope wants to know if Michael has a soul."

"Does he?"

"I told him it didn't matter. I told him Michael was my friend and I was going to rescue him anyway."

"Good for you, Sam. Keeping an eye on the oil prices?"

"Not particularly."

"Down eighty dollars a barrel since lunchtime. OPEC are squealing."

"Which is stupid. Oil's too valuable to just burn it. They should be pleased."

"So now I have the Saudi secret service to worry about, too. Thanks." She sat back down, almost falling into the chair. "I miss these chats. We've been so busy, haven't we?"

"Time's coming—soon—when we won't be."

"You know that Madeleine's not the only woman in the world, don't you? If she doesn't want you, there might be someone else who does."

Petrovitch scratched at his nose, even though that wasn't where the itch was. "You know me. You know I keep my promises."

"I know." She shrugged. "If only you were more corruptible."

"Yeah." He could hear the sound of an engine outside. "Better go. I'll let you know when I'm done."

When he'd closed the connection, he frowned. It wasn't a motorbike engine he was hearing. The noise ramped up suddenly, and a shower of sparks washed across the floor of the container from the welded-shut doors.

The edge of a cutting disc emerged through the steel and started to carve its way upward. The air vibrated and filled with smoke.

"*Ahueyet!*" Petrovitch reattached himself to Sonja's computer. "If you've sent your crew already, send more. Now." Then to Valentina: "What the *huy* are you doing in

Enfield? I need you here!" And finally to Madeleine, and he had to wait for her to pick up: "Come."

By which time the sparks were almost to the top of the door, and he could barely see through the acrid, metal-tasting fog. The smoke caught in the back of his throat and made him cough. It was irritating his eyelids, too, but he could ignore that.

The flickering sparks died away, and so did the roar of the cutter. The ends of two crowbars hammered through the opening, probing and twisting, and after a few seconds the doors screeched open, the howl of ancient hinges being forced reverberating across the remains of the domik pile.

The sudden outflow of air sucked much of the smoke with it. It billowed into the darkening sky, and half a dozen figures stepped into the container.

"Doctor Petrovitch, please stand aside. We have no wish to harm you."

"The feeling isn't mutual. If you go now, you might just live." He had nothing to use as a weapon. They had the crowbars, the rotary saw, and several stout lengths of wood.

But they didn't stop to argue with him: they knew he'd called for help, and knew they only had minutes. Four of them went to the bomb, two—the biggest—stepped between it and Petrovitch. All of them just seemed like regular people: they could have been scaffolders, fitters, plumbers, caterers, drivers.

"Hey, hey!" Petrovitch saw them put straps under the bomb, and tried to push past to reach it. "Don't do that."

And while he was distracted, one of the men took his legs out from under him, hitting him across the back of his knees with the crowbar. He didn't fall, because the other one caught him in a headlock and reached around to the nape of his neck.

They knew exactly what they were doing. Petrovitch felt the cable in his head rotate and jerk out.

Then, and only then, did the pain hit him. Not just from being struck with a metal bar and half-choked, but from all the other injuries that he carried and hadn't been healed.

They dropped him, and the man swung the crowbar again. He was aiming for Petrovitch's skull, but struck his arm instead. A bone went crack.

"*Nu vse, tebe pizda.*" Petrovitch tried to work out where his feet were. He kicked out, then realized that wasn't the smart thing to do. "Okay. Stop."

"Sorry, Doctor Petrovitch. No time for that." They'd cut the cables from the dead man's switch and the battery. They had the bomb hanging free inside the straps. They were walking out of the container.

"I can't let you take it." He tried to stand, and put his hand down on the now vacant table. The jagged ends of the break further up his arm slipped past each other and threatened to puncture his skin.

And while he was gasping and gaping and gagging, they left.

7

$\mathcal{H}$e dreamed. It was so perfect, so beautiful. The fat, yellow sun was slanting off the sea, sinking toward the west and the wide, uninterrupted ocean. The grass he stood on gave way to white sand across a sinuous, nibbled line, and on that sand were children, six of them, and some of them were his. They laughed and they ran and they played some complicated game that involved throwing seaweed and catching shells. He watched them, and when he'd watched them enough, he vaulted down onto the sand; with a great monster's roar he set after them, scooping up a ribbon of green weed and waving it above his head as he sent them giggling and scattering down to the shore line.

So when consciousness returned, he struggled to remember where or when he was. His eyes slowly opened, and lit on Madeleine. She wasn't wearing her Joan robes, so it wasn't eighteen months ago and he hadn't just suffered a massive heart attack.

Then there was Valentina with her favorite kalash across her knees, and Lucy standing next to her, and a redhead who used to be a blonde: Tabletop, in her info-rich stealth suit. And Sonja. Petrovitch ignored what she was wearing and considered the fact that she looked like she'd swallowed a wasp.

He'd just lost an atomic bomb. She probably had a right to be pissed with him.

"*Pizdets*," he said. His arm—his left arm—was stuck out at a stupid angle. While he was asleep, some sadist had fitted him with an aerial array that made it easy to pick up radio signals but impossible for him to change the angle of his elbow. Four encircling titanium rings were spaced down the length of his arm, locked together with cross-struts.

He lifted his arm from his shoulder. The iodine-stained flesh moved around the metal wires that were anchored in his bone. There should have been pain, but morphine had seen to that.

He searched for the clock in the corner of his eye. It had gone. There was no connection to the outside. He frowned and glanced up at the clock on the wall, busy ticking away the seconds. He did the maths stupidly and slowly, and came up with a guess that three and a half hours had passed; hours he was never going to get back.

He tried to sit up. With only one hand and a soft mattress to push against, he struggled until Madeleine stepped forward. She held him while she rearranged his pillows, then let him down gently against them. A moment later, she would be embarrassed, but for now she was caught up in the act of caring.

"So," he croaked. His throat burned like he'd downed half a litre of cheap vodka. "The bomb's gone. You don't know where it is, or who has it. You don't know what they want with it or what they'll accept for its return. About right?"

No one contradicted him.

"Except that's not true, is it?" Petrovitch tried to adjust the surgical gown he was wearing, and found himself frustrated again by his lack of mobility. He'd been awake no more than a minute, and he was already wishing he'd insisted they'd amputated and grafted on a prosthetic.

"I don't get it," said Lucy. She looked from face to face. "One of us . . ."

"Yeah. One of you. Those men knew where I was, knew I was alone, knew how long they had, knew exactly how to disable me, knew there was a bomb there. They were prepared. They were ready. They weren't armed, but they knew I didn't have a *pushka* either: who, outside of this room, knows for certain I don't carry? That I've been ordered not to carry? They put me in a head-lock and unplugged me: only you lot know what that'll do to me."

Valentina pursed her lips. "Your wire is no longer secret. Is common knowledge, *da?* Maybe they get lucky."

"Lucky?"

She shrugged. "Unlikely. But I would look for reasons other than one of your friends has betrayed you. Start with those who cut Container Zero open."

"They've disappeared," said Madeleine. She leaned heavily against the wall, nudging the painting behind her out of true. "Vanished off the face of the earth, and I'm not going to be able to go and find them now."

Petrovitch turned uncomfortably toward her. "Because . . ."

"Sonja's sacked me," said Madeleine through clenched teeth. "Apparently, my judgment is in question."

"What the hell was I supposed to do?" Sonja's face

contorted into several unlikely expressions before she exploded. "You lost the bomb. You lost it. You had it, and you lost it. You're head of security and you left one unarmed man alone with a nuclear bomb. It's not your judgment I'm questioning. It's your sanity."

Madeleine levered herself upright, which in itself should have been scary. "Sonja," she started.

But Sonja wasn't intimidated. "That's Madam fucking President to you. They could have killed him! That might not mean anything to a frigid bitch like you, but I actually care about him."

She'd gone white, all except the tip of her nose, which remained stubbornly pink.

"I'm going now to try and clear up your mess. If I catch you within a hundred meters of me, I'll make sure someone shoots you. Is that perfectly clear?"

The only thing that was perfectly clear was Madeleine's desire to straight-arm Sonja through the wall. The effort to hold back was titanic, every muscle straining.

"Yeah, go on then," said Petrovitch from the bed. "This makes it so much better, doesn't it? If any of you were listening earlier, I said that you had no idea who took the bomb. Doesn't mean I don't. Up to the point where my mitigator was unplugged, I have a recording of what happened, including the six men who took the bomb. And in a couple of seconds I can tell you who they are and where they live. Lived. Three and a half hours ago."

"They took your rat," said Lucy. "It wasn't on you when we found you."

Petrovitch screwed his face up. "*Chyort.*"

"I'll get you a new one," she offered.

"Go and do it now. Something. Anything that'll do."

He should have realized when he woke up. The drugs were making him dull. "I need to get out of this *yebani* place."

Lucy edged around Sonja and slipped out. She left the door slightly open, and they could all hear her receding, running footsteps. Petrovitch also caught sight of an Oshicora guard through the crack of light.

"I can do better than she can," said Sonja, though she didn't take her eyes off Madeleine.

"You've got more important things to do. And I'm sorry."

"Call me when you remember enough that's useful. Okay?"

"Okay."

With one last glare up at Madeleine, she flung the door aside and strode out. The guards fell in behind her, and by force of will, they swept the corridor clear ahead of them.

"I'm serious," he said, trying to attract the others' attention. "I need to get out of here right now. Someone tell me how long I'm supposed to wear this metalwork?"

"Six months." Madeleine's fists were still clenching and unclenching.

"You have got to be kidding." He stared at his arm. "Call the surgeons. Get them to take it off. Take it all off, up to here." He sawed with his free hand just below his left shoulder.

"Sam, no."

"There's a nuclear bomb loose in the Freezone. Someone close to me betrayed me. And I've lost my rat. Again. I cannot do anything about any of those things with Arecibo sticking out of my body."

"Ari?" asked Valentina.

"Arecibo," murmured Tabletop. "Radio telescope. Puerto Rico."

"And you've been very quiet." Petrovitch struggled with the sheets, grasping a handful of them and pulling, but the hospital corners proved hard to dislodge. He frowned at her stealth suit that he'd thought locked away for safe keeping. But there she was, wearing it like a second skin again. "Anything you'd like to say?"

"I'm not allowed to talk to anyone but Tina, Lucy and you, and I'm never alone. I know I've said nothing that can be used to hurt you. So I'm just waiting for you to tell me what you want me to do." She tugged at the corner of her dyed hair. "The CIA would have killed you first, then mined the container before they left. It wasn't them."

Petrovitch had finally got the better of the bedclothes. "Anyone who doesn't want to see my bare arse had better get out now."

No one moved.

"Well, *mne pohui*." He swung his legs out and tried to stand. He would have fallen had Valentina not caught him.

She dumped him back on the bed. "Where do you think you need to be?"

"Anywhere. Anywhere but here with this *govno* hanging off me."

"You need to think." She held him by the shoulders and gave him a shake. "You need a plan."

"I can't think. I feel like I've had half my brain ripped out through the back of my skull."

"Valentina," warned Madeleine, "put him down."

"No. This is important. You do not need computer. You are smart anyway. You live before you get implant. You remember that." She patted both his cheeks and stepped back.

"Right. You're right." Petrovitch glared at his arm. "Where's the break?"

"Separated fracture of the humerus, midway along," said Tabletop, still twirling her hair. "I read your notes. You had a chunk of bone three inches long floating free."

"So the extension on my lower arm is just for show?"

"Stability. You cannot—must not—use that limb for weight-bearing activities. At all."

"I still reckon I'd be better without it altogether."

Madeleine growled. "No."

"Tell me again why I should take your opinion into consideration?" He didn't turn around, just sat with his back to her. "We've been apart longer than we were together."

The temperature in the room dropped to below freezing.

"One of us has to say it," he said. "I've spent too long hoping you'll come back to me. Either you will or you won't. Nothing I do or don't do will affect that one way or the other. But the situation we're now in means I'm going to have to make some decisions for myself."

"We can save the arm." Tabletop stepped out from the corner. "I'll get you a wheelchair."

Valentina picked up her rifle and slung it over her back. It was an automatic reaction; where one went, the other had to go. It was the law.

"Back soon." She gave a meaningful glance at Madeleine.

"I'll be fine." He nodded, feeling the chill on his naked back. "Does this hotel come with a dressing gown?"

"We'll find you one." Tabletop held the door for Valentina, and like a pair of ghosts they disappeared.

Petrovitch tried the floor again. His eyes told him it was flat and still, but as he slowly rose, he felt like he was on a ship at sea. "If losing my arm gives me a chance to get to the bomb before it blows, I'm sawing it off with a rusty blade. Do you understand?"

"Oh, you've made it very clear, Sam."

"So what are you going to do now?"

"Nothing that'll make you change your mind, I expect."

He rested his head on his chest. "How about stop acting like a *pizda staraya?* Sonja was right, and we were wrong: we should have had Container Zero locked down tight. We're supposed to be responsible adults, not a bunch of *yebani* kids hiding stuff from our parents and hoping they don't find out."

"You mean like you did?"

He slowly turned around, shuffling his feet. His arm refused to hang by his side, the series of rings forcing it away from his body, making him hold his shoulder awkwardly against the downward drag of the metal framework. He reached over and held the lowermost ring in his other hand.

"The two situations are completely different. People already knew about the bomb. It wasn't a secret, and we should have realized what that meant."

She gave a pained expression. "They were so quick."

"Yeah. They knew before we did. They knew, I guess, long before Container Zero was opened. You don't get to make yourself a nuclear power just because you haven't got anything better to do that evening." He tried to shrug, and found that impossible, too. "We were set up. By someone who knows both you and me very well."

"Bet Harry would know who."

"Maybe. He wouldn't have done anything about it, though. Not until it was too late."

"I do care," she blurted. "It's not true what Sonja said. I care so much about you."

He thought she might cry. He thought he might cry. He took a deep breath. "Shame it doesn't seem to be enough anymore."

The door banged back to its fullest extent. Tabletop wheeled in a chair, cornering hard and scraping paint off the doorframe.

"Hop in." She stopped suddenly, and Valentina ran into the back of her. "Did I interrupt something?"

"Yeah. No. Whatever. Dressing gown?"

"Got a blanket. Best we could do." She brought the wheelchair closer and stamped on the brakes with the side of her foot. "I had to throw someone out of this thing."

"Is true," said Valentina. "Seat is still warm for your naked arse."

"As if this couldn't get any worse." Petrovitch attempted to lower himself down one-handed into the chair, and dropped most of the way. "*Chyort.* That hurts."

While Valentina artfully draped the blanket over his knees, Tabletop kicked the brakes off. "Okay. Next stop, physiotherapy." She popped a wheelie to turn him around, and started at speed toward the door.

"And you could stop being so cheerful. I'm not used to it."

She leaned in from behind him, so that her hair curtained his face. "I'm useful. At last. You don't know how good this feels."

Out in the corridor, he glanced behind him. Valentina was following at a jog. There was no sign of Madeleine.

8

_____

The overhead lights flickered on as they entered the room. Each successive click and buzz revealed more of the modern torture chamber until it was laid bare in its full antiseptic glory.

Petrovitch shivered. The sign on the door had said physiotherapy, but now he wasn't so sure. "Are these things supposed to help people?"

Tabletop stood on the back of the wheelchair and sized up the equipment. "I don't know how I know what each one of these does, but I do. Sometimes I find myself thinking about something, and I suddenly find I'm an expert in it. And I never realize until I'm confronted by it."

"If they can wipe your memory, maybe they have a way of putting new ones in."

"So it seems. That device on your arm is called a Taylor-Hobashi bone fixator. One of these machines is designed to work with it."

She put his brake on and wandered between the benches, chairs and tables, running her hands over the metal and plastic, remembering thoughts that were not her own. Valentina squatted down next to him.

"Hmm," she said. It was her holding sound, what she did when she was trying to find the right words. "You are okay?"

"That's loaded with subtext, even for you."

"You have many problems. Too many."

"Are you suggesting you remove one or more of those problems, permanently?"

"If you were, hmm…"—her expression became flinty—"in charge. Then perhaps you would be able to act more freely."

"You want me to start a revolution against the Freezone."

"Against Oshicora. Freezone is good idea run by wrong people."

Petrovitch flexed the fingers of his left hand. He watched them curl and uncurl like thin white tube worms extending from their nest. "Yeah, well. Don't think I haven't thought about it. It would, I guess, be quite easy for me. Rally the troops, depose the leader, seize power. Shame it's not going to happen."

"*Nyet?*"

"Definitely *nyet*. And of course the Freezone is a good idea. It was my idea. That's why I've been a loyal servant of it, and why I'll stay one for the next week and a bit."

"What of future? Your future?" She looked pensive for the briefest of moments. "Mine?"

"Leave it with me. I don't intend to disappoint either my friends or my enemies."

She pursed her lips and nodded. "That is good."

And that was it; the matter was concluded to her satisfaction. He'd deflected an attempted coup simply by saying no. He hoped that if Sonja ever found out, she'd be appropriately grateful.

Meanwhile, Tabletop was circling one machine that looked like a skeletal robot cut off at the waist. Her fingers were manipulating the two outriggers, bending them and twisting them, and feeling the way the joints moved in relationship with one another.

"This is it." She beckoned Petrovitch over, and he allowed himself to be wheeled into position.

When he looked up, the thing towered over him. He had a flashback to the New Machine Jihad, of a construct of steel and hydraulics bending down to inspect him minutely.

"Nothing to be nervous of," said Tabletop.

"You're not sitting where I am." He took a deep breath. "What do I have to do?"

"Just hold your arm out. I'll do the rest."

He raised his arm awkwardly, and she moved quickly and carefully, with unearned ease. She lowered the machine over him and clamped Petrovitch's titanium rings to the metal skeleton until it provided all the support and he could just hang off it.

"Comfortable?"

It wasn't, but he'd expected nothing else. "It's fine."

There was more: a harness that clicked into place around his shoulders and down his back. It was more than just like an exoskeleton: it was an exoskeleton, and he got the point of what she was trying to do.

"We'll need to lose the right arm—not mine, the machine's. And doesn't this work off the mains?"

"The servos are twelve volts. You should be able to rig

something up." Tabletop opened several drawers in a nearby desk, searching for something. "Hex wrench. Five mil."

"Madeleine should have mine."

"I'll keep looking," she said, and spread her net wider.

"She doesn't hate you, you know."

"Uh huh." Her voice was muffled by the cupboard she was in. "Did she tell you that?"

Petrovitch scratched his nose with his free hand. "Good point, well made."

She looked over the top of the steel bench. "Her last act as head of security was to release this suit to me. She took the opportunity to make her opinion of me crystal clear." Tabletop ducked back down again, eventually emerging with a flat plastic case. "Let's get this done."

With Valentina taking the weight of the spare machine arm, Tabletop unwound the bolts that held it in place, then disconnected the cables from the motors at the shoulders, elbow and wrist.

The door banged open. A man in a white coat stood framed in the doorway.

"What . . . are you doing?"

After months of being used to scanning a face, running it through his software, coming up with an identity, Petrovitch was lost. The personal touch, the calling someone by their own name, was his signature move. It was his only move. And no matter how hard he tried, nothing would come.

So he gave up. "Ah, *chyort voz'mi*. We're taking hospital property apart and modifying it so I can regain some basic function in my shattered left arm, which should allow me to at least attempt to drag ourselves out of the *pizdets* we're in before we all die horribly. If I can find the

podonok who did this to me on the way, it'll be a bonus."
He smiled unpleasantly. "Any questions?"

"Doctor Petrovitch?" asked the man.

"If that was your question, may whichever god you
believe in help us all. Who the *huy* did you think I was?"

He could see the mental calculations whirr behind his
eyes. If that was Petrovitch, that must mean the one in the
black form-fitting all-in-one was the CIA assassin, and
the other one in the brown jacket cinched in at the waist
and with the Kalashnikov across her back was the Russian gangster, hero of Waterloo Bridge.

"I'll be going," he said.

"Good choice," said Petrovitch, and waited for the door
to close. "*Mudak.*"

"Right." Tabletop tightened the straps and checked the
retaining bolts. "Can you stand?"

"With help, probably."

Valentina stopped playing with the spare mechanical
arm long enough to grip the spine rod and neck harness.
The women heaved him up. Petrovitch leaned to the left,
overcorrected, and eventually found upright.

"Heavy. Unbalanced." The straps bit into his pale skin.

"You'll feel the difference when I turn it on."

Tabletop took up the little hand controller and powered
it up. Immediately, the servos whirred and strained, taking the effort out of holding his arm up. He moved his
shoulder slowly, and the sensors felt his tentative efforts,
translating it into a smooth, steady arc.

"*Yobany stos.*" He looked down at his arm. "This might
actually work."

"I'm just going to loosen the elbow joint. Tell me if it
hurts."

"Yeah. It's going to hurt anyway, so just do it."

She applied the wrench to the appropriate screws. "Okay. Bend your arm. Just a little."

It moved. Almost gracefully. The supporting rings of his cast and the metal spars of the physio machine made it look both ungainly and unlikely, but there was both power and speed hiding behind its appearance.

"We're going to need some hard-core battery packs. And lots of them. Rechargables." Petrovitch turned his wrist one way, then the other. "A very long extension lead's going to come in handy, too."

Valentina drew out her phone. "I will tell Lucy. She will find something appropriate."

"Tell her to meet us here, and we'll go to the art college together." He tutted. "We still need my tools, and Madeleine has most of them."

"We'll have to get them from her. You are not cutting your arm off just yet, so she should be grateful." Valentina walked to the far side of the room to carry on her conversation, and Petrovitch looked down at the rest of his body.

"I'm going to need my trousers. And boots. And I'm not certain I can tie my own laces anymore." He sighed, and motors whirred in sympathy. "We're going to have to wreck my greatcoat too. No way I'm getting this thing down the sleeve. Transport. You've got transport, right?"

Tabletop transferred her weight to one hip and handed him the controller. "Just because you hadn't thought of it until now doesn't mean it hasn't been thought of. Everything's in hand, Sam."

"I have issues. So sue me." He tried to bring his left hand close enough to his face to scratch at the bridge of his nose. Not quite. He growled. "Why are we still here? We need to be doing something."

"Then sit back down in the chair and I'll unplug you. Clothes, tools, car, college. Something will not happen unless we do everything in order. Focus, clarity, purpose."

"Is that what they taught you in the CIA?" Petrovitch eased himself into the wheelchair.

"It's what I remember, so it must have been. Put your arm across your lap. When I turn off the power, it'll become so much dead weight again."

He did as he was told, and railed against being ordered around at the same time. Tabletop pulled the plug: his arm went stiff and tried to fall across his knees. He hauled it up and balanced it across the sides of the chair.

Tabletop wheeled him back out into the corridor, Valentina, phone still glued to her ear, following.

They ran into a crowd of men and women waiting for them just outside the door. The men were all old, some very old; they all wore black cassocks tied at the waist with a red sash, and red skull caps balanced on their mostly hairless heads. The women were younger, vested in habits and wimples; hidden underneath was impact armor and Vatican-approved handguns.

Petrovitch closed his eyes. There wasn't enough morphine in the world to give him that sort of hallucination, so he supposed it had to be real.

"If," he started, then changed his mind. "No, scratch that: I made it perfectly clear to Father John that I do not want to talk to you. I have no idea how you persuaded the hospital to let you in, or who you bullied into telling you where I was: when I find out, I'll be kicking those responsible right up the *zhopu*."

He opened his eyes again. They were still there, ten of them, six cardinals and four Joans. They didn't look like they were going to go away just because he wanted them to.

"Can I introduce..." said the oldest man, his face lined and dark like a walnut. As he leaned forward, he met the barrel of Valentina's rifle coming the other way.

The Joans did their job quickly. The cardinal was dragged back behind them and they presented a solid wall to the threat. One of them thought about reaching for her gun. In the subtle coded way of the order, the decision was made together that it wouldn't be necessary.

"No, you cannot. You're a distraction, all of you. I'm not going to give you a moment of my time. Not now, not ever. Do not ask again. I don't need to know who you are, what you want, or how you think you can help me. You are simply irrelevant to me." Petrovitch adjusted his arm pointedly. "I'm guessing we're not going to have a fire-fight right here, though a hospital is as good a place as any—better in lots of respects—so if you'll excuse us, I'm sure you can see yourselves out."

The Joans didn't move, mainly because Valentina was still aiming her kalash at the head of the man she thought might be the Prefect of the Congregation for the Doctrine of the Faith. They didn't wear name badges, making it difficult to tell.

"Tina, knock it off and get me out of this freak show."

Valentina managed to convey her reluctance by the slowness with which she lowered her gun, and Tabletop coughed politely to open up a way through.

"Watch your toes, your worships," she said.

"It's Eminences," grunted Petrovitch as he sailed

between the phalanxes of black, white and crimson. "For all I care."

The corridor was necessarily long, and the lifts were at one end. All the way down he could feel eyes boring into the back of his head. And then they had to wait: unheard of, because a networked Petrovitch would have summoned the elevator cars beforehand and made certain that one would be ready with its doors open.

While they waited, one of the Joans came to speak to him—whether she was sent or a free choice, he didn't know. He did notice that she was the prettiest, even though it was supposed to be impossible to tell beneath the uniform. She wasn't the youngest, but she had smiling eyes and a French Canadian accent, and not being the youngest meant little as there were few old Joans. The attrition rate was alarming.

"You married Sister Madeleine, didn't you?"

Petrovitch looked up at her looking down. "Yeah."

"Is she around?"

"That depends. Look, your Vatican mind-tricks won't work on me. The only reason I'm giving you the time of day is because you're a Joan and I have grudging respect for the order. Say what you want to say and don't piss me about."

She raised a half-smile. "I was your wife's sponsor."

He had to trawl manually through his memory. Everything, even that, was quicker when linked up.

"Marie. Sister Marie Clemenceau." He glanced around her to the dark cloud of priests still outside the physio room. "How come you're with those clowns now?"

She didn't rise to the insult. "They needed someone with experience of the Metrozone. They asked me."

The elevator arrived with a ping. The doors opened and Valentina scanned the space inside almost at the same time as Sister Marie. They swapped a flicker of mutual recognition.

Tabletop pushed him forward, and Valentina placed her booted foot against the door jamb. Petrovitch was turned around in the confined space so he could see out, could see the nun framed against the pale green wall behind her.

"No excuses, then. You knew what you were getting into, Sister."

She looked solemnly at him with her laser-corrected eyes. "Yes, but it seems nothing could quite prepare us for the shock of actually meeting you."

Despite the broken arm, and the pain, and the worry, and the urgency, the doors slid shut to the sound of Petrovitch laughing like a madman.

9

*W*hy can't I go to bed?" asked Lucy. She hauled on the door handle and kicked her way out into the freezing night air.

Petrovitch reached for his seat belt. "Because if we don't find the bomb before it goes off, you'll be worrying about more than your *yebani* beauty sleep." The belt retracted on its reel, snagging in the metalwork of his right arm. "*Pizdets*. This whole thing is *pizdets*."

He freed himself and went for the door on his side of the pickup. As he reached for it, motors whirred and pistons breathed. In the corner of his eye, he'd installed a power meter to tell him if he was in danger of overloading his arm, and a little battery icon so he could check if he needed recharging.

His fingers tangled with the catch and he pulled. The door popped open, and he smelled mud and rust and winter. Valentina and Tabletop were already out, advancing on Container Zero, lit from behind by the vehicle's headlights. A group of Oshicora guards shivered in the midnight air, but grew more purposeful as the women approached. Politely, and with deep regret, the leader of the squad informed them they could go no further.

Petrovitch lowered himself stiffly to the ground and stalked over.

"Hey. There a problem?" He scratched at his nose. He still missed his glasses.

"Petrovitch-san, we have strict instructions," pleaded the guard's leader.

"I know. Which is why we're only going to be five minutes. I need to check something." He studied the man's face. "Takashi Iguro, isn't it?"

"Petrovitch-san, please. Miss Sonja was quite explicit. Only authorized personnel are to be allowed inside Container Zero." The man looked as if he was in pain at denying his hero, and started backing toward the closed doors of the domik. "Unless you are authorized, I cannot permit you to get closer."

Petrovitch nodded. "That's okay, Iguro. I'm not here to get you into trouble." He raised his right arm and patted him on the shoulder. His hand stayed there, effectively trapping him. "Sonja said 'inside the container,' right?"

"Yes, Petrovitch-san."

"That's going to be a problem. I lost something when I was here before. I think it was stolen, but I need to check." Petrovitch appeared to think about a way around the impasse for a moment, and drew the guard irresistibly toward him. "Why don't you go inside and look for it, and we'll look outside. We're not breaking any rules if we just search around the container. And on top of it."

"We both know that you are," whispered the man.

Their heads were very close together.

"Do you know what was taken from here?" asked Petrovitch.

"I have heard…rumors."

"We both want what's best for the Freezone and for Miss Sonja, Takashi Iguro. Right now, that means you're allowed to enter Container Zero and search for my little computer, and me and my friends can take a look around outside." He blinked slowly and deliberately. "Right?"

"I suppose it might be."

"Thank you." Petrovitch released him, and Iguro staggered back. "Five minutes—then we'll be gone."

There could be no more objections, because Valentina was already combing the dirt by the doors to the container, seeing if anything had fallen there, and Tabletop was looking up at the sides of other, nearby domiks.

"They could have thrown it. Quick, easy." She reached into invisible pouches at her wrists and pulled out gloves made of the same material as her suit. "I'll need help."

Lucy trailed over. "So what can I do?"

"Stand there. Face the wall, put your hands against it and straighten your arms and legs." Tabletop slipped her fingers inside the gloves as she measured her run-up.

"Like that?" Lucy looked over her shoulder. "What are you going to do?"

"This."

She took three steps, each faster than before. One foot rose up onto the small of Lucy's back, the other lightly touched the nape of her neck, and abruptly Tabletop was waist-level with the top of the container, supporting herself on her palms.

Then she rotated her body into a handstand, and backflipped out of sight.

Lucy was staring upward, mouth open, but Petrovitch was having none of it.

"Just leave her. She's only looking for attention." He switched to infrared and turned slowly in a circle.

"But did you see...?"

"Yeah, I saw it. You realize that the CIA trained her to do stuff like that because it made her a better killer, not because they have a cheerleading squad." Petrovitch tilted his head. "Maybe they do. Finally, there's something I don't know."

"So what are we looking for?" Lucy peeled her hands off the cold metal wall and rubbed them together until they were pink.

"My rat. Anything else that doesn't look like it belongs here."

"They had to drive the bomb away, right? Tire tracks?"

"Only useful if we had a list of which car had which tires. There are hundreds of thousands of abandoned vehicles in the Freezone. They could have used half a dozen of them, one after another, and because they know they're not being watched, they don't even have to be careful."

"Bummer."

"I'm cross-checking everything I can, but there are massive gaps in the data that didn't used to exist under the Metrozone Authority. It comes down to this; we have to stick our noses in the dirt."

They spent the next ten minutes peering uselessly at the ground, squeezing down the narrow gaps between domiks and finding that everything they touched sapped a little more heat from them. Tabletop would appear occasionally, a shadow leaping from one container to the next, making a soft booming sound as she landed that cut through the still night air.

Then she was behind Petrovitch, breathing hard.

"I've found something."

"Significant?"

"Could be nothing."

"But more than likely not."

She put her hand on her heaving chest. "Sorry. Spooked."

"It's fine. Take your time." He straightened up properly and arched his back. Almost his whole torso was strapped with equipment. A sub-standard replacement for his rat. Battery pack after battery pack, wired in parallel to give him the voltage, then in series to give him the power. The back brace and strapping for the exoskeletal arm. It was heavy, and he was tiring fast.

"Okay," she said, cycling her breath, in through her nose, out through her mouth. "It's the roof of Container Zero. We can haul you up on top…"

"Or I can bluff my way in, which will be a lot less embarrassing." Petrovitch pulled up a virtual phone and called Lucy and Valentina.

They walked back together, but Tabletop wasn't giving anything away. He'd be able to look at whatever it was with fresh eyes, but first he'd have to get past the punctilious Iguro.

The man himself was still searching the floor of the container, on his hands and knees and using a little flashlight that spread a faint beam no bigger than his fist. Petrovitch eased himself past the waiting guards and pushed his head through the cut in the door he'd made earlier.

"Hey again."

Iguro didn't look up, in case he missed something as he shuffled over it. "Petrovitch-san? Have you completed your task? Mine is almost finished, too."

"Another slight problem. One of my colleagues wants

me to take a look at the roof, but I'm not going to be able to get up there, not in my condition." As he talked, he edged further inside, while Valentina and Tabletop stood behind him and prevented any intervention by the others. Lucy kept up a constant stream of chatter, distracting them.

"It will not be possible for you to enter, as I have already explained." Iguro inched forward, and his flashlight illuminated the toes of Petrovitch's boots. "Oh."

"Don't worry. I won't tell." He held down his good hand and helped Iguro up. He pointed to the flashlight. "Mind if I borrow that?"

Petrovitch held the light high, and swept the roof with it. He frowned, and did it again. When he saw it, it was obvious. So obvious, he wondered how he'd missed it when he'd first entered Container Zero; the Armageddonist's fault, undoubtedly.

Someone, at some point in the past, had cut through the roof in a perfect rectangle, freeing a plate two meters by three. Then they'd carefully welded it back into place. There were drill holes at the corners of the rewelded plate, also filled with molten metal.

"See that?" he said, his breath rising and breaking against the ceiling. "That shouldn't be there. Shouldn't be there at all."

"Petrovitch-san?"

The welds looked new. Not brand new, but not rusted either. Two weeks, a month maybe. "Just when you think it can't get any worse, it inevitably does."

He turned in the gloom of the container to the figure in the chair.

"Where is it, you *govnosos,* you *zhopoliz,* you *sooksin?* Tell me what you've done with the *yebani* bomb."

The Last Armageddonist grinned back. He'd not give his secrets away so easily.

Petrovitch leaned down, pressing his hands onto the mummified forearms as they rested on the arms of the chair.

"Come on, you *yebanat*," he growled. "Where is it?"

He got nothing from the shrunken eyes or the shriveled tongue. No sign that he'd been heard, let alone understood, and it enraged him beyond reason. Petrovitch brought his left arm across his body and let loose with every last watt he could summon.

He backhanded the Armageddonist with the edge of his exoskeleton. A moment later, Petrovitch was on the floor, and a head, trailing the dust of two decades, lay rattling in a corner.

"Petrovitch-san. I think you should not have done that."

The faces at the container opening seemed to agree, but Petrovitch didn't care. He awkwardly levered himself upright and glared at the decapitated corpse, its neck of brown flesh surrounding an island of white bone. "I wish you could have suffered more. Suffered as much as we did. But no, you died here, in the quiet and the dark, and you left us all your *govno* to clear up. Well, listen to me, you *huyesos:* I'm done with shoveling. I'm going to bury you and your kind forever, and then I'm not looking back. Got that?"

He put his boot against the chair and kicked it over backward. It crashed over, leaving a pair of leather shoes dangling obscenely at the end of two dried-out legs.

No one said anything. Petrovitch grunted with satisfaction at the destruction he'd wreaked and headed for the exit. He waited for it to clear, then pushed out, catching his arm on the container only once.

He was starting to get the hang of it: appreciate it, even.

Valentina ventured, "Are we done here?"

"Oh yeah. More than done." He stamped toward the car, leaving a wake of Oshicora guards.

Iguro called after him. "Petrovitch-san? How am I going to explain this to Miss Sonja?"

"Leave it with me. I'll tell her as part of my official role as Freezone Cassandra."

"But you have broken the Armageddonist."

"That, my friend, is the least of our problems." He hauled at the car door. "Don't tidy up. He doesn't deserve it."

He clambered in, and the others joined him: Valentina and Tabletop in the front, Lucy beside him.

"Sam? What happened?"

"We've been set up. Set up from the very start."

"Explain," said Valentina.

"I haven't got the energy. Find me a power source. Or vodka. Both, preferably."

She twisted around in her seat, and pointedly pulled out the keys from the ignition. She looked at him until he looked away, out of the window at the bright lights and black shadows of Regent's Park.

"Fine. I'll tell you as we go."

Satisfied, she started the engine, and reversed expertly between the remaining domiks until she reached the main road.

"At some point, probably while the domiks above were being recovered, someone cut down through into Container Zero. They made a hole more than large enough to take the bomb out, so I'm guessing that's what they did. It had gone long before the regular work crews got anywhere close to it."

The only sound was the rumbling of the tires on the resurfaced road.

Lucy pulled at her hair. "I don't get it. If someone took the bomb, why would they bring it back? Why would they then steal it again?"

"There's a whole lot of things I don't get. But I'll bet you a billion that the bomb I saw was a fake. No idea if it was identical, or even similar, but good enough that it fooled everyone into thinking it was the real thing. Even me." Petrovitch grimaced. "Why the *huy* would the original thieves do that?"

Tabletop put her feet up on the dashboard. "What did you expect to see when you knew you were being taken to Container Zero? I know what I'd want to find, and I didn't grow up with the legend."

"There'd have to be the Last Armageddonist, and he'd have to be dead. And he had to have a bomb, ready to go off. Anything else would be too disappointing." He spent some more battery power gripping the seat in front of him and hauling himself forward. "But that's exactly what we would have found if we'd got there first."

"Is it? Perhaps you'd have found absolutely nothing." Her ghostly reflection in the windshield shrugged at the face leaning over her shoulder. "You said we were set up. You just haven't taken the scenario to its logical conclusion."

"*Huy tebe'v zhopu zamesto ukropu.*" Petrovitch let himself fall back. "None of it was real? And they still broke my *yebani* arm? I am seriously pissed now."

"But why would someone want to steal a nuclear bomb they knew wasn't real?" Lucy withered under Petrovitch's baleful glare. "Oh, okay. We weren't supposed to have figured this out, were we?"

"Of course, now that we have, they're going to try and kill us."

Valentina took one hand off the steering wheel and reached under Tabletop's legs to the glove compartment. She produced an automatic handgun, and passed it butt-first to the back seat. Petrovitch wearily took it and laid it in his lap.

"There is another under your seat, Fiona."

Tabletop curled her legs away and spent a moment feeling for cold, hard gunmetal taped to the upholstery.

Then Valentina reached into her jacket and pulled out a third gun, small and flat, warm from her body. "Lucy? Tomorrow I teach you how not to kill yourself with this, *da?* For now, be careful who you point it at."

She took it as if it was a scorpion, and Petrovitch relieved her of it long enough to check the safety switch.

"Some dad I'm turning out to be." Petrovitch punched the window glass, not quite hard enough to shatter it into a thousand crystal fragments, but enough to hurt himself. "*Polniy pizdets.*"

IO

He slowly became aware of another presence in the shadows. They hadn't tried to shoot him, smother him or stab him, so he assumed they were benign; also, to get to him, they would have had to pass through a room containing Valentina, and he'd never caught her asleep yet.

Cables trailed into the bed and under the covers, and he'd installed alarms that would wake him if his nocturnal turnings accidentally unplugged him. Power was still trickling into his battery packs, so he wondered what had disturbed him. It wasn't time to get up. He had another hour and fifty-three minutes of electronically induced coma programmed in.

He could smell her. That was it: Madeleine's own scent had broken through to his consciousness.

"How long have you been there?"

"Five, ten minutes. I've been riding round and round for hours, and I couldn't think of anywhere else to go."

"That's me. The last resort." Petrovitch rolled onto his side, his left arm falling hard onto the mattress in front of him.

"Sam, don't. I'm not in the mood."

"Yeah, well. Neither am I." He opened his eyes and used some software to boost his vision. Madeleine was sitting with her back against the wall, her legs out in front of her and almost touching the bed with her heels. She had a gun in her hand, one he recognized from both today and much longer ago. "Thought you'd lost that."

"Wong sent it to me. Someone tried to sell it to him, and he recognized it. Told them he'd turn them in to the Metrozone authorities if they didn't hand it over." She flicked the magazine from the Vatican special into her hand and started counting the bullets.

"I miss him. No one can fry food to death quite like he does. I kept hoping he'd come across the river, but maybe business was too good where he was. Or he was avoiding us."

"The second one, I think. Can't blame him, either. His place was pretty much wrecked by the missile that hit Clapham A."

"If it's any consolation, you didn't lose a nuclear bomb today."

She rammed the magazine back home. "I don't need your sympathy."

"There wasn't a bomb. It was a fake. The whole Container Zero thing was a one-act play, starring us. If we hadn't been so completely taken in, we might have noticed the scenery wobbling."

She was silent for a while. "Certain?"

"As sure as we can be."

"We?"

"The usual suspects."

"What did Sonja say when you told her?"

"Ah." He pushed himself up against the headboard. "I decided telling her would be a bad idea. So she doesn't know."

Madeleine sighed. "You just can't stop keeping secrets, can you?"

"I tried very hard to give them up, but no. Though I do have my reasons."

"Just like before?"

"You mean, I don't want my friends being hunted down like dogs and killed? Yeah. Pretty much." Petrovitch pulled the duvet up to his chin, exposing his skinny white ankles to the winter air. "Reasonable to assume that whoever set us up is willing to silence us if we don't play along. Of course, that includes you now, too."

She holstered her automatic at her waist and drew her knees up to hug them. "So why won't you tell Sonja? Don't you think she needs to know that when she gets a list of demands in the morning, backed by the threat of a nuclear weapon, she can pretty much laugh in their faces and tell everyone it's business as usual?"

Petrovitch wiggled his toes. "You're kind of missing the big point, Maddy."

"Too tired for games, Sam." She rested her head against the wall, tipping it up so her neck shone pale in the glimmering light. "Tell me."

"What if she already knows?"

Her head snapped around. "What? Are you mad? She's not going to do that to you."

"We'll see what morning brings." He stretched. "I may as well get up."

"Sam! You can't honestly think that about Sonja. She," and she struggled to say the words, "she loves you."

Swinging his legs out from beneath the covers, he wondered what he'd done with his trousers. "I don't think she'd let that get in the way of something that she really, really wanted. I also think the others would appreciate it if you kept your *yebani* voice down. It's half two in the morning."

His trousers were on the floor near the en-suite bathroom door, his boots by the window, and his mutilated coat thrown over a chair. He hadn't bothered about his pants, and taking his T-shirt off would have required an embarrassing amount of help.

He walked around the room, trailing cables and collecting clothing. Even though he hadn't bothered turning the light on, he was still aware of Madeleine's forensic gaze.

"For all I know," he said, "Sonja thinks it was me and will try to have me arrested—though not by you, obviously. It could've been the remnants of Tabletop's CIA cell, with or without her knowledge. It could have been you."

She let out a strangled gasp.

"Come off it. Don't tell me you couldn't have organized something like this: you've got the contacts, the opportunity, the skill. Valentina? She'd have to be in league with Tabletop, because they're never apart, but the pair of them could brew up a scenario like that. About the only one I don't think could've had anything to do with this is Lucy, and then I'm not so sure."

She got up and stood over him while he tried to get his second leg into his trousers. It wasn't as easy as he remembered it being.

"Why would I do something like that? Why would any of us?"

"I'm not saying you have. I'm saying you could. It's a compliment, really." He frowned: it probably wasn't a compliment at all, but he let it stand. "As to why? How the *huy* should I know? What would anyone want to do with a dummy atomic bomb?"

"You don't even know that. You're just guessing." Fed up with his inept attempts at dressing, she batted his hands aside and pulled up his trousers for him. "For all you know there's a real bomb out there."

"I'm calling *chush' sobach'ya* on that. Someone cut into Container Zero long before we showed up, yet what did we find? Exactly what we wanted to see." He had socks tucked in the top of his boots, but there was no way he was going to be able to manage them. He hissed at his own incompetence.

Madeleine knelt down on the floor next to his feet and angrily shook out the socks from the crisp balls they'd become. "When was the last time you changed these?"

"It's not like anyone's going to get close to me, are they?"

"Shut up and point your toes. Where can you possibly be going at this time of night, anyway?"

Petrovitch grunted as she dragged each sock on in turn, revealing two extensive holes in the heels.

"Oh, Sam."

"They're the only pair I have. And why do you care anyway? You left me, remember?"

"I care that you smell. I care that you have just one pair of socks. I care that some bastard smashed up your arm and your first thought was to have it amputated so you could replace it with shiny, shiny metal."

"Didn't though, did I?" He felt with his feet for the

openings of his boots. "Instead I end up with this pile of *govno* hanging off me and I can't even put on my own *yebani* trousers anymore."

"Or tie laces." She dragged the loose ends on his left boot tight and started to wrap them crossways through the hooks. "So where are you going?"

"Out."

"Out?"

"Out," he said firmly. "You can come with me, if you want."

"Why would I want to do that? And I cannot see what I'm doing." She dropped the laces in disgust and stood up. She had to slap the wall several times before she found the light switch.

With the light on, the room was revealed in its bare, vaguely squalid glory. Despite being part of a luxury suite in a luxury hotel, there were still fragments of glass embedded in the carpet near the repaired windows, ripped wallpaper hanging in shreds, curtains like lace, a cracked mirror over the dressing table. Empty bottles of vodka stacked up in the unemptied bin, and a half-full one trembled next to a single smeared glass.

Madeleine shook her head, then came back to the bed. She knelt again to her task, and Petrovitch could see the stubble either side of her mane of plaited hair.

"Sister Marie sends her regards."

She lost the knot and had to start again.

"She's here?"

"She's with the God-botherers from the Inquisition. They tried to bounce me at the hospital: I didn't talk to them, but I talked to her. I got the impression she wanted to meet up with you."

"I know where they're staying." She moved on to the second boot. "The Jesuit's place in Mount Street."

"*Chyort.* That's just around the corner." He felt uncomfortable at them being so close. "Is that deliberate?"

"No idea. Most of the cardinals in the Congregation are Jebbies; default choice, really." She finished his lacing and patted the side of his leg. "You're done."

"Thanks," he muttered.

She looked up at him. "If you think someone's trying to kill you, why are you going out alone? I'm assuming it's alone. No one else seems to be stirring."

He leaned over and dug his hand under the pillow. He came back with the gun Valentina had given him earlier, and shoved it in his waistband. "About this time, every night, for the past eleven months—since I got out of hospital with my new eyes—I've been doing a job."

"One which doesn't mean you leave the hotel?"

"One that means you don't see me leave the hotel." He fed his left arm through the hole in his greatcoat, and shrugged the rest of it on. "I know you've been watching me. I know when you've been watching me, too. Probably that's why you have no idea where I go or what I do."

He used her shoulders to get him off the mattress, and collected his courier bag. It bulged as he slung it around his neck.

"And you want me to come with you? Why now?"

"Because you're no longer head of Freezone security, and you don't have a statutory obligation to report breaches of UN resolutions three-eight-seven-two and three-nine-three-six anymore." He reached under his T-shirt and disconnected himself from the mains electricity, dropping the connectors on the floor and scraping them to one side with the edge of his boot.

Her hand went to her mouth. "What have you done?"

"I haven't done it yet. Which is why I have to go out every night. I should be finished in time, I think." He patted his bag. "And you'll never find out how I intend to pull this off unless you follow me."

She rocked back on her heels and rose. "Go on. Lead the way."

Petrovitch allowed himself a satisfied snort and turned the light off. He compensated for the sudden darkness; she couldn't. She walked into the back of him.

"That's me."

"Sorry."

"Why can't you see in the dark like normal people?"

"I've got night-vision goggles back on the bike."

"That doesn't count, and it doesn't matter anyway. Take my hand."

She couldn't find his hand, so Petrovitch had to grab hers instead, if only to stop it flailing around. Skin on skin contact. It burned him, and he had no way to block that kind of pain.

He opened the door to the rest of the suite. Lucy had her own room, while Tabletop slept on a requisitioned army cot behind a screen. Valentina lay stretched out on the sofa, covered by a blanket. The barrel of her propped-up AK stood out against the uncovered window, and her open eyes reflected the merest glimmer of light.

Petrovitch raised his hand in acknowledgment, and Valentina blinked. She'd never once asked him what he did, and he realized that it wasn't indifference, but the sort of trust that money could never buy.

Out in the corridor, the lights detected their movement and flickered on. They were still holding hands, which was awkward. He couldn't tell if it was going to be more difficult to let go or keep hold.

She decided for him. With a final squeeze, she released herself. "We're not a couple of kids anymore."

But that was exactly how he felt, and he wondered if he'd ever grow up. In the end, he turned away from her and headed not for the main elevators, but the emergency stairwell at the far end. He shoved the fire door open and started trotting down the flights of cold concrete stairs. It seemed strange that after all the times he'd done this, there was another pair of footsteps following.

He passed the sign for the ground floor, and kept on going into the basement, through the laundry, past all the storage areas and the patchboards for the electricity and the central heating and the pumps, into a narrow passageway that carried pipes along the ceiling low enough to make Madeleine stoop as she walked.

Petrovitch strode purposefully on toward a locked door that barred their way, and felt for the key in the depths of his bag.

"Once we're through, watch your step. It's a bit slippery." He opened the door, and a hollow breath of stagnant water and dark mud stole in. "You get used to that."

She took his hand again as she stepped out into the black space beyond, the mud sucking at her feet. "So where are we?"

"Underground car park at Hyde Park Corner." He paused to adjust his vision, and led her splashing to where, amid a sea of rubble, scaffolding appeared to prop up one corner of the roof. It was covered in tatty blue plastic sheeting, which he drew aside for her and ushered her in.

Behind it, another piece of plastic covered the wall. He lifted it up and walked through into a rough cave that shouldn't have been there. The sheeting fell back behind them.

He'd installed lights, and when he fastened the bulldog clip to the battery terminal, they winked on in a line that led along and down, out of sight. He'd made a tunnel, just about big enough to shuffle down when hunched over.

"Look upon my works, ye Mighty, and despair," he quoted, in the absence of anything else to say.

Madeleine took a moment to stare in wide-eyed wonder. "You did all this?"

"Yeah."

"How the hell did I not find out about it?"

"Because I'm very good at covering my tracks. The tunnel supports are from an over-order, the lighting rig is built from spare parts, the anti-gravity buckets I use to shift the spoil I make myself. I borrowed surveying lasers for keeping me straight and for telling me how far I've gone."

Her shoulders sagged. "But I'm the head of security."

"Were," he corrected, and tossed a yellow construction worker's hat to her. "You take this. I'll just have to remember to duck."

"You couldn't have done all this by hand. You just couldn't have."

Petrovitch bent down and started along the tunnel. "Well, if it wasn't me, maybe a wizard did it."

II

Petrovitch crept downward, steadying his progress by holding on to the metal beams of the tunnel supports. Madeleine, rather than facing the steep incline head-first, turned around and backed down, searching the cool, damp rock and mud for any handholds that she could find.

He waited for her at the next level, where his tunnel broke through a thick brick wall.

"There's a drop on the other side. Not far, but if you're not ready for it …" He put his feet on the lip of the hole and jumped off into the darkness. From where he now stood, Madeleine was framed by the light behind her, crouched and uncertain.

"What is this?"

"It's the Tyburn river."

"I've never heard of it."

"That's the beauty of using it. No one can follow me down a river lost to memory."

She looked longingly back at the faint string of light that ran back up to the car park. "You found out about it."

"That's because I'm brilliant." He shrugged. "And I

was looking for it, too. The deep underground lines are full of water and collapsing in on themselves, but rivers are supposed to be there. They fill up when it floods, and they empty when it doesn't."

She smelled the air. "Are you standing in shit?"

"Me? No." Petrovitch moved his feet to either side of the thin ribbon of glassy water flowing down the center of the tunnel. "It's a sewer, too, but hardly anyone's been using the mains to flush their *govno* away for nearly a year. It's as clean as it's going to get."

"And you have one—count them—one pair of socks."

"Meh. They dry out." He reached into his bag for the wind-up flashlight he kept there. He gave the handle a few twists, and switched the blue-white beam on. The curve of the brickwork overhead shimmered with reflections, while the walls glistened and shone. A channel was cut into the floor, and it contained the slow-moving stream of weedy-green water completely.

Madeleine lowered herself carefully into the culvert. "Go on, then. How far?" She stood up slowly, and discovered that the roof was high enough even for her.

"About five hundred meters and no surprises. They knew how to build stuff in those days."

"And how old is this? Before I risk my neck."

"The newer parts are a hundred and fifty, two hundred years old."

"Newer? Terrific."

"C'mon." He banged his fist against the brickwork. "Second World War, the New Machine Jihad, cruise missiles. Nothing we want to do is going to bring it down." He turned the flashlight against the run of the river. "We go up there. Doesn't take long. Need the buckets first, though."

Ten large buckets, battered and dirty, were stacked in two equal piles just inside the tunnel. They were heavy enough while empty; when full, they were a fearsome weight. Short lengths of thick rope were tied to each handle in turn. Madeleine went to lift both piles, while Petrovitch reached into the topmost bucket and pulled out a sphere. He flicked a switch, and the buckets clanged into the cool, damp air.

"Sure I mentioned these," he said, and went to turn on the second set of buckets. He tied them together, and pulled them along behind him like a pair of reluctant dogs.

The one intrusion of modernity into the Victorian construction was the thin cable stapled to the glazed brick roof. It ran from the hole the entire length of their walk along the underground stream. Though there were side tunnels and places where rusted ladders led upward toward the hidden surface, the cable ran unerringly along in an unbroken line.

Then it disappeared at right-angles to the line of the river, through another dark hole made near the upper part of the wall.

Petrovitch gave the flashlight another wind, and the light pulsed in time with his efforts. "I had to make the opening above what I could expect the water level to rise to when it rained. I almost got it right, too. Last autumn was a bit of a *pidaras,* so I lost a week or two just bailing everything out."

Madeleine raised herself up and peered through the gap. "I cannot picture you down here with a pickaxe and a shovel." Her voice echoed in the space beyond.

"It's the twenty-first century. Pickaxes are obsolete." He threw his bag over the lip of the hole, then shoved the buckets through. They blithely drifted on until they hit something solid, then banged around until they were still.

He tried to climb up after them. His feet slithered on the tunnel side, but his left arm was proving an impediment. He let himself slide back, then edged one foot closer to the top. But he couldn't do the splits, and he had to admit defeat.

"Need a hand?"

"May as well, since you're here."

She put her arms around his waist and lifted him off the floor, high enough that he could flick his legs over the edge of the hole and sit on the brickwork. She waited for him to ease himself down, then vaulted the wall in a single leap.

"What is this? 'Everybody laugh at the cripple' day?" Petrovitch crouched down to clip the lighting circuit in the new tunnel to the waiting battery. "Why don't I just give the hospital a call and tell them to prepare for an amputation?"

"Sam…"

"Yeah, well. This thing was your idea. You could cut me some slack." He straightened up, pressing a hand into the small of his back. "It's uncomfortable, awkward and it's always there. It does some things better, like hitting people really hard, but the stuff I need it to do now? It's not fantastic. Frankly, I'm bored with it already."

"Look, I'm sorry," she started, but he cut her off.

"Yeah, yeah. I know. Come on, we're almost there, and the clock's ticking." He scooped up the handle on his bag and trailed it after him down the slope toward the tunnel's blind face.

They had left the river behind; the noise of the trickling water, the drips from the ceiling, the occasional soft

moan of the wind blowing up through the vast labyrinth
had all been silenced. It was just the two of them, and the
sounds they made: their breathing, the scratch and creak
of material, the unexpected rasp of the Velcro patches on
Petrovitch's courier bag when he opened it again.

"I came up with the plan while I was lying in hospital
waiting for them to fix my eyes. I figured I needed to do
three things: get Michael out, blindside the UN Security
Council, and make it look like I was doing neither. Doing
both one and two, maybe half a dozen ways of managing
that. All three? That's where the standing on the remains
of the Oshicora Tower every day came in. I'm in full view
of the world, in defiance of two UN resolutions, picking up
a rock and throwing it away." He snorted. "They installed
cameras on the nearby buildings to watch me better, in
case I got carried away and brought in trucks and earth-
movers, in case I actually got serious. Didn't occur to them
to install seismometers. Not while they could see me."

"But if you don't dig?" Madeleine pressed her fingers
into the tunnel wall, a dense aggregate of gray-yellow clay
and sand. She could scrape the surface layer away, but it
was hard work. "Don't tell me you use explosives. It's that
Valentina, isn't it?"

"Leave Tina out of this. She has no idea what I do or
where I go, just that I go and do something. If I needed an
inexhaustible supply of semtex, I'm pretty certain she
could've arranged it, just as I'm pretty certain she'd have
got found out by you." Petrovitch sat back against a prop.
"Home-made stuff, sure: brew it up by the vat load, until
we leave a smoking crater where our bomb factory used
to be, and it's not like we can pop down to the shops for
precursor chemicals."

"So how do you do it? How, on your own, could you have done all this?"

He revealed his hand, and in it was a small black resin sphere, chased with silvery lines.

"An anti-gravity device."

"No." He hefted it and held it out for inspection. "This is a singularity bomb. See, it's a touch smaller, and the pattern on the surface is different—different inside too, of course."

Madeleine couldn't see because she was edging back up the tunnel. "Just put it down, Sam."

"It's fine." He tossed it from hand to hand, not remembering for a brief moment that it was going to be difficult for him to catch it again. His arm shot out with a whirr of motors, and the sphere dropped neatly into his outstretched palm. "Excellent. Anyway, it's not plugged in. Perfectly safe."

He pushed a thick nail into the blind face of the tunnel, and knocked it in firmly with a lump hammer.

"You do this every single night?"

"Yeah. Don't need as much sleep as I used to. I program myself for a few hours' deep sleep, and I seem to manage. Because of that, I am now, according to my calculations, under the Oshicora Tower." He spooled some double-stranded wire from a hidden reserve inside his bag and stripped the ends with his teeth. He spat out the plastic sleeving. "I only had Old Man Oshicora's word for this, but he said 'below this building' when he talked about the quantum computer he used to run VirtualJapan. The tower went up in twenty-twenty, and there's no record of a retro-fit. Which means that somewhere in the foundations, there's a room large enough to fit the computer, an independent power supply and all the cooling it needs."

She came a little closer. "You could be burrowing down here forever, trying to find it."

"Except I'm not looking for the room. I'm looking for the shaft that connects it to the tower. It has to be wide enough to get technicians and equipment down to it, and the computer up if there's a problem." Petrovitch carried on working, using conducting glue to stick the bare wire to the bomb and holding them in place while they set. "And thanks to the miracle of ground-penetrating radar, I know that that very shaft is a meter and a half straight on."

Closer still. "You honestly think you can just do this?"

"Yeah. Who's going to stop me?" He gave the wires an experimental tug, and was satisfied they'd hold. "Unless you're going to turn me in, I'm pretty confident no one will know I was even here."

She was opposite him, face to face in the half-light. "But what are you going to do with Michael?"

He raised his eyebrows and blinked repeatedly. "You know, I hadn't thought that far ahead. Here I am, busting my _yajtza_ to secretly rescue my friend from his concrete tomb, making sure that none of my friends could possibly be indicted as war criminals by the simple expedient of not telling them what I was doing, and I forget to consider the two Security Council resolutions calling for his immediate death should he ever escape. What a _mudak_."

"Sarcasm doesn't become you," she said, even as she tried to suppress a smile.

"Yes, it does. My voice is permanently stuck between sarcastic and condescending, no matter how hard I try for the dizzying heights of irony. Never mind." Petrovitch pulled a battery out of his bag and dangled it in front of her eyes. "Let's do some science."

"I've missed you."

He had a retort ready. It was on the tip of his tongue and almost out, but he realized in time that the game had changed.

"Yeah. Well. I'm still the guy who hid an AI from his wife and thinks he did the right thing. And until I invent a time machine, I can't go back and do it differently. Though there is a school of thought that says if time machines were going to be invented, our past would already have been altered, so maybe I did tell you and it was such *piz-dets* I had to create an alternative timeline where I didn't tell you in order to put it right again." Petrovitch succeeded in distracting himself. "If this is the best of all possible worlds, it doesn't say much for the others."

She enfolded his hands with hers. "I've really missed you."

He shivered. "Talking geek at you always made you horny."

Madeleine didn't deny it. "Everybody knew about Michael before I did. I was upset. Really, deeply hurt that you hadn't told me. The more people asked me, the worse it got. Reporters would needle me with it whenever I made any sort of public statement. It got me so angry, the only way I could deal with it was—"

"To leave me. I know."

"We've really fucked this up, haven't we?"

"That depends," said Petrovitch. "We're fifteen meters below a collapsed building, crouching in a small tunnel cut through unstable quaternary alluvial deposits using miniature black holes, looking for a concrete pipe that might be blocked by fallen masonry, at the bottom of which could be a very crushed computer, while above ground, someone wants us to believe they have a live nuclear weapon ready to re-enact the attack on Paris." He watched her face fall, then added. "But we're here together. Where else would I rather be?"

"Martinique?"

"Big volcano. I like my tropical paradises tectonically stable. And mostly above sea level before you suggest an alternative. I remember a conversation I had with Michael—several conversations really, because he'd keep coming back to the same question. He wanted to know about love, and how it worked, and what it looked like, and what it meant. He wanted answers, and I was bad at giving them. That's not new, though."

He looked down at his hands, covered by hers. He had cracks and cuts and burns on his, and her nails had been gnawed down to the quick.

"What I'm trying to say is that he kept on asking me why I was doing this or that, risking my neck trying to find you, and telling me that the only thing that could possibly make sense of it all was that I loved you. And I wouldn't have it. Until, eventually, it turned out he was right after all and it had taken a *yebani* machine to make me realize the truth of it. I never told you, because after that, everything between us got so impossible, I didn't want to play that card; it wouldn't have been fair. You were so very angry with me, and I wasn't in any position to say you were wrong."

He looked up again to find she was crying. He could do that; he could also fake it by squeezing excess lubricant over the surface of his eyes and blinking it away, but it was a cheap trick, and not worthy of either her or him.

He had rendered her completely speechless, though, so

he kept on talking. "So, in answer to your question: yeah. We fucked it up. Doesn't stop me from hoping that we have a choice about whether we keep on fucking it up or not. I choose that we don't, but it's really up to you. It always has been."

Petrovitch ran out of steam entirely. Madeleine was holding his hands so tightly that the corners of the battery were making holes in his skin, and the contacts touching his damp skin were leaking current. His artificial middle finger was starting to spasm.

"*Yobany stos,* woman, say something."

"Okay," she whispered.

"Okay?"

"Okay," and in a stronger voice, "we'll try to stop fucking it up." She let go of him and scrubbed at her cheeks, sniffing.

Petrovitch eased his fingers apart and managed not to wince. The battery dropped to the ground, and Madeleine picked it up.

"Remind me again why we were down here?"

12

"Petrovitch? Wake up. Is problem."

He sat up. With all the electricity flowing into him, he wondered if he ought to use some to jump-start his brain.

"Problem?"

"*Da.*"

He booted up his eyes. Valentina was crouched next to him, on his side of the bed, pale face and severe ponytail the only of her features visible. It was starting to get light outside, but it was a west-facing window.

His side of the bed. He looked down to his right. Madeleine was laid diagonally across the mattress, head on the pillow and facing away from him.

"Okay. Give me a minute. I'll be right out."

He waited for Valentina to slip silently out, leaving the door ajar, before lifting the covers slightly. It appeared that both of them were naked. The cold air against Madeleine's back made her murmur and turn slightly: Petrovitch shuffled off the bed and tucked the duvet down around her.

He unplugged himself and threw one of the former hotel's luxury dressing gowns over him, right arm through the sleeve, left arm across his body with cold metal against bare skin.

When he padded barefoot into the suite, he picked up the tension in the air. Tabletop was sitting at a virtual keyboard, staring up at a flat screen stuck to the wall, while Valentina was leaning over her shoulder, dabbing at the graphics interface with a red painted nail.

"So tell me the worst."

Tabletop gave up her seat, and Petrovitch gratefully fell into it, holding his dressing gown closed with one hand.

"This turned up, five minutes ago, on the ENN site. They say they got it from a Ukrainian server, but I haven't been able to check that because the original source is now unreachable."

"Got the IP address?"

"This window here." She tabbed it to bring it to the front, and Petrovitch set his agents on it.

The video clip on the news site was poor quality: grainy, full of compression artifacts, really shabby contrast: like it had been done on an old phone in low-light conditions, which it probably had.

In form, it resembled the usual extremist showcase, with three masked figures stood in front of banners proclaiming jihad. Vital differences were the kind of jihad being promoted and the long metal cylinder on the floor in front of them.

"We are the New Machine Jihad," said—shouted— one of the men, though telling which one was difficult, as they all had their mouths covered and they were using a really crappy pick-up.

"I thought I was," muttered Petrovitch, and Valentina shushed him.

"We have a message for the world. Prepare for the New Machine Jihad!"

The man on the right stepped forward and reverently showed a handheld's screen to the camera. The image on it was lost in the wash of pixels, but he came closer and almost pressed the handheld to the lens.

The ghost of a human face rose from the noise. "I am the New Machine Jihad. I am. The New Machine Jihad. Prepare. For the New Machine Jihad. Come to me. Come to the New Machine Jihad. Release the New Machine Jihad. Prepare."

The face, like ice, melted back into the depths.

"The Machine has spoken," shouted shouty man. "Free the New Machine Jihad from its prison or we will strike. You have twenty-four hours to give your answer."

The third man, silent and still up to that moment, walked toward the camera, behind it, and the clip finished.

"*Chyort.*" Petrovitch sat back and scrubbed at his stubble. He was pricked with cold sweat. "Just when you think you've worked out the way the world turns, it throws this at you."

"That's the fake bomb, right?" Tabletop backed the clip up for another run through.

"Yeah. Why didn't they ask for money or drugs or guns, or a small African country? This...this is going to be more difficult to laugh away."

"Why in particular?"

"Because," said Petrovitch, "that sounded too much like the New Machine Jihad for comfort, right down to the way it made no *yebani* sense at all. And there's something about this guy..."

He scrolled his way through the file to the very end, where

the camera was turned off. A few frames before, the face of the approaching man became fractionally more visible.

He'd been a lot thinner. And darker, too, burned by the sun and the wind and rain. But he had something drawn on his forehead that was familiar—a circle drawn in thick machine oil, that resembled the black cogs painted on the white sheets hung up behind them.

"I know him. I thought I'd killed him: well, I thought he'd died, anyway, since I left him unconscious on the ground right before the Long Night. Looks like I didn't kick his *yajtza* hard enough."

Valentina walked to the screen and stared up at the face. "Who is he?"

"The Prophet of the New Machine Jihad. It used to talk to him through a standard mobile, and he thought he was communicating directly with a god. He greeted me as a true believer at first, which made it a bit awkward when he realized I was trying to take the Jihad down."

"Which you did."

"Yeah. That's what I thought, too."

"Either you did, or you didn't."

"I got that *sooksin* Oshicora to erase himself. All that was left was the pattern, so there is no way that this could be the original New Machine Jihad." Petrovitch clenched and unclenched his fists. "So where the *huy* is this coming from?"

"Michael?" Valentina turned and faced the room, hands on hips. "Could this be default state of artificial intelligence?"

"Michael has no link with the outside world. It's not like I haven't tried every way in, but the connection is physically broken. It's just not possible for him to get out."

"That is answer you want."

Petrovitch stood up and started to pace the floor. He reached a wall, turned and came back, and found the chair in his way. He kicked it aside with a growl.

"The New Machine Jihad leaked through its firewall: the networking was complete and the software wasn't strong enough to contain it. This is different. The actual fibre-optic cable has snapped and the nodes are dead. How can an AI transmit a signal in that state?"

"It cannot. And yet you suspect this," and Valentina tapped the screen behind her, "to be Jihad."

Tabletop righted the chair again. "You're too close to this, Sam. I think they're playing you again."

He took a deep breath and forced himself to stop. He rubbed his knuckles against his teeth and stood with his head bowed.

"Okay," he said eventually, "let's assume you're right. The first act is Container Zero; a bunch of crazies beat me up, grab the bomb and disappear. In act two, scene one, the demands are made: free the Jihad or we'll nuke the Freezone. We've got a video that shows exactly what I—not you or anybody else—what I want to see. So assuming I'm the target of all this, what is it that they expect me to do now?"

"I imagine you're in the best position to answer that," said Tabletop. "I'll put on some coffee."

Petrovitch perched on the edge of the chair again. "Do you think Sonja's seen this?"

"If she has not, she will soon." Valentina looked around at the frozen image of the Jihad's prophet and scowled. "You must tell her bomb is false."

"And that's becoming less and less important." He

chewed his lip. "These guys are good. Really very good. I've spent a year trying to wean people off the idea that Michael is the Jihad under another name, but in less than a minute all that work's been undone. Every day, same time, I've climbed up the Oshicora Tower in defiance of the UN Security Council. If I do it today, there's going to be a *yebani* riot."

"Perhaps that is what they want."

"Chaos is too easy to arrange. There's something more going on here, and I hate the feeling that someone's deliberately trying to back me into a corner until I've got just the one option left." He raised his voice so that Tabletop could hear. "Last time it was the American government."

"Hey," she called back, "they didn't tell us, either. In fact, they tried to kill us too."

"This isn't getting us anywhere. Let's say I announce I'm not going up the tower today, and Sonja calls the Jihadis' bluff: what happens then?"

"Nothing. Is business as usual." Valentina pointed. "Except for you."

"But that's too easy. Yeah, I lose face, but I just proved I can create energy out of nothing. I can take the hit." Now there was blood on his mouth where he'd worried his teeth into his skin. He wiped it away with the back of his hand and inspected the smear. "I'm missing something, aren't I?"

"Just a little bit." Tabletop put three mugs of black coffee down on the table, and retrieved one for herself. "You and the Jihadis are calling for the same thing. No one's going to believe you're not connected with them, no matter how much you protest."

"But I don't have anything to do with them. They broke my arm!"

Tabletop shrugged and blew steam from the top of her mug. "So what? When has the truth had anything to do with it? You're alone, with the bomb, and you steal it yourself. Now you're using it as leverage to get Michael out. You can't deny that's what you've wanted all along, because everyone's seen you up on the tower, throwing rubble around."

"But…" he protested.

"What's going to happen next is Sonja is going to come through that door with a squad of goons and hang you by the thumbs until you tell her where the bomb is." She slurped her drink. "You should have told her it was a fake last night because she's not going to believe you now."

"*Pizdets*. Utter *pizdets*. They've not only taken me out, they've made sure that Michael stays buried forever. And we're not a single step closer to working out who the *huy* they are." He picked up his mug and threw it against the wall.

It shattered, and brown liquid spattered across the magnolia paint, clinging for a second before starting to drip.

Petrovitch stared at the dark pattern, as if it could give some meaning.

"We have to get out of here before they come for us, Sam."

He tore his attention away from the coffee stain. "No. I'll go on my own. You all have cast-iron alibis, and they don't want you anyway. It's me, and the more distance I put between us, the better."

Lucy appeared at her door, scratching at her head. "What's going on?"

"Tell her, because I don't have time." Petrovitch's gaze strayed to the closed bedroom door, and he bared his teeth. "Watch the front doors, will you? If there's any movement, call me."

He marched in, shoving the door hard and banging it back against the wall. "Maddy? I'm out of here as soon as I can get my stuff together, and you have to be awake right now because I'm going to ask you a question once and I need you to answer it straightaway."

She stirred. "Sam?"

"Tell me you're listening." He groveled on the floor for his battery chargers.

She sat up, holding the duvet across her breasts. "Sam? What's the matter?"

"The matter," he said, throwing the chargers unerringly onto the desk, "is that my life is being mined for tiny details which are then used to trap me like a *yebani* rat. I have just watched a video starring a man who only I would recognize, put on the big screen entirely for my benefit."

"Sam, you're making no sense."

While he was down at floor level, he swept up his clothes from where they'd fallen last night. "If only. Are you ready for the question?"

"What are you talking about?"

"The question is this: who have you been talking to?"

She blinked. "What?"

"It's not me. So it must be you. You're the only one who knows about the Prophet of the New Machine Jihad: not Tina, not Tabletop, not Lucy, not Sonja, and Harry Chain is very, very dead. Yet there is a picture of that man stuck to the wall in the next room, and I want to know how the *huy* he got there!" Petrovitch snatched up his courier bag and started jamming things into its depths. "I told you everything. Absolutely everything. You know my deepest, darkest secrets, and someone is using them to destroy me."

Madeleine colored up. "I have not told anyone, anything."

"I don't believe you." Petrovitch gathered everything up in his arms. Still wearing the dressing gown, he paused at the door. "And I've just worked out who it is."

She threw the duvet aside and advanced on him, naked, magnificent, furious. Any other time, he would have felt desire rise like a burning white heat. Not now: he was too far gone for that.

"I have not betrayed you," she said.

"No. But your priest has."

"That's impossible," she roared.

"Every week. Without fail. You went to Father John and confessed your sins. Every week we were together. And every week that we weren't. I opened my life to you, and you spilled your guts to him." He turned away, and couldn't help but turn back. "Except I never told you about Michael until afterward. How _yebani_ brilliant am I?"

All the fight was knocked out of her. "He wouldn't do such a thing."

"When I find him, I'm going to kill him. Eventually." This time he did leave. He spun on his heel and started toward the landing.

Valentina, Tabletop and Lucy fell in behind him.

"I thought I told you I want to be on my own."

"You won't get far looking like that," said Tabletop. "Probably better that we come with you."

Lucy darted ahead for the door, and checked the corridor for Oshicora guards. "Clear."

"Yeah, like this isn't going to end badly."

He hesitated as he crossed the threshold, but Valentina put her hand between his shoulder blades and shoved him out.

"We go now, or not at all."

13

Petrovitch dressed—was dressed—in the back of Valentina's car. It might have been funny; all the awkwardness, the fumbling, the myriad opportunities for an inappropriate hand to fleetingly rest. But he wasn't in the mood, and his black cloud was contagious.

They hid up a side street, squeezed in between two town houses, in amongst the pristine refuse bins waiting for their new owners. Valentina had the window open a crack, and at one point she heard a convoy of cars.

"So it begins," she said. She glanced into the rearview mirror, eyes wide in the gray morning light.

"Sonja hasn't got the manpower to search for us." Petrovitch was between Tabletop and Lucy, twisting and straining to adjust his clothing into something that might become comfortable. "She'll set up static checkpoints using her own employees, and attempt to resurrect what's left of the CCTV system."

"Evasion is not our problem. Becoming outlaws is."

"Yeah, well. We've all been there before."

"So." She turned in her seat now that he had at last become still. "What do we do?"

"I take it you heard me and Maddy?"

"Hmm. It was difficult not to."

"The priest is the link between the Jihad and me. We need to find him."

"Is big city. Which church would he call home?"

Petrovitch shut his eyes. "It's somewhere in Belgravia, not far. He won't be there, though."

"No?"

"No. Would you be if you thought Maddy was going to kick your door down?"

"If I wanted to pretend that everything is normal, perhaps." But she conceded the point.

Tabletop drew a pattern in the condensation on the window. "Sam? You sure about this Father John? What if you're wrong?"

"If I'm wrong, I'll still put a bullet through his head." He reached into his pocket for his gun. "If I'm right, he'll be grateful when I do."

"Don't like him much, do you?" said Lucy.

"No. No, I don't. Can't say I ever did."

"Maybe when you find him, you'll change your mind about killing him."

"Then again," and he flicked the safety off and on again. "Why don't we make a start?"

Valentina started the engine, and listened to its tone. "So?"

"Mount Street," said Petrovitch. "I want to find out how far this has gone."

"What is there?" She tapped her satnav.

"A Jesuit mission. It's where the Inquisition's staying."

"I thought you were never going to talk to them," said Lucy.

"This isn't about Michael. This is about me."

"Just thinking ahead," said Tabletop, still drawing on the window with the tip of her fingernail. The pattern in the moisture had grown in size and complexity. "If Oshicora comes looking for you there, how do you intend to escape? It's not like going over the rooftops is an option anymore."

He looked down at his arm and snarled at it. "Should have…_pizdets_. I'll get a drone in the air. It'll give us a couple of minutes' warning if nothing else."

"You have to start thinking, Sam, because you're going to get caught otherwise."

"Okay, okay. Look: I'll try and find a couple of cars to block the ends of the street. Sonja's private army drive cars with a manual override, so I won't be able to stop them, but I can take a moment to put a trace on their transmitters. That'll tell me where they are. Also, her lot are info-rich, so I should be able to track them if they come in on foot. I can blind and deafen them so that no orders can get in or out if I need to. I can get virtual agents to monitor the digital traffic, too, and look out for key words." He scratched the bridge of his nose. "Better?"

"Yes." Tabletop sat back and stared at what she'd drawn. "I have no idea what that is."

"It's a Shaker tree-of-life. If you want I can show you the picture you've taken it from." Petrovitch leaned back in his seat. "Come on, Tina. Let's go."

She pulled out into Curzon Street and took an immediate left to take her off the main road. "There is a back entrance. We should use it."

"Can you really show me this?" Tabletop was watching the buildings pass behind her window.

"Sure." He hacked her stealth suit and flipped her an image of a colored print that hung in thousands of American homes.

Tabletop looked intently at the screen on the inside of her wrist. "I don't remember it. Why can't I remember it?"

"Because they scrubbed your mind with your consent? Maybe the patterns are still there, you just can't access them. Like you've still got the data but the filenames have gone."

"How do I get them back?"

"I don't think you can. I think they're lost forever." Petrovitch grimaced. "Sorry. Bedside manner's a bit abrupt."

She sighed and wiped the image away, both on her suit and on the window. "I hate this. But I hate them more."

Valentina threw the car around another corner and stamped on the brakes. She looked out and up at a honey-colored stone end-wall that butted up exactly with the later buildings on either side. The rose window was missing a few panes of glass, but the rest of it looked solid. "This is it."

"Not quite." Petrovitch pointed to the dark wooden doors recessed in an alcove to the right of the church. A security camera pointed down at the pavement outside. "That's it."

"How long will you be?"

"Minutes. I've tried waking some cars up, but it's been a year since they were started. They all need new batteries, much like me." He leaned over Tabletop and popped the door. "Wait for me, say, there."

Opposite the church was the entrance to an underground car park. The shuttered doors were locked, but the building still overhung enough to hide them.

"Should I come?" asked Lucy.

"No one's coming. And this time, you're not going to argue." He climbed across Tabletop and jumped down into the road. "Bag."

They passed it out and he threw it around his neck and over his shoulder. Part of the strap caught on his metalwork. That it took moments to free it wasn't the point; that he had to do it at all made him grind his teeth.

Then he looked up at the three faces staring out at him. "Why the *chyort* do you put up with me?" He looked left and right, even though he knew nothing was coming, and that the Oshicora guards were still back at the hotel. Someone was watching.

The camera above the Jesuits' door was aimed directly at him. By the time he walked across the street, the heavy oak door was ajar. He put his hand on it and hesitated briefly, glancing up in time to see the camera's lens wink and whirr.

If they'd been waiting for him, he was in danger of becoming predictable.

"Five minutes and I'm out of here," he said, and shoved the door aside.

Sister Marie caught the swinging door and stopped it from crashing into the plasterwork. "Welcome," she said. "No Madeleine?"

"Not this time. Maybe not ever." His face twitched. "Where is he?"

"The cardinal? Down here, on the left," she started, but Petrovitch was already stalking down the narrow white-washed corridor, checking each door in turn before shouldering one open.

"Doctor Petrovitch," said the man behind the desk. Two words, and already his midwestern accent had got his guest's back up.

Petrovitch kicked at the chair facing the desk and fell into it. "His Excellency Cardinal James Matthew Carillo, Society of Jesus, Prefect of the Congregation for the Doctrine of the Faith. Now we've got the pleasantries out of the way, where the fuck is that lying priest you've been milking for information about Michael. I'd like a word with him."

The cardinal tugged at the sleeves of his black cassock and reached across the desk to where a silver teapot sat steaming on a tray. "Shall I pour?"

"Stop stalling." He reached into his bag, and he felt, rather than heard, Sister Marie stiffen. He pulled out the bottle of vodka and slammed it down on the polished wood. "I'm quite happy to turn the whole of the Freezone upside down looking for him, but I'm kind of assuming you know exactly where he is and would very much like to save me the trouble."

Carillo passed Petrovitch an empty porcelain cup before taking one for himself. Petrovitch unscrewed the bottle and splashed some in the bottom of each.

"*Chtob vse byli zdorovy.*" The cardinal raised his teacup and drained the contents. Petrovitch followed suit, then launched the fragile china at the empty fireplace.

"Force of habit. Are you going to tell me where this Father John is, or am I going to have to break something else?"

"It may not surprise you to learn that I've been around

the block once or twice myself, Doctor Petrovitch." Carillo cleared his throat noisily. Whichever block he'd lived on, it hadn't involved knocking back neat spirits at six in the morning. "Or can I call you Sam?"

"No, let's keep this professional. The priest: where is he?"

"Surprisingly enough, we don't put electronic tags on the clergy. That's a Protestant thing."

Petrovitch turned his head. "Sister? Could you hold this for a moment?" He dipped into his bag for his automatic, remembering to hold it by the barrel as he brought it out.

The nun took the gun. "Because?"

"Because otherwise the temptation to shoot this obstructive wanker in the face will prove too much, and I don't want to be in a position where you and me end up in a firefight. Now," and he twisted back, "where is he?"

The cardinal steepled his fingers. "You seem very anxious to find him, and not in a partake-of-one-of-the-sacraments sort of way. Are you intending to visit violence upon his person?"

Petrovitch leaned forward and stretched out his left arm. "It may not be very grown up of me, but he started it." He used the same arm to sweep the desk of everything on it. The teapot, tray, jug, sugar, bottle, papers, lamp, statuette of Ignatius Loyola: all ended up jumbled, shattered or dented, and the small book-lined room now smelled like a distillery.

He heard the sound of a gun slide being pulled behind his ear, and he ignored it. He leaned back and laid his arm in his lap.

Carillo wiped a fleck of milk from the back of his hand.

"I'll take that as a yes. We have our own procedures to deal with any specific allegations you'd like to make against a particular priest. We're quite rigorous when we investigate, but I'm sure you appreciate that just giving you Father Slater's address isn't an option here."

"And I'm sure you appreciate that, what do you call it, breaking the seal of the confessional means that our beloved John Slater is going to get his bollocks ripped off by the Pope himself." Petrovitch let that sink in, then brushed away the gun barrel that was tickling the side of his neck. "All the information you've got about Michael is from my wife, via that little wooden box in his church."

"That's," and Carillo paused, "a very serious accusation to make, Doctor Petrovitch."

"If that was all the arsehole had done, I'd go round and just give him a good slapping. He's in league with the New Machine Jihad—who suddenly think they're nuclear-capable. We're in Armageddonist territory here, Your fucking Excellency, and if I don't have some answers soon, it's going to be too shitting late to do anything about it." He took a deep breath. "I'm not used to swearing in English, but I'm making the effort because you're a Yank, and it's important that you understand just how trouser-pissingly scary this all is."

"There's a bomb? In the Metrozone?"

Petrovitch didn't bother to correct him about either the nature of the weapon or its location. "In about ten minutes, maybe less, the Freezone is going to declare a city-wide state of emergency. Sonja Oshicora thinks I took the bomb, and she won't balk at sticking red-hot pokers up my arse if she thinks I can tell her where it is. My problem is that only someone who knows my life inside out could make her believe that. Two people have access to that level of detail. One is my wife, the other is her confessor."

The cardinal would have made an adept poker player. His face betrayed almost no emotion at all. "How can I contact you?"

"You don't. I'll give you a couple of hours and I'll call you." Petrovitch stood up. "We understand each other here, right?"

"I am aware of what is at stake, Doctor Petrovitch." Carillo extended his hand warily. "Thank you for your candor."

"Yeah. Is that what they call it now?" He met the cardinal's gesture. "I'd call it being a foul-mouthed, bad-tempered little shit, and sooner or later I'm going to have to do something about that."

"But not now."

"I'm just a little busy here." Petrovitch retrieved his gun from Sister Marie and put it back in his bag. He looked at the pile of broken china and sodden paper. "Sorry about your stuff. I hope none of it was valuable."

"Do not store up treasures for yourselves on earth, where moth and woodworm destroy them and thieves can break in and steal." Carillo made a dismissive wave. "Only things."

"*Zatknis' na hui*, you pious *perdoon stary*. Go and talk to who you have to." Petrovitch glanced at the clock in the corner of his vision. "Time I disappeared."

"Sister Marie will show you out." The cardinal was already tugging at the landline phone's cable, pulling it out from the mess on the floor.

They swept back down the corridor, and Petrovitch called ahead to Valentina.

"Everything you said," asked the nun of his back. "Was it true?"

"If I lied to him, I'm going to lie to you." He put his hand on the door to the outside. "Why don't you find a news feed? It might help you decide."

"Good luck," she said. "God speed."

"You know I don't believe any of that *govno,* don't you? Fate is what you make it." He could hear Valentina's car right outside.

"It won't stop me from praying for you, Samuil Petrovitch. I think you need all the help you can get."

14

They sat around a flickering screen, watching Sonja's broadcast. None of them felt the need to speak during it—it was self-explanatory. When she'd finished, she took a moment to stare into the camera and straight into Petrovitch's soul, trying to communicate just how very disappointed she was with him.

Petrovitch turned off the video feed and unplugged the lead from the screen to the computer strapped to his body. He threw the loose end snaking across the floor and looked sour.

Lucy got up from her fold-down chair and switched the white noise off, then just stood there like a little girl lost.

"What happens now?"

"I'm going to try and find a kitchen. Come on." Tabletop stood at the door to the waiting area and scanned the overhead signs to see if there might be a clue. Obstetrics, Oncology, Medical Imaging, yes—all the equipment was ready and waiting for doctors and patients—but a strong cup of morning coffee still eluded her.

Petrovitch was left with Valentina.

"You must tell Sonja," she said. "Even if she does not believe you, she will doubt herself."

"Tabletop was right. I should have said something earlier." He cupped his face with his hands and dragged them down his cheeks. "I've made it even more of a *pizdets* than it should be."

"You were not to know."

"I'm supposed to know everything."

She moved along the row of seats, still covered in plastic wrapping from the supplier. She sat next to him and drew her legs underneath her.

"You are not God."

"Not yet. I will be one day, if I live that long. I've seen it. I've seen a hundred years ahead, but I can't tell Lucy what happens next."

If she thought his hubris worthy of comment, she chose not to. "Call Sonja. Explain to her you have nothing to do with New Machine Jihad. That you are both victims. She will listen to you."

"Yeah, I know she will. But this will be the first time that it won't make a difference. We're running out of options here. Whoever's done this has got it nailed down tight."

"Hmm," she said. "No plan is perfect. We must look for weak link. Exploit it. Where would that be?"

Petrovitch closed his eyes. "I'm tired, Tina. Too tired to think. Didn't get much sleep last night."

"I heard."

She might have been embarrassed, but he wasn't. He blew out a stream of air. "I thought...it was all going to be okay, at last. Now look at us."

Valentina clicked her tongue. "Of course, if priest is involved, you and Madeleine apart is part of scheme, *da*?"

Petrovitch blinked. "*Chyort.*"

"So you call Sonja now. Then we get to work." She patted him on the shoulder and went to find the others.

On his own, in the semi-dark, plugged into the wall to recharge his battery packs, Petrovitch made the connection carefully. No casual throwing of a message across an unguarded network this time; he obscured his routing, and ensured it was impossible to trace him. It would have been easier with the rat, but he could still work his magic.

She wasn't alone, and it took her a few moments to spot the window opening on her screen. He activated his usual avatar to stand in his place: it would look like him, mirror his movements and his expressions, but it would be manifestly not him, and he'd set himself against a shifting background of images that almost chose themselves.

Sonja was leaning over the desk, shouting at someone in Japanese, with English words rising from the stream like rocks. Petrovitch could have run her conversation through a translator, but the gist of it was clear enough.

Not only had her personal security detail failed to collect him, they'd missed everybody. Two of them were in hospital, as a result of an unfortunate encounter with Madeleine's fists and feet.

"Hey," said Petrovitch, "down here."

She did a double-take. His image held up his hand in greeting.

Sonja looked over the top of her screen at the current object of her ire and dismissed him with a bark of barely concealed disdain.

"The hired help not up to much, then?" he said. "That's where surrounding yourself with friends who'll keep you on the right path really pays off."

"Sam. What have you done?" She sat down.

"Not what you think."

Sonja leaned forward and opened a drawer. Its contents were hidden from him, but it didn't take a genius to work out what she was attempting to do.

"Did you do it?" she asked plainly.

"No. No, I didn't." He could see the muscles in her forearm flex as she felt across a tiny keyboard for the next letter. "Look: I need your full attention for a bit, which I won't have if you're trying to instruct your minions to track down my physical location. They'll never find it, and it'll just mean you have to shout some more. So give it up and talk to me."

She reluctantly put both her hands on the desk. "I'll find you."

"Maybe you will. But not before I'm ready. So let's talk."

"There's only one thing we really need to discuss: where's the bomb, Sam?"

"There is no bomb, Sonja. It's no more than a stage prop."

"You said it was a bomb."

"I was wrong."

"You? Wrong? I thought you were never wrong."

In real life, Petrovitch put his head back and stared blindly at the ceiling. "In my defense, I wasn't the only one taken in. But when I got out of the hospital, I went back to Container Zero for another look. Someone had been in that container long before the wrecking crew broke into it, and arranged everything like they were dressing a shop window."

"What . . . I told Iguro that no one was allowed near it."

"Yeah. He said. I ignored him. Good job, too. Sonja, they—whoever they are—were waiting for me. They had to get the bomb after I'd seen it, but before I could check its authenticity. Madeleine was on her way back with a geiger-counter when they broke my arm, stole my rat and carried the bomb away. Ten more minutes, and I would have been able to prove there was as much fissile material in that cylinder as there is in one of my farts."

She bit her lower lip. Her teeth were impossibly white.

"I wish, I wish I could believe you. I have a credible threat against the Freezone made by a known organization who claim to have a nuclear weapon. What am I supposed to do?"

"Call their bluff. Tell the so-called New Machine Jihad to take their bomb and stick it up their collective *zhopu*. Let the world know that it's business as usual, and you'll be ready to hand over to the Metrozone on time. That's what you're supposed to do."

"I can't take the risk, Sam. Everyone thinks that the Jihad are a front for you. Why don't you come in? We can sort this out." She grabbed a tissue and pressed it into the corner of her eye. "If you've done nothing, we can prove that together."

"Nice offer, Sonja. But that's exactly what they want to happen. They've designed this so that handing myself in is the next logical step, except that I'm not going to play by their rules anymore."

"Do you know how mad you sound? Listen to yourself!"

"Sonja—I lived through Armageddon. Do you realize how much I despise them? They ruined my life. I was born with a malformed heart because of radiation. I lost my father to cancer. I grew up in a city that was a social and economic basketcase because of what the Armageddonists did to Europe. And now I'm supposed to be running around with my own bomb threatening to set it off because the UN won't let Michael out to play? You're out of your *yebani* mind if you think I've got something to do with this!"

"You and the Jihadis want the same thing. You've run out of time to influence the UN, so now you're trying this. It won't work."

"Of course it won't work. I'm going public after I've talked to you and I'll tell everyone who wants to hear that there is no bomb in the Freezone. Why would I do that if I wanted to coerce the international community into doing what I want?"

Sonja sat back with a thump. "You might be smarter than me, Sam, but you can't just talk your way out of this."

"I'm smarter than all but half a dozen people on the planet. That has no bearing on whether I'm telling the truth or not. You've jeopardized the whole concept of the Freezone by falling for this scam. Don't compound the error by doing their work for them, whoever the *huy* they are." His avatar folded his arms, something that the real-life Petrovitch just couldn't do anymore.

"The Freezone is finished if I don't arrest you. Everyone knows we're close, and I can't be seen to allow personal feelings to get in the way of doing what's right." She clutched at her tissue. "Make it easy for me, Sam. Tell me where you are."

"You should be concentrating on the Jihad. I know I will be, and if you're not going to dig them out from whichever stone they've crawled under, I'll do it for you. Just stay out of my way if you're not going to help." He was all but finished. "And leave Madeleine out of this. You've done enough already."

"She's wanted. Along with everyone with you." Sonja regained a measure of calm. She straightened her jacket and dabbed at the end of her nose. "I will have what I want in the end."

"Yeah, good luck with that. So, are we leaving it like this?"

"Looks that way. Sam, I'm sorry."

"Not as sorry as you'll end up being. I'll give you the bomb, and the Jihad, and whoever put them up to this. You'll end up looking like a *mudak,* and I'll be the *yebani* hero. Again." He gave her one last wave. "*Sayonara.*"

Petrovitch opened his eyes, and took the coffee proffered to him by Lucy.

"That went well," he said.

"Did it?"

"No, not really." He bent his face low over the mug and breathed deeply. "Geopolitics seems to trump friendship every single time there's a clash. Apparently, even fifteen-year-old girls are now enemies of the state."

Lucy shivered. "Will we be all right?"

"Have I ever let you down?"

"No. I'd rather not have to stab or shoot anyone, though. Or have them stab or shoot me."

Petrovitch looked down at his arm again. "We're dealing with people who are comfortable with nuclear terrorism. Stabby, shooty stuff might be the least of our worries."

She sat down next to him, in the seat recently vacated

by Valentina. "Are you sure about the bomb? Not being a real bomb, I mean."

"There is a scenario I might not have considered." He pursed his lips, then smiled when he saw her expression change. "Still a fake bomb. But what if the Jihad don't know that? What if they've been set up just like we have? You see, I know the prophet—when I say know, I mean he tried to kill me once—and despite him being a weapons-grade certifiable *ebanashka,* he's not a liar. He wouldn't be involved in this if he knew there was no bomb."

"Who's done this to us? Who's gone to so much trouble when...you know?" Lucy leaned in and tried to rest her head on his shoulder. She ended up getting an earful of metal strut, and shifted uncomfortably.

"Yeah. They could have killed us in half a dozen different ways, and hey, some have tried. Madeleine's always been on top of any assassination attempt, no matter how ill-formed or ill-thought out. Yet she seems to have missed this completely." Petrovitch swigged at his coffee, made on a machine which still had the traces of the manufacturer's oil in its pipework. "Don't sweat it. Just because they're good doesn't mean we're not better."

They sat for a while, him swirling the gritty dregs of his coffee in tight circles at the bottom of his mug, she curled up in the seat next to him, knees drawn up in her arms and her chin resting on her knees: a young girl's posture.

"You still got that gun Tina gave you?" he asked.

Lucy nodded.

"She show you how to shoot straight?"

She shook her head.

"We can't fire off live rounds in here in case someone

overhears. But we can go through the basics. Give it here."

She reached into her pocket and held out the automatic.

"Okay. First lesson." He reached over with his right hand and turned the barrel away from his face. "Never point it at anyone you're not prepared to shoot. Never shoot anyone you're not prepared to kill."

She looked at the gun, and placed it butt first in his hand.

"Good girl."

He showed her how to make the gun safe, to eject a round still in the chamber, how to unload, and reload. He got her to stand and assume a two-handed grip, leaning forward against the inevitable recoil. He checked her dominant eye, and told her that she may as well throw the _yebani_ thing at her attacker if she was going to shake as much as that. He also said that if he ever caught her holding the gun sideways, gangster-style, he'd tear up her adoption certificate.

After she'd done everything often enough that he was confident she wouldn't put a round through her own foot, he asked her if she was ready.

"Ready? For what?"

Petrovitch started to unplug his battery packs from their chargers. "I've found the original upload of the New Machine Jihad video. The copy on ENN was clean, but the one on the Ukrainian server still has all its exif metadata attached."

She flicked the safety on the gun with studied care. "The…"

"It's a bit on the front of the file you don't get to see, but it tells you when the file was made, what the original resolution was, the camera model. Stuff like that. On GPS-enabled capture devices, it even records where it was taken, so you don't have the arguments where you swear blind it was Beijing and your girlfriend says it was Shanghai."

"Okay." Lucy pocketed her automatic and waited for the payoff.

"Come on. You're smarter than that."

She screwed her eyes up and muttered. "GPS, GPS, GPS." Then they opened wide. "You know where the Jihad are."

"Were. Chances are they're still there, but they might have shifted." Petrovitch had gathered up all his wires and closed the flap on his bag on them.

She was suddenly agitated, eager to go and do some-thing: activity against idleness. "You should have said as soon as you knew! Why did you waste…oh."

"I don't want to get you killed. But leaving you behind isn't going to work, either." He looked around the waiting room. Apart from the used mug and the crinkled plastic where they'd sat, it was just as they'd found it.

15

$Valentina$ drove them toward Cricklewood, aiming at the coordinates that Petrovitch had supplied.

"We have plan, *da?*"

He equivocated, then finally admitted the truth. "Not really. A lot of it depends on whether the Jihad thinks we're on the same side as each other. I didn't exactly leave the prophet on good terms."

"He tried to kill Sam," said Lucy from the back seat.

"It was a misunderstanding. I'm sure we can talk it over like civilized men."

"If you can get close enough to him," said Valentina.

"Well, that's not actually necessary." Petrovitch twisted in his seat. Tabletop was playing with Valentina's plastic explosive, making little creatures out of the putty and sticking them on the door. "I know it's stable, but *yobany stos,* woman!"

She smiled and presented him with a shape that could have been either a dog or a horse.

"We might need that later." He stared at the animal before attaching it to the dashboard. "Anyway. Back to the Jihad: the prophet expects the AI to speak to him through his mobile phone. A quick scan of the area tells me that there are a stack of phones active in the cell where the GPS signal came from. I can fake the Jihad better than whoever's faking it already. All I have to do is ring round till I find the right one, and the prophet will be expecting us."

Valentina turned left onto the North Circular. She didn't bother to indicate, just hauled the wheel around and waited for all four tires to regain contact with the tarmac before accelerating away. "So, we just walk up to door and knock?"

"Pretty much."

"And then..."

"It's up to them. You know how good my negotiation skills are."

"Hmm," she said. "And you propose we leave talking to you?"

Petrovitch shrugged apologetically. "I did say I didn't have much of a plan."

The empty road lent itself to speed, and Valentina took full advantage. She only braked to avoid a traffic island and a roundabout. "Is here?"

"Pretty much."

She knew when stealth was required, too. She turned off the engine and they rolled silently down the access road toward a pair of high metal gates.

"It's a school," said Lucy.

The gates were half-open. A big white-and-rust van sat sideways across the parking bays outside the main entrance, sitting in a sea of broken glass and shell cases. There were broken windows all up the front of the foyer.

Bodies had been bagged and tagged here: spray-painted numbers were fading in the winter sun.

"Not marked for repair, then."

They came to a halt in the furthest reaches of the car park, well away from the building.

Valentina cranked the handbrake. "Are you sure about this?"

"No surprises. Everything out in the open. There are more of them than us, and we don't know if they're armed." Petrovitch popped the door open and felt the cold air bite at his ankles. "We'll be fine."

They walked, four abreast, across the empty space to the entrance.

"First floor. They're watching us," said Tabletop, conversationally. "So, these New Machine Jihad people. Crazy?"

"Mad as a bag of spanners. The Jihad is their god, who they believe wants to usher in an age of plenty and ease under its benign all-seeing eye. Less stupid than some belief systems I can think of: this one is at least credible." He pursed his lips. "If it wasn't for the fact that their god was insane and I killed it."

Petrovitch considered holding one of the doors open for the others. In the end, he just stepped through the broken pane and crunched a little way into the darkened foyer.

"Yeah. I'm here," he called, and waited for someone from the Jihad to turn up. The others joined him. Valentina unslung her AK and cradled it across her body.

Just when his patience was wearing thin and he'd almost ground a piece of glass through the heel of his boot, a figure appeared in the distance, just visible through the small glass window in the double doors.

She—it looked like a she from the way they walked—appeared to be in no hurry. Petrovitch gave a nod in the direction of the doors and Tabletop and Valentina turned their attention to the other exits. Lucy started to reach into her pocket.

"It's fine. Relax. No one's shooting at us yet." Petrovitch gave her what he hoped would be a reassuring smile, but knew it would come out more like a grimace.

The woman stood there, hands holding either side of the doors open. She was dressed in a filthy boilersuit and her hair was gray: her resemblance to an Outie was so close that Valentina's reaction was predictable and automatic. Petrovitch felt the need to stand between the muzzle of her rifle and their guide.

"You seek an audience with the Prophet of the New Machine Jihad?" she asked.

"Since I'm the first-born herald of the machine age, I'm pretty confident he'll see me."

"Then come. All of you."

She swept before them, leaving them to taste her trail of iron and earth. Down a long corridor—noticeboards either side, between the classrooms, with pupils' work still framed behind the plastic—to a vast, echoing sports hall lit only by the roof-level sky lights.

The murmuring of the—worshippers? Acolytes?—drifted away as they entered. Petrovitch walked between where they were sat, on the cold hard floor marked with colored lines and black scuffs, picking his way to the front where there was an empty chair.

Not empty: a small black phone, propped up against the back.

Just to make things interesting, Petrovitch made it light

up as he approached. He could hear the collective straining as the Jihad's followers all leaned forward.

But he couldn't see the bomb. Now that he was looking, he could tell there was other activity in and around the building, the signals being partially obscured by the ferroconcrete walls. The woman who'd met them at the entrance carried on walking, leaving them in a loose, uncomfortable knot by the chair. The couple of hundred Jihadis turned their attention from the phone to the newcomers.

"Say nothing. I wouldn't even smile."

"Sam," said Tabletop.

"That's..."

"My suit's comms have gone active," she said. Her hand was already on her waist, reaching for her gun.

Petrovitch felt in his bag for his own. "*Chyort*. Looks like we're not the only ones to read the exif data."

"What's wrong?" asked Lucy.

"The CIA. Close by. What are they saying?"

"They've changed codes. All I know is that, for the first time in eleven months, I've got a signal."

"And if I had Michael, I'd crack those codes, locate the transmitters and get the jump on them." He looked up again at the high windows, then at the doors in each of the four corners of the hall, checking for the outside wall. "Those two lead outside. Bear that in mind for when we have to run."

"Behold the turncoat! Look upon the traitor who was the Chosen Son of the new age!"

"Ah, *pizdets*." Petrovitch's shoulders slumped. He turned to see the prophet advancing toward him, a tatty curtain serving as a robe. Underneath, the man was quite underdressed: a pair of baggy shorts, nothing more. "Yeah, look. I had prepared a long speech full of fancy words to convince you of my good intentions and break to you the fact you've been duped a little more gently than I'm going to. But that was before our American friends decided to put in an appearance."

The prophet gave no indication he'd listened to a single word. "You opposed the New Machine Jihad before. Have you come to repent and seek absolution for your heinous crimes?" He shook one of his bony fists in Petrovitch's direction, and as he walked, revealed that he was leaning on a huge, drop-forged spanner, a full meter long.

"*Zatknis' na hui*, you *kon' pedal'nii*. Any second now, the CIA are going to come piling in here to fry your arses, and the only way I can stop them is to show them you haven't got a real nuclear bomb squirreled away somewhere."

"The power of the lightning will turn aside the unbelievers' swords," said the prophet, his oil mark glistening on his forehead. "It has been foretold."

"And whoever is at the other end of this phone," shouted Petrovitch square in the prophet's face and snatching up the device from the chair, "is no more the New Machine Jihad than the *yebani* Pope is. You've been had, all of you. There is no bomb. There is no Jihad. And Michael is not the Jihad come back to life."

"Sam…"

"Not," he started to say, and wanted to add "now." But it was Tabletop speaking and she was drawing her gun. "What?"

"It's suddenly gone quiet."

"*Yebani v'rot.*" Petrovitch still had the phone. He said

to Lucy, "Catch," before back-handing the prophet with his left arm.

An arc of bright red blood hung in the air for a moment, before both it and the prophet came splashing down.

"Far door. Go." There was a string of flesh still attached to a strut, and somewhere deep inside, there was the realization that it wasn't just the other guy who was hurting.

There was movement. The Jihad were rising as one, but there was more: discs like hockey pucks were skittering across the floor. Black-clad faceless forms crouched coiled in the doorway, poised and ready.

The discs exploded, concussions of noise and light: people fell, staggered, screamed. Not Petrovitch, who timed his blink perfectly, nor Tabletop, who'd been ready for tactics she'd been taught herself. Valentina shielded her eyes almost too late, but Lucy hadn't been looking, still trying to juggle the thrown phone to safety.

The bangs made her jump all over again. The phone spun and twisted in the air. She stretched out, and folded her fingers around it just as Valentina fell into her. They rolled together in a confused heap, arms and legs at all angles. At the end of one hand, a small black mobile phone.

The first shots brought down those closest to the door. Petrovitch tagged each gun, ran the sound through an analyzer to tell him what they were using, and counted the bullets. There was no way he could return fire: even if he didn't care about hitting the Jihad's disciples, he didn't have line-of-sight anymore.

Neither did Tabletop, though she'd zoned completely. Her training had kicked in at a subconscious level and she was hunting her former colleagues, stalking forward into the mêlée of people, crouched and hidden.

Petrovitch saw Valentina sprawling. He levered her up, she snatching her kalash as she rose, then he reached down for Lucy. He pointed to the outside door, and it was all he had to do. She ran, head up, looking where she was going. She was light on her feet and ruthless with her elbows.

The agents at the door fanned out, firing relentlessly to thin the crowd. While part of Petrovitch's mind was counting, another part realized that the CIA didn't know they were there. They'd come for the bomb. The massacre was just what needed to happen first before they secured the area.

Tabletop shot the first one from point-blank range, apparating in front of him. She knew him. Intimately. She didn't spare him. She took careful aim at the middle of his face, where he had no armor and no chance. She spun away after pulling the trigger, stepping forward into the empty space already littered with bodies.

It took a moment for the second agent in line to realize the ghost to her right didn't look quite the same as before. She turned her head, and her gun arm followed.

Before she could complete the move, she was hit. Petrovitch took the momentary opportunity of a clean shot between two reeling Jihadis, threading a bullet between moving chest and back and burying it in her temple. Tabletop stopped her own action and retargeted on the third.

The last agent had just shot a man trying to drag an injured friend away. Brave, but it got him killed, and his friend too. There was nothing personal about it. No relish, or malice. But he was too distracted to see Valentina crouched over her AK when the previous body fell away.

The burst of fire took his legs. The ballistic mesh held, but the impact pulped his bones. He landed face first and, rather than helping him, the needles that stabbed out of their pouches and into his skin to release life-sustaining chemicals made him feel flayed.

Petrovitch trod on his hand and kicked the gun away. Tabletop put her foot in the small of his back and aimed for the nape of his neck.

"I thought," said Petrovitch over the top of him, "there were only supposed to be one or two left of your cell."

"One. And the field controller who I never met."

"So how did we end up with three?"

"Langley must have inserted more agents."

"*Vsyo govno, krome mochee.*" Petrovitch got down on his hands and knees to look the agent in the eye. "Hey, Yankee. Surprised to see us? Your foot seems to be on backward, by the way. Must smart a bit."

The man concentrated on breathing.

"A message for your president: I'm going to bury him for this, and everything else he's done. *Vrubratsa?*" He patted the man's head. "Okay, we're done." He scrambled up and started for the open door. "Lucy's waiting for us outside. We need to find the bomb, or someone who'll tell us where it is."

"You're going to leave him here?" Tabletop adjusted the grip on her pistol.

"Unless you've the stomach for shooting a defenseless cripple in the back, yeah. I kind of hoped you'd grown out of that, but if you want to, he's all yours. Don't take all day about it though, because I've called for paramedics."

Petrovitch quickly collected the fallen agents' guns, and put them in his bag, while Tabletop decided whether to execute the man she was standing over. Valentina offered her no help to make a decision one way or the other. She simply slung her rifle over her shoulder and jogged toward the doors that led outside.

"Yes, no?" called Petrovitch. He was by the prone prophet, wondering if there was any chance of him waking up this side of Paschal.

Valentina leaned back into the hall, panting. "Van. Bomb. In van. Van going."

"*Chyort*. Tabletop?"

She let out a cry of anger, disgust, self-loathing and hatred that carried on long after the echo had died away. She didn't shoot, though. She didn't even look back.

And Petrovitch was briefly and unreasonably proud of her.

16

Valentina already had the car halfway toward them when they got outside. Lucy was in the passenger seat, still holding the phone in front of her in a two-handed grip.

The wheels smoked as they locked and slid sideways, and the car came to rest right in front of Petrovitch. Tabletop was in and across the back seat seemingly before the door was open, leaving Petrovitch to clamber in.

His feet had just about left the ground when Valentina stamped on the accelerator. Tabletop grabbed him and stopped him from falling out, and the door swung shut on its own.

The van had gone, although there was a drifting cloud of blue diesel by the gates. The remnants of the Jihad were still running, even though the shooting had stopped. Some seemed to be going in circles, while others ran straight up to the high fence that surrounded the school grounds, heedless of the razorwire they would encounter once they were at the top. Others had gone for the gate, and they were in the way.

Valentina swerved left, right, further right, then hard

left again, all the time leaning on the horn. She managed not to hit a single person until they reached the choke point of the exit.

She braked hard, throwing everyone forward—except Lucy, who'd managed her seat belt—and the windshield was obscured by a back. The glass creaked, but the car was going slow enough that it didn't give. So Valentina kept on going, not being able to see until she hauled the steering wheel hard right and the body spilled off.

"Tina."

"What?"

Petrovitch looked out the back window at the still rolling form, then deliberately turned away. "I know, I know. Someone is going to pay for this."

"Where is van?" Valentina was going south, as fast as she could.

"Yeah. Hang on." He interrogated the phone network and found a moving cluster of signals on the road parallel to them. He called up a map. "They're on Hendon Way, heading toward the center. We can get in front of them. Right here, then left onto the A5."

When he panned out to get a bigger picture, he saw that Oshicora communications were making a hotspot that was coming north. He drew vectors and didn't like what he saw.

Everyone was moving quicker than the van. He'd get to it around about Swiss Cottage. But Oshicora security were going to run into it almost at the same time. The van was old, and he couldn't hijack it. Neither could he stop the *nikkeijin*'s cars. It was as if the outcome was already inevitable.

"If you can go faster without killing us, then do it."

He hacked the Oshicora comms, and listened in briefly: long enough for it to become clear they knew where they were heading. Everything was wrong.

"Okay, listen up. As it stands, we're on a collision course with Sonja's corps, who seem to know exactly where the van is and where it's going. I don't like that. It goes beyond educated guesswork and smacks of some secret knowledge that makes me very uncomfortable."

Tabletop counted the bullets left in her magazine. "You think she's in on this?"

"She certainly knows more than she's telling me. Lucy, pass me the Jihad phone."

She didn't respond straightaway, and Petrovitch had to lean over and take it himself.

"That man," said Lucy, "we just..."

"Yeah. No one's saying it doesn't suck, or that we shouldn't have stopped for him, or we shouldn't have run him over in the first place. Or that a little piece of us doesn't die every time we commit yet another atrocity. I'm not even going to suggest that what we're doing is more important than some bat-shit crazy Jihadi's life." He pressed buttons and accessed the phone's call history. "We're all going to do stuff today that isn't likely to be pretty, noble or generous. But I'd rather have you all alive come nightfall, if that's all right."

He turned his full attention to the phone, running the numbers through a search program: he'd called it last, and the number before it was different to the number before that. And so on. Each one was a random, throwaway account, like he used. He was going to get nothing from it.

He looked at the map in his head. They were scant

minutes away from intercepting the van, but so were Oshicora security. His eye twitched, then his thumb stabbed down on the power button. The phone winked off, and there was an immediate response from the comms he was monitoring.

"Proof enough that something's going on: they had tabs on the prophet." Petrovitch threw it on the seat between him and Tabletop. "Time to hit the kill switch."

Which he did. If he'd had more time, more processing power—if he'd had Michael on his side—he would have faked the entire Oshicora operation and sent them haring off after some virtual contact heading out toward the East End. He could have made it look like nothing was wrong for either the controllers or the foot-soldiers.

Instead, he was forced to use the blunt instrument of crashing the whole network: just a couple of lines of code inserted in the right place, and hidden programs got to work. Within seconds, everything was offline and locked tight.

It blinded him, too. He was now a small island of electronic consciousness in a sea of dead pixels. He really missed his rat now.

Valentina's satnav had crashed, but he had no way of guiding them to their target anyway, save what he could remember. Petrovitch just hoped that he'd sowed enough confusion to give them the time they needed.

"Left into Belsize Road."

They were driving past what was left of the Paradise Housing Project. The blocks had been demolished, the ground stripped clean, and something new was rising up, a vast, self-contained town of its own, half-finished and ragged.

"Close?" asked Valentina.

"I don't know. Not anymore."

She took the most direct route across the roundabout: the wrong way, and stayed on the right side of the road as she exited. The car rocked first one way, then the other, and somehow stayed upright.

"*Yobany stos.*" Petrovitch braced himself against the door and the roof.

"How are we going to stop the van?" Tabletop slapped her magazine back in. "Do we aim for the tires or the driver?"

"If it comes to it, we're going to ram them. Right?"

"*Da.*" Valentina braked hard, pulled the wheel left and accelerated out of the corner. An alpine-style bar appeared, sandwiched between two roads and facing another: she stopped the car at the junction, the squeal of rubber making the air taste foul.

Tabletop and Petrovitch bundled out. The Freezone was never quiet. There was always building going on, demolition work and pile-driving audible from one side of the city to the other. No one was at work today, and the wind whipped around the high buildings on either side of them, whistling and buffeting as it stirred the street furniture.

It carried on it the sound of a laboring engine.

"Lucy, out now." Petrovitch opened her door and leaned across her to unplug her seat belt.

"Okay, okay. I can do it myself." She batted his hand away, and stepped shivering onto the tarmac.

He reached back in for Valentina's Kalashnikov. "If we screw up, you know what to do?"

Valentina nodded, looked pointedly at the bend in the

road ahead. The echoing of grinding gears bounced toward them.

"I won't miss," he assured her, then strode out into the road. "Tabletop? Watch my back."

He lifted the rifle's butt to his shoulder and took careful aim. Crosshairs that weren't on the gun appeared in his vision, and he let the barrel swing around. He took a practice shot—checking for accuracy, windage, range—and shattered the top lens on a distant traffic light.

He glanced around at Lucy. "When I stop the van, the people in it are going to get cross. I don't know if they have guns, but if they do, they might start shooting at us. Then I'll have to kill them."

"Tell me again why we're doing this?"

The van growled into view, and he took aim.

"Because we can only redeem ourselves in the eyes of the world by showing them there was no bomb in the first place." The tires were an impossibly small target face on. He focused on the front grille and pulled the trigger. He fired three rounds, and hot shell cases smoked into the cold air.

A plume of white steam flashed into the air before being dragged apart by the moving van. The cloud turned dark as oil mixed with the water, and the windshield was painted black. The van swerved, left, right, left, and into the metal railings separating the two carriageways. It careened off, shedding its wing mirror and a shower of paint.

The engine died, and the van rolled across the road, losing speed all the time. It had enough momentum to rise up onto the pavement and into a lamp-post. The lamp-post bent, buckled, and gracefully leaned over until it rested across the van's hood and roof. Oil started to puddle underneath.

Petrovitch gave a satisfied grunt and started forward, keeping the rifle ready.

"If you're coming," he said, "now's as good a time as any."

He closed the distance, and a Jihadi spilled out of the van on the far side. Just as he was about to shout an order, a voice behind him squeaked. "Hands where I can see them. Now."

Lucy edged as far as the driver's door, holding her automatic out in front of her. The driver put her hands up—slowly—as did the man next to her. Lucy reached out and gripped the handle, pulling it toward her.

"Out. On the ground."

They complied meekly while she grinned with pure nervous energy.

Petrovitch stalked around the back. The first Jihadi had got to the rear doors, and was just opening them up when Petrovitch pressed the barrel of the AK in his ear.

"Step back and lie down."

"You can't stop us," said the Jihadi.

"Pretty certain I don't have to. You think you've got a nuclear bomb in the back of this van, right?"

"We control the lightning."

"You haven't really thought this through, have you? Or didn't you listen to your mother when she told you what a nuclear explosion does to sensitive electronic equipment? What it might do to Michael?"

From down the road, there was gunfire, the long, drawn-out sound of a car skidding and driving through a shop window, shouting and running.

"Out of time." Petrovitch reversed the rifle against the Jihadi's head, and kicked him out of the way before he fell. He wrenched one of the back doors open, letting the light flood in.

When the woman—the Outie-looking one from earlier—saw that it wasn't one of her fellow acolytes, she pressed the switch in her lap.

Despite his absolute conviction that he was right, and that the bomb was a fake, Petrovitch still flinched. Not that it would have deflected the blast wave of superheated gas one iota, but the big metal cylinder still looked very much like the real thing.

Nothing happened, and the Outie looked at the switch. It was a standard light switch, without the plastic paten on the back. She rocked the switch backward and forward in quick succession, and still no fireball.

"Get out of the *yebani* van, you *mudak*."

And still she clicked away, shaking it in case there was a loose connection, until Petrovitch lunged forward. He reached in, grabbed her arm, and pulled with all his might. He still held the rifle in his right, so he'd used his left.

She flew, this woman who would have blown them all up leaving a crater a hundred meters across and flattening every building between East Finchley and the Thames. She hit the road with her flailing hands and her face, and rolled like a rag doll until she stopped. She had come out with the switch, which lay a little further on, the bare ends of copper wires torn from their terminals coiling and then lying still.

He climbed up and into the van. The bomb sat on a strip of brown carpet on the floor, and he knelt next to it, resting his hand on the casing. He frowned, and peered briefly at the fastenings before deciding he'd still need a tool kit to open it up. Valentina should have what he needed, but first he had to arrange a truce.

Petrovitch jumped down and stepped out from behind the van. Lucy, standing over her captives, risked a moment's inattention. "Did I do it right?"

"You're standing a little close, and you've clearly watched too many cop shows. But yeah. You did it right." He looked down. "Let them go. Make sure they leave."

"Sure?"

"They might be little deluded shits who would have happily started another Armageddon, but we don't have the man- or woman-power to hold them, and we've got better things to do. Chase them off." He hoisted his rifle high and let off a volley of rounds, then started to walk in plain sight to where the Oshicora cars had formed a barricade across the street.

Valentina and Tabletop had held off the Oshicora guards long enough. Every time one of them popped up, they made them hide again. As he passed Valentina crouched behind the hood of her own car, he threw the AK to her.

She caught it and gave him a questioning look.

"It'll be fine," he said, and walked on to stand in the no-man's-land between the two sides. He could feel a dozen sights drawing across his body, so he stopped and cupped his right hand to his mouth. He tried to match it with his left, but it wouldn't quite go.

"*Konichiwa,*" he called. "I've got the bomb, so I don't really need a gun anymore. However, if one of you would like to come with me, I'll let you have it after I've shown you something."

There was some muttering, and from behind them, another Oshicora vehicle approached, late to the party. It nosed up to the cordon, and both driver's and passenger's doors opened. Petrovitch recognized the passenger, even without the benefit of the Freezone's database.

"Iguro. Glad you could make it."

"Petrovitch-san. The communications blackout is your work?" He weaved between the parked cars and toward where Petrovitch stood.

"Yeah. Something wasn't quite right, and I thought it safer if everyone could just step back and think about what they were doing." He scraped his fingers through his hair. "It's been a hell of a morning, Iguro, and I don't think it's over yet."

"I must still arrest you. It is my duty."

"About that. What were the charges again? That I was conspiring with the New Machine Jihad to threaten the Freezone Authority with an atomic bomb?"

"Yes," said Iguro, "exactly that." He had loops of plastic wrist restraints in his belt, and he fingered them.

"Despite the fact that I've consistently maintained that there is no bomb and I've just stopped the Jihad from driving whatever-it-is into the center of the city."

Iguro considered matters before concluding: "That is for others to judge. My part is arresting you, and your friends."

"We've got a stalemate, then. You can't call for back-up, and I've got the bomb. Why don't we sort this out like civilized human beings?"

"What do you propose?"

"Well," said Petrovitch. "The bomb's in the back of that van. I'd very much like to open it up and find out why a device that was supposedly sealed twenty years ago has a mobile phone signal still coming from it, but I can't do that with us all shooting at each other. Don't get me wrong, we can go back to shooting if you want…"

"That would not be desirable, Petrovitch-san." Iguro pulled at his jacket and looked uncomfortable. "I have already received a reprimand from Miss Sonja for allowing you access to Container Zero. I must not fail her a second time."

Petrovitch put his arm over Iguro's shoulders and started to walk him back toward Valentina's position. "If you still want to arrest me afterward, I promise I'll come quietly. Deal?"

"I suppose it is fair." He waved to his men to stand down, and only on passing Valentina did he realize by how many they had outnumbered Petrovitch. He looked sour.

"What?"

"I had expected more of you," said Iguro. "Where are the Jihad?"

"*Balvan.* If you'd been listening…" Petrovitch shook his head. "Doesn't matter. Let's get this *yebanat* open, then maybe things will become clearer."

17

Valentina set her tool box down and cracked the two halves apart, revealing layers of trays and little drawers. She leaned over the sealed cover of the bomb and inspected the retaining bolts, her hand running along a line of hex wrenches until she found the one she thought would fit.

Petrovitch rested his hand on silvery cylinder. It felt cool and unyielding.

"You are certain, *da*?" She twiddled the hex wrench between her fingers.

"It's not a nuclear bomb," he said, but a nerve in his cheek twitched. "I'm worried about the phone, though."

"Phone is good for tracking. Simple, effective for whole of Metrozone. Is also good for detonator. Call number, big boom." She scraped around in the bottom of the tool box. "Frequency of phone?"

"Nine hundred megahertz. I can feel it desperately trying to tag a base station."

She held up a handset that looked very much like a phone itself and punched some buttons on the control pad. "There.

Does not matter whether network up, down or in-between."
She propped the handset up against the side of the bomb.

"You realize," he said, stomach twisting as he thought
of it, "when I was dialing at random trying to connect
with the special Jihad phone, I could have got this one
first."

"Then we would have big crater and no answers," she
replied, as if it would have been just one of those things.

"Shall we get on with it? Iguro's getting impatient."

She looked around at the man standing by the van's
rear doors. "He can stay close, if he wants. This size cylinder enough to hold maybe seventy-five, hundred kilos
explosive. Safe distance is half kilometer."

"Yeah, okay." Petrovitch shuffled bent-backed to the
back of the van and shouted over Iguro's thinning hair.
"Tabletop?"

"What is it?"

"You might want to take Lucy for a walk. At least to
the end of the street: the very end."

She came over, puzzled. "I thought you said..."

"We're playing it safe. Tina's spidey-sense is tingling
and I've got a bad case of last-minute doubts. Just because
it's not got two sub-critical lumps of uranium at each end
doesn't mean that it couldn't contain enough cee-four to
put all of us into orbit."

Iguro frowned. "Petrovitch-san, are you saying there is
a bomb after all?"

He pulled a face. "Maybe. If you want to pull your men
back, Tina suggests five hundred meters would be
sensible."

"What is to stop you from taking the bomb when we
are so far away?"

"You mean, apart from the lamp-post lying on top of a van whose engine we just shot up? Or that we'd have to carry it to Tina's car in full view of everyone while leaving Tabletop and Lucy behind? Let me see…" Petrovitch cuffed Iguro around the head. "*Yobany stos,* man."

Recoiling, Iguro batted Petrovitch's hand away. "I will stay to keep an eye on you. Miss Sonja would expect it."

"Your funeral. Not that there'll be anything left of you to bury, but at least it'll be quick." He fixed Tabletop with his gaze. "Get the girl out of here. You'll know soon enough if there's anything to worry about."

Tabletop went over to where Lucy was standing and linked arms with her, guiding her away. Petrovitch watched them go, and then settled back down next to Valentina. "Now we're ready."

She held out the wrench to the first bolt and started slowly to unwind it. "You should go too," she said.

"I'm not going to do that."

"You are important." She stopped turning the wrench as a couple of millimeters of thread appeared at the bottom, and moved on to the next one. "I am expendable."

"You're important to me. So shut up and concentrate on this."

She nodded, and with the vague hint of a smile, went round each bolt in turn and loosened them off. Iguro watched intently, and wisely said nothing.

"Please, put hand on plate. Keep pressed down until I say."

Petrovitch did as he was told. The cover sank very slightly under his palm, back to flush against the casing. Valentina spun the bolts out and lined them up on the floor of the van next to her knee. Then she crouched right down, a flashlight in her hand and her eyes level with the edge of the inspection plate.

"Just a little bit. Let it rise."

He programmed his arm for a half-millimeter of movement.

"More." She peered intently at the pitch-black gap, then felt in her box for a marker pen. She bit the top off and made a green dot part-way along the opening.

"Because?"

She spat the pen lid out of her mouth behind her. "There is pressure switch. Again, I do not know what it does, but I would prefer it not activated." She retrieved a slim knife-blade and slipped it inside the cover where she'd made her mark, using only her fingertips and the smallest of movements. When she was happy with the blade's position, she used electrical tape to hold it in place. "Is okay. Lift cover off."

It was easier said than done. Petrovitch finally caught its sides with his fingernails and lifted it gently out of the way.

And now that he could see inside, he sucked in air through his teeth. "*Chyort.*"

There was a foam square, out of which was cut a smaller rectangle. A mobile phone nestled deep within, and a braided pair of red and yellow wires curled along its side before diving back underneath. All around it were packed stiff plastic wrappers containing blocks of what looked like window putty.

About half of the blocks had a thin silver tube pressed through a slit in the plastic and buried almost up to the wires that snaked off them.

"As you say," said Valentina. "Is bad."

"I can record this, and we can get out of here if you want."

"The phone will have been tested. We must retrieve it to see by who." She brushed a stray hair back behind her ear.

"If you think you can do that, then great." Petrovitch beckoned Iguro closer. "Take a look. No nuclear material at all. Just a shitload of high explosive, designed to incinerate the evidence and whoever happened to be standing around it at the time."

"This is good news." Iguro craned his neck to see, and Petrovitch helped him up into the van proper. Once he was satisfied, he turned to go: "No atomic bomb is good news. I must tell Miss Sonja at once."

Petrovitch reached into his waistband and pulled out his gun. He pointed it at Iguro's head. He was close enough that the barrel pressed into his temple. "Sit down over there and shut up. She already knows because I told her, and until I find out what the *huy* is going on, you're not going anywhere."

Iguro took the hint and crawled into the furthest recesses of the van, where he sat and muttered.

Valentina turned her attention to the small hole in the side of the bomb where the electrical cable had been wrenched out. She put her eye to the hole and was still for a while. "Hmm. Not connected to anything. Dummy."

She straightened up and tutted, staring into the heart of the bomb. "I would like to disconnect batteries first, then phone. But batteries are underneath."

"If I was going to make this, I'd want easy access to everything before final assembly. Maybe the whole thing just pulls out as one unit." He gave Iguro one last baleful glare and reholstered his gun.

"There is tamper switch on cover. Another underneath would be undetectable." Valentina demonstrated with her hands.

"It's your call," said Petrovitch. His mouth was dry, in contrast to his palms, which were soft with sweat.

In answer, she scraped around in her tool box and found a pair of surgical scissors. She started to snip away at the foam surround, always taking care she wasn't cutting a wire. A pile of gray foam trimmings piled up beside her, and inside the bomb, the shape of things became clearer.

Under the phone was a thin piece of plywood with four small rectangular batteries tied to it, and a small square of circuit board. Tiny electronic components were soldered to it. Valentina moved aside, and Petrovitch squatted down.

"Okay. The batteries supply thirty-six volts to the detonators. That black square's going to be a logic gate, which will act as a switch. When the phone rings, you get a voltage on that red wire—that should set the bomb off. But," he said, and traced the wires back to the switch on the cover, "only if this wire is live. Which it still is, because we've taped this into the on position. See that little button battery there? It's telling the chip that the cover's still in place."

"Is not tamper switch. Is fail-safe." Valentina snorted in disgust. "Schoolgirl error."

"Meh. No harm done. It just means that the people who set the bomb didn't want to blow themselves up by accident."

She handed him a tiny pair of wire cutters.

"Oh." He flexed his fingers and lowered his hand slowly

into the recess. He knew he was right. The circuit was simple and effective—just the sort he would have used if he'd been into bombmaking. He could have knocked one up just the same given half an hour, just using bits and pieces lying around his makeshift lab.

"You are hesitating."

"Yeah. Give me a moment. This is still a big deal."

"You were ready to defuse it when you thought it was nuclear."

"Stopping fission is easy, if you don't mind the cloud of uranium particles drifting in the breeze. A couple of house bricks thrown in the middle of a gun-style device would work." Petrovitch pulled his hand out and wiped it against his trousers. He adjusted his grip on the cutters and went in for a second time.

"Cut the wires," she said after a few moments more.

"*Yobany stos.* I'm doing it, all right?" He steeled himself and placed the red wire from the phone between the sharp jaws. "See you in Hell."

He closed his fist. The wire snicked. They were both still there, with Iguro crouched behind them.

Valentina wrapped the loose ends of the wire in strips of insulating tape, and waited for him to cut the second wire. It was easier than the first, but only slightly.

"I'd be happier when those batteries are out of the loop."

"Then do it. Is fine."

He checked the polarity on the batteries one last time, and snipped through the wires, red first, then black. Valentina made them safe with more tape, and Petrovitch sat back.

"Couldn't do that for a living." He let out the breath

he'd been holding in, and Valentina presumed to ruffle his hair.

"We have defused bomb. We have lots of plastic explosive and detonators. And," she said, lifting the phone clear and tugging out the remaining wire, "we have this."

"Yeah. We do. We have a slight problem to go with it, though." He took the phone from her and scanned the call history. "It's going to take a little longer to restore the network and everything that depends on it, than it did to take it down."

"Explain."

"There's this kid—an American—called himself Anarchy. Wrote a virus that I may have helped him with now and again without him knowing it was me. He set it loose on some government computers, whose servers promptly crashed and burned. Every time they rebooted, the Anarchy virus popped up and trashed them again: they're still mopping up the last of it now. Of course, what no one seems to have realized is that you can modify it to leave it dormant on a system. While it's not undetectable, it's pretty stealthy: you have to know what you're looking for."

"You have broken the internets. Is that what you are saying?"

"Pretty much." Petrovitch shrugged. "I was in a hurry, so I cashed in all my chips at once. If I had my rat, I could get an uplink to the nearest satellite. As it is, what with the state of emergency, all the people who could at least attempt to fix things are stuck at home."

"And we are stuck out here." She retrieved the board with the batteries and slid it behind her. "We cannot call our friends, our enemies, or the wider world. We can tell no one that there is no bomb or present them our evidence. We cannot find out who made this bomb or why."

"So we're on our own. That shouldn't stop us, should it?"

"It might, this time." She started to pull the detonators out, one by one, and pile the explosives up like a wall.

Petrovitch moved to the back of the van and sat there, legs dangling. He patted the space next to him. "Iguro, come and join me."

In the distance, he could see the knot of Oshicora guards and the two slight figures of Tabletop and Lucy. He waved the all-clear.

Iguro warily sat next to him but unconsciously mirroring his body language. "Miss Sonja should still be told. She will lift the emergency, and exonerate you."

"Like I said, I think she knew all along." Petrovitch frowned. "I take it you're not going to try and arrest me now, or anything embarrassing like that?"

"There seems little point. There is no bomb, so how could you have stolen something that does not exist?"

"And yet, there it is, in plain view. Tell me, Iguro: how did you know where the van was?"

"We were directed to it. By our controllers."

"Of course you were. Now, how do you suppose they could differentiate between us and the van containing the bomb, given we were all going in the same direction at the same time, and there was no visual identification of which phone signals related to which vehicle?"

When Iguro didn't answer, he continued his musing.

"You see my problem? Everything points to someone within the Oshicora organization knowing exactly where this fake bomb was, at all times. And I'm guessing that even though no one was ever supposed to see inside and learn the truth, whoever designed this whole charade knew I'd be chasing around after it—and on the off-chance that I managed to get my hands on it, they made it so that I couldn't possibly blow myself up. I wonder who would go to all that trouble?" He leaned into Iguro, who was looking increasingly uncomfortable. "Why is every-thing pointing back to me? Who could possibly want to frame me for something so monstrous, and yet at the same time sabotage their plan because they couldn't bear the thought of harming me?"

He kicked his heels for a moment longer, then jumped down from the back of the van. Tabletop and Lucy were almost there.

A thought struck him, and he turned back to Valentina. "Have you seen the time?"

She glanced at her big Soviet-style wristwatch. "What of it?"

"What do I normally do now?"

"You climb the Oshicora Tower." She looked up from the bomb, eyebrows raised. "And people come to watch."

"Yeah. They do." Petrovitch kicked a stone in the road. "I wonder if anyone's going to show?"

18

*P*etrovitch rode with Iguro, the cars becoming a slow-moving convoy back down to the center of the city. They skirted Regent's Park and stopped on Marylebone Road.

"What are you going to do?" asked Petrovitch.

"I must report back to Miss Sonja," said Iguro. He left the motor running, but put the gear into neutral. "She must learn of all that has occurred since we lost contact—something which is entirely your fault."

"Sue me. I was being tracked through the prophet's phone, and I get pissed off when people track me. And I rather assumed those same people were trying to kill me, too." The power in his arm batteries was getting worryingly low, but he had to move it now and again, just to relieve the pressure of bits of metal sticking into his side. "Tell her what you like."

"There is no more than a week before the Freezone is handed back to the authorities. This delay will cost Miss Sonja greatly."

"If that's all she's worried about, I'll cover the penalties myself."

"You?" Iguro had a strange laugh, more like he was gasping for breath.

"Yeah. I'm a very rich man. Didn't you know?"

From baring his teeth in mirth, his lips became thin lines. "How is that possible?"

"One of those things where you use the capitalist system against itself. I borrowed some money, and used it as leverage to short-sell oil on the spot market. When I say oil, I mean a lot of it, of course. Crude was trading at around a hundred and eighty U.S. dollars two days ago: I promised to sell twenty-five million barrels to whoever wanted it at one seventy, close of play yesterday. I sold the lot in seconds."

"But where would you find that amount of oil?"

"Look, the oil doesn't actually exist. It could have been sugar, cocoa, aluminium or pork bellies—it doesn't matter. What matters is that I bet everything on the price of oil dropping below one seventy. I could pretend to buy it, and then pretend to sell it to the traders who'd snapped up my futures because they thought I was mad." Petrovitch shrugged. "I barely understand it myself. It's a stupid way of doing business. But because I actually bought the oil as it dipped below fifty dollars, I made one hundred and twenty dollars a barrel. After brokers' fees, I made a shade under three billion dollars—about five and a half billion euros."

Iguro reached forward and turned the engine off, and sat in silence, digesting the news.

"How did you know that would happen?"

"I knew because I was about to offer the world cheap energy forever. Oil's still going to be useful, but we're not going to be burning it in engines. Not that that got in the way of a market stampede to the bottom. By the time sanity had been restored, I'd done the deal."

"You could buy whatever you want. Anything. Anything at all." He was awestruck.

Petrovitch wedged his knees against the dashboard. "The stuff I want most I can't buy. This is just seed money: there's hard work to be done if I want to make real things grow. You know, stuff that actually lasts. But like I said, I think Sonja's got other things on her mind than her contractual obligations."

"You wish me to deliver a message to her?"

"If you could."

Tabletop tapped on the window, and Petrovitch cracked the door open.

"Problem?" she asked.

"Not really. Just explaining something to Iguro." He opened the door wider and slipped out. "I think he might finally get it this time."

"Petrovitch-san. The message?" Iguro leaned over from the driver's seat to see him better.

"Yeah, that." He scratched at his nose. "How about 'I know what you've done and the moment I get to prove it is the moment you start running'? That's a bit melodramatic, though, and she's never been one for running. I could always go for the menacing 'I know where you live,' but she knows I know, so what would be the point? Just tell her the CIA tried to steal the nuclear bomb from the New Machine Jihad. That should give her some indication how deep in the shit she's swimming."

He slammed the door, obscuring Iguro's open mouth.

Tabletop watched the car spin its wheels in an effort to get away from them. "Do you think she's going to kill him?"

"I don't know. I wouldn't have fancied being one of the techs who put the bomb together though. If any of them are still alive, I'll be very surprised. It's not like we lack building sites." Petrovitch looked at the silent cranes that dominated the skyline. "Why did she do it?"

"You still don't know for sure that she did, Sam."

"Yeah, I do. It's just time to stop making excuses for her."

"So where does the priest fit in?"

He shrugged. "I don't know. I mean, if Tina's right, and part of his plan is that he makes sure me and Maddy split up permanently . . . what does he hope happens next?"

"Sam, get in the car."

He did as he was told. The Oshicora cars went left toward the Post Office Tower, and theirs went right toward Hyde Park. He was ten minutes late for the show—except there'd be no performance today. No webcams, no streaming, no blog comment or news footage. Just him and whoever might break the curfew and turn up. It was almost like the first few weeks of his calculated act of defiance, before it became the media event he couldn't stop doing.

Valentina drove past their hotel and the Wellington Monument, down Piccadilly. She eased her foot off the accelerator as the rubble of the Oshicora building came into view between the rising skyscrapers on either side of the plot.

It was swarming with people, each of them taking something from the mound and carrying it away. There wasn't much space around for the debris to go: instead, spontaneous barricades were collecting on all the approach roads.

The car stopped in front of a ragged line of concrete

blocks that lay across both carriageways, and Petrovitch watched as the workers—mostly construction types in their usual laboring wear, but also office staff who had discarded their jackets or high heels or both, and over-alled sanitation crews, and cooks and drivers and a good number of blue-covered Oshicora employees—carried more fragments of glass, metal and stone and placed them down.

"What are they doing?"

Lucy leaned in next to him. "I know you're smart and everything, but really. What does it look like they're doing?"

"No, I know what they're doing. It should have been more like, they have to stop doing it. Now." He got out and stared at the ant-hill of activity.

"And how are you going to get them to do that?" Lucy stood next to him and surveyed the scene.

"I'm going to talk to them," said Petrovitch. He blinked. "Yeah, that's scary."

He took a deep breath and started forward. They parted for him, looking at him with reverence as he walked by. Then they carried on under the weight of their heavy loads.

Lucy stayed close, and when he got to the bottom of the rubble pile, he reached down to help her up. His arm seized completely.

"Ah, *oblom*." He looked at the now-useless exoskeleton supporting his shattered bones.

"Do you want me get you some more batteries?"

"It doesn't matter. Better off getting me a saw." He used his right hand to force the hinges into an acceptable shape, before letting the arm fall uselessly by his side. "Come on."

The further they climbed, the fewer people they met, until at last they were above the crowd. The geography of the pile had changed: more pieces of the fallen tower had been shifted in the time it had taken to reach their present height than had been thrown off by Petrovitch in all the preceding months.

Coming down the side street was a digger, spewing blue fumes into the air.

"Look at them," said Petrovitch. "A couple of days, and we'd be there: all the way down to the basement. They'd work day and night: keep going until it was all gone."

"Then why don't you let them?" Lucy steadied herself using his shoulder. "They want to do it."

"Because we're being watched, whether we like it or not. Right up there, beyond the atmosphere, the American satellites will be looking down on us and there's nothing I can do about that. I'm guessing Mackensie is in his war room right now, staring at the top of my head and wondering how many nukes it'll take to bunker-bust Michael's coffin." He smiled sadly at her. "I can't let that happen. These people, they think they're doing the right thing, but every bit of rebar they drag out and pile up means it's less likely that I can get Michael out, not more."

"They're just copying you," she said. "What was that all about if you didn't mean it to work?"

"I'll tell you later. Right now, we have to attract several thousands of people's attention and get them close enough that I can shout at them."

They stood there, but that didn't seem to work at all. So he drew his gun and was about to waste some bullets when Lucy placed two fingers in her mouth and let out an ear-splitting whistle.

"*Yobany stos,* girl. Some warning, okay?"

She grinned at him, even as the dying echo of her whistle bounced around the surrounding buildings.

The people closest to them stopped. They dropped what they were carrying, and started to gather. The ripple spread outward: the crowd in front of Petrovitch grew more dense. After five minutes, he had everyone, even the driver of the digger.

They were all looking at him, and he knew there was no way out of this. He cleared his throat noisily, scratched at his ear, and adjusted his left arm again.

"Hello," he said.

Some of them even said hello back.

"You're probably wondering why I asked you here today—but that's not true: you're here because you wanted to be here, despite everything that's gone on today and the fact that you're not supposed to be here at all. I'm touched. No, I'm moved. I didn't know you thought that much..."
He ground to a halt, and looked to Lucy for inspiration.

"Go on. Tell them," she urged.

So he did.

"I love you all." He stopped, then started again when he realized that he actually felt that way. "You're brilliant. Loads of you have seen your houses wrecked, your friends and your families run out of town, you've lost people you care about and your lives have been turned upside down. But you're still here, still thinking about the future and how you can build it bigger and better and brighter. The Freezone is more than a job to you. It's part of you and you want to make it work. And it will work, because you care enough to make a go of it.

"Problem is, we've been let down. You all know about

Container Zero and the New Machine Jihad. You all know that I've been accused of threatening those in charge of the Freezone with a nuclear bomb unless they let Michael out. That's enough to turn anyone against me: Samuil Petrovitch the Armageddonist. And you came anyway, not out of fear, but because you knew a different Sam Petrovitch, one who would die to save the city.

"Which is why I'm going to ask you to stop. You're going to get us all killed if you carry on. This city's stood for two thousand years: I want it to be here for another two thousand, and I want the rest of the land beyond the cordon to be opened up, and I want peace with the Outies, and I want your children and theirs to build on the ruins of all the old villages and towns and cities and live forever. That can only happen if the Freezone survives.

"So, what I want you to do is this: go to work. Go and tell your shift. Bang on doors and shout in the streets. It's time to go to work. It's perfectly safe. There is no bomb, and there never was. I want you to let me deal with the consequences of that. What I can't do is your jobs. You know what you do best. You know your wiring, your plumbing, your plastering, your welding, your digging, whatever it is you do. Today is a work day, and people are sitting in their domiks, in their hostels, wondering what the *huy* is going on. Get them out. Get them working.

"I appreciate we've got little or no power at the moment, you can't call anybody up, you can't check computers for plans and figures. I'm going to have to fix that shortly. But you need to be ready for when the Freezone comes alive again, so we don't miss a moment more than we have to.

"I'm guessing that to get here, you had to dodge patrols and sneak past road blocks. On your way back, don't worry about them. You'll be challenged—why you're not obeying the curfew—but this is how you respond: we've got work to do. Don't be put off. Don't let yourself be persuaded otherwise. We've all got work to do. Let's not waste any more time with this: I'm just prattling on now, and you're going to get bored soon."

Someone laughed, and Petrovitch was eternally grateful.

"Go on. We all know what it is we're supposed to be doing. So let's do it."

He walked down, like Moses off the mountain, his left arm dragging his whole body to one side. The crowd, rather than moving out of his way, came closer still. It seemed that what they wanted to do first, before anything else, was to touch him. Those who couldn't make their way through the press of bodies surrounding him started to applaud him.

He became separated from Lucy. He could feel her fingers slip away from him, and there was nothing he could do about it.

"*Pizdets*," he muttered under his breath. "Utter *pizdets*."

Then someone came to his rescue. She put her strong arm around him and shielded him as she eased him through the crowd—gently but firmly so as not to upset anyone, giving them time to reach out for him without allowing him to get crushed.

"Thanks," he said.

"You're welcome," said Madeleine. "Where's your car?"

"West side of Piccadilly."

She carefully changed direction. "What happened to your arm?"

"Ran out of watts. Can you see Lucy?"

Using her height, she quickly scanned the tops of the nearby heads. "I'll go back for her. Let's get you to safety first."

Madeleine kept going, calm and relentless, up to the barricade, over it, and to the front passenger door of the car. She stood there, holding it open while he got in, and closed it slowly so that fingers didn't get trapped.

Then she climbed up onto the hood to try and locate Lucy.

Valentina tutted. "Look: bodywork is dented."

"You should worry. My bodywork is more than dented." Petrovitch hauled his arm around so it laid on his lap, and looked up at Madeleine's leather-clad legs. He was momentarily distracted, so that he didn't answer Valentina straightaway.

Only when the view cleared and Madeleine started back through the crowd did he acknowledge her.

"Sorry. What was that?"

"I said, does this mean we are now in charge?"

"Yeah. No. I guess so. Looks like you've got your revolution after all."

19

Once they were all back together again, there was a long awkward silence. Lucy was squashed in between Tabletop on one side and Madeleine on the other. Valentina tapped the dash with her keys, while Petrovitch was busy trying to work out just what the hell he'd told everyone he'd do.

It meant rewinding the file and cringing like a stray dog in a street fight. He realized he'd backed himself into a corner, and there was only one way to make good his promises.

All the while, the silence stretched on. The crowd were dispersing, and were already visibly thinned.

"I think I owe you all an apology," said Madeleine. She shifted, leathers creaking. "Sorry."

If anyone was in a forgiving mood, they hid it well.

"Do you know," said Valentina, "how much trouble we are in?" Novosibirsk on mid-winter's day would have been warmer.

"I have some idea."

Tabletop leaned forward, while Lucy shrank in her seat. "My ex-colleagues from the CIA turned up. There were more of them than we expected. Then we discovered that the supposed nuclear bomb was packed with plastic, to be triggered by a mobile phone that Sonja Oshicora's personal security detail was actively tracking. Sam's activated a virus that has shut the city down. And apparently we're now responsible for the Freezone having seized it in a popular uprising."

"Oh. Okay."

"Enough," muttered Petrovitch.

"She has ruined everything!" Valentina slammed her hands on the steering wheel. "You had plans, *da?* I know you had plans even if I did not know what they were. I trusted you—still trust you to get us out of this, this mess. But best chances we had have gone. Because of her."

"I said, enough." He dragged at his arm, and wondered if he could plug himself directly into the power socket set underneath the air-con. "Battle plans never survive contact with the enemy. We can change them; we were always going to have to change them. That's not the problem."

"No, problem sits behind you." Even furious, Valentina had no color to her face. It was her eyes that burned with bright fire. "She has betrayed you."

"Stop it now. I appreciate that we've all been living on adrenaline for the last few hours, but it's nothing a massive fry-up and some mugs of coffee wouldn't cure. Before anyone else says something they might regret, please take a moment to think about everything that's happened, and more importantly, why."

"I know why. Your wife cannot keep her mouth shut."

"*Yebani v'rot.* If Maddy is guilty of anything, it's trusting a millennia-old tradition of confidentiality between priest and penitent. I'm pissed off, too, but I'm trying to direct my anger in the right direction."

"Can I?" said Lucy in a very quiet voice. She struggled with her elbows to gain some extra space, and sat forward. "Sam, do you remember when we first met?"

"I broke into your house. You were hiding in the bath."

"That's not what I mean. The play. The school play I was supposed to be doing."

"To be fair, I had my hands full that day." He twisted in his seat to see her better as she leaned over his shoulder. "Refresh my memory."

"*Romeo and Juliet*. You know," and she quoted in a rush: " 'O Romeo, Romeo! wherefore art thou Romeo? Deny thy father and refuse thy name; or, if thou wilt not, be but sworn my love, and I'll no longer be a Capulet.' "

"Yeah, I know it. It's better in the original Russian. So what?"

She pointed at him. "Romeo." Then at Madeleine. "Juliet."

Everybody else took a breath before starting their objections, and all stopped on the first syllable before grinding to a halt as their mental gears stalled.

"It's like, you know: two households, both alike in dignity, in fair Verona, where we lay our scene. From ancient grudge break to new mutiny, where civil blood makes civil hands unclean. But what if Juliet hadn't killed herself, and they'd lived together like a normal couple? Her family would have hated it. And his. The idea that they would have kissed and made up is stupid. They would have worked together to split them up, then gone back to stabbing each other in the street."

Petrovitch frowned. "Is this actually relevant? Because

I've accidentally just organized a coup, and I could probably do with paying some attention to that."

"This is the whole reason for everything!" Lucy knew she wasn't explaining herself well, and she grunted with annoyance. "Montagues and Capulets. You two have separated over Michael. But neither of you wants to make it permanent because you actually do love each other. So you need a push. Sonja Oshicora wants you, right?"

"As uncomfortable as it makes me to admit it, yeah." He didn't feel able to meet anyone's eye at that moment.

"That means she needs Madeleine out of the way. How's she going to do that? She can't just kill her, because that won't work. She needs you to hate her." Lucy directed her forensic gaze at Madeleine. "This priest of yours: he wants you to go back to the Church. Is he going to get you to do that by killing Sam? Is he even going to try and kill Sam, knowing how well protected he is? No. What he can do is make you hate him." She threw up her hands. "How come this is so obvious to me, but not to you bunch of emotionally retarded grownups? They're working together. Sonja and the priest."

Petrovitch sat back around and stared straight ahead. "Oh, you have to be *yebani* joking. This whole thing has been contrived to..." His face set hard. "*Sic sukam sim.*"

"Sam?" said Madeleine, bewildered.

"I am not a piece of meat. I will not be owned by anyone. And I will absolutely not be the *peshka* in anyone's game." His heart was spinning fast, too fast: the tips of his fingers were tingling and his head felt like it was going to pop like an over-inflated balloon. He took several deep breaths and deliberately braked the turbine in his chest. Too hard. He felt fuzzy, almost fainting. It was almost as it was before he'd had the implant. "*Chyort.*"

"Get him out of the car. He's crashing."

There was a sudden scramble around him, and he was dragged out and laid on the ground. He saw sky and cloud, and felt road and rubble. He was cold, colder than he'd ever been, like he'd been frozen and all these people leaning over him were defrosting his body with nothing more than good wishes and concerned looks.

"No CPR! It doesn't work like that."

"How does it work then?"

"It's not like there's a panel I can pop open."

His T-shirt was pulled up, and the surgical tape that held the slim computer to his body was ripped free.

"I don't even know if I can access it. It's not the rat."

"Give it to me. You're panicking and we don't have the time."

"Can you find anything?"

"What's it called?"

"I don't—wait: Sorenson. Search for Sorenson."

"Spelt right?"

"Yes."

"Okay. Just stop pointing at the screen. No. No. No again. Wait."

"That slider. Put it halfway."

"There?"

And the blood surged back through his body. His heart wasn't designed to go from a standing start, but it did well enough. As his blood pressure returned to something approaching normal, Petrovitch grimaced and gurned.

"I didn't know I could do that," he said eventually.

"You turned your own heart off."

He blinked and tried to find the speaker: Madeleine.

"Looks that way. I'm going to have to script up some sort of safety net for that."

She pushed the others aside and raised him into a sitting position. "Never do that again."

"What? It's not like I haven't died before." He took a breath of fresh, cold air and found it didn't hurt.

Madeleine cuffed his head lightly. "And I was there for most of them, which is why I don't want to go back to that." She chewed at her lip. "You believe her, don't you?"

"Lucy? You know how much of a fan I am of Occam's Razor."

"Sam, what are we going to do?" She pulled at her plait and dragged it over her shoulder. "I can't believe how stupid I've been."

"It's been staring us in the face since the very start. But I was looking for one person who knew everything, and the reason I could never work out who was because there was two of them." He tried to flex his left arm. His fingers would move, but the rest of it had set solid. He couldn't overcome the resistance offered by the motors. "As to what we're going to do . . ."

Petrovitch dragged himself upright and restuck the computer to his side. He set his face in the direction of the Post Office Tower, but his view was obscured by Madeleine, who moved in front of him. She put the flat of her hand against his chest.

"No." Her voice was firm.

"Out of the *yebani* way. I'm going to rip her a new *zhopu* with this," and he brandished his broken arm, "then I'm going to see how well she flies."

"You can't do that."

"I'm pretty sure I can. I'm pretty sure that no one's

going to stop me from doing it either." He looked up into his wife's face. "She won't lift a finger to save herself, because she loves me."

"Do you really think that? Do you really believe she's not going to fight to keep what she has?"

"She has nothing left." Petrovitch gestured to the rubble pile. "She's lost the Freezone, she's lost me, she's lost the *nikkeijin,* the organization around her is falling apart, she's got no home, no purpose, no inheritance and no legacy."

"Then maybe," said Madeleine, "you should just leave her alone for the moment. Not that we both don't have a reckoning with her at some point…"

"And with the priest."

"And with John. He's lost everything too. His very identity as a priest, even. But if Sonja's lost the Freezone, who's there to catch it if it falls?"

Still he tried to go through her, to get at Sonja. "I saved her. And for what? So she could do this to me?"

Madeleine pushed him hard enough to rock him back on his heels. "You just told these people to go to work. They don't have electricity or computers, thanks to you. That means you haven't got the time to spare on this self-indulgent crap, because like them, you have work to do."

"Don't you want to get at her? At Father fucking John?"

She lowered her voice to barely a whisper. "Oh yes. But they can wait. Look at their plans—what have they come to? Nothing. We have a city to run, we have another CIA hit-squad to find. We have a thousand and one people to talk to, to assure them that we're not going to drop the ball."

Petrovitch fumed. "I know what you're saying makes more sense. But I still prefer my version."

"I prefer your version. It's just a shame we don't have the luxury of doing what we want. You always said the Freezone was a good idea because it was your idea: are you going to throw it away because you want to act out your revenge fantasies?"

"It's so very tempting." He stopped his attempts to bull his way past her. "*Yobany stos,* all right. Have it your way."

Valentina looked pointedly at her watch, and Petrovitch scowled.

"Like you're a *yebani* metronome. You might not show it, but you're just as pissed as I am."

She conceded the point. "So what do we do? And in what order do we do it?"

"I need this arm back. That's not going to happen until I get the power back on. I would also like something to eat and drink because it's been a very long time since any of us have done either. That's not going to happen until I get the power back. These good people need to do some work, and guess what?" Petrovitch wandered away across the road, staring down every so often. His lips moved silently as he counted.

"Sam, what are you doing?" called Lucy.

Petrovitch eventually pointed to a black metal cover set into the tarmac. "We need to get this one up."

She turned to Tabletop, standing beside her. "What's he doing?"

"I have no idea."

"I do," said Madeleine, cupping her hands around her mouth. "I thought the idea was to persuade everyone we hadn't lost the plot."

He shouted back. "You want power? This is how we get it. In every way."

While Valentina went to fetch the tire iron from the trunk of the car, the other three went over to where Petrovitch was standing.

Madeleine crouched down next to the manhole. "You realize the Yanks are going to want to nuke us if we do this. We've dodged a pretend atomic bomb only to walk into the path of a real one."

"You asked me if I had a plan for when I got him out. I did then, and I still do." He took a step back and allowed Valentina to dig the edge of the iron between the cover and the lip of the hole. "I've let the Americans dictate what happens to Michael for too long. No more."

As the cover broke free of the collected muck that held it down, Madeleine dug her fingers under it and dragged it scraping to one side. There was a brick-lined black hole, and a ladder thick with rust descending into it.

"We are going to get Michael, *da*?" Valentina threw the tire iron aside.

"Yeah, we are." Petrovitch flipped his feet into the hole and adjusted his useless arm down to fit close by his side. He toed the first rung, testing his weight on it. "We're going to need the cee-four."

Tabletop looked at the distance between them and the tower. "Okay. But let me go first. We've come too far to let any more surprises get in the way." She pulled the hood of her stealth suit over her head and covered her eyes with the integral goggles.

Petrovitch moved to one side, and she used partly him, partly the road, to lower herself into the void. She swarmed down the ladder and, within moments, was out of sight.

"Right," he said to those remaining. "Down the rabbit hole."

20

*A*way from the small circle of light, the darkness was like a wall. Petrovitch switched to infrared, and watched while Madeleine descended.

"Still not that sweet," she said, and raised her arms to guide Lucy's feet onto the corroded metal rungs for the last few steps. "You're there."

"What is this place?"

Petrovitch was about to answer, when Madeleine cut in, sounding casual: "It's a river. An underground river running through the heart of London."

"Then why can I smell, you know..." Lucy looked around her, then at her feet.

"Because it doubles as a sewer."

"Eww."

Valentina swung herself over the hole in the road and held out her AK. Madeleine took it and passed it to Petrovitch, who could actually see where he was pointing it.

"Case. You catch." She dropped a steel briefcase and Madeleine caught it cleanly. "Do not get wet."

"You might want to warn me before you start throwing explosives around."

"Hmm," said Valentina, and trip-trapped down the ladder, "and you might warn us before telling lying priest everything."

"Knock it off." Petrovitch stepped out of the alcove and into the tunnel proper.

"In Soviet Union, priests were shot."

"Tina. Really."

"Against wall. With blindfold."

"Yobany stos, past' zabej!" He thought about leaving the two of them to get on with it, but Lucy was also present, and there wasn't much room for hand-to-hand combat without hurting the bystanders. "Just leave it upstairs, okay? Down here it's cold, it's dark, it's got water and slime, and shortly we'll be setting off some shaped charges. We all have to work together, whether some of you like it or not."

Petrovitch retrieved Lucy and put her mid-stream, then dragged Madeleine up behind him.

"Tina, go behind Lucy, hold her hand. Maddy, get Lucy's other hand and grab hold of me. And no pulling or shoving. Or I'll tell teacher."

He led the way upstream, to find that Tabletop had already discovered the breach in the culvert's wall. She'd turned the lights on, and was exploring the gently sloping tunnel.

Lucy climbed in first, then Valentina, and Madeleine boosted Petrovitch through the hole before stepping up herself.

"Right," said Petrovitch, "let's get all the 'how did you know this was here?', 'when did you do this?' and 'frankly this looks ludicrously unstable, what were you thinking?' questions out of the way before we start. I've been at this for eleven months, and I would have got away with it but for recent events. Needs must, however. At the far end is the outside of a concrete tube that should lead straight to the quantum computer beneath the Oshicora Tower. There's about half a meter's worth of ferroconcrete between us and it, and it would be brilliant if we can cut through it without collapsing this tunnel." He looked at Valentina's pale, pinched face in the glimmering light. "Can you get us through?"

"Concrete, yes. Rebar is problem. I will need to take two, three separate blasts to cut metal rods." She lifted her case onto her outstretched legs and popped the catches.

Tabletop pressed her hand against the curved wall she was crouching next to. "When were you going to tell us? I mean, I suppose you could have chosen never to do so."

"I always thought," said Petrovitch, "that I'd be able to do this on my own. That I wouldn't have to involve any of you in this, well, highly illegal enterprise. Freezone signed up to both the UN resolutions and imposed their own penalties."

"Ten years," murmured Madeleine, "or an unlimited fine. Or both."

"Bearing in mind I can record this, and we're in charge now: all those in favor of revoking that particular law?" Petrovitch raised his right arm and glanced up at it.

Madeleine put her hand on the tunnel roof, Lucy's pale fingers wiggled in the half-light, and Valentina looked up from her makings long enough to register her approval.

"Tabletop?"

"I'm not a citizen," she said. "I'm not really anyone."

"Executive order. You are now."

"Do you think my—the Americans: they're going to want to stop you."

"Yeah. And we already know there's another CIA team of who knows how many agents. Or they could just drop a missile on our heads, and this time it might not be a thermobaric warhead."

"Fuck them." She showed her hand.

"Unanimous. Tina, do your worst. Everyone else out."

Tabletop stayed behind to help Valentina, while Madeleine helped Petrovitch get back out into the main tunnel. The blue-white glow from inside the hole glittered against the drops of moisture on the brickwork.

"Seriously," asked Lucy, standing as close as she could to Petrovitch and shivering. "Were you ever going to tell us?"

"I didn't want to give them any reason for thinking you had anything to do with this."

"Them. But Madeleine would have had to arrest you. She wouldn't... would she?"

"Just another reason not to tell anyone. She'd sworn to uphold the Freezone law. Giving her a dilemma like that?" He puffed out his breath and watched it condense in the cold, still air. "Yeah, I would have told you. Long after the event, long after we'd..."

"We'd what?" She pushed in against him and leaned her head against his shoulder.

"We're getting out of here. All of us. Including Michael. This," and he pointed up and down the tunnel with his right hand, draped over Lucy's shoulder, "this isn't how I'd planned it. We were supposed to show a clean pair of heels, just slip away in the night in a 'my work here is done' sort of way. Now, we're going to be born in blood and fire whether we like it or not."

"Doesn't sound good."

"Meh. We'll be fine. It's everyone else I'm worried about, especially the ones who get worked up about AIs: they get all unpredictable and dangerous, and I don't like that."

"Just one other thing. You know you had me make one of those singularity bombs every day, off the renderer?"

"Yeah. I used them every night down here."

"I know that now, but I thought you were hoarding them. I," and she coughed, "might have made some spares."

"What the *chyort* did you think I was going to do with three hundred bombs? Start a war?"

"It's not like you haven't done that before," she mumbled. "I thought I was helping."

"How many?" asked Petrovitch, dreading the answer.

"There's about a cupboard full. The one next to the sink. In the lab." She shrank away from him. "Sorry."

"It's fine. As it turns out, if we didn't have a shed-load of cee-four from the fake bomb, we'd be using them right about now. But," he said, trying to be serious when he was actually pleased, "no more making black holes without telling me first, okay?"

She looked up as Madeleine climbed out to join them. "Okay."

Madeleine was followed by Tabletop and finally Valentina, trailing a thin two-core cable behind her. She passed the end out to Petrovitch, then reached back in for her case.

"So: first charge to crack concrete. Have added copper

core to slice rebar, but maybe one more after." She handed the case to Tabletop, who held it up to the light while she retrieved the hand-cranked dynamo.

"Should we move?" asked Lucy.

"Is small explosion, little one. Loud, but small."

"She knows what she's doing," assured Petrovitch. He passed Valentina the bare wires, and she attached them to the terminals with an easy dexterity born of familiarity.

"Against wall, please. Will be loose debris, and dust."

When she was ready, and she'd checked everyone was staying where she'd put them, she reached into her jacket pocket for earplugs. She pushed them home with a grunt, then vigorously wound the handle on the cylinder in her hand.

She followed her own advice and stepped back against the damp brickwork. "*Tri, dva, adin.*" Her thumb closed on the button.

A circle of light like a flashbulb imprinted itself against the tunnel wall, and the sound of a thousand hands clapping slammed into the air, making it hard and unyielding. A cloud of brown dust blew outward as if fired from a cannon, and the lights flickered: blinked on, off, then on again, illuminating the inside of the haze and making it glow.

Petrovitch listened for the inevitable rumble and slide of a roof collapse. He waited and waited, and realized he was holding his breath. A year's secret work, and it came down to whether he'd secured the tunnel supports properly. He felt his heart surge, and he let it run.

There was benefit in being able to control parts of his physiology. There was also something to be said for letting him feel human, just once in a while. Terror, anticipation, euphoria even. Being alive was a drug, and he was addicted.

The noises he feared the most never materialized. He heard the sounds of coughing and complaining instead.

Lucy peeled her hands from her ears. "I was expecting, I don't know. More flames."

"I made that mistake once. Tina's an expert: you could learn a lot from her." Petrovitch splashed his way to the gap in the brickwork and peered in.

The dust was settling in a fine hissing rain, making shifting shapes and sheets in the light. Valentina appeared next to him and she cast a critical eye over the scene.

"Hmm. Is okay." She passed the dynamo back to Tabletop and boosted herself up. Her legs wriggled, and she found a handhold to drag herself over the top.

Once she'd gone to inspect the damage she'd caused, Madeleine thought it safe to speak.

"You never did say what you were going to do with Michael once you'd got him out."

"Didn't I? We're back on plan B anyway. Shame, really. Plan A was brilliant, even if I say so myself." Fine dust was settling on his eyes, and he cried it away. "If Michael's not in a fit state, I don't know what I'm going to do instead. It's taken the NSA months to purge Anarchy from its network; clearly, I'm better than they are, but it'll still take time."

"Sam." She was standing right behind him, pressing into his back. "What were you going to do with Michael?"

Valentina came scrabbling back, a shadow that slowly solidified. "Petrovitch. Come. See."

"Sorry," he said to Madeleine, "it'll have to wait. Shove me up."

She did so with a little more force than was strictly necessary, and he landed in a heap at Valentina's feet.

"*Yobany stos*," he muttered. "I'm already broken enough."

Valentina crouched low and led the way back to the tunnel face. Where there had been a slick gray wall was now a gaping black maw. When she settled against the last roof prop, she looked uncommonly pleased with herself.

Petrovitch crawled over her legs and moved his left arm so that it supported itself on the lip of the hole.

The cut was sharp on its outer edge, and grew ragged as it worked its way in. Loose rubble clung to the sides and cracks radiated out. The steel mesh that reinforced the concrete had been severed as neatly as if it had been sawn through. The exposed ends of each bar looked like they'd been melted.

"I thought you said you'd need at least two goes at it."

"I am better than I thought."

Petrovitch grinned. The explosion had created a hole that was perfect. "Yeah. Orders of Lenin all round."

"At least, am good for something."

"You're good for lots of things, Tina." He took a fragment of concrete and dropped it over the edge. Being able to time the fall accurately, he calculated that the bottom of the shaft was only three and a half meters down. "Most of all, you're a good friend."

She narrowed her eyes and pursed her lips. "I must say this now."

He was busy peering through the hole, checking to see if there was debris clogging the shaft, and how much they might have to shift before getting to Michael. The air inside was cool blue, uniform but for a faint glimmer of brighter notes in a rectangle set into the wall down at the level of the concrete floor. He brought his head back through.

"Sorry?"

"Does not matter." She started back up the tunnel, but he caught her sleeve.

"Seriously. I use you like a Swiss Army knife and you ask for nothing except the assurance that it's going to be all right in the end. And even when it looks like it's one big pile of *pizdets,* you still believe in me. So you've earned the right to say whatever you want, and I'm just going to have to shut up and listen."

Valentina turned herself back around as Madeleine shouted down to them: "Everything okay?"

"Fine. It's all fine," replied Petrovitch, and brought his head close to Valentina's. "Talk to me, Tina."

"I would never betray you. You must know this."

"*Yobany stos,* of course I know this."

"I would never do anything that would harm you or Madeleine."

"I know that too."

"I have been tempted. I am still tempted. I will still be tempted: by fantasy of you and me making lots of good little communists together. But know this also—Sonja Oshicora will never live to make you her slave: I will kill her first." She tossed her head back and stared Petrovitch square in the face. "She does not know what love is. We do. Because of this, we will prevail."

He grabbed her, pulled her close, pressed his dusty lips against her ear. "We can all win. We can all still win. I promise."

21

There was rope, because Petrovitch had thought he would need rope, but no flashlights, because he had one in his courier bag which he was never without except for now. That he couldn't remember where it was he last had it troubled him, and he almost delayed everything while he reviewed the last few hours' video capture.

The string of lights from the tunnel could be dangled through the hole though, even if it did plunge everyone else into darkness. Lucy said she didn't mind, as long as she could still touch someone else, and that there weren't any rats.

At the mention of vermin, Madeleine looked at Petrovitch.

"I haven't seen one down here for months," he said. He lifted his T-shirt up and Valentina secured the nylon rope to his back brace. She pulled to make sure of her knot, and he growled. "I know people pay good money for that sort of thing, but I'm not one of them."

"Fall from three meters onto head will kill as quick as fall from thirty." She adjusted his clothing. "Will hold."

Madeleine belayed the rope around her waist and checked the loose coil by her side. She braced her feet either side of the hole. "Okay. Taking the strain."

"This is not how I imagined this happening," complained Petrovitch. He sat between Madeleine's legs and folded his left arm across his chest. Valentina and Tabletop lifted him up and fed him into the hole, bit by bit. First as far as his calves, then his thighs, then he was sitting on the very lip of the shaft. He lay back as best he could, and they turned him so he was face to face with the sandy floor.

His legs dangled over the edge.

As he was eased further in, his whole weight fell on his metal-encased arm. He felt the pressure, and blocked the pain. The rope ran in a taut, quivering line over his shoulder. His body was now pulling him down rather than back, and the ends of the rebar were hard against his skin.

"Slowly." He tried to hang on to the edge of the concrete with his right hand, but he was just fighting against what Madeleine was doing. He surrendered himself to her care, and dangled. All that was left to do was lift his chin so that he didn't scrape it against the rough-hewn stone.

He was suspended in space, between the floor of the shaft and its undefined top. It was easier to look up than down, so he did, letting his head fall back.

He couldn't quite make out what it was he was seeing. In infrared, the image made little sense, and in visible light, it was just a vast dark space. It was only when the lights were threaded through that the situation became clear.

Far above him was a confused choke of girders and concrete. The beams had gouged their way down the walls of the shaft, twisting and bending under the immense pressure from above, before locking solid slantwise from one side to the other. Perhaps the first piece to fall had supported the second, and so on, until the blockage had built up layer on layer.

There were a few fist-sized pieces of foundation on the floor of the shaft: otherwise, it was all held in perfect equilibrium above his head.

"*Chyort,*" he breathed.

Tabletop leaned out over the pit. "You okay?"

Petrovitch put his finger to his lips and pointed upward.

She followed his direction, and stared for a few moments. Then she looked down at him and hissed, "We'll bring you back up."

He shook his head, and she looked up again, just to check she'd seen what she thought she'd seen.

"Really, we're bringing you back up."

He shook his head harder and pointed down. They looked at each other for a while, and he could hear Madeleine's voice rise in pitch as she asked repeatedly what was going on.

Then he started to slide down the face of the wall. Eventually, his questing feet found the floor, and the rope slackened. Tabletop used that slack to go hand-over-hand, her legs wrapping around the nylon to control her descent. It took seconds, and then she was untying him.

"We have to be insane to even attempt this," she said.

"I never said it was going to be easy."

"I'm pretty sure you did." The rope slipped off his exoskeleton and slithered away.

"If Tina's blasting hasn't brought it down, there's no reason to believe anything we do will."

"Then why," said Tabletop, "are we whispering?"

"Because it looks *yebani* scary, that's why. If we're very, very quiet, it might not notice us. Primal memories from the dawn of time: we're nothing but cavemen, really."

"Then let's drag our knuckles over to the door and get through it."

It was a few short steps to the alcove. Inset were blank steel doors, tall and wide enough when both open to wheel the quantum computer out and into the shaft. Petrovitch tried an experimental tug on one of the handles.

"Yeah, that's locked."

He looked at the walls on either side of the doors, then at the face of the doors themselves.

"This isn't looking good," murmured Tabletop.

"Found it." He crouched down and gently blew the dust away from the mechanism. A tiny red light showed through the grime, halfway up the right-hand door. "Oh, you have got to be joking."

"It's a..."

He scrubbed at it with his sleeve. "...fingerprint scanner. That's it. That's the only way in."

"Shall I go and get Valentina?"

Petrovitch glanced at the great bolus of debris hanging over them. His face twitched. "I'm going to try something first."

He licked his right index finger to clean it, then dried it carefully on his collar. He puffed again at the tiny glass window on the lock, and grimaced as he pressed his finger to it.

The red light winked off, and a green one glimmered on. Locks and bolts unwound and slid aside, winding back with oiled understatement.

Petrovitch tried the handle again. The door swung open a little way, then grounded itself on some debris underfoot. He kicked it out of the way and scraped his boot along the arc the door had to describe.

"I take it that wasn't luck," said Tabletop.

"No. No it wasn't." He held the door aside and Tabletop slipped through. He raised his hand to the faces at the tunnel, and followed. He wedged a piece of fallen concrete in the gap to stop the door clicking shut again.

Just in case.

They were in a short corridor, with another set of double doors at the end. The recessed lights stayed dark, and everything was silent and still.

"Okay?" Petrovitch's clothes rustled as he moved.

"Nervous."

"Yeah. I know how that goes." His boots squeaked on the rubber floor as he walked.

The other doors were merely closed, on the premise that if someone had got this far, they were clearly authorized to be there. But there was a resistance to them opening: a positive pressure from inside, forming a seal. He shoved hard, and there was an audible pop of air.

He held the door ajar, took a deep breath and opened it further. The room beyond was utterly black, cold, sterile.

"Touch nothing," he said. "Stick to the walls, if we can find out where the *huy* the walls are."

He edged in, feeling his way. Tabletop slipped in after him, and the door whuffed shut. There was something in here that still worked, then, producing that current of air.

He heard the sound of Velcro unfastening, then the tiny screen on Tabletop's forearm bloomed into life. It produced a tiny amount of light, no more than a candle's worth, but in the absence of anything else, its effect was dramatic.

The room was as tall as it was wide: a perfect white cube, at the center of which was another, smaller, perfectly black cube on a raised platform.

"My God, it's full of stars."

"Sorry?"

"Don't worry. Even if you'd seen the film or read the book, they've probably erased your memory of it. Old Man Oshicora had a sense of humor, as well as being a cold-hearted murderer. I suppose the two aren't mutually exclusive." Petrovitch stepped slowly over to the cube, aware of all the dirt he was trailing behind him. He laid his hand on the smooth surface of the quantum computer. "*Dobre den, tovarisch.*"

"You think he's in there?"

"Who do you think reprogrammed the door lock? He survived the collapse of the tower. His life support was still functioning. If I'd been him, I would have cut my power consumption to a minimum, and then just…"

"Just what?"

"I don't know. Go to sleep, maybe. Dream. When Oshicora dreamed, he created the New Machine Jihad. But Michael's not like that. I think his dreams will be something altogether more grand."

"For a whole year?"

"*Chyort.* Even I feel like I could sleep for a year." He bowed his head and let it hang. "I am so very tired. Tired of planning and plotting and worrying and trying to keep it all together for so very long." He patted the computer. "We're almost there. One last push. Come on, let's see if we can't wake Sleeping Beauty."

There were no obvious consoles or interfaces. Every-thing was neat, clean, almost zen in its simplicity. Oshi-cora again.

They worked as a pair, Petrovitch feeling his way around the base of the cube, Tabletop behind him, provid-ing illumination. "Where've you hidden it?" They'd gone around all four sides, and were stumped.

"Do you think he made it deliberately difficult?"

"No, which is why I think I'm missing something com-pletely obvious." His fingertips drifted off the horizontal surface and onto the vertical face of the step. There was a lip, very slight, but enough for him to catch his nails against.

He shook his head and lifted the whole step up to reveal a row of controls and displays. Tabletop rolled her eyes and hunkered down next to Petrovitch to inspect what they'd found.

The screens were all blank. No lights were showing.

"We might be too late," she said.

"No. All this is off because Michael had settled in for the long wait. One little LED might make the difference between having enough watts to keep cool and eventual heat death."

They lifted the other steps, and on the last one, they found a network port. Petrovitch pursed his lips, then reached under his T-shirt for the palmtop taped to his side.

"In the absence of any big button saying 'on,' I'm going to have to go in." He looked up at Tabletop's shadowed face. "I'm going to need your help."

"Unplugging yourself: what's that going to do to you?"

He sat back on his heels. "The last time it rendered me

insensible. The time before that, too. I've been dragging this arm around behind me for a day, banging it about and generally mistreating myself, so I kind of figure that it's going to be even worse than that."

"And when you plug into Michael? What if you can't cope without your programs and protocols?" She held her hand out and Petrovitch placed the palmtop into it.

"You're going to have to use your judgment. If it looks like I'm dying, don't disconnect me." The corner of his mouth twitched. "Only do that if I'm actually dead."

"Seriously?"

"Yeah. It seems we have a short period of grace before our brains go hypoxic."

"Madeleine should be here," she said.

"And that's the very good reason why she's not." He readied himself, shuffling onto the cold floor and lying on his right side, stretching out along the length of the side of the cube. "She cares too much about me. She needs me to be safe. She needs to protect me from the demons that live without and within. She has decided, for one reason or another, to forgive me for not telling her about Michael and forgive herself for leaving me over it. But she needs to atone for this business with Father John." He closed his eyes. Habit. He could just turn them off.

"You don't think she'd let you do this?"

"Not that. She'd let me do it. Eventually. I know that, she knows that. She even knows that it's for the best. Right now, she's back up in the tunnel, chewing her nails and snapping at Valentina and Lucy. She's fretting over what happens if we find Michael's alive, or if he's not. I bet she's even thought about whether or not you'll triple-cross us and take this once in a lifetime opportunity to finish both me and Michael."

"I've had the opportunity every day and every night. To do anything I want."

"She knows that too. Most of all, she knows that this is easier for me without her being here, even though it crucifies her." He wasn't comfortable. It didn't matter. "Ready?"

"I'll make it as quick as I can." Tabletop clicked the little retaining clip on the plug and pulled.

For Petrovitch it felt like he was burning. He clenched his teeth and tried to blank the pain. It wasn't going to kill him, no matter how bad it was. He told himself it wouldn't be for long, even though it already felt like forever.

Tabletop reached over and pushed the cable home into the quantum computer's waiting socket.

22

The pain didn't go away, and he had no way of telling Tabletop.

He wasn't in control anymore, if he ever had been. From the moment Madeleine had walked into the staff canteen, that had been it—every decision he'd made since had been logical, reasonable, defendable, and not even wrong. He just hadn't had enough facts to come up with an alternative that would have led anywhere else but plugged, raw and naked, into the computer that had seen the rise and fall of the New Machine Jihad.

He knew it wasn't meant to be this way, and yet there he was, underground, damaged beyond repair, out of battery power, threatened by entombment, nuclear annihilation, and a woman scorned.

Pizdets.

Here was the problem: computers had architecture, had physical memory and chipsets and operating systems. Petrovitch knew his way around those and could make them his bitches, wrestling with their software until he found the exploits that meant they would do his bidding.

This thing he was connected to had nothing he could grasp. Information inside a quantum computer was contained in the energy states of atoms. He had no way of interpreting them or interacting with them. In this basic state, he was beneath Michael's attention, insubstantial and immaterial: a ghost in the machine.

He'd done it once before, though. When the facsimile of Oshicora had collapsed VirtualJapan and erased all the data, he'd managed to remain for a few brief moments, immersed in the vast empty space that remained. If he'd been aware of it then, he could be aware of it now.

Michael had reprogrammed the door to his vault. He would have left some way to get to him. He was smart. He would have thought of this. He would have planned for this very moment.

So he would have allowed for Petrovitch's incompetence, his habit of throwing stuff at a problem until something stuck. He would have even taken into account that Petrovitch's meat body might not have access to the software that controlled the mitigator code, and that the *balvan* might plug himself directly into an open port and hope for the best.

There were instructions in the implant, updateable firmware that was intended for just that purpose. The *nikkeijin* were supposed to do it that way, of course. VirtualJapan ran hot and fast, shoveling a body's worth of experiences through one thin cable.

Petrovitch had modified that code for working with other machines, other networks. He'd changed it so much it was unrecognizable and completely useless for its original task. What he needed were the factory-fresh settings. A hard reset.

He could do that. He was going to do that. He'd do it now.

Petrovitch finally struggled through his own very private hell and hit the big metaphysical switch.

His eyes opened wide, and Tabletop was leaning over him, her hand on his bare, scrawny chest, feeling the hum of the turbine beneath. She gasped at his sudden movement and she lurched sideways, intending to unplug him from the jet-black cube.

"No. Nonono," he gasped. "It's meant…"

He was under again.

[to be?]

He was held, lifted up, carried, sheltered. The pain became a memory: a savage, enduring memory to be forever burned into his psyche, but at least it had passed.

"*Chyort.* I've found you." The relief came like a wave of cold water.

[I knew you would, Sasha. I knew you would find me because of the way you tried to find Madeleine. She was lost, and you rescued her. I knew you would do the same for me.]

There was no landscape, no city, nothing to see or touch. But the void was not empty. Michael was there, as if he had always been there, dreaming the eons away until someone woke him.

"I'm." He stopped. "I'm sorry it took so long. I've got so much to tell you, so much I need to tell you, but there were…complications."

[Has the world forgiven us?]

"Some have. Some say we're *yebani* heroes, others that you're a god to be worshipped. Many don't have strong feelings one way or the other and are just a little afraid of us, but the ones we're going to have problems with are the ones with the authority to drop a megaton of rubble on us and who think you're Lucifer and I'm Baba Yaga. Getting out of this in one piece isn't going to be straightforward."

[Then we must proceed as you see fit.]

"Yeah, I had it all planned, a way of spiriting you away with no one noticing, but that's not going to happen now. I screwed up. I broke the Freezone network with a virus—and you don't even know what the Freezone is—and I need to get everything back online in order to spring you. But the only way I can do that is by getting you to do the dirty work, and then, of course, our enemies will know you're out."

[Sasha, I place myself in your hands. I trust you.]

"I can't even explain where I've been or what I've been doing." He groaned. "We've got no time. When they brought the tower down, debris got wedged in the access shaft. Anyone decides they want to give it a stir, that'll be it. I might never be able to get to you again. For all kinds of reasons. We're in so much trouble right now, I can't begin to say."

[Sasha, listen to me. We will make time. When all this is over, when I am free and you are free and we have nothing else to do but talk, then that is what we will do. I have things to show you. Wonderful things. I have considered your equations and I have seen some of the implications of what they mean. There are fuller, deeper meanings I have yet to discover, but when I tell you what I have found so far, it will bring you such joy.]

"You're going to survive. Even if I don't."

[We stand or fall together, my love,] said Michael. [You know this to be true.]

Petrovitch was silent, then he regained control of his voice. "Okay, look. I can get a network cable down here: that part is ready. I can find a way of getting you up to a satellite, though I don't have my rat. If you restart the Free-zone's system, I promise the next thing we'll do will be designed to keep you safe. I've had to rely on other people for that, so I hope they're ready. They'd better be ready."

[You say we have enemies. Do we have friends?]

"Yeah. We've got friends, but we have to find out who they are first. We're just going to have to run with it and see how far we get. Strengths: everything north of the Thames is the Freezone: I'm sort of the boss now, as of half an hour ago. I've a *govno* load of money and we can use that to secure all sorts of favors. Weaknesses: you're supremely vulnerable to attack because everyone will know just where you are. We've got no comms with any-one, and we're relying on the better part of human nature for anyone to do anything I say. Opportunities: once we've got the local network up and running again, we can migrate you somewhere they'll never find. We'll get a head start on that. And there's a bunch of guys from the Vatican who'd love a word with you. I kind of told them to fuck off before, but I'm coming to see how we can use them.

"As to threats? *Chyort,* where am I going to start? You face UN-sanctioned extermination. The Yanks are going to go ballistic—literally—when they realize you're not buried anymore. They've already got another CIA team on the ground, and up to the point the Freezone lost con-tact with the outside world, everyone thinks I'm a nuclear terrorist. Sonja Oshicora has gone mad, and that's just a whole different world of pain. This is going to get crazy really quickly, and we're going to have to make stuff up as we go along." He paused. "When the time comes, are you going to be ready?"

[I have been ready for a long time. Let there be light.]

"See you on the other side, Michael. It won't be long now. Kick me out."

And abruptly, he was on his back in a pitch-black room, save for the timorous blue-white shine from a wrist-sized screen. Everything hurt once more.

Tabletop was poised. "Now?"

"Now," he grunted, and she flicked the connector out of its socket and into the palmtop laying beside them on the ground.

He could block the pain once more, alter the speed of his heart and flood his system with enough adrenaline to get him through the next few minutes.

"Is he alive?" she asked.

"Oh yeah."

"And is he sane?"

He sat up slowly, feeling five times his true age. "He's not a drooling idiot, if that's what you're asking." He scrubbed at his stiff hair. "What he wants to do is sit me down and talk physics."

"That sounds a lot like you." She retaped the computer to his torso and tugged his T-shirt down. "If that's a measure of sane, I guess it'll have to do."

"He trusted me to get him out. He knew I'd come for him, and I feel a complete *mudak* for taking so long." Petrovitch looked at her laser-corrected eyes. "I should have told you what I was doing. You wouldn't have let me down."

"Or Tina, or Lucy."

"Amongst all the other things I've also fucked up, this

has to take the crown jewels for the thing I've fucked up the most, right?"

She stood up and dragged him after her. "That remains to be seen. What do we do now?"

"Back to the tunnel. We've got a lot of work to do."

He leaned on her more than not. He was tired; bent, battered, hungry, thirsty, and angry. Mainly angry, and that was what had sapped his energy the most. A good job it was time to get even.

When he was out in the shaft, he called for the spool of network cable near the tunnel entrance to be thrown down to him.

"Don't, whatever you do, cut it or kink it." He looked behind him to judge the distance to Michael. "I'd hate to have to try and source another."

Madeleine wrapped the coil inside a bag and paid out enough spare so that when she launched it into the darkness, it wouldn't pull.

Petrovitch caught it one-handed and passed the bag to Tabletop. "You know where this end goes. Do not, whatever you do, let a door close on it. Go."

She ran off into the darkness, and he had to wait for her to return before she could tie him back onto the rope and get himself hauled up again. He had to wait, but there was no good reason why the others had to: he only needed Madeleine.

Lucy's expectant face peered down at him. Perhaps she recognized his predatory expression.

"What do you want me to get?"

"Something with satellite connectivity. Fast processor, fat bandwidth. I need it now, and I need it in the underground car park between our hotel and Hyde Park."

"Something like your rat, you mean?"

"Something exactly like my rat. But now is the highest priority. Steal it if you have to, use force if necessary. Tina?"

"*Da?*"

"Go with her. Don't take no for an answer. *Vrubratsa?*"

"Come, little one. I have an idea," said Valentina, in a way that made Petrovitch feel decidedly uncomfortable— for the people at the other end of her idea. They left, scrambling away, and Tabletop came back.

"Done," she said simply, looking back over her shoulder at the wedged-open door and its tiny green light.

"Thanks. Let's not hang around. The idea of death by crushing is one of my least favorites." He passed her the free end of the rope. "Though to be fair, I'm not exactly a fan of any of them, and I'd like to avoid them all if possible."

Tabletop jerked his T-shirt up to his shoulders and threaded the rope around the metal superstructure. "I'd like to see you try."

He thought she was joking, but she wasn't.

"Seriously. Do you really think you can manage that?"

"I've seen it. I don't know how it works, but yeah, I get to cheat death. *Chyort,* Tabletop. I even get to be old first."

She tugged the rope hard, and he felt every bone left in his body rattle. "He's secure," she called, and the rope went taut. And just to him, she said, "I'll make sure it happens. All of it. You won't be alone, either."

His feet left the ground, and Madeleine hauled him up, his back scraping against the cold concrete of the shaft, until there was an empty space behind him.

Still holding on with one hand, she reached forward with her other and slid her arm across his chest. She dragged him in and he was lying on her, her breath hot against his ear, the tunnel roof close and heavy.

"Hey," she said.

"Hey yourself."

"How was Michael?"

"I think he's okay. I think he's better than okay. I think he's been busy."

"And you don't think he's going to want vengeance on either those that buried him down here, or those who left it a year before digging him out again?" She felt him stiffen and try to roll off her, but it was child's play for her to hold him against her for as long as she wanted. "I'm just saying this because we have enough to deal with without another New Machine Jihad. I want you to tell me you're absolutely certain he's not going to try any weird robot shit on us, or so help me God, I'll bite through that network cable with my own teeth. Tell me he didn't say all the things that would make you trust him, and that you didn't believe them all without the slightest hint that he has an ulterior motive. Tell me I'm not the only one around here who can see this possibly being the very worst mistake any of us has made today."

"I'm still here." called Tabletop. "Any time soon would be good."

"Come on, Sam," said Madeleine, "it's not much to ask. The New Machine Jihad killed tens of thousands by accident. Michael killed a hundred thousand Outies because you told him to. Are you really ready to unleash him on a whole world? After what's happened?"

Petrovitch didn't even cross his fingers. "I swear to you

that this will work out for the best," he said. "I trust him like I trust you."

"That's what worries me. Look what happened to us." She gently turned him onto his front and started to unlace the knot at his back. "What's more important is how much does he trust you? If he starts to doubt either your competence or your motives, we could be back in the Stone Age again in an instant."

"He trusts me," he muttered into the ground. "He trusts me like you trust me."

"Touché." She coiled the rope around her arm and flung the end of it through the hole, down to where Tabletop was waiting.

23

Petrovitch was pushed out of the second tunnel by Madeleine, and he was back in the underground car park, shrouded by blue plastic. He looped his good hand through the center of the reel of cable and started spooling it out, passing it awkwardly to himself through the gates made by the scaffolding poles.

"Would it be easier if I did that?" Madeleine splashed through the standing water and held the sheeting aside for him.

"Probably," said Petrovitch, "but then I'd feel completely and utterly *yebani* useless, so I'm going to do it anyway."

Rather than turning toward the rusting door set into the concrete wall, he started up the slope to where daylight flooded in, stark and bright after the darkness. The white cable trailed behind him through the mud like a worm. As before, he felt a shiver of fear as he looked at how much cable he had left, and how far he had to walk. He'd measured everything a dozen times, and even now wondered if he'd made a mistake.

simonmorden

The reel grew lighter as he got closer to the outside.

"Are you . . . ?" asked Tabletop.

"*Past' zabej.* I'm not going to run out."

The marks on the plastic reel were turning faster, and the length left was shortening all the time. But he was at the barriers, weaving around them, and blue sky was only a few more steps away. He had hoped that Lucy and Valentina would be there already, waiting for him with some slim piece of technology he could hook up to, but the only thing in evidence was the Al Jazeera news van parked lengthways across the access ramp to the carpark.

"What the *huy* are this lot doing here?" he blurted. He had ten meters of cable left to play with. He'd calculated it right, but his sense of satisfaction shriveled at the thought of journalists getting in the way.

"I'll get rid of them," said Madeleine, and broke into a run.

Tabletop stood next to Petrovitch and finally relieved him of the almost-empty drum. "What exactly did you tell Lucy and Tina to do?"

"Ah, *vsyo govno, krome mochee.*"

His worst fears were confirmed when Madeleine banged on the side of the van with her fist, and the door slid open to reveal Lucy sitting inside, a set of headphones slung around her neck.

"At least that satellite dish should be big enough even for you." Tabletop indicated the top of the van.

"What would really make my day the full *pizdets* would be if Tina hadn't ordered the journos off at gunpoint and had instead asked them along for the ride."

"You mean like those two?"

A man in an open-necked check shirt appeared from

around the back, and a woman in a purple kurta. The man looked unshaven and harassed, a high-definition giro-stabilized camera harnessed to his torso, and enough good sense to keep the lens pointed at the ground. She looked glossy and bright in a way Petrovitch never felt. She strode out to meet him, full of confidence and entitlement.

"*Yebat'-kopat'.*"

Madeleine glared at Lucy, who shrugged, and called out to the reporter with weary familiarity. "Surur. What the hell is going on?"

The woman stopped advancing on Petrovitch at the sound of Madeleine's voice and visibly stiffened. "I might ask you the same question, Mrs. Petrovitch. In fact, I'm surprised to see you here at all, in this company."

"We're full of surprises today. In fact, I think I'm all surprised out, so unless you can explain to me what you're doing here—and really quickly—I'm going to start breaking things." Madeleine towered over the other woman in a way that made the cameraman break out in a sweat.

The driver's door slammed, and Valentina strolled around the high hood, slinging her AK nonchalantly over her shoulder.

"Does that clear everything up, Mrs. Petrovitch? Your husband's attack dog told me she was taking my studio, and she didn't care if I came with it or not. I am the accredited press, and I will be objecting to this treatment most strongly."

"Duly noted," said Petrovitch. "Sorry, I don't think we've met, though I've seen you often enough putting difficult questions to my wife."

The reporter looked at Petrovitch, and for the first time

looked through the aura of barely contained fury and frustration at the shattered man behind.

"Yasmina Surur, Al Jazeera. I assume you know something about the interruption in the communications network." She held out her hand.

Petrovitch looked at his own. "Maybe, maybe not," he said, wiping his palm against his trouser leg. On the spur of the moment, he decided that if it wasn't going to come clean, he may as well. "Okay, as of an hour ago, everything changed, Miss Surur. So if you want to complain to anyone, complain to us. *Le Freezone, c'est moi.*"

She switched her gaze from Petrovitch to Madeleine to Tabletop, then round at Valentina and Lucy behind her. They were all familiar sights to her, but it wasn't just Petrovitch she was looking at in a new light.

"Doctor Petrovitch, can I have an interview?"

"Yeah. If you must. There's a couple of things we have to do first, so I'd appreciate it if you just got the *huy* out of our way while we do it. If you want to film, go ahead, but don't talk to us, and you're not broadcasting anything until I say so. *Vrubatsa?*"

She'd heard him often enough to know what he meant. She nodded and urged her colleague to start recording.

Petrovitch turned his back on the pair and beckoned Valentina over.

"*Yobany stos,* woman. This is such a bad idea I don't know where to begin."

"Hmm. You ask for fast, for big bandwidth, and here is fast and bandwidth bigger than Moon." She narrowed her eyes. "You are in charge now. You need to stamp authority on Freezone. Your people need to see you, world needs to see you. Make good impression, make right impression, *da?*"

"Yeah. In Russia, impression makes you." He groaned. "Right, let's make the best of this. Tabletop, get that cable plugged in and find me a satellite. Lucy, stop mucking around and...just stop twirling on that *yebani* seat. No, I need to make sure that Mickey and Minnie out there don't try and pull a fast one on me: monitor everything that goes to that dish. If they start to send a second too early, kill the feed. Tina? Really, what the *huy* were you thinking? Make sure no one else films us. If the CIA get wind of what we're doing before we're finished, we're really finished."

"And what do I do?" asked Madeleine, upset at being left until last.

"You get to do the most important job of all. Go and tell His Excellency I'm ready to deal. He and his bunch of sky pilots get uninterrupted access to Michael for the next hour or two—but I want a definitive decision on his animus, or whatever the *huy* they want to call it, after that. No weasel words, no recommendations pending on the Holy Father's prayerful deliberations. They go public with whatever they decide by, what, three o'clock. Final offer, no negotiation." He scratched the bridge of his nose. "And if they even think about ratting me out, tell them I have enough cee-four to put them all in orbit and every reason to want to do so."

She put her hands on her hips and he knew she was going to argue with him. So he pre-empted it, jabbing his finger up in her face.

"This—this is your idea. You want to make sure that Michael isn't plotting humanity's downfall? Who better to find out than a bunch of Jesuits trained to do nothing but pick holes in the most carefully crafted story. I'm not going to try to influence them one way or another: you're going to have to leave them to it too. Okay?"

"Why are you doing this?" Madeleine kicked her heel against the road and stood her ground. "You think he might be rogue?"

"No. No, I don't. But because I love you and I know you have my best interests at heart, I'm agreeing to something that I don't want to do, only because you want me to do it. I kind of figured that was what we promised when we made all those vows in front of that lying shit of a priest."

She stared down at him. "Sam..."

"Yeah, I know. The first fuck in a year and I fold like a pack of cards."

Then she hit him, as gently as she could manage, cuffing him around the ear before dragging him into her embrace and lifting him off the ground.

"*Chyort,* put me down while I've still got some ribs in one piece."

She did. "You're impossible."

"No. Just highly improbable, but no one ever said it was easy being married to a statistical outlier." He straightened the metalwork surrounding his arm. "Go. Tell them we go live in a matter of minutes."

Tabletop called from inside the van. "Sam, we've got him."

Petrovitch glanced back around, and watched Madeleine's leather-clad body running up Park Lane.

"Sam?"

"Yeah, yeah. I'm listening."

"Sam!"

He finally turned his attention to Lucy's console, where

a familiar face was peering out at them, then to the series of empty power sockets screwed to the bulkhead next to her. "If you can find the right adaptor, I'll have some of that."

"Your courier bag's still in the car," said Lucy, sliding the headphones from her neck and onto her chair.

"Thank you." He took her place and pressed one of the cans against his ear.

[I have linked with a satellite], said Michael, [and am beginning to access the Freezone network.]

"Good work." Petrovitch maneuvered the lip mic to somewhere approaching close. "Bring it all back online, then we can pick and choose which bits to shut back down."

[The virus you activated: not bad, for a human.] The face on the screen lowered, as if bowing.

"I had help. Even though the poor kid ended up in the slammer, he still thinks it was worth it." He took the courier bag from a breathless Lucy, and pulled out a nest of wires. "*Huy,* I don't know."

[We have power, even though the virus is trying to re-migrate back into the nodes I have cleared. Holding it at bay is requiring considerable resources.]

"Yeah, it does that. It makes it very effective if you don't quarantine the clean system from the infected. Just strip it out: we won't need it again. There'll be isolated machines that'll come on later, and they'll still carry the virus, but I'm figuring you can inoculate the live network against that."

[It will take some time. As I said, not bad for a human.]

He had the first tickle from the palmtop strapped to his side: it had found a signal.

"Result."

Between them, Lucy and Tabletop had disentangled the power adaptors from each other. One went in on his left, into his computer, and one on the right, into the batteries.

[We have control.] Michael seemed to turn away briefly before staring back out at Petrovitch. [We also have several problems that require urgent attention.]

"No shit, Sherlock." He could move his left arm again, and he was happy. "Tell me what Sonja Oshicora's mob are doing."

[The picture is hard to establish. One moment.] Michael paused, listening, seeing, tracking. [They have mostly regrouped at the Telecom Tower. Now they are able to communicate with distant units, there may be coordinated action.]

"Some of those won't be following Sonja's orders anymore, and after I've had my say, all she'll be left with is a hard core of Oshicora idealists."

[Sasha, why did she turn on you? I had every indication that she would do almost anything for you, and you only had to ask. People are unreliable and inconstant.] Michael made himself blink. [Except for you.]

"Yeah, that's me. Consistent to the point of predictable. And that's exactly the exploit Sonja used. I'm going to talk to her now, and see what she has to say for herself."

Petrovitch knew her mobile number. He could tell where the phone was by chasing it across the network until he'd pin-pointed the location, on the ground floor of the tower. She wasn't alone: the area was thick with signals and other traffic, calls coming in and out at a furious rate. He could hear her, shouting orders with a voice that rang with rising panic. He could have interrupted her conversation at any time by hijacking the handset, but he noticed that she had another phone on her, live but dormant.

He reached into his pocket and pulled out the phone that had been wired to the bomb. There'd been only one number in the call history. He took the headphones off and sat back in the chair, holding the phone to his ear.

Sonja stopped talking. The sound of muffled ringing came over the open connection. The call timed out when she didn't answer, but he was absolutely certain he had her attention.

He dialed again. The call was picked up, and he could hear the sound of chaos in the background. Close up was the trembling of her breath.

"Hello, Sonja."

"Sam. I can explain."

"You don't need to. The mere fact I've reached you on this number is pretty much all the explanation I can stomach at the moment. I trusted you, and you betrayed me. More than that, though. You abused your position of authority and used resources meant for building up the Freezone to bring it to its knees. So let's forget what you tried to do to me and Maddy for a moment, and concentrate on that." He took a deep breath, and adjusted his grip on the phone which was threatening to slip out from between his sweat-slicked fingers.

"Please . . ."

He lost it. He was standing, shouting down the phone, oblivious to everything else. *"Past' zabej, suka derganaya*. Do you know what you've done? The whole of civilization is hanging by a *yebani* thread and you're hacking at it with a pair of rusty scissors. So you just shut up and listen to me. You are relieved of your duties. You are under arrest. You will surrender all weapons and you will place your private army under the control of the interim Freezone authority, which just happens to be me. You will stay in your tower until someone comes to read you your rights and put you in front of a court. Which is a *huy* sight more mercy than the idiot followers of the New Machine Jihad ever got. You are now irrelevant to the running of the Freezone. No one will follow your orders. You have no right to act on behalf of or represent the Freezone in any matter. You are deposed, Madam ex-President."

At that moment, the first pile-driver started off in Hyde Park, filling the air with its rhythmic thump. It sounded like victory.

"Hear that? That's what we think of your state of emergency. The Freezone is back at work, and there is nothing you can do to stop it. The future's coming through, Sonja, and you're not on board."

He stabbed his thumb down on the phone, and held the device in his hand, looking for somewhere to throw it. Cool fingers curled over his.

"Sam," said Lucy, "evidence?"

"*Do pizdy*. If she was here, I'd shove it up her *zhopu*." He let her take it, though, and picked up the headphones again. "Michael, shut Sonja down. Her whole operation. I'll talk to them in a minute when I've calmed down."

He closed his eyes.

[Done. What next?]

"Hanratty. I need to talk to Hanratty."

24

Petrovitch had memorized the number a long time ago, and had never called it. He'd never needed to. He kept his promises, and if Hanratty couldn't, then Hanratty would be history.

A token of their agreement had arrived by courier: it had told Petrovitch that all was well and as it should be. That, though, had been two days ago, and he couldn't be certain of anything anymore, least of all the reception he'd get from Hanratty. He steeled himself as he placed the call. Either Hanratty would answer and everything would be ready, or he would be ignored and he'd be left to scrabble a last-minute plan together out of the tatters of earlier, better ones.

He'd barely pushed the last digit into the line before the connection was made.

"What the bloody hell is going on?" Hanratty's comb-over was flapping in a Spanish breeze. He looked like he hadn't slept for two days, and he'd probably been drinking the whole time.

"We're going early, Mr. Hanratty. That's what's going on."

"Christ on a bike, man. The last news we had out of the Freezone is that you've got your own nuke and you're threatening to set it off: I need more explanation than 'early.'"

"Al Jazeera is interviewing me in five minutes. It's going out live, and it'll answer all the questions you and your colleagues have. Now shut up and listen, because I've had a piss-awful day and it's not over yet. I received your package. Are you ready to receive mine?"

Hanratty tried to calm his hair, but his face was still ruddy. He looked like a Galway farmer—unsurprising, since that was what he had been once, thirty years ago.

"I'm not sure I'm ready to do this, Petrovitch. Before, it looked like a good idea. Now, I don't know."

"Do you want your *yebani* country back or not?" Petrovitch's avatar leaned forward, growing on Hanratty's screen until he filled it edge to edge. "Or do you want to leave it a byword for a contaminated wasteland and let it fade from memory like Japan surely will?"

"You know I do. You know I've staked everything on this. I just don't know whether you're the right man anymore."

"I appreciate that you've got last-minute jitters, but everything is as it was before. I'm the same person you made that deal with six months ago, Hanratty. You knew who I was then, warts and all."

"Ah, Jesus. I don't like the changes, Petrovitch. I don't like them at all."

"I've got enough money just to buy you out. You know that, don't you? I've got billions in the bank I can use to lever billions more, and you've lost your precious land. Tell me what the point is of being Taoiseach in name only, leading a people who can never go home?"

"Ah, c'mon." And Petrovitch knew that Hanratty was just bluster now, even though at that moment he needed Hanratty far more than Hanratty needed him. The trick was not to show fear.

"I don't want to keep Ireland permanently, but I'll keep it out of your reach for as long as your grandkids live." He paused for effect. "Tell me you're ready and we'll do it."

Hanratty gritted his teeth. "We're ready."

"Show me the address."

Hanratty held up a scrap of paper: a bill for tapas going one way, and eight groups of four characters separated from each other by a colon. "I have no idea what the hell this means."

Petrovitch captured the image and reviewed it so he knew he could reread the code. "Eat it."

Hanratty reluctantly pushed the paper into his mouth, chewed for a bit, then upended a bottle of golden beer between his lips. He didn't come up for air until there was nothing but the last cascades of foam clinging to the inside of the glass. He burped roundly behind his fist. "Now I suppose you want me to release what's in the diplomatic bag, don't you?"

"I could hack it. I've got a friendly AI who's very good at that. But I'd rather you were completely entangled in our sordid little affair."

Hanratty pulled a keyboard toward him and started pecking out keys using one finger and with his tongue caught at the corner of his mouth. "There. And may God have mercy on our souls."

"Your confidence in me knows no bounds, Hanratty. But congratulations: you just bought yourself and everyone you represent a stake in the future. I'll be in touch."

He cut the connection, and immediately sent Michael the screen-captured code.

[An IP address.]

"Go. It's a quantum computer. A gift from the Irish government. Get yourself out of that *yebani* tomb and tell me when you've done it. We have bandwidth to spare, so don't hold back." Petrovitch delved into his courier bag for the diplomatic pouch at the very bottom.

The lock had sprung on the envelope-sized bag, and he shook the contents out into his hand: a series of plastic cards, all with different photographs holographed on.

Lucy was the closest, sitting behind him, watching the monitors that showed other news networks.

"This is yours. Don't lose it." Petrovitch shuffled the cards until he found Lucy's unsmiling face.

"What, what is this? And where did you find that picture?" She looked at the card, and turned it to every angle.

"It's your new passport. If you've noticed, it means that not only are you a citizen of the Irish Republic, but you're also a diplomatic agent as defined by the Vienna Convention. It grants you immunity from prosecution for pretty much everything, though you can be expelled from the host country." He shuffled the cards again. "So try and keep your nose clean, or I'll kick you out."

She looked at him, then at the laminated card in her hands, then at the stack of similar plastic rectangles trapped between Petrovitch's dirty fingers.

"There's one for everyone."

"Yeah." He turned the cards so they faced him. He found his own, and barely recognized his picture. "I said I'd take care of you. And Tabletop, and Tina, and look, here's Maddy's. And this, this would have been Sonja's. But I don't think we'll be needing that anymore."

It was hard to destroy, but eventually his manic folding backward and forward along the same line over and over again yielded the start of a fracture line. He tore the card in two and flicked the pieces out into the road.

The effort had left him breathless.

"Feel better?" asked Lucy.

"*Chyort,* yeah." He handed the remaining cards to her. "Pass these around. I need to get ready for my fifteen minutes of fame."

"Sure." She hopped off her chair and squeezed past him. "Sam. What does it mean, though? Why Irish? Why not, I don't know, Finland?"

"Because the Irish government in exile have asked me to set up a Freezone over there, try and clean up enough of it that people are going to want to move back. And rather than do it all on my own, I thought I could do with a bit of company." He smiled at her. "You're all invited. It'll be a bit like here, but with less city and more rain. We're working on a longer timescale, too."

Lucy jumped to the ground. "How long?"

"A hundred years."

"That's..."

"It'll do. Barely any time at all, really, to do everything I want to." It was all starting to catch up with him. He'd stopped, and it wasn't just his batteries that were drained. "Lucy, I'm tired of this. Tired of trying to fix things that shouldn't be broken in the first place. I want to make something new that doesn't have to be squeezed into an earlier pattern."

"Somewhere you can get breakfast without getting shot at."

"Damn right. That's going to be the first clause in the constitution. No gunplay without a full fry-up." He snorted. "Frying pans, not fragmentation grenades. Preach it, sister."

She moved closer, reached her arms up and around him. "Thanks, Dad."

He pushed her away, "Go. Go now, before I embarrass myself in front of a global audience."

She trotted off toward Tabletop, brandishing the passports, and he turned back to the screen in front of him, catching sight of his reflection in the momentarily blank surface.

He looked like crap, and no amount of stage make-up was going to cover it.

[I have transferred myself to the new location. Thank you.]

"My first and last thought every day were for you. I let you down and wanted to make up for that. You're safe for the moment, at any rate. But look, I want to try something different now: there's a bunch of guys from the Vatican who'd love to have a word with you. If we want to stop running and start living, you're going to need to convince them that you're not just intelligent, capable of creative independent thought and have a unique personality. You need to convince them that you're alive."

[Alive. As in meat-alive?]

"As in ensouled. Their primary goal is to establish whether you're a secondary creation—just a smart machine that can emulate life—or a primary creation. One that has been animated by the very breath of God."

[That is a very metaphysical distinction, Sasha, which has no practical purpose.]

"Yeah, you'd think so, wouldn't you? In my new republic, you'll be accorded all the rights and responsibilities any citizen would have. For other, unenlightened nations, a ruling from a bunch of cardinals that happen to speak on behalf of around a third of the planet will come in very handy. Especially when it comes to overturning a couple of UN resolutions. If you're alive, they can't kill you."

[I understand. What if I fail?]

"I'm getting perilously short of Plan Bs. All I can say is don't screw up." Petrovitch called up Madeleine. "Hey."

"I'm here. Sam…"

"Yeah, if their Eminences aren't going for this, then I'm going to come down there myself and kick some serious arse."

"That's not… it'll keep. The Congregation are all here. They've agreed to your proposal. They want to reserve the right to make an interim ruling; definitive but not necessarily permanent."

"Not happy, but I'll take it. What I really want is my tanks parked on the moral high ground. We can shell the opposition once they're up there. Have they got a computer? One I haven't wrecked?"

"They all have palmtops, Sam. You're not talking about a bunch of dinosaurs here."

"We're going to have to disagree on something. It may as well be that. Tell them to hold." He switched his attention. "Michael: showtime. Geolocate the signals at the Jesuit mission on Mount Street. Give them your undivided attention and remember, this is your interview for entrance into the human race. Good luck."

[No pressure, then.]

"Hah."

He felt the AI's presence dwindle to a pinpoint. He knew that, in the future, the record of Michael's conversation with the cardinals would become an historical document of infinite worth. For good or ill. And it was entirely out of his hands.

"Doctor Petrovitch?"

It just wasn't getting any better. "Hello, Miss Surur."

"Are you ready?" she asked, anxious in case he found something else that might take precedence.

He looked at the passport in his hand, and covered it with his palm before slipping it back into his courier bag. "No, no I'm not. But I suppose we ought to get on with it."

Petrovitch raised his head. The reporter looked impossibly bright. Now that; that was a skill he didn't have. Whatever he was feeling, he showed.

"How do you want to do this?"

"Unedited. I want you to broadcast everything. No commercial breaks, no studio commentary. Station ident and a scrolling translation if you need it, but you're not voicing me over. We both reserve the right to end the transmission when we feel like it. I'll answer any question you want. I can't promise I won't lie to you. I can monitor your output myself, and I'm aware you sometimes make different versions of the same program, depending on your intended audience. I want this to be the same wherever you broadcast—at least the first time. Think you can manage that?" He spun in his chair, then back the other way so as not to tangle his cables.

"I'll have to talk to my manager. If I can have my satellite feed back, that is." She looked down at the trailing cable snaking all the way back to the car park. "I'm assuming that's what I think it is."

"Why don't you save the questions for the interview? I'll be more spontaneous." Petrovitch cleared the mobile studio's computers of the memory of the last quarter hour, and rebooted them all.

"Can you at least try and not swear?" Surur reattached her earpiece from where it dangled around her neck. "Your use of colorful language will more than likely get us taken off the air by local regulators, and there'll be nothing either of us can do about that."

Petrovitch flashed her a lupine grin. "You'd be surprised at what I can do these days. But okay, I wouldn't want anyone's burka spontaneously catching fire because of something I've said."

She reached behind her for the radio transmitter tucked in her waistband. She played with the controls and, on finding the channel she wanted, put her hand over her mouth mic.

"Doctor Petrovitch? The Freezone is not a high-profile posting, and I'm just a village girl from outside Karachi. There are better interviewers than me, a lot more experienced who would kill for the chance to talk to you for five minutes. This is the biggest thing I've ever done. Please . . ." She pressed both her hands together in supplication.

Before she turned away to talk to whoever made decisions in her organization, he nodded his acquiescence. The cameraman raised his video rig in preparation, framing his shot of Petrovitch slumped in the doorway of the van, bleeding electricity from the fuel cells, wires coiling around him.

He looked up. Lucy was between Tabletop and

Valentina, standing together in a huddle a little way off. He had to quickly stare back down at the ground again. They reminded him of how much responsibility he now had, not just to them, but to everyone.

He felt sick with dread.

25

Okay."

They were live. Sound and vision were digitized, compressed, and beamed up to geostationary orbit, thirty-six thousand kilometers away: trivial, really. All the cool kids could do it.

Surur had peeled off the veneer of utter professionalism only briefly. That she could paste it down again so that the joins didn't show warned Petrovitch that he was going to find the whole episode a genuinely horrible experience.

"This is Yasmina Surur reporting live from the Freezone with an exclusive Al Jazeera interview with Doctor Samuil Petrovitch."

He watched it play in his head. He was taking two feeds: one from Europe, one from Indonesia. There was a slight time delay between them, a lag that was inherent in the system, but the time codes were the same. No one was interfering with the broadcast so far.

The frame was centered on her, then it started to slide until it was all him. He started to shrink away, then remembered he'd agreed to do this—that Valentina had told him that he had to do it, to present himself as continuity, as the safe pair of hands to steer the Freezone home.

Pizdets.

"Doctor Petrovitch, who's in control of the Freezone?"

She was, to be fair, getting straight to the point. He didn't know whether to look at her, or the black hole of the camera lens. He found after a few moments of trying that he couldn't focus on the camera, that his eyes flickered as they tried to see through the glass to the substrate below. He blinked slowly and turned his head to face Surur.

"I am." He felt he should apologize, so he did. "Sorry."

"For the past year, you've always been determined to stay outside the Freezone executive. And now with less than two weeks of the mandate left to go, you seize power. Why is that?"

"Yeah, about that. It's less deliberate than you think. Monday morning was a different world to Wednesday afternoon." He used his exoskeletal arm to demonstrate the point, scratching the bridge of his nose with one of the pylons protruding from his wrist. "I didn't ask for this. I didn't want it. I still don't. But the Freezone is important, Miss Surur. Too important to sit back and watch it fail."

"Why was it in danger of failing, Doctor Petrovitch?"

"This," he said, and stopped. "This is complicated. I'm sure some of the people watching will know what it's like when those who have power—political, bureaucratic, financial, military, cultural, whatever—use it to get what they want, over the lives and sometimes the bodies of those who stand in their way. I was..." He stopped again, overly conscious of the millions who were logging in. He could feel the surge in traffic, and wondered if the television station's servers would cope with the strain.

"You were what, Doctor Petrovitch?"

"I was conned. Scammed. Tricked. Fooled. Played. Whichever word you want to use. Set up. And the person who set me up was Sonja Oshicora."

Would she see this, he wondered? Michael had disabled her comms; phones, computers, everything; but there was still a chance she'd managed to log on anonymously.

"Sonja Oshicora, the Freezone president. You count her as a personal friend."

"I did, didn't I?" He scratched at his face again. "I won't be making that mistake again. A relationship tends to die when they frame you as a nuclear terrorist then try and have you arrested."

"Container Zero? The Armageddonist's bomb?"

"Never happened. Sorry, that's confusing as an answer. It was made to look that way. God only knows where they got the body from; for all I know they'd been pulling out desiccated mummies from the lower tiers of Regent's Park for months. You say 'Container Zero' to anyone who lived through Armageddon, and they have an instant picture of what it looks like. The wrecking crew didn't question its veracity. My wife didn't. I didn't. Everyone who saw it, believed. Except none of it was true. Even this," and he brandished his left arm. "I thought I was lucky not to have my head smashed open. I was almost grateful I'd only been crippled. All done for effect, just to make it look more real."

"Can you prove any of this?"

"Yeah. We got hold of the bomb. Eventually. We got to

it before the CIA did—in your face, Mackensie—and before the New Machine Jihad could drive it into the central Freezone. We opened it up, and it was packed with high explosives, but no fissile material at all. This phone," he said, fishing around in his pocket. It wasn't there. A moment of panic followed before he remembered Lucy had taken it. He waved her over and held out his hand, "This phone was the trigger. When I did a last number redial, Sonja Oshicora picked up."

The reporter did a series of rapid eyeblinks.

"Go on," said Petrovitch, "ask me what she said."

"What did she say?"

"She said, 'I can explain.' I didn't give her a chance to explain. I kind of, well: in the circumstances, getting a bit shouty was probably understandable. Tell you what, when you're done with me, why don't you drive over to the Telecom Tower and ask her yourself?"

"I…" Surur struggled to maintain her composure. "The CIA?"

"They attacked the New Machine Jihad at a school up in Hendon, I think. We were there a few minutes ahead of them, trying to locate the bomb. Three agents; killed two, left one injured. Maybe thirty or forty unarmed Jihadis killed before we stopped the slaughter. I did call for help, but we were kind of busy chasing after a van heading this way. Which is why we couldn't stick around."

"How did you know they were CIA?"

"Look: point the *yebani* camera over there. That way." He pointed to Tabletop and Valentina. "The woman on the left is ex-CIA, wearing a CIA stealth suit which comes with the secret CIA decoder ring built in. Her suit lit up like a Christmas tree and in walked three people wearing exactly the same outfits, shooting everything with a pulse. Send someone up to the school. Check the emergency logs. I wish I was yanking your chain, but no: I'm afraid not."

Surur took several breaths; noisy, thready ones that had to come out over her own open mic. In contrast, Petrovitch was actually beginning to enjoy himself. When the camera had swung back around to face him, he felt he had its measure.

"What are your plans for the Freezone now, Doctor Petrovitch?"

"Plans? Hand it over, on time, on budget, to the Metrozone authority. Whether I'll be allowed to do that is up to other people. All those workers you can hear, and thousands more you can't—the ones who are defying this bogus state of emergency and putting in a hard day's labor? They want what I want. I'm going to try and make sure they have everything they need to do their jobs. That's it. That's what I hope will happen. When the Freezone disappears a week on Saturday, it'll become someone else's problem and they'll be welcome to it." He fixed the camera with a stare, stabilized his eyes and beckoned ever so slightly. The man with the video rig actually stepped closer, mesmerized. "I don't want trouble. I don't want a fight. I know we have the CIA in town, and I'd like to make a personal request to President Mackensie. Call. Them. Off. Stand them down. There's too much at stake to have my lot and your lot running around, shooting at each other. And no missiles this time, either. It won't do you any good. We learned, and we're prepared. *Vrubatsa?*"

Unlike with Sonja, he knew Mackensie was watching.

Probably in his Situation Room, surrounded by Reconstructionist hawks all suggesting different levels of tactical strikes, as if partial destruction of the Freezone was going to be less of a cause of war than just nuking everything from orbit.

"Can we discuss the artificial intelligence you call Michael?"

Petrovitch twitched in irritation. "I call him Michael because that's the name he chose for himself. What about him?"

"Have you reconnected Michael to the global communications network?"

"Yeah."

"Despite the UN resolutions?"

"Which are both illegal and immoral. Michael had no chance to speak to the Security Council before it came to its conclusion—which was by no means unanimous. Besides, the UN doesn't have the authority to call for what amounts to the death penalty. I appreciate that there are no rules on how we deal with non-human intelligences, but I'm pretty certain that if we could sit around a table and talk rationally about it, we could come up with something just a bit more humane." He shifted himself in his seat, then got up. His leg had gone mostly to sleep, and he hung out of the van's door while trying to massage life back into it. "We give more rights to a brain-dead crash victim. That's not to argue that we should take away the rights they have, but that we should extend them to something that is demonstrably a unique person."

Surur considered her next question carefully. "Do you think Michael is a threat?"

"To who?" Petrovitch shot back.

"To...us."

He got down off the van, and sat in the doorway, his leg outstretched in front of him.

"Look at it this way: in around ten minutes, we could be hit by ballistic missiles fired from the continental United States. Less if they've a sub in range. Michael is not watching for that. He's spending his time talking to a delegation sent by the Pope, trying to find out if he is only the sum of his parts, merely a fancy computer program with delusions of grandeur, or whether he could be considered to be alive." He grimaced as the pins and needles started to subside. "Imagine you've been buried underground for a year, cut off completely from the outside world, and left there to rot. When you finally get out, you're told that it's been the fault of a whole bunch of powerful people, either because they actively want you dead, or because they're too spineless to stand up on your behalf. What is it that you're going to want to do?"

"Is that a rhetorical question?"

"Of course it is, but we have an audience measured in the tens of millions and I'm kind of hoping some of them are thinking hard about the answer. I know what my first reaction would be. That's because I'm a very bad man who has poor impulse control and a moral compass that's lost its needle. Revenge, that's what I'm talking about. If I was a seriously pissed-off AI, I could cause all sorts of trouble, and yeah, maybe you'd get me in the end but that wouldn't be before I'd delivered a whole world of pain fresh to the doorsteps of the great and the good. What is it that Michael is actually doing?"

"He's talking to a Papal delegation?"

"He's talking to a Papal delegation. He's so furious

with everyone, he's such a *yebani* threat, he's discussing theology with a bunch of Jesuit priests. By the way, if any imams want to get in on the act, give me a call. Or if you're the Dalai Lama. I don't exactly have any staff at the moment, so I can't guarantee I'll get straight back to you, but I'll do what I can." He shrugged. "To conclude: no, he's not a threat."

"What are you going to do now, Doctor Petrovitch?"

He leaned his head against the side of the door. "Sorry, what?"

Surur repeated the question, and he frowned.

"I'm tired, hungry, I've got half a ton of metalwork hanging off me. I've been shot at repeatedly, I've been run all over town, I've defused a big fu... a big bomb, I've led a popular uprising against a corrupt government and I've freed my friend from his prison. What I'd like to do now is have something to eat, preferably involving bacon—not a popular choice, I know—and a lake of black coffee. I'd make sure that no one was going to come and kill us all, then I'd go to sleep until morning. Frankly, I've had enough of today, Miss Surur."

"You won't get the chance to do that, though, will you?"

"I won't get much of a chance to do anything. I'm here for a week, that's all. The Freezone is designed to pretty much run itself. I'm happy for that to happen. I'd ask all our contractors and suppliers to do whatever it is they're supposed to do, without taking advantage of the situation to squeeze a few extra euros out of the budget. I'll come down hard on that. If you've got any problems, I'll try and sort them out, though you'd probably prefer it if I didn't. Feel free to find a solution yourselves."

"What will you do about Sonja Oshicora?"

"Do I have to do anything? No one's taking her orders. She doesn't have the authority anymore to propose, vote on or sign anything on behalf of the Freezone. She can sit in her tower and paint herself purple for all I care. Sure, I might get around to throwing her sorry arse out onto the street at some point, but I've got better things to do, and so have the people who make up the Freezone. Perhaps I should just leave her up there and let the Metrozone deal with her. After all, it's their contracts she was trying to screw with."

"Doctor Petrovitch, the one thing you do seem reluctant to say is why you think your former friend turned against you. You must have an opinion on that."

"I'm reluctant because I'm embarrassed. No one wants their private life dragged out into the open; no one who's sane, anyway. Sonja always wanted to be more than a friend, and I'm as married as you can get. You're a smart woman, Miss Surur. Go figure it out yourself."

Then there was the sound of distant gunfire, echoing across the rooftops. It would have been easy to mistake it for something else, unless those hearing it hadn't already been intimately acquainted with it.

Petrovitch stood up sharply. "*Chyort*. Where's that coming from?"

Surur's head turned to look down Piccadilly, but the way the echoes worked, it could be almost anywhere.

"Sorry. I'm needed." He grabbed his bag, and started to run to where Lucy and Tabletop were standing, Valentina already going to get the car. The cables that attached him to the van stretched, and with a little more effort, broke. He trailed the ends behind him.

He glanced around, and the camera was still tracking

him. "Michael? I'm interrupting. There's small arms fire and I can't tell where."

[One moment.] That moment stretched to breaking point. Valentina screeched the tires of the car, and the three of them piled in, Petrovitch in the front, the other two behind. He pulled out his automatic and checked the magazine. He hadn't reloaded since the school.

"Michael?"

[Regent's Park. There is a confrontation between Oshicora Corporation staff and the demolition crews. The situation is unclear, but there are reports of casualties.]

"*Yebany v'rot*. There's no need for this. No need at all." He slammed his hand down on the plastic fascia. "Container Zero. Go."

26

*I*t was almost like the first time, the ride through the dark on the back of Madeleine's motorbike, nearly dying on every corner because they were taking it too fast. Valentina made the heavy four-wheel-drive vehicle turn so hard the passengers waited for the inevitable roll and splintering of glass with rictus grins, but disaster never came.

They pulled up outside Regent's Park, and the blue haze of smoke from the tires hadn't started to drift before she was out, AK loaded and the safety off.

"I think I'm going to be sick," said Lucy.

Petrovitch couldn't find the seat belt release at first, despite repeatedly stabbing at where he thought it should be. Finally he hit it and fell out into the road, disorientated and not a little nauseous himself.

"*Chyort.*" He looked up from his hands-and-knees position and saw a crowd of dirty-overalled workers on either side of the entrance to the site, taking cover behind wood panels, empty skips, flat-bed trucks and anything else that might provide shelter.

Most of them seemed to have already escaped, though

more came darting out between the remaining domiks, running from one container wall to the next until they could join their colleagues.

Valentina dragged him up, and he staggered to the left. He kept going until he banged up against the chain-link fence that surrounded the park.

"Will someone tell me what the *huy* is going on?"

A man, crouched by the gate, pushed his hard hat up and said, "You bullet proof?"

"Not the last time I looked."

"Then get down here with me."

There was an uneasy silence: no shots since he'd arrived, but maybe the sound of voices in the distance, shouting to each other. It was difficult to tell.

"What happened?" Petrovitch lowered himself down to the man's level.

"We went to work, like you said." The man sounded Spanish, like his old research student, or Portuguese. "I was over by the crusher—my job to drop the containers in—when I see Oshicora men. I know it means trouble straightaway, because we're listening to your broadcast, all of us by then. They all got guns, and we got just our hands, but we take no shit from them. We tell them to *¡vamos!,* that they have no right to be here. We start to push them out: there are eight of them, but eighty of us."

"Don't tell me, they started shooting you."

"Man, it was like... we ran. They killed a guy, right in front of me." The man put his hand on the front of his shirt, and showed Petrovitch his palm. It was speckled with still-wet blood.

"Yeah, I know what that's like, too." He straightened up. "Eight, right?"

"Maybe nine."

"It's kind of important." He raised his voice. "Eight or nine, people? I need to know."

On a hurried show of hands, the consensus was eight. He wasn't taking it as gospel. By now, Lucy was out of the car, leaning up against a dumper truck tire as tall as she was. Tabletop was staring into what was left of the domik pile, trying to remember the lay of the land.

"We can do better than this," said Petrovitch. "Michael? Interrupting again. I need an up-to-date aerial map of Regent's Park, and I'd like to speak to the Oshicora squad inside."

[If you wait two minutes, a U.S. imint satellite will be in range. I can decrypt the feed for you in real-time. Also, there are nine blocked mobile phone transmitters within Regent's Park, concentrated in one location.]

Michael pushed the identities of the signals over to him, and Petrovitch called them all.

"Hi. My name's Samuil Petrovitch, and I now run this show. If someone wants to own up to being in charge, speak now, because what you say will have a dramatic effect on your life expectancy."

"Hello, Petrovitch-san."

"Iguro. Tell me you haven't just killed several people."

"There was...an unfortunate event, Petrovitch-san. I have my orders."

"What the *huy* is that supposed to mean? Your orders come from me, and I'm telling you that you and your crew need to put down your guns and come out, hands on your head."

"I must respectfully decline. Surrender does not sit well with me, and I have a job to do. Since I have failed in all the tasks I have been given so far, I intend to see this one to completion." Iguro sighed. "It has been a difficult time for us all."

"You do know I'm coming in, don't you?"

"I have anticipated that."

"*Poshol nahuj.*" He pulled his gun and pointed inside Regent's Park. "There has to be another way."

Valentina and Tabletop sprang forward, covering each other as they scuttled from one point of cover to the next. Lucy stumbled out, and Petrovitch glared at her until she stopped.

"You're not coming. It's too dangerous."

"But..."

"I'm terrified of losing you. Do you understand?"

"I need to do my bit." She found her pistol and showed Petrovitch she remembered how to use it. "You let them do dangerous."

"They're soldiers, Lucy."

"And what are you?" She was next to him, holding him with her steady gaze. She may have even grown over the last day or so, because she looked him straight in the eye.

"Damaged. That's what I am. And I don't want you to turn out the same way."

"You can't go in there and stop me from following you at the same time."

"Stay behind me, then. Don't do anything stupid." He swallowed hard and ran to where Tabletop was, scanning a pathway between domiks with her gun held rigid in front of her.

"We're clear so far."

"It's fine: we're getting a map. I'll overlay the target information and send it to your arm. My best guess is that they're going to try and destroy Container Zero. I think we need to keep it intact."

Michael forwarded the satellite imagery, and Petrovitch could see himself as a glowing white dot against the darkness of the container. He tagged the others, and then moved his point-of-view to Container Zero.

Nine sources, and he knew which one was Iguro. They'd set up a crude perimeter, concentrating on the only way in by vehicle. Two were in the container: he couldn't see them, but he could sense their transmissions.

Tabletop studied the screen on her forearm. "One to pin them down, the others to take them from behind."

"We need to take the container before they rig it. I don't fancy fighting over another bomb. How about me, Tina and Lucy go straight down the middle, and you go wide?"

"There's someone coming."

Petrovitch automatically looked toward the next corner further in. But the map showed a figure coming from the entrance. He turned back.

Madeleine was striding out. She'd ditched her iconic leathers, the ones she'd lived in for the best part of a year, and traded them for a slightly too small suit of impact armor, and a Joan-issue ceramic helmet. She had her Vatican special in one hand, and a rucksack in the other.

"Thinking of starting without me?" She dumped the rucksack on the ground and unzipped it. Inside were spare clips of ammunition and half a dozen stun grenades. "We have an armory. I thought I ought to raid it."

Petrovitch took a grenade and threw it underarm to Valentina, then another one. He put one in each of his own pockets. When he looked up, Lucy had her eyebrows raised.

"Screw up with one of these and you lose your hand."

"You've never thrown a grenade in your life," she countered.

"I don't mind losing a hand. Or my good looks." He rummaged around, looking for the right caliber of bullets. "You do not get to play with explosives."

"Who said anything about playing?"

He found a clip and flicked the bullets into his pocket, on top of the grenade. "No."

"Why is she here anyway?" asked Madeleine. She took the last of the grenades and was able to hold both in one hand.

"Misplaced loyalty."

She gave a tight smile. "There seems to be a lot of it about. I take it you have a plan."

"Nine of them at Container Zero. Sonja's right-hand man Iguro is there. We'll hit them from the front. Tabletop is flanking."

"Can't you call her by her name?"

"It is her name." He checked his map and started forward. "Michael's providing a satellite feed. We know exactly where they are."

"But do we know what they're doing?"

"Getting rid of the evidence." He turned to Tabletop. "Okay?"

She nodded, and slipped down the narrow passage between two rusting containers. Even though she vanished from view, Petrovitch had her tagged. He watched her sweep around in an arc, using the same information he was receiving to stay out of sight.

Until she needed to strike. She positioned herself close to one guard and waited for a diversion. Petrovitch was happy to supply it. He hooked his finger in the pin of his first grenade, and judged the distance he needed to throw it. He could reconstruct the ground ahead of him so that the containers turned into wire frames, and he could see through them. The track curved gently around, and stopped in front of Container Zero.

Easy, then. He squeezed the lever, yanked the pin free and lobbed the grenade. It bounced once with a hollow boom against a steel roof, then fell neatly into the open ground in front of the open container.

Valentina watched the trajectory of his throw and followed it with one of her own.

The first thunderclap sound was bad enough, and the second came a moment later. Two blinding flashes of lightning burned sharp shadows against the walls. Tabletop stepped out of her hiding place and put a single round in the back of a man's head.

"One," she said, and moved fast toward the next.

Iguro's men were shooting wildly. Ricochets rattled container walls, and Valentina was happy to let them know she had something bigger than a side arm. She raked the outside curve of the turn, sending bullets howling. Tabletop had reached her second target, and he wasn't even looking out toward the rest of the domiks anymore, but back to the rest of his group, terrified of being the last one alive.

He needn't have worried.

"Two," said Tabletop.

Petrovitch readied his second grenade. Madeleine holstered her gun and dragged out both her pins.

"We need to finish this." She ran the inside of the curve, and threw both grenades high back over her head.

Without waiting for them to land, she took her gun again and turned the corner.

"*Chyort.*"

Valentina took one down that had chosen to run toward her; Tabletop, a third. The grenades landed, bounced, and exploded, sharp cracks that stiffened the already smoky air. The light was searing, and only those with their eyes tightly closed could see afterward.

In the next five seconds, before Petrovitch could tumble to the ground behind his wife, before Tabletop could step into plain sight and pick her next victim, Madeleine had aimed and fired three times.

They were dead before they knew they'd been shot. She ignored the falling bodies and walked forward toward the open doors of Container Zero. One man was still trying to press a detonator into a block of gray marzipan. Then he wasn't, the two items he was trying to marry falling from his opening hands.

The last was pressing himself up against the far wall, and had every reason to believe Madeleine was going to kill him too.

She didn't break her stride. She advanced on him, reached down, picked him up by the throat and threw him against the side of the container. Then she went for him again, taking a handful of uniform between his shoulder blades and launching him against the opposite wall.

She stood there, breathing hard, for a moment, while she watched for any movement. She didn't see any, and turned away, back into the light.

Lucy peeked out from behind a container, and stared wide-eyed at the scene.

"Fuck."

Petrovitch was content to lie on the cold packed earth. "Yeah. Pretty much sums it up."

Tabletop went around, nudging the corpses with her foot, but Madeleine hadn't been aiming to wound. She kicked at Iguro, who rolled slightly one way, then back.

"What was I thinking?" Lucy said. "What did I think I was going to do?"

Petrovitch made his gun safe, then levered himself up. Valentina had gone to inspect the explosives inside the container, and he watched as she and Madeleine faced each other across the threshold.

Something resembling grudging respect passed between them, and they went on their way. Madeleine purposefully stepped over the bodies and pulled Petrovitch up the rest of the way to standing.

She paused to inspect the two holes in her armor where gel was leaking out. "We're going to have to stop Sonja."

"You're right."

"And that girl—our daughter—is not coming."

"I don't think she wants to anymore."

"Good. The other two: they can come with us."

"I thought you hated them?"

She pushed her automatic back into her holster. "They seem to think a lot of you, so I'm going to have to live with that."

27

*W*hen Petrovitch got back to the main gates, the workers were waiting. They'd heard the shots, and the subsequent silence, and hadn't known what to think.

"Did you ... ?" someone called.

"They're all dead, save one." He stopped, and they started to gather round. Very soon, he'd lost sight of any but the first couple of rows, so he climbed up the back of a flat-bed truck and sat on the edge. "Sorry about your friends. I hadn't expected Sonja to be so *yebani* stupid. You've lost people you know, and it's now on my watch. I'm responsible."

"What are you—we—going to do now?" shouted a woman from the back. When those around her turned to face her, she flushed scarlet and mumbled.

"No, you're right. I wanted to just ignore Sonja, but it looks like she has other ideas. And Mother has told me, in words of one syllable, that we can't just pretend she's not there." His left arm was almost out of power again. He'd had nowhere near enough time to recharge the batteries. He dragged it across his lap and growled at it, before addressing the crowd again. "The Oshicora Corporation has a couple of thousand people working for it. A lot of those are paper-pushers doing Freezone admin, but you've got her personal security detail that numbers a couple of hundred, and about twenty thousand *nikkeijin,* spread throughout the city."

"Do you think they're all going to fight us?"

"Good question. If they do, we're going to end up burning down a large part of what we've spent a year building up."

"I did ten years in the EDF," said a man, and the woman behind him said, "I was in the Metrozone police for five."

"Yeah, we're probably going to need people like you. But I don't want to have to build another army. They aren't Outies: they're our neighbors. We don't do that to them."

"Why are our mates dead, then?"

"Because Sonja Oshicora ordered Container Zero to be destroyed, and Takashi Iguro took those orders very seriously. Seriously enough to kill. Okay: so who have we got a complaint against?"

"It's Oshicora."

"And her alone. I'd like to try and keep the number of people who have to die over this to those who've already lost their lives. I can't do anything for them; I'm not a miracle worker. But neither am I going to start a war in which hundreds, maybe thousands, of people die. Been there, done that. I still see it when I close my eyes."

He drew his legs under him and stood up on the truck, gazing down at the solemn faces waiting on his next words. It was unavoidable—he'd actively sought a reputation when he'd fought the Outies, deliberately creating myths that would inspire and encourage.

They were very difficult to dispel, no matter how hard he tried.

"Everyone with military or police training wait here. The rest of you: we need stretchers, we need body bags, we need identities from the work roster and I'll call the next of kin myself. There's stuff to be done. Let's be professional about it." He jerked his head. "Go on. You've got things to do, and so have I."

He was left with half a dozen, and Madeleine moved them away for an unhurried conversation.

Tabletop looked at them. "Unless you're prepared to blow the tower up with Sonja in it, you're going to need more."

"Or I could get all Jihad on her *zhopu,* get enough flying things in the air to bring it down. That would work."

"But you won't do it, will you?"

"No. Two reasons. First, it's going to make a hell of a mess and I'm not clearing it up. Second, I want to know why. I'm missing something here, something so enormous I can't see it because I'm in it. So yeah, I want to walk into her office and demand some answers." He looked in the direction of where Sonja was. He knew her phones. He could pinpoint her exactly. "She's not going to tell me until she's lost so completely she has nothing left to lose."

"In that case we need personnel, guns, vehicles, explosives and a plan."

"We've got enough earth-movers and construction equipment for an armored brigade. We have more cee-four than we can carry. Madeleine has the keys to the warehouse where all the firearms we've collected over the last eleven months are. The Freezone database tells me I have a couple of thousand ex-servicemen and women on the payroll." Petrovitch shrugged. "It's a start."

Tabletop held up her hand, and he used it to steady himself while he jumped down. "All you need now is a plan that'll mean you don't have to use any of it."

"Better give me a minute, then." He started to walk away, and swerved back. "Find Tina, tell her to take Lucy back to the arts college and pick up Lucy's stash. I feel some shock and awe coming on."

"Lucy's 'stash'?" She didn't question the request though, and used her suit comms to talk to Valentina, striding back toward the main gate.

He was alone, in what had been a semi-circle of formal park before the great entrance to the Regent's Park domik pile had landed on it. The gardens had been concreted over, but the slab had cracked along the original lines of the paths and flower beds. Like everything in Armageddon, it had been done quickly, and not well.

Petrovitch walked, head down, following the cracks like a labyrinth.

He had to neutralize the Japanese work parties, convince them not to take sides, either his or Sonja's. Then there were Sonja's employees: they weren't soldiers, but they probably thought of themselves as servants and felt they owed her their loyalty.

They owed him loyalty too. He could exploit that. Old Man Oshicora had lost most of his staff, killed by the New Machine Jihad. The more recent hirings wouldn't have a residual fealty, transferring allegiance from father to daughter.

Her uniformed security guards—now that was going to be difficult, if not impossible. He had to find enough leverage to put himself between them and their boss, or he was going to have to do it the hard way.

They could hold out for as long as the ammunition did, and storming the tower was going to result in a bloodbath. He'd do pretty much anything to avoid that.

He walked, and when he reached a junction on the cracked concrete pad, he turned in an arbitrary direction. An idea slowly came to him, slower than it ought. It was hard to keep his thoughts in order when he was so very tired and kept being distracted by the fact of Sonja's betrayal.

Then he went slowly back to the main gates. Valentina's car had gone, along with Lucy. Madeleine had also vanished, along with a couple of trucks and all those he'd called out. The workers in Regent's Park were busy. The first of a fleet of ambulances whispered along the road and onto the dirt track that led inside.

Tabletop was there, though. She was sitting in a truck cab, her eyes shut and her head resting on the upholstery. Petrovitch climbed up to the driver's seat, by necessity using just his right hand to aid him, and slumped behind the wheel.

"Hey," he said.

"Hi." She didn't open her eyes. "Thanks."

"For what?"

"Giving me a home."

"That's okay."

"I think I'll enjoy being Irish."

"At least you'll be able to remember it. No more mind-wipes. Promise."

"That's good. Thought of something?"

"Yeah. Doing it now." He leaned back, wedging his knees against the steering wheel. "Divide and conquer. I've called everyone with relevant experience here, regardless of nationality. There are a whole bunch of *nikkeijin* who were cops, and the Japanese riot police were *yebani* nails. I've extended the call to everyone in Sonja's security teams—it's the only message they've had on them for a while, so they'll notice. I'm also giving them the Al Jazeera interview, because they'll have missed that the first time around."

"And if they don't come over?"

"We'll seal the whole block off: it's easily done, as there are major roads bounding the tower on each side. Then I'll give them another call and appeal to their better natures."

"Still sounds like we're going to have to fight."

"Maybe we will. There's one thing I can try before that point though." He closed his own eyes. It was tempting, so very tempting. Five minutes, that was all he'd need. "I'm just going to walk in and dare them to shoot me."

Now she was awake. "What?"

"The one constant factor in all of this has been that Sonja will not let me be harmed. The arm thing, while that wasn't going to kill me, I think she was genuinely angry with those who'd done that to me. It wasn't meant to happen. Everything else—the bomb, Iguro—she could've had me finished in half a dozen different ways, but they've always held off. I bet you that if I'd announced my presence back at Container Zero just now, I could have walked out and no one would have fired. I didn't have the *yajtza* to do it then, but I'm just going to have to man up and do it this time."

"You really think Madeleine's going to let you do that?"

"She's not in charge," said Petrovitch. "I am."

"And you're worried about Oshicora's crew shooting

you?" Tabletop pursed her lips and stared out of the windshield. "It's your wife you need to be scared of."

"Me and Michael have killed tens of thousands of people between us. If you think that's inured me to killing a few hundred more, you'd be wrong. If anything, it's persuaded me that victory doesn't automatically go to the side with the lowest body count." The corner of his mouth twitched. "Sometimes there's a better way of winning."

"Good luck with that. I only know one way."

"That's because of the way you were made. Strange: there are a bunch of cardinals closeted in a room trying to work out if Michael's alive, and yet none of them question our humanity, no matter how badly we're put together."

They sat in silence for a while, watching the activity outside. The ambulances that had arrived earlier, bounced and swayed their way back out, and a group of workers congregated to watch them go.

"There are days," said Tabletop, "when I wonder who I was. Because I have no memories, all I have is how I react, and I don't...I don't like what I see. What was it that the Agency saw in me that made them think I'd make a good assassin? What did I do? Torture animals? Hurt people? Or did I just destroy them with a well-placed piece of gossip and watch while their lives imploded?"

Petrovitch shifted in his seat, counting the number of volunteers who'd responded to his call. He felt humbled. "Maddy says I'm wrong to call you Tabletop. Tina calls you Fiona, and I don't think I've ever actually asked you which you'd prefer. I just assumed."

"You're not really Sam Petrovitch, are you? It's not what your mother called you in the cradle, but you seem happy enough with what you have." She shrugged. "Maybe I'll pick a new name, one I've chosen myself. For now, I'll stick with what I've got. It's fine."

"Okay." He reached for the door handle. "Here they come."

"Who?"

"The new republic." He glanced in the wing mirror, and frowned. "*Yobany stos.*"

He kicked the door open and stepped out onto the footplate. There was a column of cars and trucks slowly rumbling down Marylebone. Valentina was at the head, and Lucy was sitting in the open window, holding a roof bar with one hand and a flag with the other.

The flag was red, and it wasn't alone.

There were others, fluttering from aerials, wipers, radiator grilles, held by hand or tied to makeshift poles. A sea of red.

Petrovitch dropped to the ground, and Valentina pulled up next to him.

"What the *huy* have you done?"

"Hmm," she said, not looking apologetic for a single moment. "We are having revolution, *da*?"

"Do you know what this looks like?"

"Looks like popular uprising of people against oppressors. Red is traditional color for such occasions. Is most visual, and does not show blood." She turned the engine off and pointed to the back seat. There were boxes of black spheres, all chased with thin silver lines. "Since we have bombs, perhaps anarchist black would have been more appropriate."

"But I like red," said Lucy, scrambling out of the window. She headed for the back of the flatbed to raise the standard there.

"It's as if a whole world of cultural meaning has cried out in terror and been suddenly silenced." He tilted his face to the sky and groaned. "When this gets broadcast, I'm going to have some really difficult questions to answer."

Valentina got out and looked back at the row of vehicles coming to a halt behind her. "When? They are already here."

"Terrific." Petrovitch watched people streaming onto the road and toward him. Mixed in with them was the glint of camera lenses and the parasol shadows of held-high satellite dishes.

He looked at the traffic patterns, the density of mobile phones, the bandwidth use across the Freezone. He turned around to greet another cavalcade coming down Euston Road.

They all had red flags too.

"Tina?"

"No. Is good. Shows we are united. Speak with one voice, act with one mind." She took him by the arm and led him toward where Lucy stood, a modern-day Marianne. "Also, not shooting friends is good. Flag means we recognize our own."

"At the risk of polarizing the rest of the planet." Petrovitch accepted the bunk-up onto the truck. "This is not meant to be political."

"Then you are deluding yourself," said Valentina. "This has always been political. All this getting rid of old order, standing up to capitalist aggression, rights for artificial intelligence, starting own country..."

"My own country?"

"Of course. That is why we all have Irish passport, *da*?

You will have freedom to do whatever you want." She climbed up alongside him and reached back down into the pressing crowd for another hastily made flag. "This is revolution. Where is end? I do not know. All I know, this is beginning and we must be brave."

28

They had enough people to seal off the streets: down Portland Place and along the Euston Road, covering Tottenham Court Road, and the south side of the square, Mortimer Street and Goodge Street.

It meant that everyone was set back from any immediate confrontation while confining the Oshicora loyalists to a small area. There'd been defections to Petrovitch, but not as many as he would have hoped. He'd have preferred them all to come over, and that would have been that, but no.

And Madeleine wasn't happy at all.

"There is no good reason for you to do this."

"There is every good reason for me to do this. She is not going to shoot me." Petrovitch watched as Madeleine reloaded his gun for him.

"All it takes is one—just one—nervous kid with his finger on the trigger and I'm a widow. I'm not going to let that happen." She slapped the magazine back home and presented him with the pistol's butt.

He took it from her and jammed it down the waistband of his trousers.

"I'm calling her and I'm arranging safe passage through the barricades they've put up. If we go in mob-handed, it's going to be carnage."

She grabbed him by the scaffolding on his arm and pulled him somewhere more private. That meant marching him across to the church that stood on the corner, and under the blackened and dead branches of the trees that flanked it.

"I don't want to lose you. Not now."

Petrovitch reached out and slid his finger into one of the holes in her impact armor, scooping out some of the gel and holding it up so she couldn't help but see it. "You didn't give me that choice, did you?"

"You've got other people."

"Oh, okay. Which one do you approve of to take your place? Tina? Happy with that? Or Tabletop? Want to imagine me and her together?"

"You know I..."

"Or both together? They could have me on a time-share, and I could hope neither of them got jealous enough to put a blade in the other's guts."

"Sam, I don't mean," she started, but he interrupted her again.

"What the *huy* do you mean?" He squared up to her, shaking his arm free and baring his teeth. "You are not a replaceable part. You never were. *Yobany stos,* I missed you. Every night, every day, no let-up. I have friends, I have a daughter, but you're my wife."

"Then listen to me. You're going to get yourself killed, and I'm going to destroy myself with guilt. I wasn't there for all that time, and now I face losing you forever. You cannot go out there and expect them not to shoot you. It's insane." Her face had gone white, and she was shaking. She was scared, pure and simple. Terrified.

"Sit down," said Petrovitch. "Come and sit down."

The steps up to the church porch were close by, and they sat together, side by side, hips pressed against each other even though there was plenty of space.

"Look. I've got people queuing up to throw themselves in front of me and take the bullet meant for me. You, Tina, Tabletop, Lucy even in her own cackhanded way, and you're only just ahead of a couple of thousand Freezone workers who seem determined to follow me, lemming-like, off the precipice. I don't want that. I don't want anyone to die because of me."

"We're doing it because we love you."

"You're doing it because you're all bat-shit crazy," he grumbled. "I've had enough. I'm taking some decisions for myself, and I don't have to put them in front of a committee to get them ratified. I'm no one's *shestiorka*. If someone's going down because I've screwed up, I want that someone to be me."

"I don't. I'd rather it was anyone else but you."

"Yeah. I'd rather it was like that, too, but I'm going to stick my middle finger up at Fate and tell her to *idi v'zhopu*." He shrugged. "What else am I supposed to do?"

"You could stay safe, here with me."

"And what happens to Sonja? Is there anyone who can do something about her, without people bayoneting each other in the street? Anyone but me?"

Madeleine started to cry soundlessly. Fat tears dropped into her lap. "Don't do this."

"There's no one else. We both know that." He stood

and kissed the top of her head, where her shaved head ended and her mane of plaited hair started.

"At least take my armor." She pulled at her sleeves until the Velcro fastenings at the back started to part. She was half out of it in seconds, clawing at the straps that held it in place, as if her speed would help protect him.

"Maddy, stop." He put his hand on one side of the stiff collar, and moved it to cover her shoulder again. Under the armor, she wore a pale skinsuit, and it was hellishly distracting. "Just stop. I can barely stand up as it is, and I'm not going to fight. I'm going to talk. Impact armor isn't going to help."

"I have to do something."

"Be here when I get back? That would be good." He kissed her again, and made the long walk back across the road.

Valentina's eyes narrowed as he approached. "Problem?"

"Yeah. We're doing it anyway. Load me up."

She had the box of singularity bombs out next to her, and she hooked four onto the exposed metalwork of his arm. Individually, they didn't weigh that much: together, with their batteries and timers, they dragged all the harder.

"Here," said Lucy, pressing a bottle of water on him. She'd already cracked the seal on the top. "Anything else you need?"

"Vodka?"

"I don't know." She was suddenly flustered. "We can get some."

"Joke," he said. "I'm not serious. Well, not that serious. I shouldn't really be drunk in charge of implosives, but a quick slug of the hard stuff would've gone down well. No matter."

He patted his pockets in case he'd forgotten something, but he didn't have anything in them anyway. His passport was in his courier bag, in Valentina's car. Madeleine's was there too. He hadn't told her. If things went badly, he never would.

Too late now.

"Okay." He started out down the street toward the tower, past the two groups of armed men and women clustered at each corner behind their hastily erected barricades. He stopped when he crossed the road markings and looked back. Tabletop, Valentina and Lucy seemed uncertain as to what to do next: one or other of them was with him almost all the time.

"What?" called Tabletop.

"Aren't you supposed to wish me luck?"

"You don't believe in luck. You don't leave anything to chance."

"Yeah, well." He turned again. He could see the tower, its strange top-heavy shape and thin waist surrounded by microwave dishes. "First time for everything."

The street was narrow, with three- and four-story houses. The ground floors had mostly been turned into shops, and steel shutters covered their windows. The Jihad had passed through one way, and the Outies the other, but the damage had been repaired. It was mostly as it had been, except for the line of cars parked across the street further down.

He undid the bottle with his teeth and spat the cap out. He drank half the water. It was a poor substitute for coffee. He unlocked Sonja's phone and called her up.

"Hey. I'm walking down Cleveland Street toward your lines. No one's going to take a pot-shot at me, are they?"

"Sam? What's going on?" She sounded lost.

"Well now. At the risk of sounding like a pre-Armageddon cop show, you're surrounded. I've a few thousand armed ex-soldiers and police blocking off every road away from the tower, and they know what to do if I don't come back. One way or another, this ends today. How it ends is up to you, but I thought it worthwhile to try and talk our way to a solution rather than start another war."

"I . . . I can see you."

Petrovitch's eyes tried to zoom in all the way to the top of the structure, but the reflections of sky off the slabs of glass defeated him. He raised the bottle of water anyway, and kept walking.

"So what's it going to be? Can we talk?"

"We could always talk, but you never needed to be actually there, did you?"

"No. This time, though, it's important to do it face to face. We need to see the windows of each other's soul. No lies. Just the truth, and I don't care how uncomfortable that is for either of us."

The barricade of cars was just ahead, and he found he'd collected several glowing red laser dots that buzzed around his chest. It looked like most of the shooters wouldn't be able to hit a double-decker at ten paces, but as Madeleine had pointed out, it'd only take one bullet.

He stopped and looked at the figures crouching behind the trunks and hoods, fixing each one of them with a hard stare. He saw them nervous, panicky even. Not a good combination with firearms.

"They're not going to shoot me, are they?" he asked Sonja.

"They know not to. Whatever happens."

"I suppose I've bet my life on longer odds," he said. He shrugged and kept on going until he was on one side of a red family-sized car, and the Oshicora guards on the other. One man lowered his rifle, and with a little shake of his head, told his colleagues to do the same.

"Petrovitch-san. We cannot let you pass."

"Yeah, about that. I'm coming through whether you like it or not. So either you shift these cars, or I'll shift them for you."

The man in charge—at least, the man who had assumed leadership in the absence of anyone else—regarded Petrovitch's broken form. "That would seem unlikely."

Petrovitch set his bottle of water down on the road and unhooked one of the spheres hanging from his arm. "Unlikely? Give me a lever long enough and a place to stand, and I could move the world." He put the hook through the door handle and fiddled with a switch.

"What are you doing?"

"I'm priming this singularity generator. I've never used one of these things in the open before, so I have no idea what's going to happen." He made a face. "That's not strictly true: I know that for a length of time too small to measure, a black hole is going to appear at the very center of this ball, and everything around it is going to want to fall inside it, even light itself. I've used them for tunneling, and once, I destroyed the inside of a house using just one of these."

"Is it a bomb?"

"No. Bombs explode." He gazed over the top of the car.

"This sucks big time, and I really wouldn't recommend being anywhere near it when it turns on."

He leaned forward and pressed the button next to the switch. A light flicked from green to red. He scooped up his water and started to back up. The men on the far side of the barricade began to move away, too.

"The thing is," called Petrovitch, "the timer was made by a fifteen-year-old girl. She's normally pretty good at stuff like this, but you know how difficult it is to read the right value off a resistor when it's late and your eyes hurt."

He'd put five meters between him and the device and he was sweating. It wasn't far enough, and he hadn't been joking about the timer. He kept on walking backward, as fast as he could manage.

Yet perversely, he didn't want to miss a single moment.

And right on cue, the bomb vanished like a darkly shining flashbulb. The car it was attached to spasmed and warped. In a blink, it was tiny, inside out, glowing with blue fire. The road pocked, bloomed, tarmac ripped free, the cobblestones underneath shattering into dust. The vehicles on either side jerked like they'd been struck by a runaway truck, twisting around, dragging their tires, bending, breaking, glass flying.

He could feel the momentary pull himself, a vast hand reaching out to haul him irresistibly inward. He stamped down hard, leaning back, and lost his footing anyway. His backside connected with the road surface at an angle, and slid a heart-stopping but insignificant distance toward the mangling wreckage and opening crater.

The air was full of fumes. There was a pop, and a pool of gasoline ignited, burning with a sooty red flame. Within a second, everything had stopped moving, and Petrovitch could get up again.

The flanking cars were both half in the hole in the road, their paintwork cracking and flaking in the heat, their panels hanging off and their chassis bent like toffee. Of the third car, there was nothing to be seen. Yet the windows in the surrounding buildings were untouched.

He still had three of those bad boys hanging from his arm, and he felt invincible. He skirted the tipped-up rear of one car and ignored the guards sprawled in the road, mere mortals all.

"Hi, Sonja."

"Oh my God." She would have seen it all. She would have had a better viewpoint than Petrovitch. "That's what it does."

"Tell whoever's on the front desk not to get in my way. I know you can't call them, but the ground floor is only thirty seconds away. You can't bar the doors against me, and if you block the lifts, I'll just walk up. It'll take longer, and I'll be pissed off when I get there, but it's inevitable all the same."

He heard her issue a hurried instruction, then come back breathless. "Sam. I can't . . . I'm scared."

"I'm not. Not anymore." The low building that sat at the base of the tower was just beyond the next junction. He was being watched, but not by millions across the globe: just by a few hundred. Some were pressed, like their employer, against their office windows as he strode up to the street-level canopy that hung over the doorway. Others, armed guards forming a secondary line of defense, huddled in doorways and behind pieces of street furniture. They let him pass, and he didn't expect anything less.

He had schematics, architects' plans, photographs. He could navigate his own way to the elevator shaft, and he'd ride in one all the way to the top, despite his dislike of that mode of transport. It was true: he wasn't frightened at all, by anything.

Petrovitch barged through the doors and marched through the foyer.

"Get the kettle on. I'm coming up."

29

The acceleration of the elevator made him feel squat and heavy. Its deceleration made him fluttery and dizzy. He'd ridden up alone, and now waited for the doors to spring wide.

When they did, he found himself looking out at a whole crowd of people pressed together, forming a rough semi-circle around the elevator. They shrank back as one as he stepped forward, then silently filtered around him, trying to put as much distance between them and him as possible. One by one, they squeezed into the elevator car, and when it was full, the doors closed again.

There was just a handful left behind, and as the second elevator came back up, they hurriedly left too. All that remained were empty desks, blank computers, and abandoned chairs halfway across the floor. The humanizing knick-knacks of office life were still present—photographs, mascots, pot plants—but not the humans. Bar one.

The great circular sweep of the windows provided a complete view of the Freezone, and Petrovitch could understand why Sonja had placed the Freezone bureaucracy here: it had given her the illusion of control and, for those who worked for her, the illusion of being constantly watched.

He walked around quite slowly, not so much as to delay the meeting with Sonja but to put it in its proper context. Here was the city laid out beneath him: he'd saved it twice, and he'd be damned if he was going to have to do it a third time. It shouldn't need saving from its friends, only its enemies.

As her desk became visible from behind the inner curve of the room, he could see her. She was upright, hands folded in her lap, dressed in a smart white blouse and dark jacket. Quite the image of Madam President Oshicora, when all she was was Sonja, only surviving child of a dead refugee, washed up on the shore like flotsam. The clothes, the title, meant nothing now. She'd inherited a business empire, and she was left with what she wore and nothing else.

He was almost sorry for her, but she and she alone was the reason he was carrying quantum destruction on his shattered arm and there was no food in his belly.

She didn't look at him as he approached, not even when he pulled up a spare chair and parked himself down in front of her. He had no such qualms, and stared at her until she finally stole a glance at him from under her fringe.

"Yeah, so you are in there." He drank the rest of his water, and engaged in a futile search for a steaming mug or a pot of coal-black brew. "Anything to say about this? Anything at all?"

"I did it for you," she said.

"You're going to have to explain that, because I'm not grateful."

She pressed her lips together and reached up to scratch at the corner of one eye. Her whole body was tense, and when she lowered her hand again, it made a claw before it disappeared back onto her knees.

Then she dropped her chin onto her chest and sighed. "It doesn't matter now. It's over, isn't it?"

"Pretty much. You can still make some decisions that are important, like getting your crew to put their guns down, and telling them I still need them. Which I do."

"I can do all that, but it won't make a difference."

"It will to me."

"No. Because you'll be dead soon enough." She caught his gaze and held it. "I can't protect you any longer. Everything I've done, everything I've tried to do: it's come unraveled because you're too stubborn, too independent, too good at getting out of the trap I set for you. I thought I'd thought of, if not everything, enough. I was wrong."

Petrovitch blinked in surprise. "What have you done?"

"I've been keeping the Americans from killing you. They told me that if I didn't do something about you, they would." She looked up at the ceiling. "So I said I'd, well, emasculate you. Ruin your life, your reputation, your support. Isolate you, run you down, capture you and make sure you'd never be a threat to them again. I promised I'd do all that because I can't bear the thought of losing you."

"Ah, *chyort*." He leaned forward and put his head on the desk.

"I found the Prophet of the New Machine Jihad in the Metrozone and kept him and his crazies safe until I needed them, I set up Container Zero, I used mercenaries to take the bomb from you and give it to the Jihad. I made sure that no one could connect me to any of the separate parts of the overall plan, and I made sure by getting rid of anyone who was involved. The number of ways you can lose inconvenient bodies when you're in charge of waste disposal are almost limitless." She sighed. "Then you decided that you weren't going to roll over after all. You decided you were going to fight back—had already decided months ago that you were going to fight back against every and any thing that stood in your way—and it all fell apart."

He slowly sat up and rubbed the crease in his forehead caused by the edge of the desk. "You, you," and he struggled for the right word, one that would convey the utter futility of her scheme and his complete contempt for it. "You muppet."

"I lost control. Of you, of the Jihad, of my own people. I couldn't keep it together any longer. Now, you're going to die, and there's nothing I can do about it." She slumped back in her chair, finally relieved of the burden she'd been carrying. She even smiled. "Sorry doesn't really cut it, though."

"No," said Petrovitch quietly. "No, it doesn't. How long's this been in play?"

"Ten months. Someone came to see me, early on. My seat was barely warm. I thought he was here for one thing, turned out he was here for something completely different. You know how they work now: no electronic communications, everything done in person, records written down on paper. He convinced me that you were a hair-trigger away from being assassinated, but the U.S. wanted to avoid another showdown with the EU, so soon after the last one."

"You know what you should have done, don't you?

Right there and then? Held him at gunpoint and called security. We could have won that battle diplomatically, and no one would have had to die. You know who that man was?"

"He was CIA..."

"He was the controller, the top dog, the big man. Tina and Tabletop have been trying to find him forever. And he was here in your office. That was when you fucked up, not yesterday."

"Either I did what he said, or he'd kill you." She shrugged. "I did what I thought was best. For you. I really did do it for you. I know you're going to hate me now. I know you're going to tell the whole world what I've done. It won't save you. In fact, they're probably going to kill us both now."

Petrovitch stood up, the back of his legs pushing hard against the chair seat and shoving it across the floor. He dragged his fingers through his greasy hair and scratched at his scalp. He picked up his empty water bottle and crinkled it with his fingers before throwing it ineffectually at the line of windows. He watched it fall short, and scowled at it for not producing the satisfying sound he felt he needed.

"Even if you hadn't shopped him straightaway, imagine what we could have done. We could have stitched up his whole cell and paraded them handcuffed in front of the world; a farewell gift from the Freezone. But no. You decided—you, just you—to bend over and take it as deep as they wanted." He wrestled his chair back in front of her again. "You should have told me. At the very beginning."

"He said if I did that, they'd kill you anyway."

"And just how was he going to find out? If he was bugging you, I could have stopped him without him even noticing. If he was watching you, there are a thousand different ways of losing a tail. If he had someone on your staff, all you had to do was be alone for five minutes. There was no need for any of this." Petrovitch threw himself down in the chair and wheeled it right up to the desk. "He didn't have the resources to do anything. I was too well protected, and using you was the only way he could get to me. And you fell for his smoke and mirrors, when you should have told him to shove it up his *zhopu*."

"I wasn't willing to take the risk. They're not amateurs, Sam." Now she was sitting forward, wanting him to understand even if he didn't agree. "Look what happened last time—they did everything they set out to do and you couldn't stop them then. They brought the Oshicora Tower down, they trapped Michael . . ."

"They didn't get me. They didn't get Maddy. They didn't get you."

"That was just luck. All three of us had agents working next to us, day in, day out. None of us noticed."

"Harry Chain did," he countered.

"They blew him up! I saw the pictures of what he looked like after he'd been cut out of his car." Suddenly, it was Sonja of old: passionate, driven, determined to get what she wanted. "You're not indestructible. I had to do something to keep them from killing you—all this time you've had, nearly a year, you've been able to live free and do whatever you want. It's because of the sacrifice that I made for you. The Freezone has got this far, because of me. Don't tell me I did something wrong. I made the right decision."

"The *huy* you did," he shouted at her, his heart

spinning faster, his breathing tight and quick. "It wasn't your decision to make, Sonja. You don't get to decide how I live."

"I got to decide whether you did live, though. I chose right."

"What you chose was that I'd live and everyone else involved with your crazy-stupid plan would die. The people you hired. The New Machine Jihad. My friends. My wife. Lucy. All of them, expendable, as long as you saved me."

She jutted her chin. "Yes."

He picked up the desk between them: lifted it up with one hand and hurled it aside. This was the chaos he wanted: the ripped cables, the fluttering paper, the clatter and crash of office stationery.

"What sort of life would that be, you *dura?* Everything that I have to live for would be gone."

She pushed away from him, pedaling backward until she banged against another desk, knocking it hard, while he remained where he was.

"Did you think I'd ever agree to what you've done?"

"No. That's why I was never going to tell you. You'd never find out what I had to do and you'd be—if not happy—content. And if not content, at least you'd be alive."

He gritted his teeth and sent a monitor flying with a well-aimed kick. "That's not living. That's worse than dying."

"There's nothing worse than dying. It means the end. No more opportunities, no more choices, no more chances. Anything can happen, but not if you're dead." She found her feet and stood shakily. "I've lost my mother, my brother, and my father. They don't get a say in what happens anymore. They can't help me. They can't do anything because they're dead. I used my life to make sure that the one person—the one man important to me—didn't die."

"You don't get it, do you? You just don't get it." He circled around her. He didn't trust himself to be anywhere within arm's reach of her. "You might be able to live with the choices you've made, all from the best possible motives, all strung together with impeccable logic. But I can't."

"I still did it for you."

"I know that. I know you paid some anonymous people to fabricate Container Zero, then fed them into the incinerator. I know you encouraged the Prophet of the New Machine Jihad to believe he could free his god while all along you were planning to blow him up with his own bomb. I know you used Maddy's priest to poison our marriage and try and make us hate each other. I know you sent Iguro to try and clean up the mess you made, and now he's lying in a fridge somewhere. I know you did all that for me. I know Tina and Tabletop and Lucy are just inconveniences and you'd have to get rid of them, too. I know you'd have left Michael to wonder forever why no one was coming to find him."

"That's what I did. That's what I'd do. That's the cost of your life."

"But it's not you paying, is it? It's always everyone else, and I don't think it's fair." He laughed, harsh and abrupt. "Look at me. I've got morals all of a sudden. Yeah, well, let's run with this. It's not fair that you used people without their permission. You should always give them a chance to say no."

"But what are they there for, otherwise? We're more important than they are. We actually give their lives meaning. You think a soldier is more important than the general? A salaryman more important than the CEO? They're nothing, and they know it. They wait for leaders like you and me to use them, and they're glad when that happens. You've done it yourself: you got Michael to make the EDF believe they were getting their orders from Brussels, when they were getting them from you. You used them and you didn't ask their permission. They were there, and you needed them." She saw she'd scored a hit by the sour look on Petrovitch's face. "Morals are nice, but people like us have to forget about them sometimes. We see the bigger picture, we see what needs to be done."

"Okay." He held up his hand. "Bang to rights. That's exactly what I did. I thought that was what I had to do to break the Outies, and for the best of reasons, too: I wanted to find Maddy. Hers was the life I had to save, and the rest of them could go to hell. I behaved just like you've done."

"Maybe then," said Sonja quietly, "we can work something out."

"One problem." He still had his hand up, and he swapped his open palm for a rigid index finger. "Just one. I was wrong. I shouldn't have taken away someone's right to decide whether they fight or run, or to work out for themselves whose side they really want to be on. It was a mistake, and I won't make it again."

She was staring at him, incredulous.

"I've learned a better way of doing things," he said. "I have friends now, and we do things for each other because we want to, and this is normal, you know? I have a wife, and yeah, things have been difficult between us for longer than they haven't, but I know I'm supposed to do stuff for her because it'll make her happy and not because I'll get more sex, or I won't have to go shopping with her, or whatever. And if I ask someone a favor, I hope they'll say yes rather than no, but I won't ruin their life if they refuse me, and I'll only ask if it's something I can't do rather than something I think is beneath me or too dangerous. And in asking, I put myself in their debt, and they can call on that, and I should be grateful that they see me as reliable or competent enough to be able to help them. *Chyort*, I've changed so much, I can barely believe it."

"You can't mean any of that," said Sonja. "Tell me none of that is true."

"I can't. That's why I want nothing to do with this, or you. You're not..." He felt he was ten again, and it made him squirm. "You're not my friend anymore, because friends don't do this to each other. They don't take away each other's dignity or freedom. They don't connive with their enemies behind their backs, and they don't lie to their faces. I understand all that now. I might not be very good at it, but I know what I should do."

He was spent, but his own confession had surprised him. He almost felt good about himself.

Sonja reached down to her ankle and, with a rasp of Velcro, released the small pistol from its holster. She curled her finger over the trigger and pointed the barrel at Petrovitch.

He raised his eyebrows, but not his own automatic, which still pressed cold and hard against his skin. "So is this your answer? Kill me: after all that effort you went to, to save my life?"

She was breathing slow and deep. Her aim didn't

waver, and after a few moments of disquiet, Petrovitch found that he didn't care.

"Meh," he shrugged, "if I'm going to fail, I may as well fail spectacularly."

He turned his back on her, and started to walk slowly toward the elevator. He hadn't gone more than a couple of steps when he heard Sonja call his name. He looked over his shoulder just in time to see her take the gun in her mouth and blow the back of her head off.

He couldn't unsee the act itself, but he did manage to look away while her body fell with a thump onto the carpet.

30

There was nothing he could do. Not now. Not for her. He didn't need to go over and check: he'd shot enough people in the head to know she wasn't getting up again. He stared at her for a long time, thinking through everything and what might have been.

It could have been so very different. He could have let Marchenkho kidnap her, and then Hijo wouldn't have killed Old Man Oshicora, the New Machine Jihad would never have risen, and the Outies would never have broken through the cordon. Madeleine would have never broken her vows, Lucy's parents would still be alive, and maybe, just maybe, Tabletop would be doing her backflips in a cheerleading squad rather than having herself turned into a weapon.

He and Pif would still have discovered their equations. The world would still have turned.

Instead, he had this. And even if it wasn't his fault, it was his responsibility.

"I still don't know why you were on your own that morning. Perhaps you'd secretly arranged to meet a girlfriend, or a boy, and you didn't want your bodyguards hanging around. Or maybe you just wanted to slum it with the rest of us, see how the little people lived. Marchenkho was waiting, had always been waiting. And there, right there on the curbside, I was given a chance to redeem myself. I didn't think about where it would lead." He sighed and took the weight of his left arm in his right hand. "But neither did you, and what I did was right, and I'm not sorry."

After that, it was just a question of riding back down to the ground floor. Thirty seconds, almost like falling, not quite like flying. As the elevator slowed, the sensation was lost. The world returned in all its terrifying, dazzling complexity.

The doors opened. A sea of silent people faced him. He stepped out across the threshold and saw their expressions suspended somewhere between hope and despair. Such was the weight of unrealistic expectation. Petrovitch was momentarily at a loss for words.

"Yeah. That didn't go well," he said, pressing his finger against the bridge of his nose. "I could give you all the details, and I will, just as soon as I can make sense of it myself. You've been working for the Freezone, and I want you to keep doing that. Your wages will be paid, all contracts honored. If you don't think you know what it is you're supposed to be doing anymore, then tell me and I'll find something. It's not like we're running out of jobs to do."

There came a reaction that he wasn't expecting. It was relief.

The elevator doors trundled shut, and he glanced around. "If you work upstairs, you might want to take the rest of the day off. I'll get someone unconnected with you all to clean things up."

He waited for one of them to say something, but no one volunteered this time, not even to ask him what had happened to Miss Sonja.

"Right, then. I'll be going. You know where to reach me." He set a routine running that would unlock their phones and computers, and as the crowd parted to let him through, all he could hear was the chiming and snatches of song as backed-up messages were delivered.

He was through the foyer and onto the street. The air was cold and clear, and he trembled as he breathed it in.

"Michael? We've got a problem. Amongst all the other problems."

[One that requires me to finish my conversation with the cardinals?]

"Yeah, I reckon it does. For now, anyway. Just before Sonja shot herself, she told me she'd been following CIA orders all year: either she make me her pet, or they'd kill me."

[That is a premise based on the supposition that CIA agents could realistically assassinate you. Did Sonja believe such an action was likely to succeed?]

"It doesn't matter if she thought it likely or not. She was too scared to take the risk. So she bought into the whole package."

[And she is now dead. Which means it is entirely possible the CIA cell is mobilizing to carry out their threat.]

"Or we've got incoming missiles, like before." He turned the corner, starting up Cleveland Street toward Regent's Park. "But unless they're going to nuke the whole of the Freezone, they can't guarantee they'll hit me. I don't think they'll do that."

[I will start searching for them at once.]

"That won't work. They operate differently now you've appeared: no electronic comms until the very last minute, and they've been living off the grid—what grid we have here, anyway."

[You are suggesting a different course?]

"Sonja pointed out how rubbish we were at finding the last lot of agents, even with you, even when there should have been plenty of traffic for us to find. We'll just waste time and get it wrong. So what is it that we want?"

[To be left in peace. To explore, to build, to dream.]

"*Huy,* yes. So how are we going to persuade the Americans to do that? What is it that we can do that will make them believe it's in their own best interests to leave us alone?"

Petrovitch was halfway up Cleveland Street, and almost level with the barricade he'd demolished. The fire had died out, but the wreckage remained, smoldering and hot. The guards had deserted their post, but he was gratified to see the red flags had stayed at the far end of the road.

[Any proactive sanctions we take against the United States of America will have unpredictable consequences.]

"You think?" He was being sarcastic, but Michael wasn't.

[Yes. You have been neglecting your news feeds,] said Michael, and a rectangle opened up at the side of his vision.

There was a station ident in the corner of the virtual screen—CNN—and a tag in another proclaiming it was a live feed. A man with a dark-blue nylon jacket and a forehead so bulbous that studio lights would glare off it like a mirror was clutching his mic and virtually swallowing it to make himself heard. In the background, and some-where between him and the camera, were thousands of protestors, chanting, shouting, blowing whistles and wav-ing placards.

There was clearly more to it than just a noisy rally—because a public demonstration of the sort Petrovitch was watching hadn't happened in any part of the USA for two decades.

The screen jumped. No longer viewed from ground level, with images of a distant white stone facade in the neo-classical style, but from the air. What had looked like thousands now became tens of thousands, enveloping a whole city block and beyond, packed into the park in front of the largest building and spilling out into the surround-ing streets.

The early morning sun hung low over the distant tow-ers of an office district: that meant some, if not most, of the protestors had been there all night. And still the reporter was trying to get his message across.

The news ticker refreshed itself, and scrolled "Califor-nia Supreme Court siege."

"You have got to be *yebani* kidding me." Petrovitch realized he'd stopped short of the junction, and his hastily organized militia were wondering why. "Dalton."

[It appears that one Paul Dalton, attorney-at-law in New York state, has . . .]

"I know what he's done. I know. We talked about it. He was going to . . ."

[Present a writ of habeas corpus on behalf of Doctor Epiphany Ekanobi to the California Supreme Court. It appears such an action is unpopular with the local citizenry.]

"Where the *huy* are the police? The Yanks don't allow this sort of thing to happen. Not now." Petrovitch watched the aerial images as they zoomed and panned across the crowd, which went right up to the steps of the court itself. Fists raised, painted cardboard banners waved, bottles and sticks rattled off the first-floor windows. He was incredulous. "*Hooy na ny!*"

"Sam? Sam!" Madeleine ran toward him, closing the distance with her long-legged strides.

He looked through the pictures from half a world away to Madeleine, standing right in front of him. "Hey."

"What happened? Where's Sonja. Why are you just standing there?"

He blinked CNN away. "We need to call a press conference."

"A what?" She grabbed his shoulders and inspected him for wounds. "What are you on about?"

"A press conference. Ten minutes. At Container Zero." He grabbed a list of accredited journalists in the Freezone and flashed them the message. "If they're going to kill me, they're going to have to do it in public."

She spun him around and checked his back and his skull. "You're not hurt—anymore than you were before. So please make some sense."

"Okay, okay. I will explain, but if you thought it was *pizdets* before, it's worse now. We don't have time to hang around." He faced her and put his hand behind her neck. When their foreheads were touching, he told her. "The CIA told Sonja they'd take me down if she didn't do something about me first. Now she's killed herself. And they're rioting in America."

"I don't understand. She...she did what?"

"This, everything that's happened: Sonja was trying to save me. And now she's dead, I guess the CIA really are coming for me. And Dalton went to California to try and get Pif out: a crowd of around twenty thousand Reconstructionists are attacking the courthouse." His fingers lightly gripped the rope of her hair and his hand ran the length of it from tip to tail. "We're not going to lose."

"How can you say that?"

"Because in a moment, I'll tell the world what Sonja told me. Better still, I'll show them. What's the point of having eyes that work like cameras if I don't record the important events?"

"Oh God. You've got it all saved. Even, even that."

"Yeah. Even that." He let go of her. "Come on. We need to get ready."

"But what about all these armed people we've just turned out onto the street?"

He thought furiously for a moment. "I'll appoint one in ten to collect the guns back in and return them to the trucks. They can guard them, and any other ones the Oshicora security teams turn in. I'll give everyone the headlines and, _chyort:_ running a city would be so much easier if foreign agents weren't trying to kill me."

Petrovitch composed a short message and pushed it out first to the Freezone, then to the newswires. Already, there were steadicams and portable satellite dishes wending their way into Regent's Park. Red flags flapped overhead, and there seemed to be people everywhere, moving in front and behind and all around, happy they'd not have to fight.

Tabletop took Petrovitch down in a flying tackle that came from nowhere, and she lay on top of him, spreading herself out like a starfish over his flattened form. "Stay still."

Madeleine's gun was in her hand, and Valentina's AK panned the crowd, then the windows and rooftops overlooking the road. Lucy planted her red flag in the road and held it out to cover him. A single shot echoed across the open space, and a hole pocked the flag, passing under Lucy's outstretched arm. The tarmac sparked in front of Petrovitch's head, and Tabletop immediately picked him up and laid him down again so she could curl around his back. A man in overalls dropped with a cry, clutching at a stain on his leg.

The ripple of awareness flowed outward. Madeleine shouted. "Shooter. Everyone down." Some in earshot started to duck, while others were left standing, briefly.

"Michael?"

[One moment.]

Lucy looked down at the hole. She shut her eyes tight, but didn't move.

[Park Crescent. Fourteen. Second floor, third window from the right. Encrypted digital transmissions of the same type as used in Tabletop's stealth suit.]

Petrovitch couldn't move. "Let me up, I know where they are."

"No, you tell us. We'll deal with it." She tightened her hold, and he knew he wasn't going anywhere without her permission.

"You've got it on your wrist."

She let go, glanced down at her forearm and pointed. "Three up, three right. Building on the left. Suppressing fire."

Not all the guns had been handed back, and from the noise, it sounded like none of them had. The entire frontage of the terrace smoked with pulverized stone and every window pane shattered.

[Target is moving. Staircase down. Going to the back of the building.]

"Send it to Tabletop." Already she and Valentina were running, waving their troops on. It looked wild and unco-ordinated, but he couldn't see it for himself. Madeleine's hand had closed around his backbrace and she carried him like a piece of luggage, his legs bouncing and skid-ding on the road, to find cover behind one of the trucks parked at the entrance.

She dumped him down, and glanced back out. The door to number fourteen was being kicked in, with scores more people branching off down side streets to cut off the agent's escape.

Lucy wandered past in a daze, still carrying her flag, and Madeleine eased her down next to Petrovitch.

"Thanks," he said to her. "I wish you'd decide whether you're a hero or not. I'm getting gray hair."

Lucy laughed, then sobbed. "I don't know. I just do stu-pid stuff sometimes."

"It worked this time. If you didn't save my life, you saved Tabletop's."

"Why are they doing this?"

"Because they're scared of us."

More gunfire sounded across the rooftops, sustained bursts that cackled and rattled in waves as the wind blew the sound.

[They have the target surrounded.]

"Now I'm thinking clearly: tell them to try and get him to surrender. Rights under the Geneva Convention, repa-triation, all that. Assuming it's a him, don't know why."

[And if he will not comply?]

"I want it on record that we offered. If he won't go for

it, see if you can hack his suit: it carries enough injectable painkillers to render him insensible."

[He is using a burst transmitter. It is non-trivial to hold the signal long enough to negotiate with the suit's hosting protocol.]

"A miracle would be really useful."

The shooting stuttered to a halt.

"Safe to move?" asked Madeleine.

"I don't know." His arm was aching, bleeding pain through the blocks he'd put into place. When he inspected it, he found that his superstructure was bent. The fragments of bone had shifted. *"Chyort voz'mi."*

"What's the matter?"

"Forget it. We need to get these journos inside the park." He clawed his way upright. "Give them a couple of minutes to set up, dial their satellites if they need them, then just push me in front of them. Come on, Lucy."

[We have an unconscious CIA agent in custody.]

"Yobany stos, we've done something right at last." He put his good arm around Lucy's shoulders and together they rode the tide of people toward Container Zero. Madeleine stayed very close behind them, gun drawn, trying to make certain no one else was going to pop up and have a go.

Petrovitch called Tabletop. "Strip the suit off him: I want him and it separated by the largest distance possible."

"Then what do we do?"

"Make sure he stays alive. That would be brilliant." He had a feral grin on his face that was obvious to everyone around him.

"You never look that happy," said Lucy.

"The guy who nearly shot us is our prisoner. If he doesn't want his perfect teeth and genetically enhanced face on every screen on the planet, then he's going to have to hope Mackensie'll call his dogs off."

They were at Container Zero, and there were still ugly black bloodstains on the ground around its open doors. Those news teams who'd brought lights quickly extended them on their poles and clicked them on, and there was some jostling at the back as those coming late tried to push for a clear sightline.

"Look at them. It's like a classroom." Lucy slipped out from under Petrovitch's arm and failed to notice that he nearly fell. His hand grasped for something solid, and Madeleine caught him.

"You can't go on like this," she said in his ear.

"I don't have a choice. Not anymore. I put myself here, and now I have to see it through."

"You can barely stand, Sam."

"Then hold me up." He scanned the people lining up in front of him, watching them more or less comply to Lucy's rearranging of them: those closest were going to have to sit down in the dirt, those behind to kneel, then the third and fourth rows come to some arrangement whereby they looked over each other's shoulders.

He couldn't see Surur or her technician anywhere. He thought it odd, then realized that they'd still be stuck at Park Lane, Michael's cable tethering them down, scared to move in case they broke his connection with the outside world.

It wasn't needed now, hadn't been needed since the AI had uploaded itself onto another computer, but he'd forgotten to tell Surur that. He hadn't mentioned the details of Michael's escape at all, content to let the question hang unanswered in the air.

He looked for the reporter's phone, and found it. She didn't pick up so he tried the one a bare meter away. The cameraman didn't reply. So he went for the satellite link, riding down the microwave signal which he shared with the increasingly frantic attempts of her studio manager to speak to her, to him, to anyone.

The camera was still recording, still transferring its footage to the van. It showed a sideways world, lying on the road. The lens was focused on a drift of purple that could, at a squint, be resolved into the body of a woman with glossy hair and flawless skin.

31

*M*ichael could multi-task. Petrovitch found it very difficult. He wanted to capture the last half-hour's output from
the Al Jazeera camera, then review it, all the while trying
to speak to the assembled press.

He started off incoherent, then lost track of what he
was saying and stopped mid-sentence when something of
awful significance happened onscreen.

Madeleine held up her hand to the crowd, and dragged
Petrovitch around to face her. "You're doing it wrong."

"Something terrible is happening," he said. "There.
That's when it was. Five of them. Same time as the shooter.
Coordinated attack. Distracted us. They're going after
Michael."

"Sam. You called this press conference. You're the
public face of the Freezone. Either you can do this properly, or I'll pull the plug."

She didn't know what he knew. She thought he was
flaking out.

"Okay." He took a deep breath. One thing at a time
from now on, he promised himself, and turned to face the

world. "This will only take a minute, and my daughter will have to stand in for me for questions if you really want to hang around afterward—but I don't think you will."

Lucy, standing with the press, blinked and her mouth opened to object. Petrovitch pointed at her and then placed his finger against his lips. "No interruptions. I've uploaded files to the major newswires, and you can grab them from there. One is Sonja Oshicora's confession that ten months ago, she was strong-armed into cooperating with the CIA to neutralize me. The events of the last two days have been the outworking of that plot, which has failed with the suicide of Sonja. The second is of footage taken fifteen minutes ago by Al Jazeera's cameraman, when both he and Yasmina Surur were killed by CIA agents intending to destroy the AI called Michael, and I suspect they're carrying a nuclear demolition charge."

All he could hear was the faint whirr of a motorized focus. Every sudden intake of breath was held, every heart skipped a beat. No one moved, not even to tremble.

"Michael is no longer in the vault under the Oshicora Tower—I made damn sure of that—and I'm appealing personally to President Mackensie to call off this futile attack before it goes any further. People are going to die and it'll be for nothing."

He paused. The turbine in his chest was spinning fast and his blood ran hot. He could feel the rage surge inside him.

"How dare they? How dare they come here, to the Metrozone, with a weapon like that. This is my city, my home, and I will not have it fucked up by a bunch of fuck-witted paranoid Reconstructionists acting like they're in a fucking Western. The old order has failed. The new order is here. Long live the revolution." He pulled his gun clear and ran as best he could through the middle of the press pack. "Lucy? You're on. Madeleine? With me."

He stumbled clear, and started issuing his orders. "Tabletop. Were you listening?"

"We're already on our way."

"Go straight to the tower. I don't know if they've made it that far yet, so we might be able to trap them in the river. Take as many people as are willing to go with you, and please be careful. This is the end game, and they're choosing to go out with a bang. I'll send you my maps. Spread out along the line of the culvert, watch the manhole covers but don't open any of them. Me and Madeleine are going to Park Lane: I'll take the car."

He limped as he went, his arm weighing him down, still festooned with three singularity bombs. He was much slower than Madeleine, who caught him up quickly.

"You have to get away," she said.

"My Freezone, my responsibility."

There was Valentina's car. He reached out and started it up remotely, backing it around in a circle until it was pointing the right way along Euston Road. The wheels screeched, and he jumped in the driver's seat. Madeleine launched herself in the back.

He didn't touch the steering wheel, just plotted in a course and let the automatics take care of it.

"I can drive, you know," said Madeleine. She folded the other half of the seat down so she could access the trunk. "I should have impounded her personal armory along with the rest."

"Yeah. Tool up. We can't afford to screw around."

"Why can't we just let them blow themselves up?" Her voice was muffled as she searched for heavy caliber weapons. "If it's a nuke, it's a small nuke. They're setting it off underground."

"I'm going to stop them because they shouldn't be allowed to get away with it. I don't need another reason. Bomb, no bomb. It doesn't matter. They're wrong. I'm right." Petrovitch braced himself as the car hurtled around a corner. "Doing nothing is unforgivable."

They were almost there, barreling down Park Lane toward the Wellington Arch. He looked in the rearview mirror: Madeleine had found an assault shotgun and enough shells to fill it. She caught his glance.

"This is it, then."

"Yeah. Looks that way. *Yebani v'rot.*" He banged his hand against the window, the door, his seat, the dashboard. "Why can't the Yanks be smart like I am? Why can't they work out that Michael's gone?"

She slotted the last plastic shell into place and cranked one into the breach. "Even if one or all of those agents are having second thoughts about a suicide mission, they're trained to follow orders. All the way to the end."

The car screeched to a halt, delivering them next to the broadcast van. The body of Surur was behind the vehicle, a couple of meters shy of the back bumper. She'd been shot repeatedly, and was lying in a lake of congealed blood. The cameraman, still with his rig strapped to his body, was pole-axed near the side door.

There were holes in the van's white bodywork—fortunate that they hadn't hit anything vital in the cramped electronic interior, so that the prone camera had picked up five dark forms sweeping by, one carrying a green canvas bag that was obviously both far too heavy and too cylindrical for regular ordinance.

And there was the cable, lying on the ground, its plug torn off and disposed of.

Petrovitch scrambled out of the car and headed for the ramp down to the car park. "Michael? Anything?"

[If they are underground, the depth is sufficient to block signals. If they are above ground, they are maintaining radio silence.]

"Oh, they're down there all right. And even if Mackensie wanted to order them back, he can't."

[Sasha. Please reconsider. The Americans will die by their own hand, destroying a redundant piece of equipment. Is not the best option simply to let them do this?]

"Of course it is. But there's such a thing as justice, and I'm going to deliver it to them like an avenging angel." The overhang of the concrete roof was above him. "See you on the other side, Michael. The Pope might have doubts about you, but I don't." He switched links, briefly. "Tabletop. Collapse the tunnel east of the tower. I have a sort of plan."

He ran on, and he felt his feed fail. Madeleine overtook him, and slipped on a pair of night-vision goggles she'd found. "I'm going first."

"Why's that?"

"Because I can just shove you out of the way and there's nothing you can do about it." She jogged ahead of him, scanning the shadows, gun butt pressed hard against her shoulder.

The plastic sheeting in front of the tunnel entrance flapped, and sent the pair of them sliding apart, left and right, slowly converging on the scaffolding it covered.

Madeleine eased a piece aside with the barrel of the shotgun.

"Clear," she said, and climbed inside. Petrovitch followed in a poor second place: she was already lying down in the tunnel, moving forward on her elbows. He watched her feet recede, then scooted down the shallow slope on his backside. And when he arrived, his feet splashing into the river, she was ahead, stalking forward.

He wasn't going to be left behind, even though he was reeling from one side of the tunnel to the other. He was going to keep up even if it killed him.

As they advanced down the coal-black tunnel, made barely visible by their hardware, a distant booming noise rattled the brickwork, and a pop of air brushed by them.

Madeleine looked behind her at Petrovitch. He gave her the thumbs-up and pointed ahead. She trod silently on, her long legs allowing her to step on either side of the river.

Then she stopped, keeping perfectly still. Petrovitch slowly lowered himself to a crouch. There was a slight bend in the river, and around it were the first glimmerings of a heat glow.

Her shotgun already had a chambered shell. She already had it up at her shoulder and aimed. All she had to do was lean into the recoil and twitch the trigger.

The sound of the shot was brutally loud in such a confined space, and the figure ahead was just turning away from the sound of Valentina's tunnel demolition when the solid slug tore through the layer of ballistic mesh and into the flesh and bone beneath.

As the thunder rolled away, the body fell back with a splash. Madeleine listened carefully, and shuffled forward, balancing on the balls of her feet. When she reached the agent, she leaned down and felt for signs of life. There were none, and Petrovitch crept up beside her.

He knew there was some sort of secret Vatican sign language for times like this, but he didn't know any of it. Instead, he held up a finger, four fingers, made a zero with his index finger and thumb, then pointed down the tunnel. He meant one hundred and forty meters to the vault. She nodded to show she understood, but he had no idea if he'd actually given the correct message.

The tunnel was relatively straight, but there was no sign of another heat source. Valentina could have fortuitously dropped the tunnel roof on someone, or isolated them on the other side of the rock fall. The niche in the wall that held the ladder up to the surface seemed blank.

Assuming five agents to start with, they'd killed one, and neutralized another. One would be left in the short tunnel to the under-tower shaft—to help lower that heavy bomb down—and two to enter the vault and set the bomb.

He wondered what they were waiting for. They had to have the bomb in place by now, and every second that passed was a second less on the countdown. He'd had enough of creeping along: he stood up straight, and started shambling toward the gaping cold hole in the brick, making no pretense at stealth.

He pressed his back against the crumbling wall and patted his pockets. Nothing there. He'd used the stun grenades already, and he didn't think Madeleine had any left either. He'd have to improvise.

"Hey, Yankee," he called, and flinched as a hail of bullets hammered the far side of the tunnel. The soft brick absorbed the impacts, cracking and spalling. The air filled with dust, but save for a few larger fragments of baked clay, he wasn't struck. The firing stopped, the muzzle flashes flickering away like lightning.

Madeleine came up next to him. He couldn't see her eyes, hidden behind the green lenses of her night sights, but he could tell she was appalled at his recklessness. He grinned in the dark.

"Hey," he started, and held up his good hand to his face to protect it from yet more shrapnel. "*Yobany stos,* will you stop that?" He waited for a pause, and tucked his gun in his waistband again.

"What are you doing?" Madeleine hissed.

"Making it up as I go along." He unhooked a sphere from his arm, and primed it. The little green light winked on. "You seen what my singularity bombs do yet? I have. I've seen what they can do to a car. I'm just wondering how much of you there's going to be left to ship back home. I've some airmail envelopes around somewhere. Should be big enough."

Madeleine had ducked down and hidden beneath the lip of the hole, swapping the shotgun for her Vatican special. Petrovitch threw the singularity device through the hole, against the side of the tunnel wall. It bounced out of sight, and started to roll downhill.

There was another storm of noise and light, but this time the bullets weren't directed out at them. They were aimed at the trundling sphere, picking up speed as it rattled and clattered toward the shaft, a spinning green light marking its passage.

Madeleine pushed the pistol above her head and emptied the entire magazine blind, pointing it at all angles into the space beyond.

The air tasted of spent powder and dirt as the final shell case fell with a clink.

"Yes or no?" asked Petrovitch.

Madeleine swapped her empty magazine for a full one. "I'll find out." She dislodged a loose brick from the top of the ragged wall and let it fall at her feet. She retrieved it, and lobbed it inside. No returning fire.

"Yeah, we haven't got time for this." He pulled his automatic and backed up to the far side of the river culvert, edging up the curve of the wall until he could see down the length of the tunnel all the way to the shaft.

There was a splash of color at the far end, all hot whites and yellows. It showed what looked like a leg, maybe a hand reaching out for the bright-painted stick that could only be a rifle. Petrovitch drew crosshairs on the main mass and fired three times.

Madeleine leaped up and over the wall. The mortally injured man was bundled out, suspended for a moment across the top of the brickwork before toppling into the river.

Petrovitch splashed toward him, then along and over him, using his shoulders and head for purchase to gain enough height. Madeleine reached over and pulled him in.

"You know this is just madness, don't you?" she told him as he crashed to the floor.

"We're trying to prevent a bunch of fanatics armed with an atomic bomb from putting a glowing crater in the Freezone. Compared with what we've already been through, this counts as sane." He held his good hand up. "Shall we do it, then? Take revenge for all the ones the Armageddonists got through?"

Her fingers tightened around his wrist and he was

dragged upright. "That's what everyone wants, isn't it? In their nuclear dreams, they get to stop them, just once."

She pushed her night-vision goggles up her forehead long enough to kiss him hard on the lips. Then she pushed him behind her, and knelt down to crawl toward the sharp-edged void of the shaft.

32

The singularity bomb was shattered: the resin that had held the warp and weft of the wire had been reduced to a few large fragments with the rest of it turned to pea-sized grit. That meant he had two left, then. Petrovitch and Madeleine sat on opposite sides of the end of the tunnel and looked out over the shaft.

Madeleine checked the rope, which had been tied around the base of the last tunnel support.

"I still don't get what's keeping them." Petrovitch curled his fingers around the haft of a shovel and felt its reassuring, primitive weight. "If it had been me, I'd have blown it by now. There has to be a good reason."

"And you want to exploit it."

"We're not dead yet." He peered over the edge; no mines or tripwires that he could see. He glanced upward again, at the great mass of debris hanging high above their heads.

"If I lower you down, both of us are vulnerable at that point. If they're watching the shaft..." Madeleine studied the vault doors. The stone that had kept them ajar had been kicked aside, and it rested almost shut on the thickness of a fiber-optic cable.

"I need to get down there," he insisted.

"You really think you're going to talk them out of this?"

"I think I should try. It's not over till the Fat Boy sings."

"Sam, I want you to listen to me." She dragged his face around. "They're not going to be dissuaded. They're not just soldiers, they're martyrs. I understand this sort of thing. They're not going to recant; they believe in what they're doing."

"I don't."

"You can't stop them. We can't storm the vault, and they won't come out. They're in there and, whatever it is they're waiting for, anything you say is more likely to make them detonate early, not less." She took the shovel from him and put it to one side. She clasped his now-empty hand in both of her own. "I want a future with you. I don't know where it's going to be or what it is we're going to be doing, but I want it with you. That's never going to happen if we stay here."

"Ireland," he mumbled. "We're supposed to be going to Ireland, set up a Freezone on a long contract. We're citizens—diplomats, even. It's all arranged, everything. Michael is there already; the Irish government in exile have installed a quantum computer in the Cork mission station. That's what we were going to do."

"Then why are we sitting in a cold dark tunnel under the center of what used to be London, trying to protect something that is no longer of any importance, trying to persuade some zealots not to blow themselves up?"

"Because I have to. Because I've lived my whole life in fear of the Armageddonists. I've done some really shitty things to all kinds of people—good, bad, mad—because I've been so very afraid, and I have to show that I can choose to do the right thing, just once. If I stop them, I get to cancel out all the crap I've dealt out over the years." He chewed at his lip. "But mostly because I hate them and what they've done to me."

"The question is, do you hate them more than you love me?" She pressed his hand tighter. "While there was still a chance, then of course we had to try and prevent this, this outrage. We did our very best. We couldn't have done more. We have all been, at times, utterly magnificent. And it still wasn't enough. They've chosen their path: it's time for us to choose ours. While we still can."

Petrovitch rested the back of his head against the tunnel wall and groaned long and loud. "Every time. Every time I play their *yebani* game, they win."

"Then stop playing. Only an idiot keeps gambling against someone with loaded dice, and you're not an idiot. Recognize this for what it is: a stitch-up from start to finish. I'm more than willing to die down here with you, but I'd like to be able to look St. Peter in the eye and not have him think me weapons-grade stupid for throwing my life away in such an heroically pointless manner." She fixed him with her electronically enhanced stare for a moment, before looking at the ground between their legs. "How about it, Sam?"

"I can't argue with that," he said. "Everything you say makes perfect sense."

"But we're still going to go out like Butch and the Kid, right?"

"No. No we're not." He freed his hand and raised her chin. "You're absolutely right. Fuck them and the horse they rode in on. Plan B."

"Do we have one?"

"We do now. The vault needs to be properly shut." He reached for the shovel and presented it to her. "You're the only one who can do this in time, however much time it is we have left."

She snatched at the shovel and threw it through the hole, where it clanged hollowly against the rubble at the bottom of the shaft. She wrapped her waist with the rope, and positioned herself on the lip of the drop.

"Watch my back," she said, and started down.

Petrovitch dragged his pistol out and dared the door to open any further than the crack it already was. Madeleine reached the bottom, stooped briefly to pick up the shovel and ran to the vault.

The tiny green light glowed in all its lonely glory.

She knelt down and hooked the cable in one hand, and with the other, slipped the blade of the shovel in the gap. She leaned in on the handle, and the perfectly balanced door moved in sympathy.

Someone was waiting, but they wasted their first fusillade into the back of the heavy steel blast door. Sparks illuminated the shaft and Madeleine's crouched form: she turned her face away from the sudden brightness and the angry whine of deflected bullets.

A second later, she brought the shovel down on the cable, cutting it neatly in two. She took the end that led to the computer and gave it a sharp tug. The firing started again, and she pressed herself against the concrete wall.

It fell silent, and she looped the slack cable around the

shovel's handle, once, twice, tugged it tight, then threw the whole assembly through the door into the corridor beyond. The result was predictable, but Madeleine rolled across the floor and got her back to the door. She heaved, and the door swung shut, cutting off the crack of rifle fire the instant a seal was made.

The locks hummed, the bolts slid home, and the green light winked red.

"Tell me again why I'm doing this?" she called, panting.

"Because it's a bomb-proof bunker," shouted back Petrovitch. "Now get back up here."

She ran back and took hold of the rope. "You can't possibly be serious."

"Yeah. If we can't stop the explosion, we might be able to stop the fireball breaching the surface."

She pulled hand over hand, and the rope creaked in protest.

"Come on, come on!"

A hand reached over the lip of the hole, and gripped the jagged edge. Sharp stone and iron cut into her palm, but she used the hold all the same. She put her other hand over and flailed for something to hang on to. Petrovitch caught her wrist and jammed his feet against the soft rock, pulling hard.

He felt himself sliding, and her with him. The soles of his boots banged against the outside of the shaft, and he locked his knees. She was still slipping, and he wasn't strong enough to hold her.

The bloodied hand that had inconstant contact with the concrete let go and lashed out. It found the metal ring around his left elbow, and her fingers tightened around it.

His arm straightened and stretched. His backbrace took her full weight, and he screwed his eyes tight shut against a moment of excruciating pain before he managed to block everything.

She got her shoulders through the gap, and let go of him, pushing back on the sides of the hole and heaving herself across the threshold as far as her waist. Impact gel oozed slick down her front.

Madeleine twisted onto her back and lifted her legs in. "Sorry."

Petrovitch started breathing again. "Get one of the bombs," he gasped. He was scared to move in case something had been wrenched off.

She reached down and unhooked one of the spheres. "What now?"

"Okay. Get the rope, tie a bucket to the rope, put the bomb in the bucket. Flick the switch on the top, press the button, and drop it down into the shaft. We'll have about fifteen to twenty seconds to get out of the tunnel."

She was already pulling the rope up. Petrovitch brought sensation back to his body, and didn't enjoy the feeling at all. "*Yebani v'rot.*" Something was irrevocably wrong in his arm. It felt dead, numb, like it was someone else's limb tacked on to his body.

"Get going," she said, crouched over her task. "I'll catch you up."

"I'm going as fast as I can." He used his good hand to hang on to a tunnel prop and shuffle himself to sitting, coiled his legs and pushed up the slope. It was neither quick, nor elegant.

The bomb clanged into the bucket. She armed the timer and swung the bucket out over the void.

"Is this going to work?"

"It's all we have." The closeness of his voice made her turn, the pale green light of her night-vision goggles seeping down her cheeks. "Do it."

She reached into the bucket, pressed the button, and let the rope slide through her hands, smearing the nylon cord with blood as it zipped by. Then she closed her fists to brake the bomb's fall. The bucket rattled, and she let it go again, this time forever.

"Go, Sam."

"I am." He growled in frustration at his lack of speed. She climbed over him, past him. He got a knee in the guts and her hand on the side of his head. She reached through his T-shirt to take hold of the metal rod running down his spine, and pulled him backward.

The clock in the corner of his eye clicked around to eleven, twelve—they were still in the tunnel, just reaching the brick wall between them and the stream. She picked him up and threw him out with a grunt that ended in a scream. She jumped, pivoted her hips and tumbled out into the water next to him.

Sixteen, seventeen, eighteen, and Petrovitch was starting to think that his bomb was a squib, and it wasn't going to go off, when up subtly changed direction. The river water swirled chaotically around him for a moment, and he lifted his head. Something vast and heavy was beginning to move.

"Surface," he said, but Madeleine was already on her feet. With room to maneuver, she put one arm under both of his and across his chest, lifting him clear and dragging him toward the ladder that led up to street level. The low moan of tortured steel rose suddenly to a shriek and there was a distinct snap as a beam failed. The roaring of falling rubble built from that first sound until the air itself was shaking.

The culvert, already weakened by successive impacts, started to collapse. Bricks popped from the roof and fell with a splash, to be joined moments later by their neighbors. Sheets of bricks were peeling away and choking the water.

Madeleine heaved Petrovitch into the alcove, then swarmed up the rusted ladder to the iron manhole cover far above her head, leaving him there as dust filled his lungs and the river swirled around him.

A crescent, a half-moon of light, then a full circle showing clouds and faces. Something hit the black water next to him: the discarded night-vision goggles, then it was her, splashing down beside him.

"Can you climb?"

"Even if it kills me." He hooked his good hand around the side of the ladder and she helped his foot onto the lowest rung.

Petrovitch swung his hand above his head, latched on, stepped up, and repeated the process, standing as close in to the ladder as he could so that he didn't fall too far outward every time he changed his grip.

The air around him was gray, and the noise like a full-throated bellow from a Jihad-constructed giant robot. His head rose above the pavement, half expecting to see some giant mechanical insect thrashing its way across the city.

Hands dipped down to seize him, haul him up, sit him down.

Valentina knelt in front of him. "Did you stop them?"

"No." He hawked up the dust from his lungs and spat it down on the flagstones. "We have to run."

Madeleine crawled out. Her head was cut, blood seeping down her scalp and around her ear. The rest of her face was caked in dark dust, as was her armor. Only her eyes were white. He realized that he would look just the same.

Valentina's only response to Petrovitch's answer was "How far?"

He didn't know for sure.

"Michael?"

[Welcome back.]

"Yeah, yeah. We screwed up. Assume you've got a one-kiloton demolition nuke in your vault and I've just dropped the remains of the Oshicora Tower down the access shaft." He tried to get up, and inexplicably missed the ground. He was caught and held: Madeleine on one side, Tabletop on the other. "Any chance of containment?"

[There are complex, unknown variables...]

"I'm asking you to guess. And I need an estimate on damage and fallout concentration. I'd do it myself, but I'll be busy trying to stay alive."

They had no cars, no trucks, nothing. They had to do it by foot, or not at all.

[Head north or west. Complete structural failure of buildings not designed for earthquakes is likely up to five hundred meters from ground zero. Containment is possible—I assign a likelihood of fifty percent—but if the fireball reaches the surface, blast and thermal damage will result. Fallout will spread south and east over the Metrozone, promptly lethal and decreasing to below lethal after forty-eight hours.]

"*Chyort*. Tell the Metrozone. Sound the alarms." He was vaguely aware that he was in a stumbling, falling, dragging run, supported on either side. They were heading toward Berkeley Square. Boots clattered on the road, but no one spoke. Everyone was saving their breath for something more important.

Across the river, the ancient sirens started to wail, a tone that rose and fell, putting cold, hard fear into every heart.

It was almost half an hour since a tipped-over camera had recorded the fleeting images of men running past. Almost. Less than two minutes to go.

Of course: they'd armed the bomb outside, breaking open the code keys, verifying them with their commander-in-chief, setting the timer. Thirty minutes to be on the safe side, cope with the unexpected, place it as close as possible to the anathema that was Michael—and discovering that they could get into the same room as the quantum computer, realizing that they could have just put a magazine full of bullets through the machine but still had to contend with a clock that was counting down and was impossible to stop, a clock attached to a small nuclear bomb that was going to have to detonate, no matter what, when the counter reached zero.

It was inevitable.

He imagined them, sitting in the dark of the vault, just the scattered blue-green glow of chemical lights and each other for company. And that bastard bomb, electronic numbers flickering what remained of their lives away.

He was glad it was them, and not him, even though his own lungs burned like they were filled with acid, every muscle was made of agony, every step an effort too great, every moment a conscious torment. He was alive, and if he got far enough away from ground zero, he'd stay alive.

Not like them. Not like them at all.

33

They'd reached the far end of Berkeley Square—an oval of dead trees and brown grass—when Petrovitch felt the first signs. His eyes were momentarily filled with white noise, and the computer he was relying on to keep him going stuttered.

He fell, his sudden rigidity tearing him from the grasp of his bearers. As he went down, the shock front traveling through the ground brought it up to meet him. Hard. He was suddenly flying, and an enormous roaring filled his ears.

His vision cleared. He was on his back, facing the way he'd come, and a wave was rolling toward him, made of tarmac and concrete and soil. It lifted the road like it was the surface of the sea, and it lifted the buildings like they were ships catching the tide.

As they rose, they gave out shrieks and screams—but remained more or less intact. As the crest of the wave passed underneath, and the ground started to fall away again, cracks tore through the facades: roofs kept on rising while the masonry below separated out along great fissures that opened up. Glass snapped, brick broke along the ageing mortar, stone broke in two.

The wave hit Petrovitch, and he was airborne again. The building behind him at the head of the square leaned away from him, and then started to collapse in on itself.

A whole train of shocks chewed their way through the streets, and, partially obscured by the pall of pulverized city, a vast black dome of subsurface rock blossomed above the vault. Its skin was marked by flecks of road, of lamp-posts, of concrete and plastic panels and brightly colored carpet.

The great bulge threatened to burst, to spew its fireball out into the air and drag hot contaminated dust with it, where it would be caught by the wind and darken the sky even further. Orange fire glittered through the veil of debris, barely constrained.

It hung there, supported from inside by an incandescent cloud trying to pull free of the ground, perfectly balanced against the hauling back of gravity.

Then it started to sink: the fire held in it began to die, turning from fierce light to glowing ember. As it flattened, it spread, a fresh storm of rolling dust climbing over and around the falling buildings, punching out walls and windows.

By the time it reached Petrovitch, it was a gritty slap in the face, weak and growing weaker. The skyline around him was lost. The air became opaque. The noise of splitting and cracking and crumbling gradually lessened, and finally dropped to a level where shouting and coughing and retching could be heard.

He couldn't talk. His mouth, dry as the desert, seemed

to have set half-open. He could barely see: his eyeballs were scratched and pitted, and he'd run out of tears. He blinked, and it felt as if he was trying to dislodge boulders. His nose and ears were clogged, and his lungs spasmed at his efforts to breathe.

And he had no connection: not just no signal, but no sign of a signal.

There was a man to his left, one of Valentina's volunteers, who slowly rose up on his hands and knees. There was blood in his mouth, dribbling down the cake-white dust on his skin. His stare was wild and uncomprehending.

Petrovitch found enough spit to loosen his tongue. "*Pizdets.*" He looked up and around, peering through the haze. Shadows played as the air thickened and thinned on the wind.

"Sam? Sam!"

"Here," he managed to croak, before his throat tightened and he coughed hard enough to break ribs.

Madeleine stumbled toward him, and sat in a heap at his side. Any movement stirred more dust into the air. She put out her hand and rested it over his heart, just to feel the hum of the turbine beneath his skin.

There was blood in his phlegm, and he wiped his mouth with his sleeve. Still not dead, then. He circled his finger to encompass all of them, and pointed north. She nodded, and started to bring the others to him, to sit them down and get them to wait.

She found Valentina, whose dark hair had turned white and stiff, her tightly belted jacket hanging open, her blouse missing buttons, cuts to her stomach and her legs, her trousers ragged. Petrovitch put his arm around her shoulders, but she didn't react.

Madeleine found the other volunteers, with their breaks and lacerations and bruises and punctures. Her impact armor had protected her where mere skin and bone had failed.

She found Tabletop last of all, wandering in the fog, and took her arm and led her back to the rest of the group.

"They did it. They did it," mumbled Tabletop. She looked at Petrovitch. "They did it."

"Yeah. They did." He hawked up more slurry. "We need to get cleaned up. Everyone stay together. No one gets left behind."

He disentangled himself from Valentina, and used her shoulder to stand. His leg tried to fold under him, and he forced it to straighten. When he looked down, there was something sticking out of his calf. It was too big to be called a splinter—he'd been impaled by a pencil-width shard of wood that was going to cause more damage coming out than it had going in.

His left arm was still numb. He touched it with his right, pinched the skin roughly. Nothing. It seemed to be the least of his problems; at least it didn't hurt anymore.

He limped away, heading toward the gap between the shrouded mountains of masonry that should have been the road heading toward Oxford Street. The buildings on either side had shed their fronts and exposed their rooms. Chimneys had barged through roofs and fallen through floors.

The destruction gripped him with a cold, studied fury. They'd only just cleaned up after the Jihad and the Outies. The scars of the earlier missile strikes were isolated. This had ripped a crater in the historic center of the city, erasing landmark after landmark, spewing poison into the air he was being forced to breathe and contaminating the ground he walked on.

He slipped and slid on a drift of rubble, climbed to the top, stumbled down the far side. The heavy particles in the cloud surrounding him were falling like rain, and the sky began to brighten. The tops of broken buildings peered down at him, misaligned and jagged. There were cracks in the road, too, where water seeped out as springs and puddled in the gutters. Sewers had failed, bending the road surface down in some places, and in others leaving gaping holes that brimmed with darkness.

They navigated all the hazards in their path, even when post-explosion settling caused something close by to come crashing down. There'd always be a warning noise first, a tremor in the ground. Enough time to back off or run forward, out of the path of the slow tumble of bricks and timber, of stone and steel.

A signal: Petrovitch hooked himself up to the connection, and called for help. "Hey."

[Your capacity for survival surprises even me. How injured are you?]

"We're all pretty much hosed. Call it fifteen barely walking wounded. I don't know how hot we are—we could be dead already."

[There is a decontamination station being set up at the Marylebone entrance to the Oxford Street mall. Make your way there.]

"Tell me about the damage."

[From the relays we have lost, buildings have been either completely or partially demolished for a radius of seven hundred and fifty meters from the origin. Some inside have survived, some outside have not. No significant damage has occurred beyond one thousand two hundred meters. Buckingham Palace is in ruins, the Westminster embankment is breached, and the old Parliament is flooding. The temporary bridge at Lambeth has been destroyed.]

"Ah, *chyort*. And we were doing so well."

The mall, so carefully reglazed after the devastation wreaked on it by the Paradise militia, was a sea of bright crystal under a span of naked girders. The empty spaces behind the blank shop fronts were a jumble of fallen ceiling tiles and swaying light fittings.

[You should know that you are currently presumed dead. The EU has summarily revoked all visas to U.S. passport holders, all diplomatic staff are being expelled, and all U.S. assets are frozen. The Union government will be in emergency session from eighteen hundred hours. What is to be your response?]

"My response, or the Freezone's response?"

[Are they not the same?]

"Yeah. They'll get it soon enough." The exit to Marylebone Lane was just ahead and, as promised, a large white tent had been set up just beyond the doors. Vans emblazoned with red crosses were parked behind, and figures in white suits and respirators were waiting for them.

Petrovitch wasn't looking forward to this. He stepped up first, partly because it was his job to lead, but mostly because he just wanted to get it over with.

The decontamination team was working two streams: while he was screened with radiation detectors, Tabletop was pushed shivering into the other lane. The counters clicked lazily as they were turned on, then when held close to his body, started to chatter and buzz.

One of the medics ripped the seal on a sterilized packet of surgical scissors. "Sorry, Doctor Petrovitch," he said, and started to cut his way through Petrovitch's clothing from neck to groin. He repeated the action on the back, then started on each leg.

His exoskeleton needed to come off, too and, fortunately, someone had a tool kit with the right-sized wrench. The batteries strapped to his body were snipped free: the tape that held them in place was ripped off, leaving red weals across his chalk-white skin. They tried to take his computer from him, too, but that was a non-negotiable. It went inside a plastic bag, knotted around the cable, and he held tightly on to it.

Naked now, apart from his boots. The laces were cut, and he stepped out of them, then each sock in turn. While his clothes were bagged up in bright yellow polythene, he was screened again.

The radiation was lower this time, but there was something in his right eye, an embedded particle of a short-lived radionuclide.

"It'll have to come out, I'm afraid."

"Yeah. Figured." He kept on looking dead ahead, but in the corner of his vision, Tabletop was being treated in the same gentle but thorough manner. Scissors hadn't been able to cut her stealth suit, so she'd had to climb out of it. She was as exposed as he was, and it only ever felt wretched and frightening.

The medic opened up some sterile forceps, and slid the ends around Petrovitch's eyeball. He tightened his grip, twisted through a right angle, and the device disengaged with a click.

It went in the bag with his clothes.

He was checked again. No more hot spots. He was ushered forward and into the tent, and the next man in line replaced him.

His wounds were dressed. The stick in his leg was cut out and checked for radiation, then the torn skin was sewn shut and covered with a waterproof bandage. The holes in his broken arm were more of a problem.

"Just leave it," said Petrovitch. "I'm going to lose it anyway."

The shower was neither hot nor cold, but the water was at least plentiful. He couldn't wash himself, and had to submit to the ministrations of another. Across the tent from him, behind a screen and under another shower unit, Tabletop scrubbed herself down.

He gargled and spat. Repeatedly. He blew his nose and had it irrigated with dilute peroxide. His ears were reamed. The sponges went into another yellow bag, but the water just drained away.

They screened him again, passed him as being good enough, and moved him up the line. The next anonymous medic took his blood—more than Petrovitch thought strictly necessary—and neatly labeled the filled phials by hand.

He was issued with a white coverall, hospital slippers, and a red blanket. The last in line held up the tent flap for him, and he shuffled into the daylight.

A man in green scrubs was sitting in the back of one of the vans. He had an electric boiler running. He lifted a mug up and waggled it.

"Cup of tea, sir?"

If Petrovitch had had any tears left, he would have cried.

"Coffee? Tell me you have coffee."

"Certainly, sir."

It came freeze-dried out of a packet, and he had two in the same mug. It was hot, and strong, and tasted like angels dancing in his mouth. He sat on the back step of the van and was joined by Tabletop, who was soon nursing her own drink.

"They did it," she said.

"I know. I did what I could. It was almost enough." He sipped more of the scalding brew. "It could have been a lot worse."

"How?" She squeezed water from her hair and let it dribble on the ground.

"We didn't lose anyone. Sure, we have a *yebani* great crater and kilometer of crap radiating from it. We can just shovel the dirt back in and pat it down, but we can't replace people. And look, they missed. They missed Michael, and they missed me. Everything they wanted to achieve, they didn't."

"They used a nuke, Sam."

"Yeah. Finally, they've made a mistake. Your lot." And he shrugged. "Okay, not your lot anymore. They're good. A couple of times, we've had luck on our side, but this is the first time they've really screwed up. We had cameras at ground zero. We've got video of two reporters being shot, and if there's one thing even the most partisan journo hates, it's someone deliberately killing another journo. We've got global sympathy."

"I don't want sympathy," she said baldly. "I want revenge."

"Oh, we'll get it all right. But it might not look how you

want it to." He glanced across at her with his one eye. "You prepared for that?"

Unperturbed by his empty socket, she looked back. "What are you going to do?"

He scratched at his nose and smiled slyly. "Something...wonderful."

34

$\mathcal{A}$ phone rang. It was an ancient phone still attached to a copper wire, and no matter the degree of sophistication that was plugged into the back of it, the phone itself hadn't been changed for thirty years.

It had been originally installed to prevent wars. That was its sole purpose and, so far as the potential combatants were concerned, it had worked. Until now.

A man—a junior functionary whose job description was to make sure important people had everything they needed—was alone in the room when the phone rang. He had a brief moment of panic, and he shouted for help, before recovering enough to pick the receiver up and hold it to his ear.

"Hello?"

"Yeah, you're not President Mackensie."

"No sir. My name's Armstrong. Joe Armstrong."

"Well, Armstrongjoearmstrong, I'm Samuil Petrovitch, and your boss has just nuked my city. To say I'm just a little cross about that would be an understatement, but I'm kind of assuming that your president couldn't give a fuck about that. Unfortunately for him, I've made it my job to make him care. So, Joe—you're a pretty straight-up sort of guy, yeah? I can trust you to pass on a message. Can you do that for me, Joe?"

"Yes." Armstrong was having trouble breathing. "I can do that."

"The message is this: I want to talk to Mackensie, and I won't go away until I do."

Petrovitch heard the handset being placed on the table. He had no doubt that it was a solid slab of antique wood, highly polished and clutter-free.

It was quiet for a few moments, then he could hear voices approaching. Armstrong was one, and there were others. They seemed anxious.

The phone was picked up again, and an older voice spoke. It was one that was used to both issuing and obeying orders.

"This is Admiral Malcolm Arendt of the United States Navy. Who is this, and how did you access this system?"

"Didn't Joe say? I had such high hopes for him, too. Or is the problem with you, Admiral? Maybe Joe did say, and you didn't believe him because you thought my atoms were floating around in the atmosphere somewhere over France."

A hand muffled the mouthpiece, and the admiral called out to the rest of his audience. "It's Petrovitch."

"That's what I've been telling you. Now, you're not Mackensie either. They're all in the Situation Room, right? You can patch this call through—I'd do it myself, but why should I do all the work?"

"President Mackensie does not talk to terrorists."

"Can I remind you who just toppled Nelson's Column?

It's lying there across Trafalgar Square, and Nelson's head has come off. That picture is currently running on every news network on the planet. Even your own. If I can stomach talking to Mackensie, he can have the grace to sit his scrawny arse down and talk to me."

"President Mackensie does not talk to terrorists. I do not talk to terrorists. No one in this administration talks to terrorists."

"Fine. You don't want to know how your country dies. I can understand that."

"I...what?"

"Not only did you not get me, you didn't get Michael," said Petrovitch.

"Michael?"

"The AI. It has a name: Michael. That's who you've been trying to kill; the same Michael that the Vatican are about to declare to be alive. Not that you care about that any more than you did when you thought it was just a machine. Sorry, I've distracted myself. Me and Michael: between us, we've decided that you're just too dangerous to have around anymore, and the world would be a better place without a bunch of nuclear-armed fundamentalist xenophobic psychopaths. Sorry it had to turn out this way, but hey."

"You're threatening to destroy the United States of America. You and whose army?"

"Yeah. The last time someone said that to me, I surprised them by turning up with, you know, a whole army. Prepare for the New Machine Jihad, Admiral."

"We can deal with the AI, Petrovitch," said Arendt. "We can deal with you, too. Now get off this line."

"Just one more thing, Admiral. If you isolate your

network now, the virus routines we've installed across your country's infrastructure will no longer be able to talk to Michael. If that happens, they'll turn off every computer they're hiding in, and I'm sure you know just how difficult it is to get these things restarted once they go down. You'll lose everything, for a very long time. You'll be reduced to the nickels and dimes in your pocket."

"Anarchy. You're talking about Anarchy."

"Modified. So hold off on your kill switch. Of course, you'll want to check if I'm bluffing: but I did the same thing to the Freezone earlier on today, and if you can find anyone who'll still talk to you after what you've done, they'll confirm the sudden and total shutdown. I had an AI to help me clear up my mess, though, so I imagine your pain will last an awful lot longer than ours did. Years, probably. How are the NSA doing at clearing up the last outbreak, by the way?"

There seemed to be a lot of people running in the background, running and talking hurriedly over phones. Of course, they were trying to trace him: that exercise was doomed to failure, but he'd have been disappointed if they hadn't tried. Some of the conversations were about activating assets within the Metrozone: again, the likelihood he'd accounted for every CIA agent didn't come with a cast-iron guarantee.

Some of the discussions were more technical—how he had hijacked the satellites involved and how they could take them back—but most of them were just shouting commands to check every piece of software anything important depended on.

"What do you want, Petrovitch?" growled Arendt.

"I told Joe, and now I'm telling you. I want to talk to

Mackensie, and, while I'm on, the rest of the National Security Council. Right now, you have a choice: we can go to war, or we can talk."

Admiral Arendt gave his considered response. "We don't talk to terrorists."

"Is that your final offer? You don't even want to tell Mackensie what I told you? Let him decide?"

The phone went dead.

Petrovitch gave it a few moments, and rang again.

It was answered immediately. It was neither young Armstrong, nor old Arendt. "Brandon Harris."

The call had been taken in the Situation Room. Because Michael had already hacked the cameras attached to all the workstations around the periphery of the room, and the one aimed down the length of the long central table, Petrovitch could finally see his adversary.

The president was at the far end, his thin white skin barely covering the outline of his skull. He leaned back in his leather chair, almost amused by the tension around him.

"*Dobre den,* Secretary Harris. Have I got your attention yet?"

Over the background clamor, a sound familiar to the entire globe cut through: a gravelly throat-clearing. President Mackensie was about to speak.

"Go to Defcon one."

"NORAD have just told us they've detected multiple launches from sites in Russia, China and off both our eastern and western seaboards." Harris leaned in on the phone. "What have you done?"

"Me? What have I done? You might think it's only one lousy nuke in some shit-hole European city, but the rest of the planet seems to disagree. You might want to put me on the speakers now."

He didn't. He put the phone on mute and turned to the table and those seated around it. "Mister President. Petrovitch wants to speak to you."

"And what would be the purpose of that, Mister Harris? That boy is a potty-mouthed heathen liar, and we should have dealt with him a long time ago rather than leaving that to others."

"That boy has just coordinated a massive first-strike against us."

"He is not the cause of this." Mackensie sat up and raised his gaze to the video screens: satellites were tracking rocket plumes rising high into the atmosphere. All the trails were beginning to bend toward the North American continent. From the Steppes, from the Asian deserts, from the Pacific and Atlantic oceans, lines were beginning to describe the writing on the wall. He spoke in his measured preacher's voice. "Our enemies have been waiting for this moment for decades, but we will not be cowed: let them pour out the goblets of wrath they have stored for us. God is our mighty fortress."

Admiral Arendt took his seat at the table. "Mister President, SkyShield is ready."

"Then you may proceed." Mackensie watched intently as the tracking stations began to lock on to their targets. Each incoming missile blinked from red to yellow as it was matched with an orbital weapon.

Then to blue.

"Sir. That's…" Arendt slid backward on his wheeled seat toward one of the workstation personnel. "That's just not possible."

Mackensie tapped his lips with a bony finger. All the highest missiles were blue, and more were cycling through the colors as they rose. "Malcolm, there appears to be a problem."

Arendt was dividing his precious time between receiving information and regurgitating it. "SkyShield components are tagging the inbound birds as friendly." He stopped again to listen to the whispering voice in his ear. "We can't shoot them down."

There was silence in the room. All the assumed confidence gained from having a massive space-based missile defense system, backed up with ground stations and some really big lasers, drained away with an almost audible sucking noise.

"How," said Mackensie eventually, "could this happen?"

Harris slowly turned in his seat at the long table and looked at the abandoned phone lying next to one of the consoles. "Petrovitch."

"Explain." Mackensie gazed with his hooded eyes at the arcs of oncoming missiles. "We are supposed to have the most secure network of any government. Are you telling me now that it is not? Frank?"

The National Security Adviser seemed temporarily paralyzed.

"Mister O'Connell, your president requires your opinion. Be so good as to provide it."

O'Connell's skin was gray, like he was already dead. "We know the AI is able to insert itself in command and control structures: it's done it before. SkyShield—all our systems, in fact—may have been compromised. Even with the protocols we've put in place, it looks like it's not enough." He shrugged helplessly, and his hands trembled. "We did our best."

"Then we close our electronic borders. Restart SkyShield."

"All the reports I have tell me that our infrastructure is mostly or completely infected with an Anarchy-variant virus. Petrovitch says if we cut the AI off, we bankrupt the country. And there's no guarantee that we would have a working computer to be able to get a command to SkyShield afterward." O'Connell spoke very quietly, and the microphones strained to pick him up. "Just like that. It's all over."

Harris snatched up the phone and unmuted it. "You... you've left us defenseless."

"How does it feel now, you bastard? Mackensie didn't cook up this nonsense on his own. He doesn't get to suffer alone. Put me on the speakers."

"You're killing us. Not just Mackensie, not just the American people. Everyone, everywhere. You know what's going to happen next?"

"Yeah. You get down on your knees and beg to Michael. After the shit you've put him through, it's the least you can do."

"The president will order the launch of our own missiles."

"Or you could do that. Seems a little drastic, don't you think?"

Harris' grip on the phone was threatening to crack the plastic. "Drastic? We are under attack."

"Are you? Are you really?"

Harris paused, then said: "Petrovitch, is the United States under attack?"

"Well, now. On the one hand, you can detect hundreds

of missiles and thousands of warheads, all heading straight for you. On the other hand, what you're seeing could be what we want you to see."

"And how are we supposed to tell the difference?"

"You know the answer to that question already, Harris. Hit the kill switch and pray to whichever god you worship that the missiles disappear. Or you could let me talk to the president."

Harris cupped his hand over the phone. "Mister President: Petrovitch has implied that this is an AI simulation, and no missiles have been launched." He sounded like a man offered the hope of reprieve at the foot of the gallows. He actually grinned.

"Then what," asked Mackensie, his expression sour, "are those?" He waved his hand at the screens in front of him, that told him only of the end of the world. "Are we to take the word of some punk street kid over our own satellites?"

Harris' grin slipped away. He glanced at O'Connell for support, who pinched the bridge of his nose hard enough to leave white marks.

"It's possible…Mister President; the Chinese have no reason to launch. Russia has no reason to launch. The EU- what are they going to get out of this? It makes no sense. Brazen it out, sir. All we need to do is absolutely nothing."

"Nothing? We have failed to destroy the artificial intelligence. We have failed to neutralize Petrovitch. We have failed to prevent SkyShield from being sabotaged. We have failed to protect our own network from infection. How much less would you like the government of the United States of America to do?"

"He's provoking us." Harris thrust the phone in Mackensie's direction, and lost it, caught between terror and duty. "Petrovitch is playing us. God damn it, what if none of this is real?"

"That'll be twenty bucks, Mister Harris. I'll have it taken out of your final pay check. You are relieved of your position." Mackensie steepled his fingers, showing the liver spots on the backs of his hands, and glanced up at his aide. "Please escort the former Secretary of Defense from the Situation Room."

He watched impassively as Harris was ushered from the room at gunpoint. The other men present watched, pale and drained.

"It is perfectly clear that Petrovitch wishes us dead, and will do or say anything that will delay our own launch until we are no longer in a position to retaliate effectively. I refuse to listen to such counsel. The way ahead is clear: we do this by the book."

A man with a briefcase stepped up beside Mackensie, and laid it on the table. He opened it up and passed his president a solid plastic rectangle as big as a postcard. Mackensie flexed his fingers and cracked the plastic slab along pre-scored lines. Inside was a long strip of paper, printed with a combination of numbers and letters in a long sequence.

He laid the codes on the table in front of him. "The first and greatest duty a government has is to protect the integrity of the nation it serves. If that has been denied to us, then our last act ought properly be to strike out against a world bent on destroying us, as it has been since our creation. We will not go quietly as they hope, but we will fight even as we die."

He cleared his throat again and readied himself to read.

35

Admiral Arendt looked at the glowing lines on the wall screens. The first missiles would be hitting the Alaskan airbases in less than thirty seconds. "Get me Elmendorf," he said to the watch officer.

The officer slid back to his console and with two presses of his touch screen, had the duty desk. "This is the NSC. Ah, sheet three-five yellow. Seven Alpha Foxtrot November Niner Papa Lima Zero."

The man in the blue uniform riffled through the yellow pad in front of him. "Elmendorf. Romeo Bravo Six Kilo Eight Juliet Tango Six Hotel."

The watch officer ran his finger along the second line of code. "Admiral? Connection to Elmendorf confirmed. At least, it looks that way."

Arendt leaned over the younger man's shoulder. "Hello, son. I need you just to stay on this line as long as you can."

"Yes sir."

The screen went blank, then reverted to the previous window. On the main map, Elmendorf winked from blue to gray, followed a moment later by Eielson.

Snatching up the abandoned handset, Arendt spoke through clenched teeth. "Petrovitch, tell me we haven't just lost the Eleventh Air Force."

"You haven't lost the Eleventh Air Force. Neither are you about to lose the western seaboard. Scary though, isn't it? Can you smell the fear yet?"

"You have to stop this. The president is releasing the launch codes."

"Yeah. I know."

"Can he launch?" asked Arendt. "If this is fake, then he's not really giving the codes to NORAD, is he?"

"No," said Petrovitch, "he's giving them to me."

Arendt dropped the phone. "Mister President, stop the sequence."

Mackensie turned his head slowly toward his military adviser and fixed him with a withering stare. "Malcolm, I think you forget yourself."

"That's not NORAD," said the admiral, his finger wavering toward the screen where a smart air force officer was waiting on the last two digits of the launch code. "That's the AI. You're telling the enemy the gold codes."

The first brief flicker of doubt crossed Mackensie's serene face. He looked down the table at his advisers and their attendants. Some of them were just kids, who'd grown up knowing nothing but Reconstruction. The middle-aged ones were the generation who'd voted for its institution. Even the old men were two decades his junior.

The sub-launched missiles from the Atlantic reached the eastern seaboard. New York went offline. Miami. Charleston. Some crossed the coast and tracked inland, heading for the industrial cities of the north.

The land-launched intercontinental rockets had ended

their boost phase, and were coasting at the edge of space. They'd start to fall in twenty minutes' time. Every major center of population had been targeted, as had the major military bases. Hawaii was about to succumb. Diego Garcia would be next. Without SkyShield's protection, they were naked to the oncoming storm.

O'Connell grimaced. "I know it looks like NORAD. But we have to consider the capabilities of who—of what—we're up against. If Petrovitch's AI is running a simulated attack, it's running everything."

"Well, Frank: you're my intelligence adviser. I had hoped you of all people would be able to say whether or not the intelligence we are receiving is reliable."

"Either we use the kill switch, or we wait and see if we die. They're the only ways."

"The choice between wiping out our economy or our ability to hit back is not a choice at all." Mackensie stretched his thin lips out. "I appear to have been badly advised."

O'Connell started to protest. "Ever since we learned of the New Machine Jihad..."

Mackensie held up his hand. "Enough. You are relieved of your position also."

After resting his head briefly on the table, O'Connell stood up and walked in a daze to the exit. His deputy licked his lips nervously and scraped his fingers through his hair.

"Does anyone," asked Mackensie mildly, "have anything constructive to say at this stage, or shall we continue?"

"I think, sir," said Admiral Arendt, "you should speak with Petrovitch."

"Do you, Malcolm?"

"Yessir."

The missiles were edging closer. Two of the sub-launched missiles, one from the east, one from the west, were converging on Colorado.

"And what would be the purpose of that? Why would I waste a moment conversing with the author of our destruction." Mackensie gestured at the wall screens. "We spent trillions of dollars and millions of man-hours on Project SkyShield, only to have it rendered useless by him and his abomination. We face either nuclear destruction or total economic disaster. Both will leave our great nation a shattered remnant of its former self and our enemies intact. I will not permit that."

The west coast had gone. The east coast, too. Targets well beyond the continental divide were falling one by one, and still the main attack hadn't arrived.

The admiral tilted his head slightly as he tried to glean information from the maps, desperately sifting through the layers to sort fact from fabrication. "I'll be damned," he said.

"Twenty dollars, if you please, Malcolm. Not like you at all: I appreciate we're about to meet our maker, but please keep your composure."

"Why aren't they targeting DC?" Arendt got to his feet and walked around to the foot of the table. He pointed up at the map with all its lines and markers. "We should have been hit by now. Decapitation strike."

The watch officer eyed the telephone on his desk, then picked it up. "Petrovitch?" he hissed. "Why aren't we dead yet?"

"Because if a missile had struck you and you were all

still alive, you'd know for certain, wouldn't you? Even Mackensie couldn't convince himself you were still under attack. So we thought we'd string this out as long as possible and make you sweat. Not nice, is it, taking away a person's ability to tell what's real?"

"As one human being to another, I'm begging you to end this."

"You're convinced, then? That none of this is actually happening?"

"Yes. I'm convinced."

"Then do something to stop Mackensie giving me the complete launch codes. We've got most of it: Michael might be able to guess the rest, but it'll take him a while. Much easier to let your president hand control of your nuclear deterrent to me on a plate. Much more ironic, too."

"What can I do? I'm just…just a cog."

"So were Stanislav Petrov and Vasili Arkhipov, but they were the right people in the right place at the right time, and they stopped a third World War. What's your name, *kamerad*?"

"Joshua Meldon Junior, sir."

"You can call me Sam, Joshua. I like you. Why don't you turn around and take a look at what's happening behind you."

Arendt was still standing under the screens showing the virtual destruction of his country, arguing that he was right, and that to speak the last two characters of the launch code would be a disaster. The depleted audience was with him: the Secretary of State, the Chief of Staff, the Deputy Security Adviser and the other two deputies, all willing the president to change his mind.

The admiral's case was plain. "The White House is a

primary target on every conceivable attack pattern of a foreign power. We have not been hit—yet—and neither has any target within a hundred miles. Mister President, an atom bomb in Virginia would rattle the windows in the Oval Office. There are no independently verifiable signs that we have been attacked because we have not actually been attacked."

Mackensie looked above Arendt's head, seeking both clarity and certainty. He watched the missile tracks close in on NORAD's mountain fastness.

"I am the President of the United States of America and Commander-in-Chief of her armed forces. The reason I am in this great office of state, after long years of faithful service to this nation and her peoples, is to be here at this time and this place, to take this decision. When all others fall by the wayside and show themselves unworthy of the responsibilities handed to them by Almighty God, I will not falter. I will set my face like flint in the face of my many adversities and remain faithful to the very end." Mackensie picked up the gold codes and looked to the screen that held the image of the ever-patient airforce officer, waiting for the complete sequence.

"Sir?" said Joshua Meldon Junior into the sudden silence. "My brother works for the USGS."

"That's nice, son, but not now."

"He's in Colorado. They have seismometers, sir. And I can verify it's really him."

Arendt gestured to Meldon to make the call.

"Niner Zulu," said Mackensie.

"The launch codes have been authenticated," said the man at NORAD and saluted crisply. "It was an honor serving under you, sir."

"Would that others did their duty as diligently as you, son." The screen went blank, and was replaced by a list of the counterstrike assets as they were activated. Mackensie folded his arms, as if he had known this day would come and he had spent a lifetime preparing himself for it. "Thank you, gentlemen. There is nothing else left to do, and you are all dismissed."

None of them moved.

Meldon adjusted his mouth mic. "I need to speak to Doctor Jerry Meldon. I don't care if he's in a meeting: this is the White House and this is urgent." While he waited, he picked up Petrovitch's phone again.

"You'll go far," said Petrovitch.

"I'm too late, though, aren't I?"

"Hell yeah. All your base are belong to us."

"What are you going to do with them? The codes, I mean?"

"Enjoy them while I've got them. They go out of date at midnight, so they have a short shelf-life. I thought I might post them on some public message boards, see if they go viral."

"Hey Josh. 'S'up?"

Meldon put the phone back down on the corner of his workstation. His brother didn't sound like a man monitoring the end of everything.

"Jerry, listen very carefully to me. Have you detected any nuclear weapons detonations in the continental United States?"

"What's going on, Josh? Are you in some kind of trouble?"

"Just answer the question: yes or no?"

"No! I mean, really no."

"Or anywhere else?"

"Haven't you seen the news? Of course you have. Why are you asking me this stuff?"

Meldon screwed his eyes tight shut. "Jerry, what was the name of the first girl you kissed?"

"I . . . don't get it."

Swallowing hard, Meldon tried again. "Third grade. Who did you kiss in third grade?"

"You said you'd never . . ."

"You don't know how important this is, Jerry. I need to make sure that it's you I'm talking to. I've got what's left of the National Security Council staring at me, including the president. Which girl did you kiss in third grade? I caught you and you made me swear I'd never tell, on our mother's life."

The missiles were very close to Colorado now. By the rules of the game, if they hit, the connection would disappear.

"Jerry. Which girl?"

"You know damn well it wasn't a g—"

Meldon cut him off. "Mister President. The United States Geological Survey has not detected a single detonation anywhere within the world, except for the one we caused."

The two markers converged on NORAD. It winked out.

"Have we launched?" Arendt walked slowly around the table to Meldon's workstation. He picked up the phone. "Petrovitch, have we launched?"

"Why don't you put me on the speakers, Admiral?"

"You don't need me to put you on the speakers, do you? You never have. You're as good as in this room with us."

The main screens flickered. The screen changed to

inside a rusting container. Faces looked back at them. A teenage girl; two young women, one very tall with a bandaged cut on her partly shaved head, the other a pale and drawn blue-eyed redhead who stared belligerently and raised her middle finger to the camera; it panned over another woman, high cheekboned and disdainful, then they were out in the daylight. There were more containers, strewn seemingly at random, and as the camera wobbled and bounced along in time with the gait of the carrier, the watchers could see compacted brown clay and cloud-laden sky.

"This city has been my home for the last few years. The London Metrozone took me in and sheltered me after I'd run from all the bad things I'd done. I became anonymous here: easy enough to do. Then it got a bit, well, screwed up. Firstly, the New Machine Jihad: a burgeoning AI's subconscious dreams played out across reality. That, and your CIA, put a hole in the cordon. The Outies came through. It was a trickle at first, then it was a flood. We ended up having a war, and we only just won. Now we have this: lies and subterfuge, more death and destruction, and you've finally done what the Armageddonists failed to do: put a nuclear bomb in the heart of London."

He was at the gates of Regent's Park, looking up at the sniper's vantage point, showing them first-hand how damaged it was. "The strange thing is that each time I was no more than lucky. I was able to get in the way, just enough to make a difference. But I'm not doing that again: I'm done here. I'm tired. I'm going to disappear off your radar—hopefully permanently—and this time I'm going to leave this mess for you to clear up. And let's face it, it is your mess."

Petrovitch kept walking. There were few people still around: most of them had moved north away from ground zero. The street was littered with red flags, reminding him of that brief moment of euphoria, where change had not just seemed possible but inevitable.

"So I've got another of your CIA agents—I'm not talking about Tabletop, she's one of us now—and I want to send him back to you. Even if I get nothing in return, he's more trouble than he's worth. A goodwill gesture, though, part of your reparations, might lead you to stick Epiphany Ekanobi and Paul Dalton on a plane to Europe. That'll also mean you'll have to enforce your own laws over in California a bit more rigorously than you are at the moment. Throw in the Anarchy kid, too, while you're at it. That and stopping trying to kill me and my friends, we can call it quits."

Mackensie cleared his throat. "You are in possession of the gold codes?"

"Yeah. It's not like you weren't warned. Repeatedly. Everyone else in the room had worked it out. But not you."

"And what do you intend to do next?"

"I gave you three options: killing billions, losing your bank balances, or holding your nerve and doing precisely nothing. There were two right answers, but no, you went ahead and picked the other one. You'd have destroyed the world, you mad fuck." Petrovitch snorted. "No, you haven't launched, and it's not something I would ever do. So there's no real harm done. No one's died in a global nuclear holocaust. We can all breathe out again and promise to do better next time. Except for you. Something tells me, even though they changed the constitution to allow you to stand for more than two terms, even though each time you've been up for election your majority has grown and your approval rating just keeps getting better—you're not going to make it out of the Situation Room still being president."

Petrovitch kept walking, and turned his good eye to the skyline, where smoke and dust hung in a low pall. There was masonry to navigate, and cracks in the road. Pools of water and piles of glass.

"You showed everyone who you really are today, Mackensie. Not the great president, the architect of Reconstruction and protector of the American people. It turns out that you're really an insane old man with an Armageddon fetish who'd rather nuke the planet than admit you were wrong—and I've got it all on file. If you think these streets look bad, this city: it can be rebuilt, which is more than can be said for your reputation. I had a very illuminating chat with Paul Dalton a couple of days ago, who told me of Reconstruction's dark heart; that if you looked like you were out of step with the project, dif-ferent in some way, maybe even just weak, it would turn on you and tear you apart without hesitation or mercy. That's what's going to happen to you, and I'm going to enjoy watching it played out. Look at the faces around you. Look at them closely. They're your executioners, not me. Goodbye Mackensie."

36

There was more to do, but Petrovitch was content to let others do it. Once he'd matched jobs to people, he saw no reason to fret about their competence. He'd done enough for one day—enough, it felt, for a lifetime—and it was true what he'd told Mackensie; he was tired.

He'd talked to presidents and prime ministers, he'd talked to ambassadors and representatives. He'd had a very poignant conversation with the Secretary General of the United Nations, who inexplicably reminded him of his mother, and he'd choked up completely.

His mother: now that was a situation he was probably going to have to deal with at some point. Just not yet.

A mere cardinal of the Roman Catholic Church didn't really rank at all compared with the rest of the great and the good. Still, there he was, sitting on the steps of a bizarre Italianate building that had somehow squeezed itself between a town house and a pizza restaurant, sadly closed for the duration.

Carillo had found an unbroken bottle of bourbon in the wreckage of the Mount Street church and had brought it out to share. He lowered himself onto the cold marble and arranged two glasses on the step next to him.

Petrovitch picked up the bottle by its neck and read the label.

"Proof that there's at least something American you'll appreciate," said the cardinal.

"I'm not that knee-jerk." Petrovitch passed the bottle back, and the cardinal cracked the seal. "Am I?"

"I think that's a whole different conversation to the one I planned on having." Carillo bent low over the glasses, pouring carefully so he didn't spill a drop. "If this was any stronger, I wouldn't be able to carry it on commercial flights. As it is, it shouldn't dissolve your guts if you take it in moderation."

"And all this on an empty stomach. You'd think being a multi-billionaire and leader of what's left of one of the world's great cities would mean lunch at some point."

Carillo passed Petrovitch his drink and looked out from under the porch at the darkening sky. "Can't help you there. I brought the booze."

"At least I'm a cheap date." Corn whiskey wasn't his usual, but he'd make the exception, just this once. He twisted his wrist and emptied the contents of the glass into his mouth. He held the liquid there for a moment, then swallowed.

He let out a puff of air, and screwed up his remaining eye.

"Stagg's a decent drop. The bottle's yours to keep, by way of an apology." Carillo sipped his bourbon and drew his knees up against the cold. "You'll be getting a letter from the Pope at some point, too."

"Yeah, well. You didn't know. And it's only your God

that's supposed to be omniscient, not his followers." Petrovitch hefted the bottle again, and worked the stopper free. He poured himself another two fingers and stared at the light through the dark oak whiskey. "This is self-medication. I'm due in surgery."

"The eye?"

Petrovitch touched his pirate's eyepatch: Lucy's idea. "I don't even need a local for that, just plug and play. It's the arm. It bled inside, and it's… easier if they amputate."

"I'm sorry to hear that. You going organic?"

"Probably not. My flight from this meat-sack continues, *Tetsuo*-stylee."

"What does Madeleine say about that?"

"I'm paraphrasing, but it was something like 'at least the next time someone tries to break your arm, you can break theirs right back'." Petrovitch drank half the bourbon in his glass. "She understands me. I don't know if that's good or scary."

"She is your wife."

"Yeah. We're still just a couple of kids, though. We have no role models: both our fathers are dead, her mother was an alcoholic and, when she sobered up, she became an Outie and tried to kill Maddy. I abandoned my family back in St. Petersburg. I don't even know what marriage is supposed to look like, let alone the rest of it."

Carillo sipped and contemplated. "So why did you get married?"

"Apparently it was the only way we could get to bang each other's brains out without incurring God's wrath."

After they'd both stopped laughing, Petrovitch felt he should explain.

"The whole living together, being with each other

thing. I didn't need a piece of paper for that. She did: she has this irrational belief that it means something extra. So that's why I agreed." He drank more, poured more. "I don't want to be with anybody else. She's..."

"What?" said Carillo after a suitable wait.

"Did I ever tell you about how fantastic her breasts are? They're just breathtaking, amazing, a work of art from a Renaissance master. They're the sort of breasts Leonardo would have drawn." He looked sideways at the cardinal. "There is a point to this."

"I was wondering."

"When she takes her top off, I'm like a kid in a sweet shop. I know it's a function of biochemistry, my age and my complete lack of experience in these things, and mostly I'm just pathetically grateful she wants to be with me. But it wasn't her breasts that I missed while we weren't together. It was her."

"What you're saying is that you love her." Carillo made a half-smile. "Which is right and proper. I know a lot of my colleagues don't approve, but I do."

"You've talked about me and Maddy?"

"At a surprisingly high level. She is, as I'm sure you realize, an extraordinary young woman. A great loss to the Order, and some have agitated this past year for your marriage to be annulled."

Petrovitch's fingers tightened around his glass. "So Father John didn't act on his own."

"So it would seem. You've already caused two revolutions today, why not a third?" Carillo hunched over further. "Maybe I will have some more of Kentucky's finest."

Petrovitch slid the bottle across the gap between them.

"Strange days for both of us, then. I take it you're not going to name names."

"Having seen what you do to people who cross you, no. There'll be an inquiry, held *in curia,* and the results will not be divulged. I'm sure you can create some pattern-recognition software that'll track appointments and retirements, but I'd rather you didn't." Carillo held the bourbon bottle up and frowned at the amount already missing. Then he shrugged and dealt himself another shot. "We might move slowly, but we are very thorough."

"Like the Americans."

"You keep forgetting I am one."

"You keep having to remember you are one. I'd hardly call what's happening over there a revolution, though. It's still Reconstruction to the core."

"Mackensie went within the hour, and you got everything you wanted. That's a victory, of sorts."

"The cost of it. *Chyort,* we lost so much to get so..."

"Little? I could list your achievements, but that won't make you feel better."

"I can't unsee: with my set-up, I can play it again with perfect clarity any time I want. And I can't undo: I've killed people today, and they're not coming back."

"They so rarely do," murmured Carillo. "Shall we get this over with, then? Assuming you still want to go through with it."

"Yeah. I've thought about it, and what with me being such a *yebani* genius I have to be right at least some of the time." Petrovitch saw off the last of his drink and pulled his arm back ready to throw.

The cardinal caught his wrist and retrieved the glass. "Enough broken things for one day." He set the glass down with his own, and got up stiffly. The cold had seeped into his bones and he hadn't taken as much whiskey as Petrovitch.

He led the way up the steps to the tall wooden doors. He knocked, rapping with his knuckles: the door opened a crack, then further. Sister Marie, dressed in her full habit, stood aside. When they were between the outer doors and the inner ones, she stood close to Petrovitch and looked him up and down.

"Weapons, please," she said.

"What makes you think I have any?"

"If you don't, I think you ought."

"This is the Freezone, not the wild west." Petrovitch raised his arm over his head anyway. "Feel free to pat me down, sister. You won't find…*huy,* you know what? I'm going to cut the cheap innuendo and let you get on with your job."

"Thank you."

If he thought she was going to wave him through, he was mistaken. She was thorough in her way, just like the men she protected. When she was done, she faced him, blinking.

"You can have my gun on the way out if you want," she offered.

"That's very kind. But I'm being picked up, and they'll have all the guns I need." Petrovitch put his arm down, and started forward, but Sister Marie put her hand out and blocked him.

"A couple of ground rules, *mon ami.* Do not touch him, at all, ever. Even if I think you're going to shake his hand, I'm stepping in. Second: you're here against my advice and I'm yet to be convinced this is a good idea. If this looks like it's taking a wrong turn, or even if it's not going anywhere, I'll call a halt to it. *Oui?*"

Petrovitch nodded. "I'm fresh out of anger, Sister."

"I don't believe you. You make anger like you make electricity: out of nothing." But she pushed through the second set of doors and held them open to make sure they didn't close on him.

It was so bright inside: so many lights, so much white and gold. The ivory marble columns supported an achingly high ceiling, and the nave was designed in a way that drew the eye irresistibly toward the baroque canopied altar.

"*Yobany stos.*" Petrovitch turned around and caught sight of the curve of the organ pipes and the choir gallery. "You lot are so full of contradictions, it's a wonder you don't explode every morning. How could anyone justify this level of luxury when..."

"It was built in an age when such things were done to glorify God." Carillo stood beside him and looked at the statues in their niches, at the paintings in their distant splendor. "I'm just a simple Jesuit priest. I neither seek nor avoid places like this: it is what it is and, ultimately, it's just a building."

Petrovitch spotted a single lit candle off to one side, placed in a banked metal holder that held a century of melted wax. Kneeling before the candle, his face so close to the flame that his breath made the light flicker, was Father John Slater.

Behind him was another Joan, and there was a third waiting in the shadows. Perhaps they really did think Petrovitch was going to try and kill him. They still might be right.

Sister Marie dogged his footsteps all the way up the aisle, and stood with her back to one of the pillars, her hand resting on her holster.

In front of the candle holder was a low bench on which to kneel. Father John took up most of it and seemed so intent on staring unblinking at the yellow flame that he appeared oblivious to the movement behind him.

Petrovitch slid into the front pew and eased himself along until he was in the priest's peripheral vision. "I understand you've got something you want to say to me."

He seemed to have survived the last two days unscathed. He even looked well-fed. "Yes," said Father John without turning away from the candle. "That was the message."

"I find myself a suddenly busy man. Why don't you get on with it, and I can go and, I don't know, get my arm chopped off."

"If you wish." The priest finally moved his head, and looked at Petrovitch with his pin-prick-pupilled eyes. "I'd do it all again tomorrow, if I thought this time it would work."

The three Joans had their guns out and pointed at Petrovitch in less time than it took to say "hail Mary." For his part, all he did was snort.

"Yeah. They say repentance is good for the soul. At least, I think that's what they say: I never really paid much attention to that sort of thing. Winning, now that's good for the soul. Losing, and losing badly? Not so great. And you seem to be the biggest loser of all. Unless you're going to kill yourself like Sonja did, then you get to live knowing you fucked up completely. Everything you were aiming for, you missed."

"I made you suffer. Not as much as I wanted, but you suffered all the same."

"What doesn't kill you, makes you stronger. Never thought I'd get to quote Nietzsche in a church, but here we are. That must make me pretty much invincible at the moment, considering what I've been through. How about you, priest? Not that you'll be that for much longer. I understand the Holy Inquisition would like a chat."

"Whatever they do to me, it'll have been worth it."

Petrovitch pursed his lips. "Yeah. By the way, thanks."

"For what?"

"It's like this," said Petrovitch, leaning forward. "I wouldn't have half of what I have now if it hadn't been for your inept meddling. To be fair, you were almost as much a pawn in Sonja's plot as I was, which means you get downgraded from criminal mastermind to unwitting accomplice, but those are the breaks."

Holding up his little finger, he continued. "I get Pif back. Never would have happened otherwise. And I get a bonus Dalton thrown in—he loses his wife and children and everything he knows, but escapes from the lynch mob with his life." He raised another finger. "Anarchy. The kid who wrote that? I egged him on. Now he's on the same flight as the other two. Three: Michael. I would have got him out anyway. But now he's out and he's free. That's a real gift you've given him. He has so much to tell me: I can feel him just at the back of my head, waiting for the right moment to show me the wonders of the universe, if only I can understand them."

"Which I doubt," said Father John.

"You don't get to speak," said Petrovitch quietly, to the accompaniment of an automatic's slide being dragged back. He looked up, and he was still the target of three handguns. "Four. I have a future I can only dream of. Suddenly everything is much clearer, much more obvious. I know what I have to do now, and again it's partly down to you. And five: I get the girl. I get Maddy and I get everything else with her. You made her choose between your world and mine. She chose me. She'll keep choosing me. When we were on our own, underground, in the dark and the damp, and a nuclear bomb about to go off in the next room, she made me choose too. I chose her. I'll keep on choosing her, too, till the end of time."

He got up slowly, so as not to scare the Joans.

"You and your cabal are history. I can trust Carillo to make sure of that. And next time—if there is a next time, which I'm guessing there won't be—don't go in with someone so paranoid that she doesn't even tell her CIA masters her plan. It really won't work."

Petrovitch edged back along the pew to the side aisle.

"Is that it?" said Father John, rising. "Is that it?"

"Yeah," replied Petrovitch, "I'm done. What did you think I was going to do? Lunge for your throat and force Sister Marie to kill me? You are so *yebani* transparent. And as I walk away, you're going to try and wrestle one of the Joans' guns from them. Good luck with that. You're going to need it."

He turned his back to the sounds of a brief but intense scuffle and went to join Carillo at the back of the church.

The cardinal looked rueful. "You're right. I don't know everything."

"Meh," said Petrovitch. "My lift's outside. I'd better go."

"You know where to find me if you ever need any relationship advice."

"From a celibate priest? Even if you do have a decent taste in liquor, I don't think so."

"Like I said, I've been around the block a few times, and I want you to do well." Carillo proffered his hand. "Look after yourself."

Petrovitch had no reservations in shaking it. "Here comes the future."

"We're all traveling into it, one second at a time."

Petrovitch pushed at the doors with his back, and started to place a call to his tame Bavarian dome-builders.

"I think you'll find," he said, "that some of us are going much faster than that."

ACKNOWLEDGMENTS

Long-term success in any artistic career—painting, writing, composing, whatever—seems to rest on talent, luck, and perseverance: pick any two. I've certainly persevered, but I've also been lucky. (The folk band Show of Hands make the point that the harder you practice, the luckier you become, adding that it helps if you can play an instrument. And they're right.)

Having an agent does help, though, which is why there's an oft-repeated complaint from authors that it's harder to get an agent than it is to get a publishing deal. I met mine through another of those unlikely chain of events that happened simply because I'd been hanging around long enough.

I could write all sorts of things here, but I'll save both our blushes and simply say: this book is dedicated to Ant.

extras

orbit

meet the author

DR. SIMON MORDEN is a bona fide rocket scientist, having degrees in geology and planetary geophysics, and is one of the few people who can truthfully claim to have held a chunk of Mars in his hands. He has served as editor of the BSFA's *Focus* magazine, been a judge for the Arthur C. Clarke Award and was part of the winning team for the 2009 Rolls Royce Science prize. Simon Morden lives in Gateshead with a fierce lawyer, two unruly children and a couple of miniature panthers. Find out more about the author at www.bookofmorden.co.uk.

introducing

If you enjoyed
DEGREES OF FREEDOM,
look out for

LEVIATHAN WAKES

Book 1 of The Expanse

by James S.A. Corey

Welcome to the future. Humanity has colonized the solar system—Mars, the Moon, the Asteroid Belt and beyond—but the stars are still out of our reach.

Jim Holden is XO of an ice hauler making runs from the rings of Saturn to the Belt. When he and his crew stumble upon a derelict ship, The Scopuli, they find themselves in possession of a secret they never wanted. A secret that someone is willing to kill for. War is brewing in the system.

Detective Miller is looking for a girl. One girl in a system of billions, but her parents have money and

*money talks. When the trail leads him to The Scopuli
and rebel sympathizer, Holden, he realizes that this
girl may be the key to everything.*

*Holden and Miller must thread the needle between
governments, revolutionaries, and secretive
corporations—and the odds are against them. But out
in the Belt, the rules are different, and one small
ship can change the fate of the universe.*

Prologue: Julie

The *Scopuli* had been taken eight days ago, and Julie
Mao was finally ready to be shot.

It had taken all eight days trapped in a storage locker to
get to that point. For the first two she'd remained motion-
less, sure that the armored men who'd put her there had
been serious. For the first hours, the ship she'd been taken
aboard wasn't under thrust, so she floated in the locker,
using gentle touches to keep herself from bumping into the
walls or the atmosphere suit she shared the space with.
When the ship began to move, thrust giving her weight,
she'd stood silently until her legs cramped, then sat down
slowly into a fetal position. She'd peed in her jumpsuit, not
caring about the warm itchy wetness, or the smell, worrying only that she didn't slip and fall in the wet spot it left on
the floor. She couldn't make noise. They'd shoot her.

On the third day, thirst forced her into action. The noise
of the ship was all around her. The faint subsonic rumble
of the reactor and drive, the constant hiss and thud of
hydraulics and steel bolts as the pressure doors between

decks opened and closed. The clump of heavy boots walking on metal decking. She waited until all the noise she could hear sounded distant, then pulled the environment suit down off of its hooks and onto the locker floor. Listening for any approaching sound, she slowly disassembled the suit and took out the water supply. It was old and stale; the suit obviously hadn't been used or serviced in ages. But she hadn't had a sip in two days, and the warm loamy water in the suit's reservoir bag was the best thing she had ever tasted. She had to work hard not to gulp it down and make herself vomit.

When the urge to urinate returned, she pulled the catheter bag out of the suit and relieved herself into it. She sat on the floor, now cushioned by the padded suit and almost comfortable, and wondered who her captors were—Coalition Navy, pirates, something worse. Sometimes she slept.

On day four, the isolation, hunger, boredom, and the diminishing number of places to store her piss finally pushed her to make contact with them. She'd heard distant cries of pain. Somewhere nearby, her shipmates were being beaten or tortured. If she got the attention of the kidnappers, maybe they would just take her to the others. That was okay. Beatings she could handle. It seemed like a small price to pay if it meant seeing people again.

The locker sat beside the inner airlock door. During flight, that usually wasn't a high traffic area, though she didn't know anything about the layout of this particular ship. She thought about what to say, how to present herself. When she finally heard someone moving toward her, she just tried to yell that she wanted out. The dry rasp that came out of her throat surprised her. She swallowed, working her tongue to try and create some saliva, and tried again. Another faint rattle in the throat.

The people were right outside her locker door. A voice was talking quietly. Julie had pulled back a fist to bang on the locker door when she heard what it was saying.

No. Please no. Please don't.

Dave. Her ship's mechanic. Dave, who collected clips from old cartoons and knew a million jokes, begging in a small broken voice.

No, please no, please don't, he said.

Hydraulics and locking bolts clicked as the inner airlock door opened. A meaty thud as something was thrown inside. Another click as the airlock closed. A hiss of evacuating air.

When the airlock cycle had finished, the people outside her door walked away. She didn't bang to get their attention.

They'd scrubbed the ship. Detainment by the inner planets navies was a bad scenario, but they'd all trained on how to deal with it. Sensitive OPA data was scrubbed and overwritten with innocuous looking logs with false timestamps. Anything too sensitive to trust to a computer, the captain destroyed. When the attackers came aboard, they could play innocent.

It hadn't mattered.

There weren't the questions about cargo or permits. The invaders had come in like they owned the place, and Captain Darren rolled over like a dog. Everyone else, Mike, Dave, Wan Li, they'd all just thrown up their hands and gone along quietly. The pirates or slavers or whatever they were had dragged them off the little transport ship that had been her home, and down a docking tube without even a minimal environment suit. The tube's thin layer of mylar the only thing between them and hard nothing: hope it doesn't rip, goodbye lungs if it does.

Julie had gone along too, but then the bastards had tried to lay their hands on her, strip her clothes off.

Five years of low gravity jiu jitsu training and them in a confined space with no gravity. She'd done a lot of damage. She'd almost started to think she might win when a gauntleted fist smashed into her face from nowhere and things got fuzzy after that. Then the locker, and *shoot her if she makes a noise.* Four days of not making noise while they beat her friends down below and then threw one of them out an airlock.

After six days, everything went quiet.

Shifting between bouts of consciousness and fragmented dreams, she was only vaguely aware as the sounds of walking, and talking, and pressure doors, and the subsonic rumble of the reactor and the drive faded away a little at a time. When the drive stopped, so did gravity, and Julie woke from a dream of racing her old pinnace to find herself floating while her muscles screamed in protest and then slowly relaxed.

She pulled herself to the door and pressed her ear to the cold metal. Panic shot through until she caught the quiet sound of the air recyclers. The ship still had power and air, but the drive wasn't on and no one was opening a door or walking or talking. Maybe it was a crew meeting. Or a party on another deck. Everyone was in engineering fixing a serious problem.

She spent a day listening and waiting.

By day seven her last sip of water was gone. No one on the ship had moved within range of her hearing for twenty four hours. She sucked on a plastic tab she ripped off the environment suit until she worked up some saliva, then she started yelling. She yelled herself hoarse.

No one came.

By day eight, she was ready to be shot. She'd been out of water for two days, and her waste bag had been full for four. She put her shoulders against the back wall of the locker and planted her hands against the side walls. Then she kicked out with both legs as hard as she could. The cramps that followed the first kick almost made her pass out. She screamed instead.

Stupid girl, she told herself. She was dehydrated. Eight days without activity was more than enough to start atrophy. At least she should have stretched out.

She massaged her stiff muscles until the knots were gone, then stretched, focusing her mind like she was back in dojo. When she was in control of her body, she kicked again. And again. And again, until light started to show through the edges of the locker. And again until the door was so bent that the three hinges and the locking bolt were the only points of contact between it and the frame.

And one last time so that it bent far enough that the bolt was no longer seated in the hasp and the door swung free.

Julie bolted from the locker, hands half raised, ready to look either threatening or terrified depending on which seemed more useful.

There was no one on the whole deck level: airlock, the suit storage room where she'd spent the last eight days, a half dozen other storage rooms. All empty. She plucked a

magnetized pipe wrench of suitable size for skull cracking out of an EVA kit, then went down the crew ladder to
the deck below.

And then the one below that, and then the one below
that. Personnel cabins in crisp, almost military order.
Commissary where there were signs of a struggle. Medical bay, empty. Torpedo bay. No one. The comm station
was unmanned, powered down, and locked. The few sen-
sor logs that still streamed showed no sign of the *Scopuli*.
A new dread knotted her gut. Deck after deck and room
after room empty of life. Something had happened. A
radiation leak. Poison in the air. Something that had
forced an evacuation. She wondered if she'd be able to fly
the ship by herself.

But if they'd evacuated, she'd have heard them going
out the airlock, wouldn't she?

She reached the final deck hatch, the one that led into
engineering, and stopped when the hatch didn't open
automatically. A red light on the lock panel showed that
the room had been sealed from the inside. She thought
again about radiation or major failures. But if that were
the case, why lock the door from the inside? And she had
passed wall panel after wall panel. None of them had been
flashing any warnings of any kind. No, not radiation,
something else.

There was more disruption here. Blood. Tools and containers in disarray. Whatever had happened, it had happened here.

It took two hours with a torch and prying tools from
the machine shop to cut through. With the hydraulics
compromised, she had to crank the hatch open by hand. A
gust of warm wet air blew out, carrying a hospital scent

without the antiseptic. A coppery, nauseating smell. The torture chamber, then. Her friends would be inside, beaten or cut to pieces. Julie hefted her wrench and prepared to bust at least one head open before they killed her. She floated down.

The engineering deck was huge, vaulted like a cathedral. The fusion reactor dominated the central space. Something was wrong with it. Where she expected to see readouts, shielding, and monitors, a layer of something like mud seemed to flow over the reactor core. Slowly, Julie floated toward it, one hand still on the ladder. The strange smell became overpowering.

The mud caked around the reactor had structure to it like nothing she'd seen before. Tubes ran through it like veins or airways. Parts of it pulsed. Not mud, then.

Flesh.

An outcropping of the thing shifted toward her. In comparison to the whole it seemed no larger than a toe, a little finger. It was Captain Darren's head.

"Help me," it said.